ULTIMATE BETRAYAL:

Revelations

CATRINA COURTENAY

Dedication

For my loves, without you nothing is possible.

Contents

Acknowledgments

My deepest love and gratitude first and foremost to my husband. Thank you for doing the laundry, cleaning the house and taking our son everywhere he needed to go while I wrote and wrote and wrote. Your patience and energy is boundless, and my love for you, limitless.

My son - You are the light of my life. I am blessed to call you mine.

For my mom, who put up with so much and got so little in return. Thank you for everything you ever did for me. And thank you for helping me make this book possible.

Mayte - You are my sunshine. Thank you for the never-ending encouragement and kind words. When I needed it, you were there. I am blessed to know you.

Ashley W. - You are more than a beta reader, or an editor, you have become a true friend. Your patience knows no bounds, and the world needs more talented, generous people like you in it. Thank you for sticking with this, even when I kept sending changes.

Elizabeth - One of the most talented artists I've ever met, who works at lightning speed. You are the best!

To everyone else who had a hand in the making of this book. Anne Glynn, Jennifer S, Stephanie, Angela P, Jane, Amanda and Cassie. You all had a huge impact on my writing, and making this book a success. You are all invaluable to me, and thank you for your support and encouragement.

♚ CHAPTER ONE

The gray morning light slowly wakes me up. It's nine a.m. on Sunday, and I've been home from my last job for less than twenty-four hours. I move my arms from beneath the warmth of my blanket. I don't want to get out of bed, but I need a satisfying I've-slept-ten-hours-straight kind of stretch.

It's the first time I've slept this late in months. Now that the police closed the Michael Cummings case, I have a whole two days to myself before I start my next job. Poking my finger through the blinds, I look out on another typical gray, foggy, and chilly San Francisco morning. But I roll over and stare at the ceiling again as I debate whether to stay or get up. But I fall victim to the comfort of my bed.

Okay, maybe five more minutes.

When I finally venture out of bed, my apartment is cold, and I step into my slippers and robe and shuffle into the bathroom. The face that greets me in the mirror looks more tired than usual, and I feel old for thirty-nine. Faint lines are etching their way into the tender skin around my eyes, and those laugh lines are permanent now.

Sarah says I don't look my age, which I suppose is a good thing. But compared to her, I'm the ugly step-sister. She's a slim, fiery redhead, and I blend into the walls with my dark eyes, dark hair, and olive skin. She says I'm a Mediterranean beauty, and my mom would love that. I look a lot like her, and I inherited her short stature, with plenty of curves to go with it. Sarah laughs every time I mention it.

1

I rub my cheeks and notice some new, wiry, gray hairs springing from my temple. The little bastards seem to multiply overnight. Maybe I need to get out of this job. The idea of walking away from Jeff and Cole Security Services scares me. At my age, I don't have many more years left as a security agent. It's a hard life that wears on most of us, causing more heart attacks and divorces than an average office job does. Starting over with a new company means working my way up from the bottom, which might take more years than I have left as an agent.

Years ago, Jeff promised me a franchise, and it's finally becoming a reality. The last few contracts have been extremely successful, and we're growing and hiring new agents. Tim Bennett worked out so well that I left him to handle Mr. Cummings' security on his own. But Jeff still finds it necessary to micromanage a little too much for my liking. His OCD ways aren't a surprise after twenty years, but they certainly irritate me.

I set no more than one foot into the kitchen when the phone rings and Jeff's name flashes across the screen.

"Morning Jeff. Checking up on me again?" I laugh into the phone. He knows my sarcastic nature, but he's used to it by now.

"Are you at home?" he asks. He has me on speakerphone, and it sounds like he's in the car.

"Yeah. Why?"

"Turn on CNN." I walk over to the couch and grab the remote. As I switch to the news channel, the anchor is in the midst of describing a breaking news story.

"We have a developing situation near the Brentwood section of Los Angeles. An explosion rocked the neighborhood earlier this morning, destroying one home and causing major damage to several homes nearby. Nothing is left of the property, which has been leveled down to the foundation. The house is owned by actor Erik Sinclair. You may know him as Axel Reed on the show *Lords of the Street*. Mr. Sinclair will play Cameron Porter in the Breathless series of films, the first of which is due out soon. Gas and electricity to nearly three hundred homes were turned off, and police are urging people to avoid the area."

"Holy crap, Jeff. Where is my client?"

"Ah, glad you bothered to ask. He moved into a new place. It's a ranch out in Santa Clarita. He put the Brentwood house on the market recently, but the girlfriend was living there. Well, I should say, his ex-girlfriend."

2

Well, this is interesting news.

"Is she accounted for?"

"Yes. From what I understand, no one was in the house. You sure you still want to take this case?" He has that be-careful-what-you-wish-for sort of tone in his voice.

"Yes, I'm fine with it Jeff." He laughs and brushes off my reassurance.

"Okay, but don't say I didn't warn you." His words raise the hairs on the back of my neck, but I ignore both them and the knot building in my gut.

"I have to go. I'm headed to the scene. If there's anything earth shattering, I'll update you. See you tomorrow."

When I return to the kitchen, I set the kettle to boil and then go through my work e-mail. Jeff sent me a message a few weeks back about this job, but the Michael Cummings case was becoming more dangerous, and I pushed it to the back burner.

From: Jeff Cole
Subject: New Contract
Date: August 15, 2013 13:21
To: Veronica Harper

I took on a new contract with Millennium Pictures/Olympus Television. Your new client is Erik Sinclair. He has been receiving threats since he was named as the lead character in the Holding On: Breathless film.

Before you chew me out, yes, I understand how you feel about L.A. The problem is that I need you here. I have too many contracts and not enough agents right now. I can't afford to lose this one. Tim Bennett can run things in San Fran in your absence.

Millennium Studios has hired temporary security for Mr. Sinclair and his girlfriend, so the situation is stable until the Michael Cummings case is concluded.

Jeff Cole
CEO, Cole Security Services
(See that title Ronnie? I DON'T WANT ANY SHIT ABOUT THIS CASE.)

I hadn't noticed the subtle love note below the signature line before, and I laugh a little. But still, the e-mail has me intrigued, why can't we afford to lose this contract?

Jeff knows of my distaste for everything Los Angelian, and if it were any other job, or any other boss, I might put up a fight. Even my love of warmth, bright sunshine, and beaches can't entice me to go back. I hate L.A., and I always will. The memories of being abducted, held hostage, drugged, and then raped day after day will always haunt me.

It was Jeff who rescued me, and I'll always be grateful for the care and understanding he showed afterward. It took months for me to recover from the abuse I suffered at Kincaid's hands. All these years later, I still get the sense that Jeff feels responsible. He put me on that job and no matter how many times I tell him that I don't blame him, I still see the guilt in his eyes.

I shake off the unsettling memories and go through several months of mail Sarah collected for me. Tossing the junk, I set the bills aside before opening the large Priority Mail envelope Jeff overnighted me a few weeks back. It's the dossier on my new client.

I pour a bowl of cereal and take my cup of tea and the file into the living room. CNN is playing in the background, but it's political white noise.

I flip open the dossier and read the lengthy bio on my client. Mr. Erik Sinclair is thirty-one, six-foot-two, with black hair, blue eyes, and no identifying marks. He's British, but he moved to the United States in early 2000. No arrests, no repeat trips to rehab, and no sex tapes. He's "clean", which is a rarity in Hollywood.

On the popular television series *Lords of the Street*, he plays Axel Reed, the charismatic, good-looking underboss of a violent street gang. Until recently, he'd taken smaller roles in several unremarkable Indie flicks. Landing the role of Cameron Porter in *Holding On: Breathless* is his first stint as a leading man in a major film.

Setting the folder on the table, I get comfortable on the couch and reach for the remote. Today is the perfect day to binge watch my client's television show, and I start from the first episode of season one. The opening scene is dramatic and shows four men on Harleys racing along the highway. When another rival gang catches up to them, bullets start flying, and one character lays down his bike, flipping and rolling into the brush. He stands and pulls off his helmet. It's my client.

Damn. He's young. And hot.

Holy hell he's hot and I'm screwed.

The hours tick by as I watch eight episodes. There are two classic themes to the show: the struggle between father and son and the fight between good and evil. It's the driving force behind Axel Reed's desire to take control of the gang, and I'm enthralled watching him. He's a talented actor, and he covers up his English accent well. When I finish the last episode of the first season, I'm left shaking my head. It's the most violent show I've ever watched.

I grab my laptop and do a few Internet searches on the show. It has a huge following on social media, and several of the cast members interact with fans during and after each episode. My client, however, does not. He's not interested in social media or being accessible to his fans twenty-four hours a day via Facebook or Twitter. While he isn't opposed to signing autographs or taking selfies with fans that wait for hours outside the set to catch a glimpse of him, he remains protective of his private life. "I'm not the Hollywood type," he says in interviews, and is often absent from industry events, preferring to spend his time with a group of close friends. "I'm all about the work," he says.

Flipping to the back section of the file, there he is—my insanely gorgeous client. He looks older in this picture compared to the young man I watched on television all day, but it only adds to his beauty. It's clear to me there's a bit of American Indian in his blood, and the long, jet-black hair along with a strong jaw and cheekbones give it away. His cerulean eyes are stunning, and the bad boy goatee adds to that sexy, dangerous quality. My God, those blue eyes.

I set the laptop down and continue watching another season of the Lords of the Street. I quickly become immersed in the plot, subplots, and violence. Not to mention, my client.

I wake up, startled by my phone. As I reach for it, the dossier falls off my chest. "Hello?" I mutter as Sarah's over-excited voice thunders through the line, forcing me to hold the phone away from my ear.

"So, are you ready for tonight?" I laugh at her. She's ready to party. It's been far too long since we've had a girl's night out.

"Hi Sarah. Yes, I am. I need to get a quick shower, and then I'll meet you downstairs."

"Perfect. I'll see you then."

Sarah's friendship has been one of the most important of my life, besides Jeff. She's more than just my friend and downstairs neighbor—she's a lifesaver. If it weren't for her, I might be sitting in a padded room, wearing a straitjacket, drooling and twitching in a corner. When Jeff helped me move out of Los Angeles, he was reluctant to leave me alone, but I assured him I would get help. That help came in the form of a loud, opinionated, and funny redhead named Sarah. Awakened by terrifying screams coming from the apartment upstairs, she came pounding on my door in the middle of the night.

That was one of my more severe nightmares, and when I finally let her in, she stayed with me for hours, talking me out of the panic and fear that always follows those horrible dreams. Sarah became my savior, and over time, a close friend. With her background in clinical psychology, I came to rely on her expertise with PTSD, anxiety, and depression. Even though she's a professor at the university, she's a licensed therapist, and if it weren't for her, I might not be alive today.

I lean over and retrieve the dossier from the floor. It's still open to the picture of my client, and I'm instantly caught up in his stunning features. He's the kind of guy that has women all over the world dropping their panties, and if I stare at him any longer, I might become one of them.

Better get a move on, Harper.

Shuffling into the bathroom, I jump into the steaming hot shower and mentally prepare myself for this evening. As much as I like going out with Sarah, crowded clubs can sometimes trigger anxiety. Thanks to Sarah's coaching, it's better than it was but still not completely gone.

I scrub myself down and rinse off quickly then jump out, wrapping myself in a towel. When I wipe the layer of steam off the mirror, my less than stunning features are staring back at me. I'm nothing special, and my chestnut brown hair and matching eyes are boring compared to Sarah. She has the confidence I lack, and the fashion knowledge to play up her best assets. She knows clothes; I know guns. We're polar opposites, but that's why our friendship works, I guess.

I retrieve my best outfit from the closet–it's one Sarah's seen many times–black dress slacks and my one fancy shirt of dark purple silk. She never says anything, but I know she'd just love to take me shopping. I slip into my clothes and then shrug on my black trench coat as I head out the door into the frigid night air. When I reach the bottom of the stairs, Sarah's door is already open, she's waiting.

I peek my head inside. "Hey, are you ready?" I ask. Dressed to the nines and looking beautiful, she's wearing a snug emerald green dress and heels.

"So what do you think, Japanese or Italian?" She grabs her purse and keys off the counter and then locks up while I wait.

"Um, Japanese. I don't want to go dancing after a heavy meal of pasta."

"But you're Italian," she giggles, as we walk across the courtyard to the parking lot. I roll my eyes, she knows how I love my pasta, and it's a rare occasion that I turn it down. Sarah hops into the seat beside me, and I back out of my parking spot while she fiddles with the radio. There's a Beyoncé song on, "Single Ladies". The beat is relentless and thumping, making it a great song for dancing.

"Love her," she yells over the music. "You need to get a job protecting her!" If she knew what it was like protecting these egomaniacal celebrities, she might change her mind.

We end up on Market Street, which is almost deserted on a Sunday night, and I find a parking spot right in front of the restaurant. Inside Shoji Japanese, Sarah and I sit on the red satin couch, perched just in front of the giant portrait of two Geisha's painted on the wall while we wait for a table. When the young hostess guides us through the restaurant, we pass through a maze of shoji-screened booths. Each booth is lit with a paper lantern, which is decorated with Japanese Plum tree branches dotted with bright red blooms. The seats are upholstered in red and black leather that complement the overall theme.

Even though the street was empty, the restaurant is full, and I can hear patrons laughing and clapping as the hibachi chefs perform their tricks. The hostess leaves, and our server arrives to take our drink order. Once he's gone, Sarah questions me.

"So, what is your new job about?" she asks, getting comfortable in her seat.

"He's an actor. I have to fly into LAX tomorrow morning."

She raises her eyebrows, wide eyed and concerned. "Are you prepared for this?"

The waiter returns with two glasses of water and menus. "I'll give you ladies a few minutes." He runs off again, and I'm left with Sarah's question.

"Yes and no. The nightmares have started again."

She nods. "Anything you want to talk about?"

"No. It's nothing new, just the same thing I dream about all the time."

She takes a sip of her water and continues to look over the menu. The waiter reappears with Sarah's white wine and my soda, takes our orders, and disappears again.

"So what's the client's name? Anyone I'd know?" Sarah says, keeping her eyes fixed the menu in her hand. Normally I wouldn't hesitate to tell her about a celebrity client, I know I can trust her to keep that information quiet. But this time it's different. I'm dreading her excited reaction when she realizes I'll be protecting one of Hollywood's most gorgeous, eligible bachelors.

"Ah . . . his name is Erik Sinclair." The menu flops down on the table, nearly overturning her glass of wine. Her smile and her eyes are huge.

"You mean Erik Sinclair as in *Lords of the Street*—Erik Sinclair?" I nod, holding up my index finger to my lips.

"No freaking way!" Her voice gets louder, and I scan the room nervously, hoping no one overheard her. She retrieves her phone and immediately Google searches his name and hands it to me.

"*This* Erik Sinclair?"

The picture is an artful black-and-white shot highlighting his stunning torso. He has broad shoulders and his well-defined chest is in perfect proportion to his narrow waist, with only a smattering of hair below his navel. His well-oiled, silky looking skin reminds me of the flawless white marble of Michelangelo's David. He's ripped, brooding, and magnificent.

The man is sex on legs.

She snatches the phone back from me and coos. "Ooh, here's another nice picture." She flips the phone around to show me yet another shirtless photo—this time in color. He's wearing a large Gothic cross suspended from a chain around his neck, hanging almost down to his navel, which has Sarah practically salivating. "Oh my. Now that's a very happy trail!"

Her naughty sense of humor makes me laugh, and I almost choke on my soda. But I play it off and shrug my shoulders.

"Oh, come on! He's smoking hot!" Sarah stares at me, exasperated by my lukewarm response. Apparently, four years of therapy has not made me any more agreeable to the idea of a relationship with a man, even a super-hot one. However, my disinterest isn't about my past getting in the way, it's because I can't protect someone I'm lusting after. And right now, Sarah's not helping.

Forget those blue eyes.

Returning her attention to the phone, she swipes through a few more pictures before slipping it into her purse.

"So how are things with Jeff?"

"Okay, I suppose."

"You suppose? What's going on Ronnie?" She takes a bite of her entrée that the waiter just placed on the table. She stares at me for a moment, and I'm not sure what to say.

"I don't know, Sarah. He's been very irritable. I'm not sure what's going on." I sip on my soda.

"Have you asked him?"

I nod. "Yes. But he says everything is fine. I'm worried about him."

Right now, I feel tense and helpless. My best friend is going through something, and I can't help him with it. I can't even get him to talk about it.

"So when are you going to try dating again? Don't you think it's been long enough?" Her quick shift in topic leaves me speechless. It's the ninety-ninth time she's asked me, and every time my answers are the same: I don't have time for dating. I'm never home. My job has become my whole life, and my crutch. The long hours and jobs far away from home make it easy for me to avoid the whole problem of men and relationships. Giving up the protective shield of my job would force me to admit the truth. I'm still afraid.

"Listen, you've been telling me that for five years. It's time to get out there honey! Now, what about your client? He's super-hot!" I drop my chopsticks and stare at her.

"Okay, you've officially lost your mind! I can't go fucking my client, no matter how cute he is!"

She covers her mouth and laughs at my indignation. "I knew it! You think he's hot, admit it!" She points a finger at me.

I'm busted.

I should know better than to hide things from Sarah.

Monday mornings at San Francisco International always seem to bring out a rush of business travelers. The airport is jammed with them, all pressed and neatly coiffed in their business suits and tight pencil skirts. My flight is in an hour, and I have some time to kill.

Finding a newsstand, I walk inside and browse the various offerings. The shelves are lined with souvenirs, t-shirts, and a plethora of snacks and drinks.

It's food that I'm after. Last night's excursion with Sarah had us rolling in the door at two a.m., and the last thing my stomach can handle is overpriced, greasy airport food. I should have known better. Sarah starts slow, but once the music takes over, she can pound back the shots like a salty sailor.

Spying some trail mix on a shelf, I grab a bag and head toward the cooler for a drink. With my food in hand, I turn and see it—*Holding On: Breathless.*

Almost one whole corner of the store is devoted to the three novels, lined up in neat rows from the ceiling to the floor. The monochrome covers catch my eye, and I wander over to the wall as my curiosity takes over. Just as I pick up the book with a red flogger on it, a bright-eyed sales girl approaches me.

"Have you read the first one?" The girl is young and obviously well acquainted with the books. I shake my head, embarrassed to admit I'm the one person on the planet who hasn't read this.

"Really? They're fantastic! You should totally start with this one. It's the first of three." She reaches for a book with the bed on the front and hands it to me.

"Thanks," I say as she scampers off, leaving me to find a quiet spot in the corner where I can flip through a few pages. The heroine, Bianca Wright is young and naïve, and falls for Cameron Porter, who's rich, spoiled, and reckless. Seems like the standard, formulaic romance novel—which ordinarily wouldn't interest me—but I take it, hoping to understand the hysteria surrounding my client.

I pay for my items and head toward the gate, trying to maneuver in the fast moving crowd. When I find a seat, I pull open the book, and read a few more pages, but the obnoxious businessman talking loudly on his phone next to me is distracting. I pull out my phone and load my playlist, looking for something upbeat, and "Up All Night" by Alex Clare is at the top of my list. My choice of music is ironic considering last night.

Within a few minutes, the attendants call for VIP boarding, and I gather my belongings and head down the Jetway. I make my way to business class, and as I'm stuffing my carry-on in the overhead bin, I hear a voice behind me.

"Excuse me ma'am, I'm in seat A." I turn to find a dark-haired young man in a navy suit waiting with his ticket in hand. He's attractive and probably fresh out of college with an MBA. I'm relieved when he pulls a slim laptop from his carry-on and then slides past me into his window seat.

Thankfully, he'll spend the flight typing away on some new business plan or a project outline instead of talking my ear off.

I slump heavily into my seat, stuffing the bag with my book into the seat pocket. My bag of trail mix crinkles loudly, catching his attention. He eyes the back of the seat for long seconds and then smiles at me. Mr. Junior Executive must be familiar with the book, and he smiles at me nervously as his eyes dart back and forth from me to the book.

Pervert.

As the flight attendants prepare for boarding, I pull out the dossier and read up on my client:

> Millennium Studios has selected Mr. Sinclair to play the lead role of a spoiled playboy with a fetish for BDSM in the movie Holding on: Breathless. Fans of the best-selling book disagree with the choice of Sinclair for the lead. Within days, several Internet petitions (see: change.org) have sprung up demanding other actors be considered for the part. Mr. Sinclair has received virtual threats through Social media as well as physical threats left at his home and work. Millennium Studios, backer of Holding On: Breathless, has hired temporary security for Mr. Sinclair and his live-in girlfriend, Miss Catriona O'Neill. The threats consist mostly of letters mailed to the home of Mr. Sinclair, with some arriving in boxes containing lingerie. One box containing a threatening letter was left at the Lords of the Street set on September 10, 2013 [See enclosed pictures].

The pictures of the evidence are interesting. At best, they look like a kindergarten project. Words and letters cut out of magazines to form sentences, glued to paper. *Amateurs do this kind of shit.*

The text of the first two letters is typical, saying things like he should drop out if he knows what's good for him, and if he doesn't want to see his girlfriend hurt. The third letter, however, is more disturbing and unique, making explicit reference to BDSM:

> You have no business aspiring to play a BDSM Dominant. You're just a paltry substitute for the real thing. One must learn to submit before they can dominate. One must experience the pain before they can inflict it. Are you prepared to experience the pain of losing everything?

At the bottom of the note is a picture of a woman shackled to a Saint Andrews Cross, her back is raw and bloody from a severe whipping. The memories come back in a bitter torrent, and I flip the page, trying to stem the rising panic. The next page is more pictures of evidence, mainly the boxes of shredded lingerie that arrived with the notes. Each piece appear to be high end, and not the type of thing the average overeager fan would spend money on only to shred and leave on someone's doorstep. Whoever bought these is serious.

Someone wants to be noticed.

♚ CHAPTER TWO

I wake from my catnap as the plane hits the runway, and I'm out of my seat as soon as the fasten seat belt light is off. As Mr. Junior Executive gathers his belongings, he watches me surreptitiously. I turn and walk out the door, but halfway down the Jetway, he catches up with me.

"Ms., you left this. Ms.!" He shouts at me, and I turn.

"That's okay. I don't need it." His eyebrows lift, and he turns with a huff. When we reach the gate, I watch with amusement as he tosses the book on a seat in the waiting area.

LAX is jammed as usual, and I make my way through a sea of tourist, passing by the occasional throng of paparazzi hounding some celebrity. After a long walk, I reach the lower-level baggage claim, and my tension level rises as the city looms closer. It's as if I'm descending into my own personal hell, which lies just beyond the glass doors. The lump in my throat feels like cement, and I swallow hard as I step off the escalator. I move with the mass of foreign voices and jockey for a position near the carousel.

When I exit, the bright Los Angeles sunshine and smog hit me in face, and it fills my lungs with dread. But as soon as I spot Hunter standing next to the car, my nerves settle down. He's tall, muscular, graying at the temples, with trusting green eyes that are made more prominent by his tan skin. Hunter is the strong silent type, a former Marine, and he's lost none of his military spit and polish over the years. He never strays from his high and tight, his crisp black suit, and no-nonsense demeanor. Even though he rarely smiles, his quiet and steady demeanor is welcoming to me.

13

Hunter pumps my hand as I step off the curb. "Good to see you, Ronnie!" he exclaims as he reaches for my bags. He slams the trunk closed, and I slip into the back seat.

"How was your flight?" The dull thunk of the driver's side door signals the start of the ride to the Cole Security offices.

"Mostly uneventful. I had some time to read up on my client though."

He nods at me in the rearview and then pulls out into traffic. Hunter filled my spot as Jeff's right-hand man when I moved to San Francisco, and I'm grateful. Relocating may not have been possible if not for him. Left to his own devices, Jeff could easily drive off employees with his overbearing managerial style. For years, I served as a buffer between him and the troops as his Staff Non-Commissioned Officer. I managed the day-to-day mentoring of the junior NCOs while Jeff handled the brass. Together we were a good team.

After he agreed to let me work out of San Francisco, our relationship changed. We weren't best friends and co-workers anymore, and it took a while for both of us to get used to it. Instead of seeing each other daily, we called each other every day, but over time, that waned and was slowly replaced by texts and e-mail. Our relationship became more formal—less like buddies and more strained. Even with the substantial increase in revenue from my office, the change in his demeanor over the last few months has me puzzled. He should be happy.

When we arrive at the Cole Security office, Hunter pulls open the door for me. "Jeff is waiting for you. I'll take care of the bags Ronnie."

From the outside, the Cole Security building looks a lot like a warehouse. No one would suspect just by looking at it what goes on inside. I walk up to the double doors and scan my employee badge. Beyond the doors, the office is cold and sterile. The black marble floors and white walls add to the ominous feel. The heels of my shoes click along the floor as I walk, and the smell of the leather furniture fills my nostrils.

I pass the reception desk as Marci waves hello. She looks the same, all primped and pulled together with her tight bun and pencil skirt. While she's attractive, Jeff wouldn't hire the typical blonde bombshell executive assistant you see everywhere in Hollywood. Marci is smart, efficient, and reliable enough to keep the office running, even if Jeff is out of town. Between Hunter and Marci, they provide a nice buffer between Jeff and the rest of the employees.

"Can I get you something Ronnie?" She asks politely. I shake my head, and she points to Jeff's office. "Go ahead. He's free."

Taking a deep breath, I ready myself for an uncomfortable meeting with Jeff. It's the first time I've seen him in more than six months. He won't discuss what is bothering him, not today, and not in front of Hunter.

I exhale sharply and step into the office, and when Jeff moves in to hug me, I stiffen automatically. He grasps my arm in his one hand and looks me over to see if I'm still the same.

"How are you my friend?" He asks as he backs up, sitting on the corner of his desk with one leg dangling like a snake from a tree.

"I'm good Jeff. You call me enough, you should know."

Jeff smiles, ignoring my sarcastic wit. "So I received a wonderful report from Michael Cummings. He's very pleased with your service." He wears the look of a proud papa on his face.

"I'm glad things turned out well. He's a nice man." I pick at some lint on my pants as I try to mask my apprehension.

"He's very happy to keep Tim Bennett around. If we weren't stretched so thin, I'd have him back you up on this job as well. He was a great hire, Ronnie."

"So why is Millennium hiring this one out anyway?" I ask abruptly, feeling uncomfortable with his praise. I don't get it. If he's so pleased, why is he so crabby?

"They're not. It's Olympus Television and the producer, Mark Cohen, who want additional security. After the last threat was received at the set, he figured it was time to tighten things up."

Jeff stops speaking as Hunter approaches the door. Waving him in, Hunter sits on the black couch opposite me. After sliding off the desk, Jeff retrieves a brown folder from the drawer. When I reach for it, I notice Hunter's expression. His shoulders stiffen, his jaw locks, and the tension rips through him.

"Here, have a look at this. This is a bigger problem than Olympus Television," he says. The folder is heavy in my hand, and the emblem on the cover page is recognizable as the FBI's. My blood runs cold as I flip through several pages, skimming through the IT Forensics report, noticing words like hacked, spoofing, and Cole Security.

"We got hacked? By whom?"

He sits on the corner of the desk again, watching me as I read. "I'm not sure." He crosses his legs, one over the other and sighs. "We found a message on one of our servers, more like a sick love note actually." He points to the folder, and I flip the page.

"As long as Sinclair plays Cameron, he's not safe. I'll find him, no matter who's around him, no matter who tries to protect him."

"Is the actress playing Bianca a target?" I ask, confused.

Jeff shakes his head, looking grave. "No. I don't believe so. She hasn't received threats of any kind. That message was left on the server in your personnel folder."

I suddenly feel as if my stomach has been launched out of my body and over the top of the Empire State Building. It's a warning to both me and my client, but why? How would anyone know to target me? I look at Jeff, and he reads my expression immediately. He shakes his head as he turns and sits in his chair.

"I don't know. Hacking was not Kincaid's thing. I've got everyone here working on it, and I'm in constant contact with the FBI, so as soon as I know, you'll know. Your buddy over there, John Grilli, is working the case." This calms my jangled nerves a bit. I've known John since childhood, and he's become like a brother to me, someone I know will always be there for me. He's not just a peer, and I trust him with my life.

"We need to take extra precautions until we find out who is behind the threats. I've put a rush on the security for the set, but judging by the size, the Santa Clarita house will take more time." He hands me another brown folder.

"This is the property layout for Mr. Sinclair's ranch house. He moved in a few weeks ago." The photo of the thirty-acre lot worries me. His house sits in the bottom of a valley, surrounded by outbuildings and a heavily forested ridgeline.

"This place is a stalker's dream. The ridgeline is perfect cover, and the buildings offer plenty of places to hide," I say.

Jeff nods his head, but he moves on to other matters. "So far we have nothing on the Brentwood house. I spoke to the Fire Marshall, and he doesn't think it was a gas main leak. We won't know anything until they finish the investigation."

He rubs at the stubble on his chin. Since leaving the military, he's given up on shaving regularly. It suits him though. "I spoke with his ex, Catriona

O'Neill." He mentions casually. My eyes shift from the property layout to his face.

"Is she a person of interest?"

He shakes his head. "No, not at this time. She didn't notice anything unusual before she left yesterday. She has been living at the Brentwood house since she and Mr. Sinclair split up three months ago. He moved out to Santa Clarita before the threats started."

Jeff sounds unconcerned by the issue of the ex-girlfriend, and in his mind, only one body to protect means only one agent. But for me, it's a cause of anxiety. I'll be alone with him. All alone with a make-me-weak-in-the-knees, newly single piece of man candy. *Lord help me.*

"You'd better get going." Jeff raises an eyebrow, silently asking where I had drifted off to. When I don't offer up an explanation, he continues. "Hunter will get a Cadillac Escalade ready for you."

Hunter rises from the couch, causing the leather to squeak as he moves. He's gone in an instant, and I make myself busy packing the new folder containing the details of Sinclair's property in my bag.

"Stay safe, please," he says, rising from his chair, looking concerned.

"Always Jeff." He hugs me again, tightly. Even with one arm, Jeff gives an amazingly strong hug. He's managed to overcome his injuries and what they cost him. Not long after he recovered, the Army discharged him. But it was losing his wife of barely two years that almost broke him. When Amy left, he went to a very dark place, drinking and nearly overdosing on heavy-duty painkillers. Whatever brought him back from the edge, I'll never know. But I was happy to have my friend back.

I wiggle nervously from his embrace, and he seems distressed by it. He knows being close to people, even him, unnerves me. The pained look on his face makes my heart ache, but I can't help how I feel.

I turn and wave a hand as I walk through the lobby. Now I understand the reason behind his odd mood, the hacking attempt is enough to put him on high alert. Jeff would never have put me on this case if he thought Kincaid was behind those threats, but if he has hacked into our network, he might know I've moved out of Los Angeles. The thought of him, lurking, waiting for his chance halts my steps, and the sense of safety I've had all these years drains away.

"Your bags are in the back, along with the ammunition." Hunter nods and hands me the keys before opening the door so I can climb into the SUV.

"Thanks, I'll see you soon."

The GPS screen flickers to life, and I punch in the address of the North Hollywood set. The annoying GPS bitch starts giving me directions, demanding I turn right in three hundred feet. *Yeah, sure lady. In this traffic, that distance will take twenty-five minutes. How about you make yourself useful and get me a burger and a beer?*

As I pass through several neighborhoods, the streets look familiar. The set is almost an hour from where I used to live, and far from the Cole offices, but not far from where my ill-fated job took place. The close proximity raises the hairs on my neck, and instantly, I'm back there. Fighting for my life.

As I approach the street, I notice the warehouse where Kincaid took me is gone. In its place is a shiny new shopping center, complete with a restaurant, a nail salon, and a bank. They could have built Disneyland on this very spot, but for me, the awful memories will always be there. I interrupted Kincaid's plans for Miranda Cassidy–I look like her, so for him, I was an acceptable substitute. And I certainly paid the price for it.

When I finally arrive at the set, I'm disappointed to find it's not one of the swanky, high security major studio lots. In fact, it's nothing more than a dirty looking back alley, surrounded by a standard, six-foot chain-link fence. The guard, a rather rotund looking man, sits on a stool ten feet from the street. I suppose I should be happy there's a guard, but he's unarmed, and looks like he couldn't catch anything except his lunch. As I turn into the driveway, the heavyset guard greets me. Handing him my ID card through the open window, I introduce myself.

"Veronica Harper from Cole Security Services, I'm here to meet Mr. Erik Sinclair." As he checks my ID against the clipboard in his hand, his lips tighten into a knot, accentuating his chipmunk-like cheeks. He nods at me as he returns my ID.

"Let me open the gate," he says as he walks away. Pulling a set of keys from his pocket, he opens the lock on the gate and stops to lift his radio to his mouth. "Ms. Harper is here to see Mr. Sinclair," he says then lowers the radio to give me directions.

"Pull in and make a left, Ms. Harper. You can park in one of the empty spaces behind the trailers."

I drive through and park behind the first trailer. Once I turn off the car, I grab my messenger bag, and when I make it around to the front of the trailers, I notice how close they are to the gate. With no more than fifty feet between the fence and the first trailer, it would be easy for anyone to toss a threatening note or a box of ripped up lingerie right over the top. They're lucky it wasn't something explosive. When the security guard meets me, I'm informed that I'm standing in front of my client's trailer.

"You can wait here. Mr. Sinclair should be done soon." I nod at him, and he turns around to leave.

Really? You're just going to leave me here alone? He lumbers back to the main gate, and I turn, taking a look around the set. There is a long row different sized trailers, probably for wardrobe and crew, with the permanent buildings situated at the far end of the lot. One has a blue sign that reads "Axel's Pub" at the top. Another building across from the pub is heavily damaged and pockmarked with bullet holes. Jagged shards of glass cling to the window frame and the door is missing.

Jeez, we really need to step up security around here.

I look around, and except for the gate guard, the set is almost empty. Yet, even with the lack of activity, I would never allow a guest to wander around the set or trailers unaccompanied. I climb up the steps, have a seat on the landing, and I pull out my files. There's no time like the present to get some work done. Studying the property layout is a priority so I grab the photo. The house is large, and it takes time to plan a security installation. It's not long before I'm lost in my work, and perhaps ten minutes passes, maybe more.

"Excuse me, may I help you?" The deep, urbane voice surprises me, but when I look up, the person standing before looks intimidating. Disregarding the files, I let them slip from my lap as I stand. My hand instinctively reaches inside my jacket and wraps around the grip of my Glock as I assess him. He looks like a criminal; the low-slung jeans, plaid shirt, and black leather jacket all add to his gang member appearance.

"Who are you?" I demand as I stand my ground.

He smiles subtly and looks back toward the thick-necked bouncer behind him. Then I notice it. Sewn on the front of the leather jacket are the words "Lords of the Street." I close my eyes for a mere second and relax my stance, letting my hand slip off the grip. It's *him*. It's Erik Sinclair.

"Sorry, I didn't mean to startle you," he says, looking up at me with bright blue eyes, evidently unaware that he was seconds away from being shot.

"I'm Erik. And you are?" Before I can form an answer, the breeze picks up, and the noise of scattering papers catches both of our attention. With one hand, he pulls off the beanie cap as he bounds up the stairs two at a time. As he passes me, I inhale his scent. It's an interesting mixture of motorcycle exhaust and leather along with something spicy, citrusy, and very masculine. I step down to just beneath the landing and gather the papers that fell.

"Here, let me," he says with a hint of an English accent. He looks very different from his headshot, more scruffy and dangerous. But it's him all right. The very same one who's well-defined torso made me weak in the knees. My brain downshifts into neutral as I watch his long, graceful fingers arrange my papers into a neat pile.

"And you are?" It takes a few seconds for my head to clear, but this time, I manage to introduce myself.

"I'm sorry, Veronica Harper, from Cole Security Services." He nods as I extend a hand, but he doesn't take it. His hands are full of my papers.

"Pleased to meet you. Come inside." He turns to open the door, but can't, and turns to face me again. "Here, these are yours." The soft warm skin of his hands meets mine, and the contact is electric. White-hot sparks erupt between our fingers, and I hold his gaze, I think for a few seconds moment, but it could be longer.

He pulls his hands from underneath the pile, but I'm caught in his unwavering stare. The slightest tightening of the soft skin around his eyes says he's aware of it too. Turning around on the cramped landing, he opens the door and walks into the trailer. It's dark and dreary inside and nothing like the luxury accommodations I imagined. The mostly brown furnishings are sparse and worn, and the carpet has been repaired with duct tape adjacent to the door. Setting the pile on the small dinette, I watch as Erik slips off his leather jacket. The bulk of it along with the baggy jeans makes him look much larger and more intimidating. With just the layers of flannel, he looks like any other guy, but perhaps more handsome than most. *More like impossibly handsome*, I think as my mind wanders to the photos Sarah found last night. The man in those photos resembled a marble statue, carved by some Italian master, perfect and unattainable. Instead, the man before me is real. No Photoshop, no makeup, and no special lighting.

"I'm Dan Royce." The thick-necked, red headed bouncer reaches out a hand, returning my thoughts to the present. He's tall and powerfully built, wearing tan chinos and a pale blue shirt, which is just a bit too tight around his biceps. I shake his hand, and he retreats, taking a seat on the couch.

"You must work for Millennium?" I ask, and he nods at me with an air of confidence that belies his actual importance.

"Please, take a seat." Erik sits next to Dan, and I pull out a chair at the dinette, giving myself some room to breathe.

"I noticed pictures of my house in your papers. What is that for?" He scratches at his shiny black hair as he waits for an answer.

"It's a property layout for the security system, Mr. Sinclair."

He suddenly looks perturbed, even confused. "I don't understand. Why is a security system necessary?" It seems no one from Millennium or Olympus is keeping him briefed on the threats or procedures necessary to keep him safe.

"Mr. Sinclair, after the explosion at your Brentwood house yesterday, we need to take extra precautions. Your Santa Clarita property sits in a valley surrounded by a heavily forested ridgeline. You wouldn't know you were under threat until it was too late." My blunt assessments tend to frighten even the most difficult clients, but not him.

"I still don't understand. That explosion was probably a gas leak. Besides, no one is going to come all the way out to Santa . . . " He looks annoyed when I shake my head, his lip crinkles, and his eyebrows bunch.

"The investigation is still ongoing. Until we have a report from the Fire Marshall, we have to treat the incident as suspect. And yes, Mr. Sinclair, a person who wants to hurt you would indeed make an effort to come all the way out to Santa Clarita."

Dan's eyes grow wide, and he huffs loudly. He exchanges a dubious glance with Erik before he speaks.

"I can't believe all this would be necessary." Dan's interjection is unwelcome, and it takes a force of will not to dress him down and leave him whimpering in a corner. When I stand and slip my papers into my bag, I give him a professional, yet concise response.

"If you prefer to forgo the security measures, I'd be happy to leave you in Dan's capable hands." I sling my bag over my shoulder and wait. When Erik looks at Dan, he cocks his head toward the door, and Dan rises. As he closes the door behind him, it's obvious they've developed a rapport with each other over the last two months. We're suddenly alone, and my heart rate skyrockets as his demeanor turns icy.

"Ms. Harper, Dan may not have your expertise or resources, but he's done a good job over the last few months. He deserves a little respect, don't you think?" He stares at me with a raised eyebrow.

21

His commanding tone leaves me withering inside. Only one person dresses me down, and that's Jeff. Yet, my boss's reprimands don't leave me in a puddle. It's suddenly very warm in the trailer, and it seems to get hotter as he rises from the couch and moves toward me.

"Mr. Sinclair, please take a look at my résumé. If you'd rather go with Dan's expertise in security matters, be my guest." I stare him down, but his focus never wavers as he steps closer. He reaches for the paper that I've pulled from my bag, and our fingers touch again. He feels it too—the connection. I can see it on his face as he quickly drags a finger across my knuckles then pauses for a few brief seconds before pulling away. I swallow hard and step backward, but the distance does no good.

Dammit, breathe Harper.

The need to escape his presence builds as he goes silent. His eyes move over me, touching every inch of my frame as he paces around me.

This is almost unbearable.

"I'll step outside while you . . . "

He turns abruptly. "No, please. Don't go," he says in a gentle tone, tipping his head to the side. The tingles rocket through me, and I wonder how is it that just a few words uttered from his beautiful mouth makes everything okay? *Does he have this effect on all women or is it just me?* I sit down and watch his slow, lithe movements as he walks around immersed in his task, while I kick myself for not having stepped outside.

"You spent fifteen years in the Army? Why didn't you stay the full twenty?" he asks as he looks up from my résumé.

I gulp hard and gather my wits. He's noticed the gap in my employment history, and I have no choice but to explain it. "Mr. Cole recommended me for the FBI. They were doing a lot of hiring in the mid to late '90s." A look of confusion quickly washes over his face. He stares at the paper then back to me.

"Mr. Cole? So you knew him before you worked for Cole Security?"

"Yes. We served in the same battalion. He was my commanding officer." His eyebrows dart upward and his mouth crinkles as he nods. His reaction strikes me as odd. Why would he care how long I've known Jeff, and why the frown? I smile to myself a little as I stare at my hands. Maybe he's wondering if me and Jeff . . . *No, don't be stupid Harper.*

♟ CHAPTER THREE

My smile must rattle him, and when I look up again, he's partially crumpled my resume in his fist. "He . . . um . . . he obviously values your skills, if he chose to hire you outside the military," he stammers then takes a seat at the small dinette, closing the distance between us. "So how long were you with the FBI?"

"I was only with the FBI for a year." I don't elaborate, hoping he will take the hint and move on to other questions.

"Why such a short employment? Working for the FBI is a prestigious job."

I stare at my shoes and explain one of the most embarrassing chapters in my employment history. "Dealing with the layers of management, procedure, and governmental red tape was a bit difficult. It wasn't the best fit for me," I admit, hoping he accepts my answer and moves on.

"I see. A rebel." His mouth softens into a wicked smile, and it's a smile that could take me to another planet. I fidget, laying my hands in my lap and weaving my fingers together tightly.

"No. I'm just impatient." Those blue eyes are staring a hole right through me now.

"Low tolerance for frustration?" he smirks in reply.

I shrug. "Perhaps."

He's picking me apart, and I'm not sure why. Any more of this intrusive questioning and that frustration he's picked up on might make an appearance. "May I ask to what these questions tend?" The words fall out of my mouth, laced with a bit of sarcasm. He pauses, never taking his eyes off me, and a slight smile rises at the corner of his lips.

"Merely to the illustration of your character. I'm trying to make it out," he says, letting the melodious ring of his English accent come out.

His words have the familiar ring of something well known and loved. As I search my brain, the words flash before my eyes. He's quoting a book. Cheeky bastard! Perhaps he thinks I'm some literary heroine. A Jane Eyre, a Tess, or a Scarlet, all romantic and swooning, one leg rising as she's kissed by the object of her desire.

Maybe I should lay my gun on the table.

I raise an eyebrow and give him a sly smile before answering. "And what is your success? Mr. Darcy?"

He laughs heartily, throwing his head back. "Well done, Ms. Harper, touché."

Apparently, this conversation has devolved into a game of flirtatious brinkmanship, instead of an interview.

"Do you always quote Jane Austen when conducting interviews, Mr. Sinclair? Should I expect Shakespeare next?" I smile, but then stop, realizing I'm being drawn into his playful game.

He laughs again, this time setting my résumé on the table. "No, Ms. Harper. No more classic literature, I promise. However, I won't apologize for trying to figure you out," he says, as he draws a finger across his bottom lip.

"The only thing you need to know about me is if I'll take a bullet for you, Mr. Sinclair. Whether I'm an impatient person or not has no relevance." He nods and stares at his lap, thoughtfully forming his reply.

"Ah, but I disagree. If I'm to spend the next several months with you, I'd prefer to find out now if you have a taciturn personality." He looks at the table and lightly taps at the résumé with his fingertips. "I mean, your work history speaks for itself. You have an impressive background in military tactics, surveillance, and security. Not to mention, you're probably deadly with a gun."

He gives me a sideways glance, and every muscle in my body goes weak. This man can take a simple sentence and make it into something sexy, even vaguely erotic. *How is that possible?* He pauses again, and I open my mouth to thank him for his generous assessment of my skills, but there's a knock on the door.

"Erik, Mr. Cohen is here." Dan steps inside, followed by another man. He's short and rather mousey looking. His neatly trimmed brown hair is laced with gray, and his black rimmed glasses dominate his small face. He approaches me and extends his hand.

"Ms. Harper, nice to meet you. I'm Mark Cohen, executive producer of Lords." He's very polite, but I sense that he's a potent force around set. He's in charge, acting as head writer, producer, and director. Tagging along behind him is a woman, probably in her fifties. She's the epitome of a Hollywood bombshell, with miles of long blond hair and enormous fake breasts that are propped up precariously underneath her snug blue sweater.

"This is my wife, Beth." She has a warm smile and a firm handshake for me.

"I'm glad you're here." She smiles, and I appreciate her attempt to make me feel welcome.

"I was just going over her résumé," Erik says as he joins the Cohen's on the couch. I sense the interview is not over, and I take my seat at the dinette again.

"So you're going to protect Erik?" he asks. I try to speak, but he ignores me and continues. "Pardon me, but how is a pretty little lady like you going to protect him? What are you? All of a hundred pounds, soaking wet?" Cohen laughs, but Erik looks a bit embarrassed, and Beth appears mortified by her husband's chauvinistic, sarcastic tone.

I try to mask my anger, gritting my teeth behind my lips. While he may be the boss around here, I have no intention of putting up with his insults. But years of being reprimanded for my sharp tongue slam back into my brain, along with Jeff's words: "Watch your tongue soldier." I decide to stow it, and when I don't answer, he looks toward Erik for agreement.

"I can't see how she's going to protect you, man." The embarrassment on Beth's face quickly changes to horror, and her mouth falls open. She looks at me, and tilts her head, her eyebrows turned upward as a silent apology for her husband's impertinent remarks. But it's too late. I've put up with as much as I can from him.

"Mr. Cohen, I've served in combat and hauled wounded soldiers twice my size over my shoulder. Perhaps you should—" It's all I can get out of my mouth before Beth steps in.

"For the life of me, Mark, I cannot believe the shit that just came out of your mouth! You should be ashamed of yourself." Beth snatches my résumé from Erik's hand and continues her rant.

"This little lady has one hell of a background. As attractive as she is, she could probably beat the shit out of half the guys on this lot. Want more do you want Mark?" She glares at him, waiting for an answer. He pulls the paper from her hand and smiles hesitantly at her before looking it over.

I stand in amused silence as she looks at me and smiles. "Don't let them intimidate you honey," she says with a wink. Her words are genuine and encouraging. I like her, a lot.

"Look, don't get me wrong, Ms. Harper, I have a vested interest in his safety. Millennium wants him for a few months, but I need him for the next two or three years." I understand his point, but his delivery leaves a lot to be desired.

"I appreciate your concern, Mr. Cohen." My focus shifts to Erik, who's nervously raking his hair from his eyes. "The final decision is up to you, Mr. Sinclair. It all depends on who you feel comfortable with."

Erik nods. "I think Mark makes a good point. We may want to keep Dan around for some muscle, just as backup. Would Mr. Cole consider hiring him on a part-time basis to help out?"

His suggestion doesn't offend me. He's developed a relationship with Dan, and his presence may be useful after all. Perhaps my client will think twice about flirting in front of Dan.

"I'll call him and ask. Is this a deal breaker?" Cohen nods and Erik follows suit. "Let me step outside and call Mr. Cole. Excuse me, please."

Once I step outside, I inhale the cold air, trying to cool my temper. I'm annoyed by the complete change in attitude, when only minutes ago, Sinclair admitted that Dan lacks experience. But I shrug and write it off. Sinclair is probably trying to appease Mr. Cohen.

I dial Jeff and when he answers, I explain the situation. As expected, he's irritated that Mr. Cohen would question my skills, and by extension, his judgment as CEO. Although, refusing Cohen could cost us the contract and as he said—we can't afford to lose this contract. It doesn't take much to change his mind however. With the lack of security and the long hours Mr. Sinclair spends on set, this job requires to agents. He sighs and agrees to make the arrangements with Millennium without much of a fight.

Stuffing my phone into my pocket, I climb the stairs, and when I walk into the trailer, Mr. Sinclair, Beth, and Mr. Cohen are discussing my résumé. He and Erik seem relieved when I tell them Jeff will arrange to keep Dan on staff. Dan, of course, appears thrilled. Mr. Cohen stands, and Beth follows. Stopping in front of me, he looks over his glasses as he speaks.

"No offense, Ms. Harper. Just making sure my bread stays buttered, if you know what I mean."

"I understand, Mr. Cohen." He moves toward the door as Beth stops in front of me. She gives me an encouraging smile. "If you need anything, please, let me know."

I nod at her in thanks as they leave. Thank God that interview is over. Erik looks relieved as he stands up and follows Dan to the door. They are arranging lunch, and my stomach growls noisily at the thought of eating something other than trail mix. A burger and a beer sound good right about now, but I'll have to be content with a Chicken Caesar Salad.

"Ice water is fine for me, Dan." He nods and jogs down the wooden stairs, rocking the flimsy trailer from side to side.

"I'm sorry about all that. I hope you're thick-skinned. Mark is . . . an acquired taste." His voice lilts as he speaks, and his blue eyes twinkle a bit. "He has a unique sense of humor and absolutely no verbal filter. You just have to get used to it. He meant no harm really." he says, motioning for me to take my seat again.

"I understand his concern. You, however, will need to learn to trust me, Mr. Sinclair." He looks up at me with a faint smile on his lips and looks almost intrigued by my request.

"Please, call me Erik," he says.

I'm surprised. Clients almost never ask me to call them by their first name. It's not professional, and Jeff would not be pleased if I did. Becoming too chummy with a guy as good looking as him could cost me my job. My eyes settle on his mouth, but I quickly recover my wits, pulling the dossier from my bag again.

I run through my list of information I need from him: the phone number for his publicist, what cast appearances he has scheduled, and the vehicles he owns. But a sudden knock at the door puts an end to my nervous ramblings. It's Dan coming to drop off our food. Erik rushes to the door and takes the boxes from Dan and sets them on the table before retrieving our drinks

My hands shake slightly as Erik offers me the large cup filled with ice water, and he notices. He stares boldly into my eyes, and there's a slight crinkle of recognition at the corner of his mouth. I suddenly feel naked, holding a drink. Erik sits down, and his focus shifts to his food, and I'm grateful his attention is off me. Perhaps I'll calm down if he's not boring a hole into my skull with those blue eyes.

When he tears into his salad, he picks up where my ramblings left off. "So that's a long list of security precautions. I don't like all the idea of tracking equipment and cameras in my house." He shovels another large forkful of lettuce into his mouth and chews loudly.

"Well, we can forego all the security and you could end up as someone else's prisoner." I shrug at him nonchalantly as I take a bite of chicken. His eyes immediately widen, perhaps in reaction to my bluntness. You'd think he'd be used to that with Mr. Cohen's smart mouth.

"I don't think that'd be much fun for you, would it, Ms. Harper?" He smiles, and that mouth captures my attention. His lips look soft and kissable. "Look, all of this is incredibly intrusive. I had no idea my life would change so fast when I got involved with this movie. It seems a bit too much to me."

He's humble and hot. This is not good.

Before he digs his heels in any further, I change direction. "May I ask about Miss O'Neill? Are you in contact with her?" He shifts uncomfortably in his seat and rests a fisted hand on the table before sighing.

"No, not really. Just the occasional text message. There are still a lot of her things at my house."

I suppose leaving things behind is the perfect excuse to return and to keep contact going. Smart, very smart. But if I were her, I might do the same thing.

"Do you think she has anything to do with the threats? Or maybe the explosion at the Brentwood—" I freeze mid-sentence when I see the change in his expression. He sits back in his chair and the anger emanates from him like a blast wave. His shoulders tense and the muscles in his jaw clench, he's turned to stone.

"No, she doesn't. Next subject, Ms. Harper." I drop my fork in the box and straighten my spine. I hit a nerve, and apparently, it's a very raw one. He shifts again, and the crackling tension between us lingers, hanging in the air like a thick fog. I try to gather my thoughts and remember my list of questions I typically ask clients, but before I speak another word, the door swings open.

"Erik, you have fifteen minutes," Dan calls out sticking his head in the door briefly.

"Thanks, Dan." He turns back to his salad without looking at me again.

His departure is relief. I'm used to being a constant companion, never alone. But this one rattles me. The sexual tension is suffocating and a potentially dangerous distraction. He makes his way out the door, and Dan waves at me. I nod at him, allowing him to take the reins for the time being.

Dan is in and out of the trailer at various times throughout the day, and I gather his appearances correlate with Erik's schedule. Since Erik is the lead character in the show, filming can last twelve hours a day, sometimes more, I'm told. In hindsight, having Dan around is a benefit, as it leaves me free to take care the security system layout and make calls to Erik's "people". My first call is to his agent, and my brief conversation with Mr. Alessandro De Luca is very productive. He is happy to keep in contact with me about any future projects, interviews, or appearances.

With Dan supervising Erik at the makeup trailer for the next hour, I make a call to his publicist, but my conversation with her is less than productive. My recommendation to check with me on any interviews or appearances didn't go over so well. Getting her to agree that his safety is far more important than press releases was nearly a ten-minute battle.

Once I finish with my calls, I head out of the trailer. Dan is sitting at a picnic bench outside a large white trailer.

"Hello, Ms. Harper," he says politely. He seems a little hesitant after our exchange this morning, so I smile, trying to put him at ease.

"Call me Ronnie. So where is Mr. Sinclair?"

He looks past me and points to the blue building, Axel's Pub. "They're filming inside. It'll be awhile before they're done. They're doing a black out scene." He looks at me as if I should know what that means. I shrug.

"It's when they remove a former gang member's tattoos, by force."

I nod, horrified at the images that rush through my head. Lord knows how they go about doing such a thing outside of a doctor's office. I guess my expression amuses Dan because I hear him chuckle as I look over my shoulder at the Pub.

"Yeah, it's pretty gruesome. Mark Cohen has a sick imagination."

I stand up, figuring now is a good time to get a working knowledge of the property. "So can you show me around the set?"

He stands, and I follow. We walk between the set dresser's and craft services trailers then toward the cast parking area. After a minute of walking, I finally get a good look at the damaged building I noticed earlier.

"So what happened here?"

My question elicits laughter from Dan. "Oh, that was part of the show. There was a drive by targeting the Lords."

My mind swims for a second, trying to remember if I watched that episode. I hadn't. Although I'm relieved that someone didn't target the set and try to kill my client, the security on set is sorely lacking.

We end up back outside craft services, and we sit for maybe an hour before the door to the pub finally opens. The entire cast and crew walk out and the large rolling cameras follow. Erik notices Dan and me sitting at the table, and when he reaches us, it's not his appearance that is disconcerting, it's his smell. He reeks of gasoline, and he looks exhausted.

"Hi. Everything going okay?" I ask.

"Yes. Those scenes are rough," he says, forcing a smile. "I'm done for the day, so we can go if you're ready?"

I nod. "Yes. We were just waiting for you to finish up." Dan and I get up from the table, and I follow as the two of them chat about football on the way back to the makeup trailer.

"I've got to stop at wardrobe and then get this crap off my face. Dan usually hangs out in the trailer until I'm ready to leave." He climbs the stairs and disappears into the large makeup trailer first. I start to follow him, but Dan stops me.

"There's not enough room inside for all of us. I usually wait outside."

The constraints this set places on security is beginning to frustrate me.

"I'm not convinced that our rotund friend Michael is up to the task of securing this place. Is there anyone else responsible for security around here?"

He shakes his head. "No, not since I've been around."

"How often does Mr. Sinclair go out and sign autographs?" I ask.

"Hmm, usually every day. Why?"

That frustration Erik remarked on is building fast. Dan should have known enough to cut back on the personal interactions since all this started. "We're going to have to curb that, Dan," I say as I watch his mouth press into a frown.

He nods, and I take advantage of his undivided attention. "While I'm on the subject, we need to make some changes. You and I can split up the driving duties. Do you know how to use a SecPro?" I ask.

He scratches his chin. "A what?" he asks.

"It's a security camera for checking the undercarriage of vehicles. We'll use it on the Escalade or his car."

"For what?" he asks. I raise my hand to my forehead and rub my aching temples as he stares at me. *Maybe he's joking.*

"For bombs and tracking devices," I reply, astonished.

His eyes grow wide. "Wow. You think this is all necessary? I mean, it's just a few boxes of ripped up lingerie right?"

For some reason, Dan knows nothing about this case, and I can't imagine why his boss at Millennium didn't brief him fully.

"So where does he park his car," I ask, hoping to get the SecPro out to check it and give Dan a lesson.

"He drives a motorcycle," he says.

I look at him in disbelief. The minute he started receiving threats, that motorcycle should have been garaged. "Okay, well that needs to stop. We'll be driving him everywhere, and security is amping up to twenty-four hours a day. After we talk to him about the changes, you can take off to get your gear, and I'll follow him home." Dan is speechless, and his mouth hangs open. "What?" I ask.

"He loves is bike, that's all. He's not going to like this."

I raise my eyebrows. "He's not going to like a lot of things, Dan."

Dan nods as Erik finally exits the makeup trailer. He looks less like a criminal and more like any average thirty-something drop-dead handsome California boy. As a result, I find myself a bit tongue-tied. He stares at me a moment and smiles. "Ready to go?"

He needs to gather his belongings, and so do I. We step into his trailer and he slips on a leather jacket and his backpack, but as Erik takes a step toward the door, neither Dan nor I move.

"What is it?" he asks as his eyes dart back and forth between us nervously.

"We need to discuss a few security changes before you leave, Mr. Sinclair. Have a seat."

31

He removes his backpack and tosses it on the couch as he sits. "Is there another threat or something?" His eyes widen with concern. Dan sits at the dinette, but I remain standing to give myself the position of authority.

"No sir. Dan and I discussed a few changes to your daily routine. With the situation at the Brentwood house this weekend, it's time to step up security."

He looks at me, and then to Dan nervously. "Okay, so what does that mean?"

"First, you'll need to give up the motorcycle. It's too dangerous right now," I brace myself for an explosive reaction, and I get it.

"What? Are you fucking kidding me?" His voice grows louder with indignation.

"No, sir. I have an armored vehicle. Dan and I will drive you wherever you need to go."

He stares at me for a moment, and when his eyes move back to Dan, they emanate betrayal.

"Please don't think of this as a loss of your freedom, Mr. Sinclair. Think of it as saving your life." It's one of my typical responses to clients who protest security arrangements, and it usually works. When neither of us back down, he gives in.

"Fine. What else," he demands, exasperated.

"We need to limit contact with fans and the time you spend outside the gate." I don't expect he'll give me a hard time about this. But he does.

"Seriously? They wait out there for hours!" he says, pointing toward the trailer door.

"I understand your concern, Mr. Sinclair. We'd only like to change the times you go out there, switch it up so we don't establish a pattern for anyone that wants to hurt you. It's safer for you and your fans that way. Now, the security at your house is a major issue. We need to get a security system setup right away."

Most of my clients do not object to this, but when Sinclair huffs loudly and pops the knuckles in each hand, I ready myself for another fight.

"I already told you—no freaking cameras!" he yells, glaring at me.

"Mr. Sinclair, it's for your safety and the safety of those around you. We need to make sure we have all possible security measures in place. If this person is willing to drop off threats to the set, whoever it is could do the same at your new home. If we have cameras in place here and at your house, perhaps we can catch this person on video." He sits silent for a moment, staring at his shoes. He's digesting my words and raking his hand through those silky black locks. Which I just might like to try myself.

"Fine . . . fine. I don't want cameras inside my house. Absolutely no way I will agree to that. If I want to walk around in my fucking underwear in my own home, I don't want video of that getting to the press."

I press my lips together hard, not only to keep from laughing but also to stifle the image in my head, the one I have stuck in there thanks to Sarah and her damn Google search. But Dan does laugh, and it's just enough to break my poker face.

"Fair enough, Mr. Sinclair. That's not something we usually do. However, motion sensors are standard." He nods and waves a hand in the air as a gesture of conciliation.

"Fine. Now please tell me there's nothing else." He glares at me again, and my stomach turns into a knot. This is the worst part of it all, and if my client were anyone else, I wouldn't mind the living arrangements. But since he wants to walk around in his underwear, this could be incredibly awkward.

"Well, there is one more thing. You've only had daytime security so far. It's time to step up to full-time, round-the-clock protection. So that means, Dan and I will stay with you at your house. I understand you have a guesthouse?"

He stares at me in amazement. I'm not asking, I'm telling, and there's no room for compromise.

"Wow, you weren't kidding. You really don't sugar coat anything!" He laughs, but his words are bitter, and he stares daggers at me to prove it. He huffs. "Nothing like house guests who invite themselves!"

I want to laugh at his sarcasm, but I stifle it. Dan, however, lets out a hearty laugh, and I'm almost relieved. It takes down the tension a few notches. Erik will accept that from Dan, but from me, it would be like gasoline on a fire. I'm the new girl and I need to tread lightly for a bit longer.

He looks around, suddenly twitchy and agitated, almost like a scared animal trapped in a cage. He's desperate to get on that bike and drive, and tonight is his last chance to do so.

"Can we go now?" He stands up and slings his backpack over his shoulders.

"Yes, of course. Dan will meet us at your house later. He needs to retrieve his personal effects from his house." Erik nods at Dan and zips up his leather jacket before stepping out the door. He's down the stairs before me and Dan make it outside.

"That went well, don't you think?"

Dan snickers. "Yes, like a skunk in a small room."

It's good to know my new lieutenant has a sense of humor.

He's going to need it.

♚ CHAPTER FOUR

The forty-five minute drive to the ranch house is quiet. I'm alone in the car, and the traffic isn't too heavy. Even with the lack of traffic, my client is a lane splitting lunatic, and he's getting on my nerves. I swear he's trying to lose me on purpose.

Bastard.

Just getting out of the city is a welcome thought. Santa Clarita is a small community, and his property seems far off the beaten path. Being away from Los Angeles, secluded in this sleepy little enclave for at least eight hours a day will help take the edge off my nerves. Overall, I can call the day a success, except for the hacking of Cole Security. There's no easy way to inform my client about the new threat without making the company look unprofessional and entirely unsecure.

At last, I arrive at the house, which doesn't look like much from the street. There are no street markers or property numbers, and I would have passed it if I weren't following him. Erik jumps off his bike and unchains the rusted, bare metal gate that blocks the gravel driveway from the main road. As I follow toward the house, I can vaguely make out a horse corral through the thicket of trees. The tall Ponderosa Pines that block the view of the house from the road may offer privacy, but they conceal the view of street, making the house and my client vulnerable.

The only light comes from our vehicles, and the eerie glow crawls up the trees lining the gravel driveway as we make our way toward the house. Jeff and our security technician, Alex Harris, will have quite a big job securing this place.

I park in front of the house and turn off the engine. When I step out, Erik is already in the garage removing his helmet and gloves.

"You kept up with me well," he smiles as I walk in. He's full of mischief and there's a hint of sarcasm in his voice.

"Yes. You didn't make it easy. Lane split much?" I raise an eyebrow, turning the sarcasm right back at him. It's quickly become clear that this is how our relationship will work when no one is around, a constant tit for tat. This is going to be exhausting.

He opens the door leading into the house, but I stop him. "Mr. Sinclair, let me go first, please." He stares for a moment but holds out a hand, gesturing for me to go ahead. It's going to take him a few more days before he gets used to this.

"There's a light switch on the wall to your left." He mentions as I step into the house.

I nod. "Stay here."

I pull my gun from the holster and reach out for the wall, letting it glide along the paneling as I move. When I feel the switch, I flip it on, and the fluorescent bulbs hum loudly in the empty house. I move through the kitchen, checking behind the laundry room door and then ensuring the back door is securely locked. As I look out on the back of the house, the deck and pool lie between the main house and the guesthouse, which seems small, but it will be enough for Dan or me. The deck is well lit and decorated with outdoor furniture, a fire pit, and large potted palms, but the valley beyond it is shrouded in darkness, and it makes me nervous. When I turn again, I notice the new high-end appliances and the granite countertops are covered in empty glasses, mail, and old newspapers.

The living room is partially lit by the light from the kitchen, but I turn on a lamp next to the couch. Much of the living room is paneled in dark wood, and the light casts a warm glow on the well-worn beige sofa. A glass coffee table, which is covered in stacks of scripts and papers, sits in front of it.

The dining room is next, and I notice the striking emptiness as I check the locks on the double French doors. The built in display shelves on either side of the single, large watercolor painting are empty, and there's no furniture, pictures, or any of the knickknacks you'd expect to see in a room like this. I take a quick walk down the hall toward what appears to be an office. A small lamp lights the large desk, and as I step inside, I can see the furniture is much too large for the room. The window above the brown leather couch is locked, and I turn to leave.

As I pass by the open garage door, my client is waiting, but the quirked eyebrow tells me his patience is wearing thin. I keep going, heading down the hall toward two bedrooms. Flipping on the light, the smaller of the two is equipped with a daybed, a chest of drawers, and a small writing desk.

I turn off the light and cross the hall, opening the door to the larger master bedroom. As I enter and flip on the lights, the first thing I notice is the mess. Piles of laundry, both clean and dirty litter the floor as well as the window seat that looks out on the property. But it's the scent that steals my attention. The entire room is drenched in that same citrusy, spicy cologne that is threatening to make me dizzy again. I shake my head and go back to work, checking the two large windows and then the walk in closet. Nothing here. The bathroom is clear. Beautifully appointed, but clear.

"Mr. Sinclair? You can come in now."

I switch off the light and step into the hall. He's standing at the end of it with his backpack at his feet, waiting.

"Am I allowed in my house now?" He says a sarcastically as he reaches down for the backpack and smiles as he looks up at me. It's a killer smile, which I'm certain causes women all over the world to drop their panties in an instant. He walks into the living room and drops his backpack next to the couch as if nothing was bothering him. Well, except the condition of the house. Immediately, he launches into a litany of apologies and explanations for the messiness, rambling about how he's not used to handling the domestic chores.

It's been a rough couple of months and he finds himself alone, after many years of having a companion. They were all but married, and while the current situation between him and his ex-girlfriend is of some interest, admittedly, it's not of a professional nature. He intrigues me, and my mind wanders back to the moment in his trailer when he took the résumé from my hands. The sensation starts again, like some automatic reaction to the mere thought of him, and I rub my hands together to quell it.

I look around, and I'm struck by how average the house is. There's no fancy crystal, no overly grand furniture, and no expensive electronics. A house and land of this size are never cheap in California, so he has plenty of money. But he doesn't seem to be the type that would flaunt it. He's happy to play the role of a quiet, anonymous neighbor living in a non-descript ranch house. Never attracting attention, so no one knows there's a celebrity in their midst.

Erik walks into the kitchen and takes two bottles of water from the fridge, and I accept one happily. "The guesthouse has a queen bed, but it's more like a flat. It's an open floor plan, no privacy." I nod and step past him, headed for the large kitchen island. Pulling out a stool, I sit, and he settles in next to me.

"One of you will have to stay at the guesthouse, I suppose." He takes a long sip of his water and leans back. "There's a daybed in the guest room. Will that do?" He looks at me to see if I have any objections.

"Yes, the room will be fine. All I need is a bed, a shower, and maybe a meal once in a while."

He laughs, apparently happy with my easygoing approach to the sleeping arrangements. "Good. I'd rather have you in the house anyway." He shifts nervously in his seat, perhaps noticing my confused reaction to his comment. "Dan won't be here for a while. I need to find the sheets and blankets so you two can get settled."

As he moves from the island, I keep my eyes on my bottle of water. Inside, my mind is swirling around his comment. Why would he rather have me in the house? It's an odd thing to say, and I wonder if it's based on a real concern or if it's just part of his flirtatious banter.

"And about that meal once in a while . . . " He walks to the refrigerator, and when he opens the door, I notice the emptiness inside. A few jars clatter in the rack as he pulls the door back and leans against it. "I don't think I can help you with that. I suppose I need to do food shopping." He's clearly embarrassed, but I dismiss it.

"That's okay Mr. Sinclair. I don't need anything tonight. We can have Dan run errands tomorrow if that's all right with you. He knows the area, correct?"

He leans against the fridge, and he rubs at the stubble on his face. "Yes. He's lived in Downey his whole life, and he's been up here several times already." I nod at him as he disappears in search of blankets and pillows.

While Erik is rummaging through closets in search of linens, I get my bags and gear out of the car. I step outside into the frigid night air, and I shiver. A cold snap this far south is unusual this time of year, and I'm kicking myself for leaving my long wool trench coat at home. Pulling the bags from the back, I take them one by one up the stairs. As I drop the last one on the porch, Erik's feet appear before me.

"Let me help you," he says. As I straighten up, my eyes travel the full length of his frame, from his shoes to his face. When I stammer an answer, a trace of a smile touches his lips. Shit, he noticed that. My cheeks flame, but the darkness and the dim light of the porch hide the embarrassment, and I say nothing when he grabs one of the bags by the handles. The contents shift and clatter as he tries to maneuver the bulky bag through the door.

"Damn, what's in here? A dead body?" He laughs. I'm not sure what is responsible for his change in attitude. He's a different person than the agitated, sullen Erik I left at the set. The charming, funny Erik is much more to my liking.

He sets it on the floor as I kneel down beside it and open the lock. I expect him to be curious, but there's no way I'm going to let him rummage through my gear. "No. I keep the dead bodies in the trunk," I say as I look up at him. He laughs as he takes a seat in the chair beside me.

"So what is in there?" he asks as I pull open the zipper.

"Tactical gear."

He raises an eyebrow. "Such as?"

"Some bulletproof vests, mace cannons, and GPS tracking units. Oh, and guns."

He smirks at me. "Oh, thought you'd just use your Wonder Woman super powers."

"Touché, Mr. Sinclair. Well played," I laugh. He smiles, satisfied that he's one-upped me. For now, I'll let him have his little victory and if it keeps him happy, I'm fine with it.

As I dig through the bag, I pull out a large, gray case, which I set on the table in front of him. I expect him to be curious, and right on cue, he reaches for it. No harm can come from him opening the case. All he can do is look since it's locked and not loaded.

"Wow. That's a beautiful gun. What caliber is this?" He pulls it from the protective foam to get a closer look.

"It's a standard Police issue .40 caliber Glock."

He rises from the chair and holds the Glock in both hands, but his stance is all wrong—probably something he learned from some acting coach. While he's busy playing with the gun, I pull a small box from the duffel bag.

"Mr. Sinclair. You'll need to keep this with you at all times."

He sets the gun back in its case and reaches for the small box in my hand. He opens it and lifts the chain and cross from the box. It's the same style as he wore in the black and white photo Sarah found. "It's fitted with a GPS transmitter."

I pull out a Kevlar vest as he slips the chain over his head. "I assume this is for Dan?"

"No, this is for you." I hand him the bulletproof vest, and he almost drops it, not expecting the weight of it.

"Wow. You really think I need this?" He looks at me with his eyebrows raised high. He still can't imagine a situation where someone might take a shot at him.

"Please, just try it on. We might need it." He sighs in disapproval, but gives in and slips his arms into the vest and then struggles with the straps.

"I don't think this fits," he says, looking down at the two-inch opening under his arm that should be covered.

"Wait, take it off and remove your flannel."

He hesitates, and looks at me for a moment, wearing a wicked smile. I can read his expression immediately; he thinks I'm enjoying this. That I'm just dying to get a better look at him. *Okay, I am, but I'll never admit it.*

I take the vest as he slips out of his red plaid long-sleeved shirt. He's wearing a white t-shirt underneath, which is just tight enough to show off his well-defined pecs and I'm fascinated watching his muscles ripple and flex as he moves. I step forward and pull the straps around from the back. It's the closest I've been to him so far, and I struggle not to lean in closer. I secure one of the straps, and he moves with my tugging as I pull it tight.

"Easy now," he says playfully. I look up for a second, and his hooded eyes are glowing with something like amused fascination, but there's no smile, just this deadly stare that makes me catch my breath. I can feel his breath on my skin, warming me from the inside out as I secure the last strap.

How is it possible that a smile and the scent of him rattles me so quickly? The instant he looks at me, I forget myself and what I'm doing. Anxious to put some distance between us, I step back from him quickly, and once I'm a few paces away, he turns in a circle, doing his best supermodel impression.

"Well, how does it look?" he asks as he runs his hands down his chest until they come to rest on his hips. The muscles in his biceps bulge and flex.

I want to devour him.

I nod and shrug. "Hmm, it's not Victoria's Secret, but it will do." He smiles and looks down at his chest, covered with black armor plating. He peels back the Velcro straps and slips off the vest, laying it on top of the bag.

"I haven't found the sheets yet. I'll be back," he says, and as he passes by me, he drags his hand lightly across my arm. That one small touch sets my skin on fire, and once he's down the hall, I exhale. His departure is a relief, and the silence gives me a moment to clear my head of unwelcome thoughts. *Forget that touch and those blue eyes.*

Before he can gather all the sheets and blankets, I hear the noise of a car coming up the drive.

"I think Dan is here," he shouts from the dark hallway. Within seconds, he's back in the living room, but I'm at the door before he can get there. Without a word, he stops and lets me check who is outside first. The frigid air hits me and my breath puffs out in a cloud, and I wish I had at least put on my light-weight jacket as I wait for the car's occupant to get out. With the lack of light, it's tough to make out who is inside.

"Mr. Sinclair, does Dan have a Hyundai?"

He answers from behind the door that it is Dan's car. The engine switches off, and Dan steps out into the cold.

"Woo, it's freezing!" Dan says with a shiver. As he gathers his belongings from the car, I return to the warmth of the house. He pushes the door open and drops his bag near the door before having a seat on the couch. As he rubs his hands together, his eyes settle on my bag and then the open gun case lying on the table.

"What's that?" He points to the gray box.

"I always bring an extra, but you can use it while you're working for Cole."

"Nice hardware. I had one of these when I worked for L.A. SWAT." I toss him the key for the trigger lock and he removes it and then pulls an empty clip from the case.

"The ammo case is over there," I say pointing to the green rectangular box near the door. As he moves forward to load his clip, Dan gives me a rundown of all the different weapons he's used over the years. While we talk tactical gear, Erik makes himself useful, looking for sheets and blankets to get us both settled.

"I don't have a vest though." Dan's admission strikes me as odd, and I zip up the bag and sit opposite him in the blue chair. A man his size would

41

usually need to order one since most companies don't keep every size on hand.

"I'll stop by the office and get you one. Hunter might need to order it. It will be a few days." He nods at me and walks into the kitchen. When he returns from the fridge with a bottle of water, I let him in on my plans for the next day.

"Mr. Sinclair tells me you're familiar with the area?" He nods as he takes a long sip of water.

"Good. You might have noticed that there's almost nothing in the fridge. I'll need you to run to the grocery store. And we'll both need keys, so stop by the hardware store and get two sets made up while you're out."

"Okay," he says as he looks around, laughing a little. "Erik is not used to being alone. I think his ex-girlfriend took care of all the household chores." A brief image flashes through my mind of someone model perfect and glamorous. But would that kind of woman go along with moving out here, tending chickens and horses? I hope she did more than sit around the pool all day.

"Well, Mr. Cole is not paying us to do chores. However, we do have to eat."

"So gimme a list, boss." He sets the bottle on the coffee table and reaches into his jacket for his phone. He taps on the screen as I talk, making a list of the groceries and errands that I mention. Dan and I compile a large list by the time Erik returns looking exasperated.

"I have no idea where she put the extra blankets or pillows," he says brushing a strand of hair from his eyes. He sits next to Dan and notices the long list on his phone. As he looks over Dan's shoulder, he reads off the first few items.

"Milk, pasta, eggs. I suppose someone is going to cook all this food?" He chuckles and both of them look at me with raised eyebrows.

"What? Why are you both staring at me?" They look at each other and laugh loudly.

"Oh, that's completely sexist! You know that right?"

Erik tries to make amends and interrupts the raucous laughter. "Okay, okay, I can cook a little."

Dan laughs. "I can barely boil water." The two of them stare at me again.

"I'm not a personal chef, Mr. Sinclair. I don't get paid for my cooking skills." From the look on my face, I'm sure he can see I'm not happy.

"I realize personal chef is not on your résumé, but I'm willing to pay you extra," he says, trying to stifle his laughter. But it's no use, both of them breakout in hysterics again, and I narrow my eyes and fold my arms across my chest. Jeff needs to pay me more money to put up with this crap!

"Fine!" I get up and grab my bag in a huff and walk down the hall, feeling stung by the two of them. When I reach the door to the guest room, the renewal of their raucous laughter burns me yet again. It's boys against girl– I get it. However, that doesn't mean I have to like it. I set my bags on the floor and look around at my new room. It's a decent size, and the room is decorated in the shabby chic style. It's not my taste, but it's functional. The white iron daybed is up against the windows, which affords an excellent view of the front of the house. Sitting on the bare mattress, I rub my eyes. It's been a long day, and the stress is wearing on me already. Although being outside of L.A. helps, dealing with my client is an entirely new kind of tension. The attraction is there, it's obvious at times, and at some point other people are sure to notice. Surviving this job will be difficult, but surviving it with my career and reputation intact will be a miracle.

When Dan calls out to me from the living room, I realize how long I've been sitting here, perhaps twenty minutes, maybe more.

"Hey, boss lady? I'm going over to the guesthouse. Erik is coming with me. I've got my gun."

"Okay. Please make sure you accompany him back to the house when you're done." I wait for his answer while I unzip my bag, and then I hear the door close. I pull out my suits first and lay them on the bed. As I fill the drawers with my clothes, my mind wanders. I'd love nothing more than a shower and sleep right now, but it still seems like this day will never end. At this point, I could pass out on the bare mattress with just a blanket.

When I open the bi-fold doors, I realize my day just got a little longer. Boxes and clothes fill the closet from floor to ceiling, giving me no room to hang my suits. Wonderful. I suppose I could hang my clothes in his closet, I laugh to myself. I'm sure he'd be thrilled at the idea of me walking in on him at any given moment, in various states of nakedness...and *stop it Harper!*

All of the clothing is high-priced, very feminine, and very tiny, maybe a size two at best. As I run my hands along the garments I notice the difference between my functional black-and-white wardrobe lying on the bed, and suddenly, my ridiculous thoughts from earlier make me wince. There's no way he'd be interested in someone like me.

By the time I turn to go, I feel like I've been snooping on him and his ex—stumbling upon the end of their relationship, and it's something I'm uncomfortable with. I wander into the living room and take a seat on the couch. There's a large pile of scripts on the coffee table in front of me, and I reach out, pulling one off the top of the stack. I'm surprised to see it's his, 'Untitled' by Erik Sinclair. Well, he's a writer too. As soon as I set the script back in its place, I hear Dan's voice at the back door. He opens it and Erik walks in with a pile of sheets and pillows in his hands.

"I found the linens. They were all in the guesthouse," he says, nodding toward the hallway and motioning for me to return to the bedroom. I walk ahead of him, and instantly I wish I hadn't. Even though I should know better, but I can't help thinking he might stare at my ass as I walk. Or maybe I'm hoping he is. But once I return to the safety of my room, those foolish ideas disappear. Surely he won't attempt anything.

I step into the room and point to the open closet without saying a word. His mouth drops open and he drops the pile of sheets on the bed. As he walks up to the closet, he rubs a hand against his cheek.

"I'm sorry. I forgot about all her . . . junk. She was living at the Brentwood house but still hadn't come to pick up the rest of her stuff. I'll get that out of here." He reaches in and grabs the lot. When he turns, the entire mound of clothes flops over, and he can barely see past the pile in his arms.

"Can you get the door, please?" he mutters, his face hidden by the clothes. I wrap a hand around his rock hard bicep, made firm by his exertion, and guide him out of the room. It's a few steps across the hall and I open the door to his bedroom, turn on the lights and open the door to the walk in closet. When he steps in, he drops the entire pile on the floor before turning on the light. Except for the additional clothes, his large walk-in closet is almost empty on one side. I wonder if he still sleeps on his side of the bed. Poor guy.

"I'm going to go hang up my things." I step out of the room, but I can hear him in his closet, mumbling and possibly cursing to himself. He was not expecting to have her things back in the room he was just beginning to think of as his alone.

Just as I finish hanging my suits, Erik reappears. "The bathroom is stocked with towels. Everything is under the sink," he says, trying to be a good host. I drop my shoes and the empty bag into the closet and turn to thank him. But I say nothing when I notice the apprehensive look in his eyes.

My belly flutters uncomfortably, and more ridiculous thoughts float through my head, but once again, I'm reminded how foolish I am.

"I'm sorry about earlier, with that chef thing. It was totally sexist," he says.

I nod and lie to him, just to keep the peace. "It's okay."

"So, I have you all to myself, twenty-four-seven?" he asks.

My lips fall open, but I press them together quickly, trying to resist the urge to gasp at the odd wording of his question. *What in the world is that supposed to mean?* I hesitate a second longer, but he's staring at me, waiting for an answer, maybe even amused by my reticence.

"Ah . . . Yeah . . . yes. I mean . . I'll be with you every day and staying with you every night," I reply, offering nothing more than a regurgitated version of his question with one huge Freudian slip thrown in. He almost laughs aloud but smiles instead, taking a few steps toward me as he talks.

"Yes. You don't miss much, Ms. Harper," he says. "What I mean is, Dan typically stays out of the way on set. He's laid back. So what's your style? Are we going to be joined at the hip for the foreseeable future?"

Oh dear God. My mind, along with my pulse is racing. There are so many ways to answer his question. Yet, I can't find one that won't get me in trouble, and the first thing that comes to mind escapes my mouth.

"Oh . . . yes. I'm a bit more hands on than . . . " My choice of words is regrettable, but he finds the humor in it, and a small twitch appears at the corner of his mouth, which spreads into a heart-stopping smile. Trying to stifle another gasp, I feel my heart thundering against my rib cage as he continues to gaze at me. I lower my head and stare at my shoes, trying to break the intense connection between us so I can breathe again.

"Right then, I'll let you get to bed. Early day tomorrow, I have a six a.m. call time." I nod at him as he suggests we get on the road by five a.m. because of the traffic.

"Good night, Mr. Sinclair."

The door closes, and I'm alone, grateful that he left.

Maybe now I can breathe again.

♚ CHAPTER FIVE

My alarm goes off at an ungodly hour, and I knock the phone off the nightstand as I reach for it in the dark. Cursing under my breath and fumbling with the blankets, I grab it off the floor and shut it off. I lie in bed for a moment longer, trying to gather my wits, but my first thought is of him. My damn imagination isn't wasting any time.

I roll over and sigh. He isn't making it easy by being so humble and charming. And those blue eyes make him hard to ignore. Oh, who am I kidding? Everything about him is hard to ignore. But I'll play his game. I'll be friendly, yet professional.

Yeah, that should work.

I swing my legs out of bed and sit up, blinking wildly as I turn on the bedside lamp. Rising to my feet, I walk to the closet and pull out my uniform of a classic black wool suit and a pale blue Oxford shirt. Once I'm dressed, my confidence returns, as if I'm wearing a suit of armor, impervious to the charms of Mr. Sinclair. But my confidence only lasts until I reach the bedroom door, and I reach for the knob with a shaky hand.

Oh, get over it Harper, I laugh at myself.

Quietly moving down the hall with my gear in hand, I slip on my holster as I walk into the kitchen. I turn on the lights and rifle through the cabinets in search of coffee, a bag of beans or even a jar of instant would suffice at this point, but I don't find either. Great. I'm at the point of desperation when Erik shuffles into the kitchen.

"What the hell is going on?"

He sounds groggy, and even with bedhead, he looks incredibly delicious in nothing but a pair of sweatpants. Swallowing hard against lump in my throat, I try my best to look unaffected, but it's impossible. I can't keep my eyes off the large set of tattooed wings that encircle his collarbone. They are stunning. *He's stunning.*

"Good morning, Mr. Sinclair." I look at him briefly, figuring the less our eyes meet the better. "I was looking for coffee. I didn't mean to wake you, sir." He strides into the room, and the muscles of his abdomen knit as he walks. Now I know what all the uproar is about. *Six packs rock.*

Opening the door to the pantry closet, he pulls out a container of ground coffee. "Here," he says, thrusting the container at me with one long, muscular arm. I reach for it, and my fingertips touch his for a split second. Jeez, there it is again, that zinging electricity. It turns me into a puddle—again. And apparently, he knows it.

With one raised eyebrow, he smirks and then turns toward the hall. "I'm going to get a shower," he calls out.

I nod to myself, trying to slap down the steamy images invading my thoughts. Images of him, stripping down to nothing but his sexy skin. Him, stepping into that über-expensive shower I spied yesterday, with the creamy stone walls and the shower heads mounted in the ceiling. It's big enough for both of us, and...

Beep, Beep, Beep.

The coffee maker wakes me from my elicit daydream, and I shake my head to clear my thoughts. My morning cup of courage is sitting in front of me, and I'm going to need every ounce. I won't have the luxury of a partner today since I gave Dan a long list of errands to complete. So that means I'm alone. With him. *All freaking day.*

Just as I pull two mugs from the cabinet, I hear Erik's bedroom door open. When he walks into the kitchen, he's less informally dressed, and I'm relieved. He nods and smiles, looking totally at ease. I pour his cup of coffee first. "Here you are, sir." I hand him the steaming mug as he walks past me and pulls a small sugar bowl from the cabinet.

"I think I asked you to call me Erik yesterday."

"Yes, you did," I say, doing my best to sound unaffected. Pulling the pot free of the machine again, I pour myself a full cup. It's easy to avoid looking at him when I'm in desperate need of coffee. But that voice, that accent, they are like the slow burn of hundred-year-old scotch as it slides down your throat, warming you from the inside out.

"Are you going to play along?" he asks with a hint of amusement in his voice.

"No." I try to smile, but my voice is weak and unconvincing. The more I try to relax, the more tense I get. He's silent while I add sugar to my cup and stir it, but I sense his impatience as he sighs.

"Are you all right? Did you sleep at all?" I realize he's mistaking my nervousness for irritability.

"Yes."

He says nothing as I stare at my cup and stir.

And stir.

And stir.

The spoon makes that irritating clink against the cup, filling up the awkward silence. I'm hyperaware of him. Yet, somehow, the awareness of his body near me doesn't include his hands, so when he reaches up and tucks a few strands of loose hair behind my ear, it takes me unaware, and every nerve in my body explodes like fireworks on the Fourth of July.

Seriously? Really? I thought that was just in the movies.

I flinch, "Please don't," I say, my voice just above a whisper. I have no idea how I'm still standing because the Earth just shifted off its axis. My mouth betrays me, my body betrays me, and everything in me is screaming 'touch me'. When he lays his hand gently on my shoulder, I'm convinced my brain is going to explode.

"Are you sure you're all right?" he asks quietly.

I nod without looking his way. He inhales a deep sigh and frowns, obviously unconvinced. After a beat, I catch the quick nod of his head, and then the hand that just caressed me disappears, dropping to his side. Taking his cup of coffee with him, he heads down the hall to his office, and I'm alone again.

Still rattled by our exchange, I move to the sofa and sit down, hoping to shake off the feel of his fingers on me. I need to let this go. How do I let him know I have boundaries he can't cross? When he returns to the living room with his backpack, he sits in the blue chair across from me.

"We should get going soon, Mr. Sinclair." He looks at me and scrunches his lips into a frown. I've recovered, and he senses it. Or maybe he's annoyed by my formality. Perhaps that's my best defense when I'm around him.

48

Willing myself off the couch, I take my cup into the kitchen. "Do you have a travel mug? I barely touched my coffee." Erik turns in the chair toward me and thinks for a second before walking into the kitchen. He pulls open a few cabinets before finding the mug. "Here you go."

I take it from him, and he plants himself next to me with his back to the sink. Watching. My heart pounds as I feel his eyes on me, and I pour my coffee into the mug as I try to keep my nervous hands from shaking. Heaving a sigh of relief when he moves away from me and heads to the front door, I take a second to collect what's left of my scattered thoughts before following him.

"Are you coming, Ms. Harper?" His words are taunting as he looks at me with a mischievous flick of his eyebrow. My mouth goes dry, and I take a sip of my coffee, which burns my tongue. Good. Maybe it will break his spell. Slipping on my jacket, I grab my cup and my gun case. When I meet him at the door, I catch him smirking as he slips on his jacket. He's quite satisfied with the effect he has on me. He's probably used to women falling into a swoon in his presence. I'm ashamed to admit, I'm one of them.

"After you, Ms. Harper." Leaning forward, he pushes the door open for me and then with a hand at the small of my back, he guides me out onto the porch. The contact is electric, and my skin erupts in thousands of tiny tingles. It's the type of thing I'd expect from a boyfriend or a husband. Not a client.

I shiver and pull my jacket closed as I hop down the stairs. Unlocking the trunk, I pull out the SecPro and turn on the monitor. The screen glows in the semidarkness, and I make a quick pass under each side of the vehicle. Erik watches from the porch, and when I'm done, he locks the door.

Once I stow the SecPro in the trunk, I get into the driver's seat. The car is like a freezer, and a fog exits my mouth as I breathe. The icy leather seats burn through the wool of my pants as I flip every switch in the car looking for the seat heaters.

"Damn it's cold," he groans as he slips into the passenger seat and closes the door. The scent of freshly showered Erik overtakes the aroma of my coffee, and with him sitting so close to me, it makes it hard to concentrate.

"You need to sit in the backseat, Mr. Sinclair."

He looks at me, bewildered and ignores my request as he reached for his seatbelt. "Why? What's the big deal?" He looks irritated.

I huff. "Multiple reasons. Most of which you don't want to know."

His lips part as if he's about to argue, but I don't let him. "Please just sit in the back, sir."

"Sir? Seriously? Just call me Erik."

"No. Now please, sit in the God damned back seat. Sir."

His eyebrows knit, but he's not moving. I've evidently awakened his obstinate side.

"Not until you tell me why," he demands.

"You will get in the way if I need to open that window to fire my weapon," I say.

His mouth drops open as he tries to imagine the various crazy scenarios where that might be necessary. To me it's old hat, I've done it before. For him, it's inconceivable in real life. It's something he'd expect to see in a wild action movie.

"You're kind of scary. You know that right?" He looks at me with wide eyes, then opens the door in a snit and slams it before getting into the back seat.

Mission: *Accomplished.*

I put the car in gear and drive down the unpaved road. The rising sun colors the gauzy clouds an orangey-pink hue, and I can just make out the contours of the corral and the gate that runs along the front of the property. The trip to the set is long, and I turn on the radio to break the silence. I'm blessed with fifteen minutes of quiet before he opens his mouth.

"So, tell me your life story."

"My what?"

I briefly look at him in the rear view. He's staring out the passenger side window, watching the dark mountains pass us.

"Tell me about yourself. We have a forty-five minute drive so you might as well keep me entertained."

"Keeping you entertained is not part of my job, sir."

He's determined to get to know me, and I'm not sure why. If he wanted to get me in bed, he certainly wouldn't need to know my story to do it.

All he'd need is one touch.

One smile.

And those abs.

He laughs and politely ignores my protest. "Where did you grow up?"

I look back at him in the rear view, and he's staring at me and waiting for my answer. Terrific. He's not going to let this go. I sigh heavily and give in.

"New York," I state blankly.

"Really? In the city?"

"Yes. In Queens."

"Is that near Manhattan?" he wonders.

"Yes."

"So what was Queens like?"

I spend the next ten minutes describing the Italian mafia enclave I grew up in and my brushes with John Gotti and the Gambino Crime family.

"That sounds like an interesting upbringing. Like something out of the Godfather movies," he says. But I bristle at the stereotypical comparison. When he asks more about my family, and why I joined the military, my patience reaches its limit. I grumble yes or no answers, reluctantly giving up information.

"Is this something you'd rather not talk about?"

"Yes."

"Why?"

I protest loudly this time. "What are you, my therapist now?"

"No. Do you need one?" He snaps.

I look at him in the rearview again and find that he has propped up his head on his fingers and is staring intently at the side of my face. He's wearing a smirk, lifting just the corner of his mouth.

"Wow, for someone who is so intensely private, you seem very comfortable digging into my business." If he hasn't figured out that I'm tired of this conversation, I don't know what I have to do.

"Touché, Ms. Harper."

Now the ball is in my court. "So you never explained why you would rather have me in the house instead of the guesthouse?"

"It's just a guy thing," he says.

No, no, that won't do. He's not getting off that easy. "A guy thing? Such as?" I can see his smirk in the rearview disappear as he looks out at the mountains. The sun has come up over the horizon now, and traffic is starting to build.

"Ms. Harper . . . if anything happens, I'd rather be close enough to help. I'd don't want you over there alone."

His meaning is crystal clear, and unfortunately, his reasoning will get him killed.

"Mr. Sinclair, you realize I have a gun, right?"

He laughs from the backseat, and I await yet another sarcastic answer, but what I get is entirely different.

"Yes. I do. And you're probably bloody deadly with a gun. It's just how my mum raised me. She taught me to protect women." He pauses, and I look into the rearview. "Even one with a gun." He stares at me in the mirror, and his eyes are burning in the darkness. I look away, suddenly aware that I'm not paying attention to the road.

"Mr. Sinclair, please don't put yourself in harm's way for me. I'm being paid to protect you, remember?"

His loud sigh from the backseat signals his frustration. He says nothing for a few seconds, but when he answers, he takes a jab at my reticence.

"Do you ever let anyone get to know you? You seem very guarded."

His words sting, but I don't reply. It's none of his damn business why I am the way I am. He has no idea what I've been through.

"Mmm hmm, just as I thought."

Jeez, the son of a bitch is goading me!

"Mr. Sinclair, I'd appreciate it if you wouldn't try to pick me apart or judge me. After all, I haven't treated you like a spoiled Hollywood celebrity, yet."

Fortunately, he gives up on his quest as I turn onto the street leading to the set. "Hmm, you're lucky we are here. We'll continue this next time, shall we?" he says confidently as he locks eyes with me in the rearview. He's teasing me.

Maybe I'm starting to enjoy it. "Fine," I grumble as I park the car. He snickers from the back seat as he gathers up his backpack. When I shut off the engine and hear the click of the seatbelt, he delivers the final blow.

"Consider it a date, Ms. Harper."

I swallow hard, and when I hear the thunk of the door, I exhale. *A date.* Did he really just say that?

He walks around to the front of his trailer, and I follow him noting that the morning seems colder than it was when we left his house. He unlocks the door, and I enter first, checking the tiny bathroom and back room for danger while he waits at the foot of the stairs.

"It's safe Mr. Sinclair," I yell from inside. It's gloomy and cold in his trailer, and the chill hangs in the air. I pull my jacket closed and button it, but it won't do any good outside. He steps inside and drops his backpack.

"Are you ready for some food?" His change in demeanor has me baffled. One minute he's testy because I won't give into his intrusive questioning and the next, he's jovial and unaffected.

"Yes." I nod enthusiastically. I'll agree to anything as long as I don't have to be alone with him. I'm almost at the door when he stops me.

"Wait, you'll need a warm coat." He unzips his jacket and holds it out.

"Oh, no that's okay. I'll be fine."

He crumples his lips and shakes his head. When he steps behind me, I look back at him to protest, and he scolds me. "Wardrobe has thick down jackets for us. Just put it on and stop fighting with me about everything." Feeling foolish, I let him slip the jacket on me.

"Thank you." The jacket is enormous, still warm from his body, and drenched in his scent. I turn around, and he looks me over.

"A little big, but it will do. Let's go." He bounds down the stairs, full of energy, and as we walk toward craft services, I notice more people have arrived on set. I watch as the crew scurries around, pulling large cameras into place for the day's first shots. Most of the actors are just arriving, and a long line of headlights stretches from the entrance to the cast parking lot. As we near the craft services trailer, I can smell the food, and my stomach reacts instantly. Inside it's nothing more than an oversized food truck with enough room for a few tables.

The blackboard by the window has a list of the day's offerings: egg and sausage burritos, oatmeal, fruit, and coffee. The young Asian man takes my order, and he shouts directions to the cook, an older woman in her sixties.

Beth walks into the trailer, and when she spots me, she waves. "Good Morning! Still here, I see?" She smiles and raises an eyebrow at Erik. "I'm surprised he hasn't scared you off. Is he driving you crazy yet?"

Oh my! How can I answer this without getting myself into trouble? The blood reddens my cheeks, as I stand there mute and embarrassed.

"You don't need to answer that, honey." She leans in close as she whispers and points toward my client. "This one is a bit of a challenge."

Erik notices the huddle between Beth and me and smiles. "Okay mum, stop putting ideas in her head." He sets the bowl of steaming hot oatmeal topped with fruit on the table along with my breakfast burrito, and I join him.

"I'm going to get some food. I'll see you later." Beth walks up to the window as I sit across from Erik. The two of us eat in silence, but I notice him watching me from time to time. I try to ignore it, but it makes me nervous. After all the things he learned about me this morning, I feel like he's lying in wait, trying to figure me out—to bring down my guard. It's unnerving, and frankly, it makes me want to protect myself even more.

"Come on. Ready to go?" He crumples up the paper bowl and tosses it in the trashcan. I follow Erik outside and cringe as the cold breeze hits my face. The sun is higher in the sky now, but it has done nothing to warm up the bitter wind. As we walk, Erik greets various crew members as they hurry to their trailers to get ready for the day's shoot. We reach the makeup trailer first, which is longer and wider than the actor's trailers. It's spacious inside and three black barber-shop style chairs sit in front of three brightly lit mirrors.

"Morning Melissa." Spinning the chair around, the woman faces Erik, then looks at me. "Melissa Tyler, this is Veronica Harper. She's part of my security team."

Melissa smiles as the makeup girl waits impatiently for her to turn around again. "Hi. I'm Axel's wife." She smiles and holds out her hand. "Nice to meet you."

She seems nice, with friendly eyes and a good sense of humor. "So how long are you going to be with us?" she asks, spinning her chair around to let the artist finish her work,

"I don't know. As long as I'm needed. When this job finished, I'll go back to San Francisco." I point my response at Erik, hoping to make it clear to him that this is just a job. When his surprised gaze settles on me in the mirror, I'm almost positive Melissa notices. She narrows her eyes as she looks at him, before focusing on me again.

"Okay Melissa. You're all set." The makeup artist removes the protective drape from around her shoulders, and Melissa stands to leave.

"Nice talking to you Veronica." She smiles and says good-bye to Erik, but he grumbles a response, and I catch an eye roll in the mirror as she walks out the door.

The makeup artist starts works on the tattoos covering Erik's forearms first, and I'm amazed to find out they're fake. Adrianna uses small brushes, carefully recoloring the image so it will look crisp on camera. Halfway through the hour-long process, another actor enters the trailer, and Erik turns toward the door.

"Morning Tom," he says as he looks over his shoulder. Tom is a tall, attractive man with a closely shaved head and a smile that shows every tooth in his mouth. I recognize that wide, dimpled grin; he plays "Jinx" Carter.

"Hey man," he fist bumps Erik, who tries not to upset the makeup artist. Before Tom sits, he notices me seated in the corner. "Hi. Who are you?" He smiles and bounds toward me, his long legs closing the distance quickly. He has a welcoming smile, and I detect the familiar sound of a New York accent. This must be the person from Manhattan Erik mentioned. I take his hand and introduce myself.

"Hi. I'm Veronica Harper."

"Tom Campagna."

"She's my new security guard," Erik adds as he watches us from the corner of his eye. Tom looks me over from head to toe, and I can't tell if he's flirting or thinking the same thing Mark Cohen blurted out so eloquently yesterday. But he retreats and takes a seat in a chair next to Erik.

"She's from Queens, Tom," Erik chuckles, as he looks at Tom, amused.

Right now, I'm regretting answering any of his questions. Tom looks my way, and his eyes are wide with surprise. "Really! Where about?"

I look at Erik and shoot him a terse glance before answering. "From Ozone Park."

"Oooh! Damn!" Tom holds a hand over his mouth as he cackles. "Dude, your girl here is from one of the tougher parts of New York. You had better watch out. She'll kick your ass!" My face flushes, but perhaps Tom's assessment of me is a good thing. Maybe Erik will think twice about touching me.

♚ CHAPTER SIX

We head out the door to the next trailer, which is marked wardrobe. Inside, there doesn't appear to be anyone here, but the smell of leather and freshly laundered clothes fills the trailer. "You back there, Cecelia?" Erik calls out.

"Hey Erik. I'll be right there," a female voice answers from the back. Another larger room is off to the left, and from my vantage point, it looks like a storage area full of racks of black leather jackets and denim. It isn't long before Cecelia makes her way to the front.

"Morning Erik! Oh, who's this?" She's a pretty redhead, slim, with green eyes. I extend a hand and introduce myself as Erik's security.

"Well, it's good to have you around then. Is everyone is making you feel welcome?" she asks politely.

"Yes, thank you," I say, taking a seat while she and Erik discuss the day's shoot. She disappears for a moment but returns with several articles of clothing on hangers. It's his costume for the day, which is Axel's leather jacket, a flannel shirt, and a pair of jeans. Erik takes the clothes from her and disappears into the changing room. Erik isn't gone long before he's calling for Cecelia. When she knocks on the door and enters, my curiosity is piqued. I sit alone in the trailer, waiting for my client's return, staring self-consciously at the walls, and wondering why the cute redhead is back there with him when he's possibly undressed. In a moment, they both walk out, in the middle of a conversation.

"Sure, I can help out. Just for the premieres?" He nods at her, and his eyes shift from Cecelia to me as she tries to talk quietly. "I'll take her with me on Friday."

When he notices I'm watching, he flushes a bit but says nothing to give away his plans. I have no idea what they are talking about, but I'm praying it doesn't involve me. When I get a good look at him, it's as if he's been transformed into a different person. He looks like a criminal dressed in all that flannel and leather.

"Oh, Cecelia, I need a crew parka." Cecelia looks at me and realizes I'm wearing Erik's jacket.

"Sure, I'll be right back." She heads to the racks of clothes and comes back with a giant black parka with the word CAST in white lettering on the back.

When we reach his trailer, I'm simmering mad. Whatever plan he's concocting with the wardrobe girl has me worried. I sit on the couch checking my e-mail as he reads a pile of script changes. I tell myself that worrying about whatever he is up to is ridiculous. Try to ignore him, I tell myself. I realize I must look like a pouty child, but right now, I don't care. He's different from any client I've had so far, and I'm at a loss on how to handle him. I'm not sure how long I've been sitting here, but when I look up, I find him staring at me. He's leaning on his hand, and his index finger is gently tracing along his bottom lip. My eyes meet his, and those usually bright blue irises have darkened into two inky blue sapphires. He stares at me as if I'm a meal, and he hasn't tasted food in a week.

"What is it?" I ask, but that finger never moves from his lip.

"Nothing." His focus never wavers, and his eyes moving over me feel like a thousand fingers caressing my body. My temperature skyrockets from normal to inferno in an instant, and that electricity sparks all around us again. It's that tingling pull between us that started the moment we met. It's impossible to ignore. He's impossible to ignore.

I lose focus on the present, imagining the taste of his lips and the feel of his hard body pressed against me. In my fantasies, all that and more is possible and the idea of pleasuring him, hearing him call my name as he comes undone has reawakened those primal urges. The ones that lead to an afternoon of wild, untamed, sheet-clawing sex, that have us grunting and sweating like animals, stopping only when we're spent and unable to move. In my head, it's a world where I have no fears, where I'm normal and whole again and where I have no baggage to send a man running.

"Are you ready to go?"

At some point, he moved from his chair, and once I notice his feet in front of me, I look up. Our eyes meet for a second, and I could swear he realizes what's going on in my head—that I'm still picturing him . . . us, naked. Before he can see my pink cheeks, I lower my head and respond, trying to sound professional.

"Of course, Mr. Sinclair."

I stand and reach for his jacket, and as I turn my back to shrug it on, it lifts behind me. One quick glance over my shoulder confirms that he's holding it up for me, being a gentleman again.

"You don't need to—"

He silences me as I shrug the jacket on and turn around. "Just because you're security, it doesn't mean I'm going to stop treating you like a lady." There's a husky quality to his voice, and it sends goose bumps racing across my skin. His words are worthy of a return appearance of the butterflies, but I turn away abruptly, headed toward the door.

"You'd better zip that up. It's windy," he says, meeting me at the door. "Here—" he steps forward and reaches for the zipper, his eyes full of mischief as he pulls it slowly up to my chin. I let him do it even though I know it will block access to my gun. He reaches up and tucks my loose bangs behind my ear, and for a moment, his eyes flash hot and deep with desire. My skin tingles, and my insides flutter madly as I watch his eyes settle on my mouth. If I stand here any longer, I just might kiss him. But I'm taken by surprise when his mood shifts, and he steps past me without saying a word. I'm left confused, with a head full of embarrassingly smutty thoughts.

"Are you coming, Ms. Harper?"

Well played, Mr. Darcy. Well played.

Erik leads the way out to the set, and I follow, walking briskly toward the bullet-riddled building. Actors, camera operators, and sound people are milling around, so I hang back, trying to stay out of the way of the various crew members. When Mr. Cohen arrives, he gives the actors direction, and they take their places as filming begins. I unzip the jacket so I can reach my gun, and sit, watching the action. Beth walks up, and I'm happy to see a familiar face. Even though I don't make a habit of becoming friendly with my client's co-workers, she's someone I don't mind talking to.

"Hi there. How are you getting along? Are you finding your way around?" she asks. She seems like a mother hen around here, always checking up on people.

"Yes, so far so good. I don't want to get in the way."

"Oh, you won't. Stick with me, I'll show you the ropes," she smiles.

"So are you an actress?" I ask. She's pretty enough, but she laughs heartily.

"Oh no. I'm one of the writers."

I'm intrigued. Even in Hollywood, a husband and wife writing, directing, and producing team is unusual.

"And I should apologize again for my husband. He sometimes forgets that the insane things he can put in a script should not come out of his mouth in real life."

I nod. "It's all right Mrs. Cohen. I understand his concern. He just wants Mr. Sinclair to be safe." She reaches over and squeezes my hand, taking our conversation from cordial to personal in an instant.

"It's Beth. And please keep him safe," she smiles nervously.

"I will."

Her affection for Erik is obvious. Perhaps that's why he called her Mom earlier.

"He's had a rough year with all the craziness with Breathless and the threats. Then there was so much back and forth with Catriona before they broke up . . . He just does not need all this."

I'm surprised to hear Beth talking about my client's personal life, and by the tone in her voice, it doesn't seem as if she liked his ex, which intrigues me. She seems to know a lot so perhaps it's time for a fishing expedition.

"You didn't like her?" My question is innocent, and it's the best way to get her talking.

"Oh no, not at all! Right from the beginning, I thought she was fake, clingy, and too dependent on him. She won't give up on him though." Erik strolls by, looking at both of us as he waves.

"There are still a lot of her belongings at the house," I mention casually.

Beth turns toward me with her eyebrows raised. "Really?" she huffs, sounding disgusted. "I suppose she knows exactly what she's doing." She cocks her head to one side and smiles at me. I know precisely what she means.

"I thought the same thing."

Beth laughs, relieved that someone else agrees with her. "And what's your story? No one in your life?" She's such a Nosy Nancy, and I didn't intend to become the focus of the conversation, but I'll give up a little information, just to gain her trust.

"No. My life is as crazy as his. I'm never in the same city for more than a few weeks or a few months at a time. My job isn't a typical eight-hour day. I'm on the clock twenty-four-seven."

She continues probing. "And you've never been married, no kids?"

"No." There's no point in bringing up my past with her. It will just get back to Erik. Besides, not wanting children isn't a lie. Kids were never on my radar. The idea of myself as a doting mommy never appealed to me, and I never met anyone I felt was worthy. Five years ago, the lingering thought that I might like to find someone to marry started to weigh on my mind, but Kincaid interrupted those plans.

Beth's focus shifts, as an older man with a large belly and long, frizzy, gray hair saunters over and has a seat next to her. He pulls out a cigar from his leather jacket and lights it up, and I watch as the blue flame shoots upward as he puffs quickly on the stogie.

"Hey, little lady, how are ya? I'm Tim Boone."

I smile back. "I'm fine, thanks."

"Um, I didn't mean that in a sexist sort of way honey," he says.

I have to laugh at him. He's good-natured and funny, and I can't be angry. "No offense taken . . . *honey*," I retort.

He gives me a wink and hearty belly laugh. "So you're gonna protect our boy, eh?"

"Yes, I plan to do just that." He takes a long drag and a large cloud of acrid smoke wafts up through his hair. "I swear, all this Breathless shit is just cra–aazy. Erik is a real laid-back guy. This movie is going to put him in like, the Brad Pitt and Tom Cruise world of fame. He is totally not used to that. I just don't know . . ." Boone takes another drag of his cigar and leans back in the chair, obscured by a cloud of smoke.

"Now, there goes trouble," Boone says, and his eyes narrow into slits as he watches Melissa Tyler sprint past us. I look at Beth and shrug my shoulders in confusion, hoping she will offer some details.

"Hmm, she's been giving Erik a hard time about Catriona." Her voice takes on a low, cautious tone, and my eyes grow wide in surprise. Our meeting this morning was entirely pleasant.

"Why?"

"She's good friends with Catriona. Melissa has gone to bat on her behalf, and she won't leave Erik alone about it," she says, shaking her head looking thoroughly disgusted.

"That's interesting. He didn't mention any problems with her this morning."

"Erik is a gentleman. He knows he has to work with her, for a few more months at least. So he'd rather keep the peace. They went a few rounds about Catriona last week," Beth admits, and her eyes narrow as her gaze falls on Melissa. I'm completely surprised by this. While I doubt Melissa would try to harm Erik, it's clear that I need to be wary of her.

Mr. Cohen calls Boone over, and he stubs out his cigar before he leaves. As they begin filming again, Melissa steps toward Erik, and he smiles at her as he takes her in his arms. They speak a few words to each other before he leans in for a long kiss. I can't tear my eyes away. It's like watching a train wreck. Even though I know they are just playing a part, I'm strangely jealous, and embarrassed to watch it. The uncomfortable feeling doesn't last long, and the scene is over quickly.

When Erik returns from his shot, he's ready to take a break, and I follow him as he walks back to the trailer.

The trailer is warmer inside than it was this morning, and the heat takes the chill off instantly. Erik pulls off his gloves and blows hot air into his fists as I sit on the couch. He retreats to the small bathroom, but once the door closes, he yells for me to turn on the electric kettle sitting on the counter. I step into the kitchen, and try to turn the little knob on the kettle, but my fingers barely function. My hands are like two blocks of ice, and I'm kicking myself for not bringing a hat or gloves with me. When he steps out of the bathroom, he looks at the pot, which is still turned off.

"I can't turn it on. My fingers are frozen," I say as I hold up my stiff hands.

He looks at me and laughs as he reaches for the small dial. The kettle gurgles within seconds, heating the water for tea. "Here." He steps toward me with his hands in front of him, but I hesitate, feeling shy about touching him.

"Come on, luv, give me your hands. I won't bite," he says with a smile. I offer one hand, and he takes it, wrapping my hand into a fist and completely enclosing it within his own. His large, strong hands are warm, and they melt the chill off my skin. When he raises our hands to his mouth and blows warm air between them a few times, my mind races. I can only imagine what those lips feel pressed against mine.

"You're lucky you don't have frostbite," he says, blowing more air into my fist. Those eyes mesmerize me and not even the gurgling and beeping of the kettle can distract me.

He releases my right hand, and then reaches for my left, repeating the process. As I watch his mouth make contact with my skin, every muscle between my legs clenches violently. Everything about him, from the way he walks, to the sound of his voice, his scent and those blue eyes could become my drug, an unhealthy addiction. He's my Mr. Brownstone, my Tambourine man, and I'm starting to enjoy the rush I feel when I'm near him. Probably a little too much.

He rubs his thumb across my knuckles, smiling. "I think you're warm enough now."

Ha, you have no idea, Mr. Darcy.

He moves into the kitchen while I take a seat at the dinette, and I watch as he makes two cups of tea. His broad shoulders are in perfection proportion to his small waist, although, it's hard to tell when he's in costume. The baggy jeans and leather hide the contours of his body. What a shame.

He carries the mugs filled with steaming water and lays the tea bags and sugar on the table. I'm not in the mood for tea, but I'll take it, even if just for the warmth against my hands.

"So I understand there's been some tension between you and Melissa. What's going on there?"

He looks at me above the steam rising from his cup, and his eyebrows bunch up in frustration. "Where did you hear that?" He pauses. "Oh, never mind. Beth told you, right?"

I nod. "And Boone."

He shakes his head and huffs, and then his face turns hard. His anger is quick to trigger, and he's gone from smiling to livid in a split second.

"From what I heard, the argument was rather intense."

He looks at me, and his stare is withering. I may have opened the wrong can of worms. "It was. And what is the point of your question, Ms. Harper?"

I hesitate, looking down at my hands, still wrapped around my cup for warmth. When I look up, he's resting his chin on his hand, and his finger is tracing his lip as he stares at me. Again. *That lip looks delicious.* I'm transfixed on his face for a moment, and I stammer. "Uh, she . . . Melissa could cause trouble."

"Well, she might. But I don't see how that affects you," he says, quizzically.

"You'd be surprised how easily she could cause trouble for me, Mr. Sinclair."

His mouth hangs open in disbelief. Erik is clearly not the sort to anticipate how devious other people can be—especially ex-girlfriends.

"How?"

"Jealousy. Women use it as a weapon all the time in relationships." To get him back, I would.

He's silent, and a slight frown appears on his face, but he nods in agreement. "Yes. Melissa has already tried that tactic."

"And did it work?" My curiosity is more about his feelings since I can't help wondering if he's still in love with her.

"No. I didn't bite. Catriona seemed to back off afterward. That's when Melissa and I got into a big row over it."

Ah, now I understand what the two of them are doing. Make him jealous and he'll come running back. Or not. I stay quiet, sipping my tea, waiting for him to come to his own conclusion. I hope. Explaining this theory would be mortifying, and I'm not in the habit of making myself part of the drama. Besides, if I suggest it, he's far more likely to dismiss the idea. I wait patiently and finally, he looks up at me, wide-eyed and amused.

"No... she wouldn't," he shakes his head, and I gulp hard, figuring I'll have to convince him. "You don't think Melissa will tell Catriona there's something going on between you and me to stir up trouble, do you?" He's propped his chin up on his hand, smiling as if it's the most ridiculous theory he's ever heard. And as I blanch, he laughs. He's making fun of me. Bastard.

I remind myself not to take offense and try to recover what's left of my pride. "Of course. It's the perfect story to make Miss O'Neill jealous. There's a new woman hanging around, and she doesn't have to know I'm security. If she flips out and it gets back to Mr. Cole, he could fire me." He shakes his head adamantly. *Yeah, he thinks you're nuts, Harper.*

"I won't have anyone making trouble like this. No one is going to get you fired," he says, sounding dismissive. "Besides, my relationship with her is over. You needn't worry about Catriona. I'm a free man."

I try to hide my shock as a huge wave of embarrassment washes over me, and the mug almost slips from my shaky fingers. Oh Jesus, what did I do?

I didn't mean to . . . *Ugh, maybe I did.*

My insides curl up into the fetal position, and I wither under Erik's intense scrutiny, which he appears to be enjoying as the smile on his face widens. *Did I hear him right? Was that an offer, or is he just messing with me? Jesus, the man is so hard to read.*

My heart pounds as I force out a few words. "I didn't mean . . . Ah. What I meant was—"

"Oh, but I did Ms. Harper. If I want to date you, I will. I don't give a rat's ass if *anyone* has a problem with it."

My heart is in my mouth, I can't speak. I stand up awkwardly and run my clammy hands along my thighs. *I have to get out of here.* Taking a step back to retrieve my coat, I take one clumsy step too far, backing into the chair.

"Whoa!" I'm teetering on my proverbial heels as Erik jumps from his seat, reaching me a second before I flip over the chair. He grabs me by the wrist and pulls me forward, hard. "Easy. I've got you," he says, pulling me forward and wrapping his arms around me in one swift movement. His splayed fingers press into my back as we move as one, away from the overturned chair. And even though I'm safe, my hands linger on his biceps and chest.

I'm speechless, utterly mortified by how much I'm loving the feel of him pressed up against me, and the way he's looking, no, staring at me. I can tell what he's thinking by the way his eyes graze my face, then linger on my mouth. It's intense and almost erotic, and my face feels warm, my breathing turns ragged, both made worse by embarrassment. We're too close, but damn, close feels really good, and I wish he'd kiss me just to get it over with. Maybe if he does, this awkward tension will disappear.

The door opens suddenly. "Hey, Erik? Are you—" Beth's eyes bulge as she sees me, still wrapped in Erik's grasp, flustered and shaky. Erik and I freeze, then separate like teenagers caught sneaking in through the window after curfew. While I retrieve the upended chair, Erik walks toward the door and talks to Beth.

"What is it Beth?"

"I'm sorry. I didn't mean to–" She doesn't finish or step inside. "Mark needs you ASAP."

"I'll be right there." He turns toward me, and he's a little red-faced as well.

"Are you all right?"

I nod at him. "Yes. I'm fine."

He walks out the door quickly, and she stands back as Erik hurries down the steps. Beth steps inside and watches me as I sit at the dinette.

"What happened?" she asks.

"Oh, nothing. I'm fine Mrs. Cohen." As I pretend to check e-mail, my mind swims with different excuses, all of which are coming up short. She knows it, and she continues to stare at me.

"It's nothing. I'm just clumsy," I mutter. She weaves her fingers together, and nods, smiling at me. She's not buying my story.

"I'd better go." She stands and smiles with a bit of concern in her eyes. "I'll see you later," she says before closing the door again.

I sit alone at the dinette for a few minutes, trying to catch my breath and staunch the embarrassment. He probably thinks . . . Thinks what? That I wanted it to happen. That I fell all over him on purpose?

I laugh at myself, *Get a grip Harper*.

The cold sunshine hits me in the face as I walk out of the trailer and scan the set for a quiet spot to sit. I find a secluded corner, which is far enough away from the commotion of the busy set but close enough to keep an eye on my client. Although I'm not searching him out, my eyes find him as he jogs from one part of the set to another then stops as he waits for the cameras to change position. That incredible tingling starts again, and I laugh to myself, wondering how he can affect me so completely. Even though he's on the other side of the lot, the intense power he has over me doesn't quit. It's as if my emotions are no longer under my control.

As I sit and watch Erik from afar, my attention turns to Beth. She's standing in front of the pub, talking to a tall blond I haven't met. I'm hoping her conversation has nothing to do with what she walked in on earlier. As they continue to talk, Melissa appears from inside the pub and stands in the doorway. She's standing just behind Beth and her friend and appears to be listening to them talk.

Erik makes his way over toward Beth and her friend, and then looks around, probably wondering where I am. I need to get my act together and do my job, but being near him right now would only raise suspicion. And Lord help me if he gets too close–this crazy mix of embarrassment and lust I'm feeling would be obvious to everyone, including Erik. Then I'd look like a fool, just another one of the millions of women that are clamoring to get their hands on him. No, I need to hang back a little longer and let the sick fascination he has with taunting me wear off.

He's immersed in another scene right now, and I can safely watch him from here. Besides, I know what I stand to lose if I give in to this attraction. There is no doubt in my mind that Jeff would fire me. He ranks dating a client just below getting a client killed. So it really should be a simple choice, but every time I look at him, my judgment disappears. In desperation, I pull out my phone and send a quick text to Sarah. She's teaching, but maybe she will have time to talk on her lunch hour.

Me: Everything is okay, but need to talk ASAP. Free during lunch? XOXO

♚ CHAPTER SEVEN

"Hello Jeff."

"What the hell is going on down there?" His tone is angry and biting. My eyes grow wide as I sit at attention. Fortunately, no one is around to hear this conversation.

"Whoa, Jeff! What's wrong?"

"I got a call from Mr. Cohen. What the hell is going on between you and Erik Sinclair?" he says, barking at me as if he were still my CO.

"Jeff, I don't have the first clue what you're talking about. What did Cohen say?" I ask, trying to sound innocent.

"Cohen said someone walked in on you and Sinclair, and you two were kissing!" He's all but screaming at me now, and if there story were true, I wouldn't blame him.

"That's a complete lie, Jeff!" *Well, it sort of is.*

"So nothing like that happened?" he asks, but his question still sounds like an accusation. I hesitate, but my integrity dictates that I tell him the truth.

"Mrs. Cohen barged into Mr. Sinclair's trailer today, but I had nearly fallen over a chair. Mr. Sinclair grabbed me before I fell on my ass. THAT'S IT! There was no kissing involved. Come on Jeff. You know me better than that," I plead. My heart pounds as I listen to the silence, and I pray he's not thinking the same thing I am. I'm not that clumsy. When he's quiet too long, I check the phone to make sure the call hasn't dropped.

"Then why did Sinclair call me and ask if you could get all dressed up for the Breathless premieres?" he asks, with a hint of jealousy in his voice. I ignore the tone in his voice, because I've heard it many times over the years.

"What? Are you kidding? This is the first I've heard of it, Jeff!" I'm astonished, and the panic rises in my belly, spinning into a giant knot.

"Yeah. I think he wants to show you off like you're his own personal piece of arm-candy. I'm not going to let him do that!" He's irate again. And while he's trying to protect me and Cole Security, there's more driving this rant than just our reputation.

"Jeff, I'm telling you. There's nothing going on between me and him! Nor will I agree to dress up like some trophy girlfriend."

"I swear Ronnie, if you make an ass of me—"

Regardless of Jeff's feelings, he should know better than to ask me something like that. I wouldn't risk my reputation or his, just to satisfy a client's ridiculous demands. But I have one last shot to convince him. "Seriously. Nothing happened." The truth is, he wanted it to, and so did I.

"What are you going to do, Jeff?" Again, he's silent for longer than I'd like.

"I'm going to call Cohen and find out what kind of game he's playing. I'll talk to you later."

My hands shake as the call goes dead. Someone is causing major trouble here, and I think I know exactly who to point the finger at. I rise from the table, propelled by my anger, thinking over the possible motives behind this mess and I stop in my tracks. I can't believe I have to devote my energy to this, and I'm disgusted with my own behavior. My judgment and integrity have disappeared in less than twenty-four hours in Erik's presence. This has to be a new world record.

As I climb the steps to the trailer, I can hear Erik voice. He's sitting at the dinette with Tom eating take out tacos, and I realize over two hours have passed since our awkward moment. Tom smiles and waves a hand as I walk inside.

"You disappeared. What happened?" Erik looks at me and my face reddens, knowing we're about to have another awkward encounter.

"I had a phone call from Mr. Cole." My tense reply is enough to tell Erik something is wrong. He nods as he chews and sets his taco in the Styrofoam box.

"Ah, Tom, could you excuse us, please," I ask as calmly as I can. Tom nods, wipes off his hands, and then gathers up his food and drink.

"See you later." Tom says walking past me, closing the door behind him. It's just me, Erik, and my already frazzled nerves.

"What happened? You look . . . " He stops mid-sentence and retrieves his phone from his pocket. "Fuck, it's her." He stares for a second while it rings, then he taps the screen and sends the call to voice mail. Already, I'm overheated and flustered, and I haven't even explained the situation. I shrug off his jacket and toss it on the couch, but when I turn back, he's in front of me.

"What is it?" His asks with concern in his eyes. The familiar electric pull is back; that vibration that starts low in my belly whenever I'm close to him. I can't think, but I have to tell him about the call from Jeff. The tips of his fingers brush along my arm from my shoulder to my wrist and goose bumps race across my skin. My insides quiver in a way I haven't experienced in years. *Dammit, I said I wasn't going to do this*. He comes closer, and my breath hitches.

I have to stop this. I back away. "What happened earlier can't happen again, sir." I'm trembling, my knees feel as if they're made of rubber, and I sit on the sofa behind me. "Ever." I add and fold my hands together in front of me, trying to appear resolute. But I don't feel that way. His lips part fractionally, and he sighs, running a hand through his jet-black hair. He opens his mouth to argue, but I stop him.

"Jeff called. Someone told him about this morning."

He inhales sharply before his mouth crumples into a frown. The muscles in his jaw flex and tighten. He opens his mouth, but once again, his phone rings. "Jeez. She just doesn't quit!" He answers this time, and I immediately hear a shrill, agitated voice, but I can't make out what the woman is saying. He looks exasperated, and he gets up from his chair. His paces the room as he listens to her yell, but I'm startled when I hear his booming, angry voice shouting at her.

"What? No! That's not true!" He exclaims as he rakes the hair off his forehead. "Who told you that? Oh wait, let me guess, Melissa."

And there it is, confirmation that Melissa is out to cause trouble. Erik paces the room as he listens to Catriona rant, occasionally pulling the phone away from his ear as she screams. There are moments of hesitation when he stops, briefly opening his mouth only to close it again as she talks over him. But there is one question that halts him, and he turns to stare at me for a few long seconds, saying nothing as he listens. Then a wicked gleam lights up his eyes as he finds an opening to speak.

"If you must know, yes, she's quite pretty," he says.

I look to the floor and suppress a shocked gasp. Admitting that to her is a huge mistake, much like poking a sleeping bear. Regardless of his bad judgment, my insides turn all gooey and giddy, and I'd love to unleash the biggest smile, but I can't. There's an obvious attraction between us, and hearing him admit it aloud is huge. But it can't go any farther. An admitted attraction and nothing more. Giving in to it would mean the loss of my job, and it could put both of us in danger.

He continues to talk about how their relationship is over and how it's none of her business who he is, or isn't dating, and I start to feel like a voyeur. I stand up and try to make my way outside without him noticing, but he grabs me by the wrist and shakes his head.

Damn.

I sit again, agitated and uncomfortable as I listen to him rant. But he goes silent and his mouth hangs open. This doesn't look good.

"You did WHAT? You had no right, Cat!" He looks at me, and the anger is palpable. As she talks, his face changes from angry to positively enraged. When he looks at me, I roll my eyes and mimic her nonstop talking. It's an attempt to lighten the mood, and he starts to chuckle but stifles it as he finds an opportunity to argue his point.

"You'll have to pay for all the damage you did. Now that I have your attention, pick a day to come get the rest of your stuff. I want it out of my house."

Damage? What could she have possibly done with Dan in the house?

He goes silent while she yells at him again, and I wonder where she'll go with all those boxes. Losing the Brentwood house means she has nowhere to turn. She better not come running back to Erik. *Jesus, did I just think that?*

As I strain to listen, my phone vibrates. It's a text from Sarah.

Sarah: R U OK? Meetings thru lunch, then teaching class until 4. Will call U After.

I look down at the phone and type a quick response while listening for the conversation to continue.

Me: I am Ok. Just need major advice. 4 is fine. TTYL

"And there's going to be an alarm system installed soon, so stay the hell out of the house." As he talks about lawyers and money, it's clear she owns half of the house, which gives her the right to block the security installation.

"Yes. I'll have someone from the security company contact you. Good-bye." He disconnects the call and stares at the phone as if it's burning his hand, and then he rakes the hair out of his eyes. Before he can say a word, I'm peppering him with questions.

"What happened at the house? Is she okay?" He looks at me and sits on the couch with a sigh. We have no security out there yet, anything could have happened.

"Catriona is fine. She found your things in the closet and flipped out." He pauses, almost choking on the words. "She got my machete and destroyed your clothes."

This has to be a joke, and I snort a quiet laugh. When the look on his faces changes from anger to embarrassment, I know it's real. I rub both my hands down my cheeks. This is the last thing I need.

"She thought you might be my new . . . " He can't say the word.

"I have a damn good idea what she thought," I snap. Without knowing it, she's not far off the mark, and admitting he finds me attractive probably made matters worse. Had he actually kissed me, Catriona's fears would be justified.

"I guess you were right. I'm sorry about all of this." He shakes his head and sighs, looking disgusted.

"This is not your fault." I try to reassure him, but I might have flipped out too if I suddenly found another woman's clothes in my ex's place. Although, I have limits. Angry, yes. Machete . . . no.

"And, by the way, where the hell did she find a machete?"

He laughs and his expression changes. His blue eyes glitter and his smile goes slack. "How do you do that?"

I look at him in confusion and shrug.

"You know how to make me laugh, even in terrible situations." His moist lips part slightly as his eyes roam my face. I feel a kiss is in my future, and every muscle in my body tenses in anticipation. My heart pounds in my chest, and I know what will happen if I sit here any longer. I stand up nervously and slip on his jacket. He watches me as I move, and the silence becomes awkward.

"Look, just try to forget about it. It's done." He nods in agreement, but he still appears raw from the experience.

"I know. But the more I think about it, the more I realize I'm ready to move on," he says, rubbing his chin thoughtfully before his gaze locks on my face. My mind screeches into neutral as I realize the meaning behind his words. He's ready to move on all right, and I know exactly whom he has in mind.

My nerves get the better of me, and I almost sprint out the door, but my phone rings. It's Dan, and I'm tempted to ignore the call. He has the worst timing in the world, but my sense of responsibility wins out. When I answer, Dan rambles for a few minutes about completing all the tasks I gave him, which strikes me as odd. Why wouldn't he just cut to the chase and tell me about Catriona? That's far more important than groceries and keys. *Jeez, who trained this guy?*

Not bothering to mention I know about Catriona's visit, my stomach goes queasy as he explains how she startled him by showing up unannounced. Apparently, she just walked into the house, and he drew his gun on her. Now I understand why she was so agitated. Between the gun in her face and a strange new woman in the house, no wonder she flipped out.

He relates the entire ordeal, but I stop him. "I already know what she did to my clothes. She just called Erik," I admit.

"Okay. Check your text messages, boss." I switch over to the text app, and he's sent me a picture. Of my clothes, my poor defenseless suits, shirts and pants which now lie on the floor, in tatters. What a bitch.

"Dan, get in the car and get down here. I have to go to Cole and get an advance to cover the clothes." I hear him close the front door and then start his car.

"Okay boss. I'll be there as soon as I can."

Erik gets up and stomps toward the door. "Mr. Sinclair, where are you going?" I demand. He turns with his hand on the door handle.

"I'm going to find out who is spreading gossip." Erik says, sounding angry. He's disgusted and determined to find out if it was Catriona, Melissa, or Beth who betrayed him.

"Everyone thinks they know what's best for me, and I'm tired of all the drama." He turns to walk out, but I spring from my chair and grab him by the arm.

"Please, just calm down. Let me call Mr. Cole. You can talk to him about his conversation with Mr. Cohen. Plus, we need to speak with him about Catriona."

He calms suddenly, and he turns from the door. Maybe it's my touch, or maybe I've gotten through to him. Either way, he relents and sits on the couch again. As I retrieve my phone from my jacket, I dial the office.

"Hi Marci. Can you put me through to Jeff, please?"

He looks at me and raises one eyebrow, but doesn't say a word. I lean against the counter as we wait for Jeff to come on the line. As I stand there, I surreptitiously type a quick text to Jeff, asking him not to bother bringing up the premieres. Maybe if we ignore it, Erik will give up on the idea. Marci comes back on the line and lets me know that Jeff is free.

"Hi Jeff. We had an issue at the house with Mr. Sinclair's ex-girlfriend."

"What happened? How bad is it?" He sounds anxious.

"She turned up at the house without warning. She startled Dan, and he drew his gun on her."

"Oh shit. Was she hurt?"

"No, Dan didn't fire his gun. He just drew it on her." I can hear him exhale sharply in relief. "She went into the room I'm using and found my clothes in the closet. She had a major meltdown, thinking Mr. Sinclair had a new girlfriend. Before Dan could stop her, Catriona destroyed all my clothes."

I pull the phone back from my ear when he breaks out in hysterics. "It's not funny Jeff!"

"Oh yes, it is! There's a ton of high school bullshit going on at that set. But hey, you wanted jobs that are more exciting. Be careful what you wish for, huh?"

This time I have to laugh. He's totally right. Part of me wishes I could go back to the boring CEOs since my life would be far less complicated right now. Jeff talks through his laughter.

"Is he there? Put me on speaker."

I walk back to the couch and sit next to Erik, who shifts closer until his thigh touches mine. I can feel his body heat through my clothes, and a tingle rockets up through my leg and straight to my sex. The gentle throb makes concentrating on business nearly impossible.

"Hello, Mr. Cole." Erik makes a point of emphasizing the word Mister as he looks at me.

"So I understand Miss O'Neill caused a bit of damage?"

"Yes, unfortunately. I'm sorry about all the drama Mr. Cole."

Jeff and Erik talk about the damage she did, and her reluctance to allow the security system installation. When Erik admits she is half owner of the house, Jeff is irritated even further.

"You might have mentioned this earlier Mr. Sinclair. Let me talk to our legal counsel. There might be a way around it. I'll get back to you on that."

When Erik addresses the outrageous rumor, I can hear the tension rise in Jeff's voice. Even when he assures Jeff there was no kiss, Jeff sounds angry and unconvinced.

"Why would Mrs. Cohen invent a story like this?" Jeff demands.

"I'm not sure, Mr. Cole. But I intend to find out."

Jeff isn't impressed. "Look, whatever is going on down there is not my problem. I won't have Ronnie down there dealing with a bunch of gossiping children. That puts you and everyone around you in danger and I have no problem pulling her off the job."

Erik's eyes grow wide. He didn't expect such an acrimonious response.

"I have a feeling I know what and whom is behind this Mr. Cole. But I can assure you, Ms. Harper has been completely professional. Nothing untoward has taken place."

"Mr. Sinclair, I can assure you, if it did, I'd pull her off the job immediately."

This could become a shouting match in a second if I don't step in. "Jeff, we will have Mr. Cohen call you when we find out how this happened."

He is silent for a moment, but relents. "Okay Ronnie. I'll see you at the office. Good-bye, Mr. Sinclair."

I stand and retrieve my coat, slipping my phone into the pocket. "I'm going to leave. Apparently, I need a new wardrobe," I quip.

"Go get Cecelia. She can help you," he smiles.

"I can do this myself Mr. Sinclair. I'm a big girl." My attempt to play dumb fails, leaving my sarcasm to fall on deaf ears.

"Well, I haven't told you yet. I spoke to Jeff the day you arrived. He thought it was a good idea for you to dress up for the premieres." He walks toward me with a devilish look in his eye.

What? No . . . No he didn't!

I stifle any reaction, hoping he doesn't realize I know. "Really? Well, he told me he didn't you using use me as—now, how did he put it? Oh yes,

74

'your arm-candy'." My indignant stare cuts him like a razor, and his eyes shift as he stammers.

"Ah, what I meant was . . . "

Yes! I've reduced the great Erik Sinclair to a stammering fool. I smile, knowing I have the upper hand, and I wait, watching him back pedal furiously, just to amuse myself.

"Look, all the security is new to me. It's embarrassing having to go to these lengths because of angry fans or a deranged lunatic. Just do this for me, please. Cecelia will help you. She knows what to buy for these kinds of things."

I let go of my delight at watching him squirm, as his reasons become clear. It's about ego. He feels emasculated by the threats, by the visible security. Having me dress up is his way of controlling the situation. But I still don't like it.

"N-No. This is not a good idea." I try to leave, but before I can leave, he spins around and blocks my way out. "Mr. Sinclair, this is unnecessary. I can't protect you in sky-high heels and a sequined dress. I go with you as your protection, not as your . . . "

For a moment, I wonder if he'll say it. But he just smiles, and it's filled with impish delight.

"This is completely unnecessary," I declare, hoping he'll give in.

"If that's the case, then why do I need protection at all?" He stares at me, all confident and cocky, folding his arms across his chest. I just want to slap him. He doesn't understand who he's dealing with. Even if Kincaid is not behind the threats, lowering our guard with a possible deranged lunatic on the loose is not wise.

"Look, people who send threats like this are dangerous. Do you want to take a chance with your life?"

His eyes grow wide. "Ah, so you agree that this is a potentially dangerous situation and it might be better to go undercover, so to speak."

Son of a bitch just talked me into a circle! I can feel my eyebrows bunch up. I hate giving in. "Fine," I snap.

"Where are you going?" He looks at me as I open the door.

"Shopping. Apparently, I have a premiere to attend."

As I walk down the stairs, Dan rounds the corner. He reaches into his pocket, pulls out a ring of keys, and hands them to me.

"Here's the extra set of house keys for you, boss." I nod at him.

"Would you mind if I borrowed your car?" I take the Escalade keys and hand them to Dan.

"No, not at all boss." He digs his keys out of his pocket and hands them to me before I let him know that I'll be heading to the office. Before I head toward wardrobe, I give him instructions for the rest of the day. Stay close to Sinclair and no autographs. When he disappears inside Erik's trailer, I walk over to the wardrobe and knock before entering. Cecelia comes up from the back. "Hi, Ms. Harper. What can I do for you?" she smiles at me.

"Oh, please call me Ronnie. Mr. Sinclair said you would help me do some shopping for the premieres?" I look at her nervously, but she smiles again, putting me more at ease.

"Oh, yes. He asked me about that. Are you going somewhere now?"

I laugh, and when I explain the real reason for my shopping trip, she is appalled.

"Well, I guess you need more than just dresses," she says, surprised. She turns and walks to the back again. "Let me get my purse."

When she comes back, she has her coat on, and we walk out and head behind the trailers to Dan's Hyundai. As I drive off the lot, I mention making a detour to the office before we hit the stores.

"I have one stop to make before we do any shopping, if that's okay." I mention.

"No, not a problem at all. My assistant can handle things while we're out," she says.

On the drive across town, I grill Cecelia about the premieres, hoping she can give me a quick and dirty education on fashion. I have no idea what the protocol is here, and if left up to me, I'd show up in something ridiculously inappropriate. She mentions a few designers I've heard of, but most of the names have me scratching my head.

When we arrive at the office, Cecelia follows me inside. "You can have a seat here and Marci will get you something to drink if you like."

Cecelia steps closer, looking tense. "This place is creepy. It's all very secret squirrel!" she says with raised eyebrows. Marci overhears her and steps from behind her desk to introduce herself in an effort to make Cecelia more comfortable.

"Can I get you something? I just made a fresh pot of coffee, and I brought in some homemade cookies."

Cecelia agrees and nods at me as I turn toward Jeff's office. "Hi Jeff." I smile as I take a seat on the couch, hoping he decides against chewing me out. He turns his chair and looks at me with suspicion in his eyes. Those normally bright-green eyes take on a dark and angry color. He reaches into his desk and hands me the Black Card.

"Don't go crazy. Just replace what she destroyed," he says with a tense nod. "So what is up with that text?" he asks.

He stares blankly as I let out a nervous laugh. "I just figured if we ignore it, it will go away." Telling him the truth of how Erik talked me into a corner would not be wise. But there's no way I can hide this from Jeff.

"Who's the redhead?" he asks looking past me toward the lobby.

"That's Cecelia. She's the Head of Wardrobe," I swallow hard. "Um, she's going to help me . . . with um . . . the dresses." I rub my fingers across my forehead, tipping my head to the side as I wait for him to explode. Jeff mirrors my reaction, and he sighs, realizing my plan was unsuccessful.

"I don't like this one damn bit," he says as the furrow between his brows tightens. I shrug my shoulders, but I'm at a loss since no client has ever demanded something like this before.

"Fine. Do it. But if he insists on dressing you up like a movie star, he'll have to reimburse us," he grumbles. "Oh, I've run into a small problem. I got a call from Alex Harris' wife today. He's in the hospital—emergency Appendectomy." Alex is our tech and security guru, and without him, the security system install at the set and the house will come to a screeching halt.

"Is there anyone we can hire on contract to do this?"

He nods and rubs at his stubble. "Yes, I'm trying to arrange something. I want to get this done before you leave for the London premiere." He looks at me and lowers his eyes as his mouth twists into a frown. "So, being left alone with the über handsome Erik Sinclair doesn't bother you?"

His question makes me nervous, and I can't tell if he suspects something or if he's joking. I figure the best option is to brush it off. "Oh, I think he's harmless Jeff," I laugh. I hope that sounded convincing.

He looks apprehensive and opens his mouth to speak, but then closes it again. Jeff normally has no trouble saying what's on his mind, but he turns his chair away for a moment, then taps his fingers on the desk a few times, thinking over his words.

"If he says or does anything inappropriate, tell me. I'll get you out of there, no questions asked. And he won't like what happens if I find out he lays a hand on you."

I nod, trying to hide my surprise, but my heart pounds in my ears. Why he'd say this at all strikes me as strange.

"Now, go back to work," he says.

I smile half-heartedly and gather my bag as I walk out the door. Turning down the hall, I head toward the armory. I swipe my employee badge through the card reader and open the door, and the smell of CLP cleaner fills the air. Hunter is hard at work on the back table, cleaning a Glock. He's out of his usual dark suit, opting for his old desert combat uniform instead.

"Hey Ronnie. Give me a minute, just installing a new firing pin," he says as he looks back down at his work. I take a seat at his desk, but it isn't long before he stores the repaired gun in the cage.

"What can I get you?" he asks.

"Do you have an extra-large vest?" I get up to look around and grab a black duffel bag. He nods and walks to the back of the room.

"Here you go." He stuffs it in the bag. "Anything else?"

I give him a laundry list, and he makes quick work of it, pulling items off shelves and retrieving weapons from behind the locked cages.

"This guy doesn't have gear of his own?" His eyebrows are raised. "Weird."

I shrug.

Maybe it is weird.

♟ CHAPTER EIGHT

Cecelia and I end up on Melrose, and as soon as I get out of the car, I feel like a slob. My two hundred dollar suit and forty-dollar shirt look like rags from the thrift store compared to the clothes I see displayed in the shop windows. Before we even walk into the store, I feel overwhelmed and self-conscious, but she takes me by the arm.

"Come on. Just follow my lead." We walk into the immaculately designed, upscale store that has a high-end price tag to match and I watch as Cecelia goes to work. She bypasses the sales girl that comes rushing up to help, preferring to look through the racks herself. I stand on the sidelines, watching her as she hunts. She's a woman on a mission, this is her domain. She likes silk and sequins. I like guns, and I don't even own a dress. Not one. Something must be wrong with me.

Cecelia finds a beautiful black-and-white gown with a twist of chiffon draped in front. It's tasteful, but the low split neckline is a bit revealing. When she hands it to me, I shrug nervously. This might be more dress than I can handle. I follow Cecelia and the perky blond sales girl in her perfect pink dress to the back of the store, and close myself into one of the small rooms. As I strip out of my clothes, I stare at the dress. It's just hanging there, mocking me. *"You don't belong here, honey."*

When I come out, Cecelia is thrilled with the fit, and she suggests I take it. Truthfully, as I look at myself in the mirrors, I have to admit the fit is beautiful, and for once, I actually like the way I look. *Hmm, that was relatively painless.*

When we leave with a huge dress bag, Cecelia is beaming. Stuffing it in the back seat, she directs me to the next location, which is a vintage store that a friend owns. We park and enter Vintage Vamp, and the owner, Mary, greets us as soon as we walk through the door. She's older, and her voice reminds me of Demi Moore as she and Cecelia discuss what type of dress we're after. Armed with ideas, Mary goes to work, and within a few minutes, I'm in another dressing room with several intimidating gowns in a range of styles and colors. Taking hold of the red dress, I can see right away it's not for me. It's clingy and red just isn't my color, so I set it aside in favor of a silver beaded dress.

When I slip it on, and not only is it heavy, but it's way too long. With the premieres only weeks away, I suppose this dress will require major alterations. While it's nice, I just don't feel comfortable in it. One of the last items is an aqua-colored chiffon creation, with an interesting geometric lattice like bodice that goes over the shoulders. Thankfully, it's not trashy. I don't do trashy. I slip it on, and manage to get my head through the strappy top without ripping it or strangling myself, I think. When I turn to look in the mirror, it all looks wrong.

"Cecelia!" I shout, begging for help. When she knocks, I open the door, and she giggles before she steps inside.

"I don't know what I did," I say, exasperated. Cecelia laughs more, covering her mouth with her hand.

"Oh my! I don't know how you did it but you've got your head through the middle of this!" She laughs and bends down to lift the skirt. "Okay, now crouch down so I can get this over your head." I do as she asks, and she carefully pulls the dress off me without ripping a single stitch.

"Okay, let's try this again."

She lifts the dress over my head, and I slip through it, correctly this time. Instead of the bodice sitting up at my neck, it falls in the correct place without a mess of loose straps hanging off my back. I turn, and she zips me into the dress. "Much better, don't you think?"

I step out with Cecelia following behind, and Mary is waiting. The two of them agree that the dress is perfect, but I'm not so sure. I didn't notice the higher than thigh-high slit in the dressing room, but she assures it could be tailored more modestly. It takes a little more convincing, but I give in. And when we leave, having spent another thousand, she's happy. Our next stop is the Beverly Center. Inside a familiar department store, I go in search of new suits, and Cecelia helps, quickly matching suits with shirts and accessories. Her choices much bolder than I would pick. I usually go for solid colors, but the color blocked and patterned shirts she chooses are understated and professional looking. I think I like having my own personal stylist.

Once Cecelia and I are finished shopping, we get back on the highway, headed toward the set. She's eager to get to work on tailoring the dresses so they will be ready in time for the premieres. As she yammers on about all the different celebrities she's dressed, my phone rings. Dan is calling to let me know that he and Erik have left the set and are on their way to the house.

When we return to the set, I help Cecelia carry the dress bags into the wardrobe trailer and thank her profusely for all her help. Just as I pull out of the gates, my phone rings and I see it's Sarah calling.

"Hi Sarah," I say happily, feeling relieved that I have a friend to talk to. I immediately launch into the events of the last few days, and she's shocked, especially about the hacking and being so near the warehouse where Kincaid took me. It doesn't take her long to downshift into therapist mode.

"Oh wow. And how are you handling this?"

"Um, I'm not. I haven't fully processed it all. The nightmares will start again, I'm sure, and I have to pass by the fucking warehouse on the way to the set every day. Every time I see it, I just want to vomit. Is that ever going to change?"

"Oh dear. I wish I could tell you yes. Living in San Francisco, your negative reaction is harder to treat. We could work on some aversion therapy if you lived in Los Angeles."

"It's a shopping center now."

She suddenly seems more upbeat. "Well, that's positive. Even something ugly can turn into something shiny and new. Think of it that way."

Yeah, sure. That sounds like the plot of every Disney movie ever made.

"Look, if you need to call me in the middle of the night, do it. I don't mind."

"Thanks, Sarah. I hope that won't happen. I have another security agent working with me on this case, so I'm not alone. That should help a little."

"Okay, that makes me feel a little better." She sighs, but I know she's still worried about me.

"And how is your client? Hopefully, he's still hot and sexy."

I can barely contain my laughter. Sarah listens intently as I tell her about my first meeting with Erik, and she's not surprised that I almost shot him.

Sarah has watched the show, so she knows they all look like dangerous criminals—even the women.

"So tell me about Erik. What is he like?"

I sigh. I know I'm not going to get off this call without telling her everything. "He's okay. Nice guy I guess," I say without a hint of excitement in my voice. Her laughter thunders through the phone, and I pull it away from my ear.

"That's it? He's just *nice?*"

I don't think a word exists that describes Erik.

"I don't know him that well, Sarah. He seems like a gentleman. He's got this chivalrous, protective thing about him. That's about all I know so far, but he appears to want to get to know me."

My answer is vague, and she's probably contemplating what I mean. I'm sure if we were in the same room, she'd be gulping down glass after glass of wine, with her eyes wide, hanging on every word. When I get to the truth of it, the intense connection between us, the way he picked me apart as he read my résumé, and his interest in my past, she offers her psychological insights.

"Honey, you realize what's going on here right? Remember when you were little and boys started pulling hair and teasing girls? His behavior is simply the adult version of that. He wants to get inside your head and see how you react to him."

I laugh at her comparison, but it makes sense, in an immature sort of way. Swallowing back the huge lump in my throat, I admit my enormous mistake. I tell her about the theory that snowballed into an "almost kiss" which culminated with Beth barging into Erik's trailer at the worst time. I'm sure she's cringing as I describe Erik's newly minted irate ex-girlfriend, the devious Melissa, the shredded clothes, and the call from Jeff. In truth it all sounds rather juvenile, no wonder Jeff reacted the way he did.

"Well, it's nice that Jeff stood up for you."

Her reaction is tepid, but that's Sarah. She's only met Jeff once, but she knows of our history. She's never figured out why I have a hard time getting close to him, even now. I'm sure she has a complicated psychological theory for why I feel that way.

"So how did you feel when he grabbed you? Were you okay, or did you have a panic attack?" Suddenly, she's less interested in Erik and his hotness.

"No, strangely, I didn't."

"And why do you think that is?"

I feel like I'm back in therapy, but I might as well explore this while I have the privacy and time to talk about it. "I don't know Sarah. Just getting close to Jeff bothers me. Why Erik? Why now?"

As nice as it feels to be the object of his attention, I'm at a loss as to why he's attracted to me. Usually, I sit safely in the background while I watch the men go after Sarah.

"Well, there's something non-threatening about him. He's flirtatious and charming, and he seems to show an interest in getting to know you. You have no history with him, and he doesn't know about your past. He's someone with whom you have a clean slate."

Wonderful. But this attraction is coming at the worst possible time. Clean slate or not, the same thing will happen with him that always happens. As soon as he finds out about my past, I will get that look. That "oh you poor thing" sort of look. Then he'll disappear.

"Maybe you're right. I just can't get involved with a client though. You know that."

"I know, hun. Just focus on the present and the fact that he's interested in you. Plus, he's the first man you've talked about feeling comfortable with since I've known you."

"But he just got out of a long-term relationship. He's probably on the rebound."

She laughs. "Yes, perhaps. Or he's just over the moon for you! You know, love at first sight happens sometimes."

There's no containing my laughter. I wonder if she actually believes that?

"I'm not suggesting you should jump into anything. Just concentrate on your job, and see where things lead. Get to know each other discreetly, take it slow."

Discreet flirting will be difficult with Dan lurking. Even if we were alone, it could take years for me to feel comfortable enough to have a real relationship, one that includes sex. Since the abduction, I haven't let a man get close to me, making it difficult to treat my phobias.

"We can get to know each other but there can't be any PDA. With the other security guy around, any kind of flirting would be career suicide."

"Do you really think Jeff would fire you? He cares for you. I highly doubt it, honey."

I want to agree with her, and I'd hope Jeff would forgive a rare indiscretion. He's my friend, but he's still the boss, and getting involved with a client ranks just below getting my client killed.

"Yes, I think he would. He sure made that point crystal clear to Erik."

"Hmm, he may have just been trying to scare Erik off. Maybe he's afraid he'll lose you. From the sound of it, Jeff is quite jealous."

She's right. Beside my client, Jeff is worried about money and hacking attempts. Those last two could ruin Cole Security's reputation in the industry. No matter what happens with Erik, I need to keep my job if not my reputation, intact. Money problems are out of my hands, and if the business fails because of it, I won't lose anything. However, if I lose my job due to risky behavior, well, I'd rather not live with that regret.

"Have you thought about how Jeff would react if you got involved with someone? I mean anyone, not just Erik?"

I think over the few relationships I've had over the years, and none of them amounted to much. Deploying for a year at a time makes it difficult to date, and I never stayed with anyone long enough to consider making it permanent. Ironically, it's better that I never did, since most of those guys didn't make it home in one piece. Jeff and I were lucky to remain together for so long, even as friends. Maybe he hoped something more would come out of that, but I never thought of him that way. As much as I care for him, I know I need to move on. I can't stay locked up in this cocoon forever.

"I don't know Sarah. He might be jealous, but I don't think he'd go crazy."

"Just remember, he hasn't had a relationship for years," she warns.

Her words are unnerving. She's not saying anything horrifying, but the implication is there. I've been on the receiving end of a jealous rage, today, in fact.

"I'll think about it Sarah. He seemed a little concerned when I saw him earlier, but nothing that would make me worry."

"That's good. I hope it stays that way. But honestly, I think if you quit and opened your own agency, you might have a better shot at a normal life."

"I don't want to leave Jeff, Sarah." In his eyes, that would almost be worse than having a fling with my client. I don't know if he'd ever forgive me.

"Look, I admire your loyalty. But if you want to get married, run a company, or have a normal life, sticking with Jeff won't get you there."

In some respect, she is right. Being a security consultant is preventing me from having a real life, and it has become my crutch. It's my way of avoiding relationships and men in general. Being the boss would give me a more regular schedule and with it, more options. However, I need to let someone near me first.

"Hey Sarah, I'm back at his house. I have to go. Listen, I've heard everything you said, and I will think about it."

"Call me if you need me. Bye."

Parking behind the Escalade, I shut the car off and hang up with Sarah. I take a deep breath, trying to rid myself of all the negativity. I'd love to go for a full throttle sweaty workout right now. A whole hour of kicking the shit out of a heavy bag or going a few rounds of sparring would clear my head and relieve stress, but I have no idea where a gym is around here.

A warm tingle spreads through me as I remember the press of Erik's very hard, toned body against me. *Jeez, get a grip Harper*. But I realize he probably has a gym membership with a body like that. Opening the door, I force myself out of the car and grab my bags from the back. When I reach the porch, Dan opens the door.

"Hey, boss." The duffel bag Hunter gave me is heavy, and Dan reaches down to take it from me. "Looks like you got everything replaced."

I nod at him, and he sets the duffel bag on the floor by the coffee table. "All the gear you'll need is in there Dan. Just give me the bag when you're done unloading it." He nods at me and then hesitates with a hint of a smile.

"Oh, you're right about that Escalade. She drives like a tank!"

Jesus, he worries me. The thought of the two of them joyriding in the Escalade all over L.A. springs to mind.

Erik gets up from the couch, with a mouthful of barbecue chips. He takes the garment bag from me but not before wiping his hands on his jeans, leaving the brownish red flavoring along his thighs.

"Wow, how much did you buy?" I ignore his question and look past him into the living room. I can see from the mess on the coffee table that the two of them have been drinking beer and watching the game.

"Chips and beer for dinner?" He glances toward the table and then smiles at me and shrugs. *Caveman*. Erik steps past me, and I can smell the Coors Light and barbecue chips on his breath as he carries the bags into the bedroom.

"Great, now that you're here, I can grab a shower." Dan jumps up and heads for the back door, but stops. "Are you cooking?" Dan asks. I look at him in exasperation, but I suppose I should. He did buy everything on my list, after all.

"Hmm. Yes, I think so. I plan on being in a carb coma by, let's see . . . nine p.m."

He laughs. "Well, in that case, I'll come back after I shower." The door closes behind him and I'm alone. I pull out the meat and the eggs, and I find the boxes of pasta stacked in the pantry closet.

"What are you making?" I hear Erik's voice and the muscles in my shoulders tense as I recall today's compromising situation. I'd rather not give him the opportunity to repeat it.

"Pasta."

"Can I get a shower or do you need my help?" Handing him the carton of eggs and the cheese, I make my point. I have no idea where anything is, and it's his kitchen.

"I see. What else do you need?" he says as he waits for instructions.

"I need a big pot. Fill it with water and turn on the burner, please." He does as I ask while I search out the rest of the ingredients.

"What next?" he asks.

"Can you separate six eggs?" He opens the package and gets two bowls. As he cracks the eggs, he struggles with separating them, but he eventually manages it.

"So what are you making?"

I take the bowl of yolks from him and set it on the counter next to me. "It's called spaghetti carbonara. Here, put the spaghetti in the pot."

He tips the box of pasta into the water and then gives it a good stir. "I thought that was the fettuccine with the grilled chicken and Alfredo sauce."

"No, it's Italian bacon and eggs over pasta. It doesn't have cream in it like Alfredo sauce and no chicken. Lots of black pepper though. It originated in the Rome area in the 1940s."

"You seem to know a lot about cooking. Do you cook a lot?"

"I used to. I'm always on the job now in someone else's home. They usually have personal chefs to do the cooking."

"I like to cook. Well, I like to learn from people who know how." He smiles at me, and I appreciate the implied compliment.

"So, are you married, Ms. Harper?" He leans against the island, staring at me.

"No. I've never been married." I instantly regret the words that just crossed my lips, and I kick myself for not saying yes. Maybe he'd leave me alone if I told him about my impulsive first marriage. If he knew I married an Army buddy just to get out of living in the barracks, he might think I'm shallow, or even better, a gold digger willing to marry anyone for personal gain. Of course, Jeff would disagree with both.

There's a loud knock at the back door, and I drop the spoon into the pan as Dan walks into the kitchen.

"Ouch! Son of a bitch!" I run to the sink and turn on the cold water, trying to wash away the scalding hot grease that's burning my skin. Erik rushes to my side to inspect my hand, and Dan looks over my shoulder.

"Ouch. You okay, boss?"

I nod at him as Erik carefully wraps a wet paper towel around my hand.

"Can you get that spoon out of the pan, please?" Dan does as I ask, and Erik jumps in. "Just give us directions, we'll finish it up."

I have a seat at the island and watch as Erik finishes cooking by my instruction. When he's done, he's quite pleased with his performance. He sets out bowls and serves the food.

"This is excellent, boss. Good job Mr. Sinclair," Dan says with a mouthful.

"Are you done?"

"Yes." As I stand and put my dish in the sink, Erik rests against the counter, surveying the damage I did to his kitchen. He grumbles, but doesn't move.

"I suppose we should clean up." He looks at me, and I shake my head disapprovingly.

"The best thing about being a cook is not having to do the cleanup." I smile and exit the kitchen, taking a seat in one of the blue chairs.

"Now that's just messed up." Erik walks to the sink and turns on the faucet again. "You're obviously the best cook in the house. But you knew that, didn't you?"

Erik laughs at my enthusiastic nod, then looks over at Dan, who is preoccupied with whatever he's found on television.

"All right Dan, it's you and me on cleanup duty." Dan turns and looks at me, then Erik, and frowns before getting off the couch. After Dan and Erik finish cleaning up the kitchen, they return to the living room. Erik commandeers the remote control and scans the television stations until he finds a football game. I sit in the blue chair, trying to make sense of a game I barely understand, and sigh.

Football is just not my thing.

A sudden knock on the door startles us. Dan is out of his chair and makes it to the door first. He looks through the peephole and then back to me. "I don't recognize this guy, boss," he says nervously. I step to the door, and through a small peephole, in the dim porch light, I make out the face instantly.

"Relax, put the safety back on," I say.

Dan nods at me as he drops his hand from his gun, and I open the door. The tall imposing man waiting on the porch smiles and I run out the door and jump into his arms.

"Hey Ronnie. It's good to see you," he says as he bear hugs me.

"You crazy fuck. What are you doing out here?"

When I turn around to welcome him into the house, Erik is standing in the doorway, watching with suspicion.

♟ CHAPTER NINE

"Mr. Sinclair this is Special Agent John Grilli from the FBI."
Erik stares at John for a moment, before extending a hand. "Nice to meet you. Why are you here?" he says, staring at John with narrow eyes.

I'm shocked at his tone and his ungracious behavior. But John is a big man, and at six-foot-four and close to three hundred pounds, most people find him intimidating. His jet-black hair and dark eyes do nothing to soften the impression that he's an old-school mafia button man instead of a federal agent.

I realize that Erik knows nothing of the FBI involvement, the hacking at Cole, or Kincaid, but that's about to change. There's only one reason John would come out here unannounced.

"Please, Mr. Sinclair, let's have a seat."

Erik nods, and Dan closes the door behind us as John and I take a seat. He pulls a brown folder from his satchel and without giving me time to warn Erik, he launches into his briefing.

"Mr. Sinclair, I've been working with Cole Security on the recent developments on your case."

"Such as?" Erik says with an icy stare, which John doesn't notice. But I do and I return it, hoping he'll back down. If he doesn't, this will become a dick-measuring contest, I can just feel it.

"I was assigned to the case a week ago, when Cole Security was hacked. But with the situation at your Brentwood home and the threats dropped off at the set."

Erik's gaze shifts quickly to me. "What hacking attempt?"

My insides curl up tightly when his gaze fixes on me. But it's not only Erik staring, John is looking at me the same way. I should have informed Erik, and I knew it would come out eventually. But now I have to explain my reasons.

"Mr. Sinclair, late last week, a message was left on the server that stores Cole's personnel files and contracts. The message seems to be directed toward both of us."

John flips the page and quotes the message verbatim.

"As long as Sinclair plays Cameron, he's not safe. I'll find him, no matter who's around him, no matter who tries to protect him."

Erik's eyebrows knit in confusion. "That's odd. Why would the threat be aimed at her," he asks, pointing to me.

John shakes his head. "It's a veiled threat, Mr. Sinclair. The file containing the message was left in her personnel folder on the server."

Dan's eyes grow wide, and Erik's expression changes so quickly it's hard to decipher what he's feeling. He seems confused, then angry, and then worried.

"How in the world would anyone know Cole Security is protecting me, or a particular agent? Nothing has been made public, at least to my knowledge. And why didn't you tell me, Ms. Harper." He stares at me for a few long, agonizing seconds, and the withering heat of his angry stare surprises me.

"I had very little information at the time. The investigation was in the preliminary stages." I admit.

"She's right Mr. Sinclair. I only had the case for two days when she arrived. We've made some progress since then."

Erik nods, and I can see he's just barely satisfied with that answer. He shifts in the blue chair and leans his chin on his hand. The muscles in his jaw are clenching and the vein in his neck is throbbing.

"Speak, Mr. Grilli."

His condescending response shocks me, and I raise my eyebrows as I look at Dan. Even he's surprised by Erik's touchy temper, and he shrugs a shoulder. Fortunately, John keeps going, unfazed by Erik's attitude. John is good under pressure. He handles unhappy superiors and distraught victims quite well.

90

"We traced the IP address backward from the Cole Offices all over the globe. The hacker was spoofing his IP. Do you know what spoofing is, Mr. Sinclair?"

I can see a slight smirk lifting the corner of John's mouth, and my mood sinks further when I realize he's taunting Erik. This conversation will become unbearable if they go toe to toe. Unaffected by John's dig, he shakes his head. Erik is smart, and he won't take the bait, even in his present mood.

"The IP address originated at a property in Henderson, Nevada." John looks to him for comments, but he only utters one word.

"Continue."

"Do you know anyone in Nevada, Mr. Sinclair?"

"No, continue."

John rearranges his papers as he speaks. "I sent a couple of agents from the Las Vegas field office to that address. It's an abandoned house. Currently bank owned, but the last listed owner was a woman named Miranda Cole."

My heart sinks to my shoes, and I clear my throat and cough uncontrollably. I feel like I'm going to vomit. "Excuse me, I need a glass of water." I get up and dash into the kitchen. Turning my back to the living room, I pull out a bottle of water, gulping down half of it while I try to calm my breathing.

Count your breaths, one, two, breathe, three . . . four . . . breathe.

John doesn't wait for me to return, he knows I can hear him from the kitchen. "The agents were able to enter the house, and they found an active Internet router. Whoever set it up spliced the Internet service off the house next door. The officers questioned the neighbors, and we feel they were unaware of the situation."

I return to the couch, a little calmer, but the shock of Jeff's possible involvement is eating at me silently. Erik's gaze falls on me and he looks me over for a moment before turning his attention back to John.

"So how do you know they aren't involved?"

"Good question, Mr. Sinclair. They are an older couple, both in their late seventies. They barely know how to start the computer their kids gave them." This time, Erik appears satisfied with John's answer.

"So how is all of this related to the threats and my house?"

"Mr. Sinclair, we think it's the same person behind all the incidents and the threats targeting you. Now, the interesting connection is this: according to the neighbors, the last they knew, Miranda Cole was in a nursing home.

The preliminary information we have so far, indicates that she is the mother of Jeff Cole, the owner of Cole Security."

I lower my eyes and cringe. Hearing John talk about Jeff and his mother being dragged into this case is the most disturbing thing I've ever experienced. Why anyone would want to involve them is mind boggling. My mind swirls, going over years of memories and conversations between Jeff and me, and I realize there's only one person who would go to such lengths. Only one person in the world carries such a grudge. *Kincaid.*

"Do you think Mr. Cole has anything to do with this Agent Grilli?"

"No, Mr. Sinclair. Jeff Cole is a highly decorated Army officer."

I'm staring at the table and clutching the bottle of water in my hand so hard that the plastic crinkles. Something about John's information doesn't sit right with me. "Wait!" I shout, gripping the plastic even harder. The memory comes back to me with the force of a speeding train.

"Have you briefed Jeff on any of this?"

"Yes, of course. Why?" John looks at me, confused. My cheeks burn, I look at my hands, and release the crumpled bottle, setting it on the table.

"John can I talk to you in private, please?" I stand and walk past Erik. He looks at me, confused and annoyed. I'm hiding information from him, but I have no choice. John follows me down to Erik's office, and he sits in the chair as I close the door, leaning against it.

"What is it Ronnie?"

"John, five years ago Jeff told me his mother died."

"Are you sure about that?" John looks at me. It's his turn to look shocked.

"Yes. I remember being surprised that there was no funeral. He had her cremated and interred."

John stares for a few seconds then exhales, looking off into the distance. He straightens himself in the chair, opens the folder again, and writes furiously in his usual chicken scratch shorthand only he can understand.

"You know what this means right?"

I nod. "Jeff is now a person of interest." My emotions are so scattered, so brittle, and fragile, I feel about ready to break.

"Did you ever meet her?" John asks as he continues to write.

I nod. "Yes, probably ten or twelve years ago."

He finishes writing and closes his folder. "If you think of anything else, call or text me. I may have to go out there myself. Do you think you'd be able to come out and verify if it's Jeff's mother, from the nursing home records?"

"I don't know if that is possible, John. We're headed to London soon." Going out to Vegas may not be a good idea. I can't leave Erik alone with Dan for that length of time.

"Think of it as a vacation." He smiles and laughs as he rises from the chair. I know him. He's trying to lighten my mood.

"Oh yes. That would be such fun! What happens in Vegas stays in Vegas? Maybe we can bury Kincaid there." He shakes his head and puts his hand on my shoulder as he follows me out the door.

"You have a sick sense of humor, you know that?" he says as he buttons his suit jacket. When we walk out into the living room, Dan and Erik are right where we left them.

"We'll be in touch if there's any new information, Mr. Sinclair," John says. With what I just told him, this puts a whole new spin on the case and there's no point in going over anything else for tonight. Erik stands from his chair, but doesn't bother to extend a hand to John before we both walk out the door. He watches as John and I step out on to the porch, seemingly irritated by John's presence, or by everything he's heard.

John unlocks his car and drops the folder on the passenger seat, but before he gets in, he feels the need to pick on me a little.

"So, is your client always such a crabby jerk?"

I look up at him, trying to mask the defensive reaction building in my gut. "No! He's not a jerk. He's charming and funny, and—" Before I can finish my sentence, I realize it. John is playing me. Son of a bitch!

"You're an asshole, John." I shove him hard, and he backs up a step as he laughs at me.

"He couldn't take his eyes off you." John has a great time needling me—just as any older brother would.

"He's just crabby because I told him no, John."

"Are you serious? Did he come on to you? You know this is not a good idea." His warning irritates me. I know this attraction between us is a problem. Even though his advice comes from the heart, I'd rather not listen to it.

"Yes, I know it is. You know I'd never date a client."

Yes, keep saying that. Maybe you'll eventually believe it.

"I know. Just be careful with him, okay?" He grabs me and gives me a big brotherly hug and a kiss on the cheek before he slips into his car. I watch him drive off, and as I turn to walk up the steps, Erik is standing stock still in the door, brooding. I'm not sure what he heard, and I shift my gaze as I walk past. He doesn't say a word as I step into the living room.

"Well, that was enlightening." Dan quips as he retrieves his gun from the coffee table. "I'm going to call it a night if it's okay with you, boss?" He looks at me as I lock the front door.

"Good night Dan," I say. Following Dan into the kitchen, I try to contain my anger and walk past Erik without a word. The dark kitchen lights up as I open the large refrigerator doors and stare inside. The whole incident has my sent my nerves into overdrive and my throat is parched—again. A full drawer of apples catches my eye, and I take one along with a bottle of water from the bin on the door.

I turn and almost plow right into Erik. "Son of a…" My pulse quickens, my skin prickles with anger and my teeth clench momentarily. When I suck in a breath, I mutter a good night as I try to move past him. But he doesn't let me. Dammit.

"Is there something I can do for you Mr. Sinclair?" I ask, hoping he'll decide not to torture me any further.

"I thought you'd want to hear about my conversation with Mark and Beth," he says calmly.

I nod, realizing John's visit overshadowed the excitement from earlier today. I give in and lean against the island opposite him, putting some much needed distance between us.

"So, you were right. Melissa was out to cause trouble." He stops and watches the smirk spread across my mouth, as he leans against the fridge.

"Go ahead, Ms. Harper. Take a moment and get your 'I told you so' happy dance out of the way," he snickers. I look up, and I can't hide a small smile. My own feeling of vindication and his ability to admit when he's wrong is impressive. But I say nothing.

"She overheard Beth talking to Sandra about walking in on us and wasted no time running to Mark about it, embellishing the story with the, well, a kiss." He hesitates on that last word for some reason, and he almost looks embarrassed by the idea. *Weird.* He sure seemed fine with it earlier today. He fidgets and crosses one leg over the other. Well, at least the call from Jeff makes more sense. Melissa's well-aimed attack was just enough to put Jeff's radar on high alert.

"Beth was very upset. She didn't mean to cause trouble. And when I told them about the call to Mr. Cole, she wanted to apologize, but you were gone. Mark said he'd call Mr. Cole and straighten everything out."

Those words are an enormous relief, hopefully putting an end to the ridiculous mean-girl antics of Melissa and Catriona. "Good. I hope Jeff won't get any more calls from Mr. Cohen?" I ask. He smiles at me and cocks an eyebrow.

"Mark promised he'd come to me, especially if it concerns Melissa. He was worried you were more interested in flirting than doing your job."

I frown. Hearing that is exactly what I was afraid of. I know it's impossible to protect someone I'm attracted to. Even the Cohen's know that. "Good night, Mr. Sinclair." I say, trying to move past him.

"So, did you find everything you were looking for?" he asks, halting me two steps from my escape. My thoughts race for a moment. He's killing me with this conversation whiplash and I wish he'd say whatever he's thinking and get it over with. When I realize he's referring to dresses, I turn.

"Yes, I did." I offer nothing more. After all, what would be the fun in that? Seems only fitting that I let him stew for a little while.

"Anything . . . fancy?" His eyes light up as I look at him. But something recoils inside me. The term "arm-candy" repeats in my head, and it bothers me.

"Yes. You won, okay? You can show me off like a trophy," I say bitterly.

The shock registers in his face, and I have the feeling he's about to tell me I'm being ridiculous. "A trophy? I could never treat anyone like that way. That would make me a hypocrite, wouldn't it?" He stares, waiting for an answer. But I'm not sure what he's getting at, so I shrug.

"Come now, Ms. Harper. Be honest. I'm sure your friends were excited when they found out it was me you'd be protecting. The 'Sexiest Man Alive' rumors have been running rampant since I took the role in Breathless."

Jesus, what a narcissistic, egotistical...celebrity. And here I thought he was humble and charming!

"I can just see it, 'Oh Ronnie. You're so lucky. He's *sooooo* hot'." Erik flails his arms, mimicking the high-pitched voice of an exited female. I want to laugh at his ridiculous display, but his mocking tone tells me he isn't amused.

"I'm treated like that every fucking day. So no, I would never treat you like a shallow, vapid Barbie doll." He stares at me, his eyes burning with indignation. It hits me in the chest, scolding me and I feel self-conscious. It's like he's been listening to Sarah and me talking, like he's secretly listening to the thoughts in my head.

I push off from the island, taking my apple and water as I try to escape once again. He reaches out a long, muscled arm as I try to pass him, and it extends across my chest, where his fingers grip my waist. In a blur, I'm turned around and my back presses against the cold stainless steel. He takes the water and fruit from my hand, placing them on the counter beside the fridge, and then I'm pinned by the gentle pressure of his hips. We're so close, that I can feel his warm breath wash across my lips and the scent of his cologne is threatening to steal all my reason.

His eyes flash with an intensity I haven't seen before, and for a moment, I think my heart is going to explode. *No, wait.* It can't...it's stopped beating altogether. Oh, this is not good. I know I should walk away, but my hands move on their own and latch onto his biceps.

"I think you know I wanted to kiss you today, Ms. Harper," he says softly as one hand reaches up to cup my cheek. "And if we hadn't been interrupted, I think you would have let me." I look up and take a sharp breath in, and what comes out sounds like a soft, mewling assent. Nothing like the denial I was going for.

He smiles a little and then tips his head to the side, and I can see the uneven rise and fall of his breathing, the rapid pulse in the vein standing out in his neck. His sandpapery stubble scratches against my cheek and the most gentle kiss presses against my skin next to my ear. The goosebumps race across my body in record time.

"I think you want me to right now. You're trembling, even more than you were this morning." He whispers, planting a soft kiss on my neck, and then another. Trying to recall whether I was trembling in his arms this morning is useless. My brain is no longer functional.

"Your body is betraying you, Ms. Harper. It's in your breathing, the flush in your skin, and your puckered nipples."

Another wet kiss presses into my flesh, along my jaw. "I wonder about the things I can't see," he mumbles as he stares at me. His lips come to rest on my forehead and for a moment, I breath. *Okay. He's not going to go any further*, I think.

Then ever so softly, I feel the rock of his hips against mine. The large bulge in his pants presses up against a very sensitive spot in the center of me that I'm now hyperaware of.

"I'd like to find out, Ms. Harper. In my bed. Making love to you all night long," he whispers as he straightens his head. The look in his eyes alone could make me rip of my own clothes and hop right into his bed, but the words–oh my–the words send a delicious shiver straight to that private place that he's rubbing against.

"Or do you need a good, hard, sweaty fucking, Ms. Harper?" His thumb brushes against my mouth and then drags my bottom lip open, exposing my teeth. That word…fucking.

Oh hell! It was unbelievably arrogant, but so sexy, so raw, brutal, and savage. So vicious and inhumane... My brain comes sputtering back to life, and now it won't stop sounding the alarm.

Danger! Danger! Will Robinson.

Erik's thumb ends up between my teeth and I bite down. His eyes fly open wide and when he grimaces, I let go, pushing him back a few steps. "Owww! Bloody fucking hell woman!"

"I told you no once already today!" I yell as I turn on my heels and sprint down the hall.

My breath heaves and with shaky hands, I close the door and lean against it, pulling my gun from the holster. I look at it, recalling how I nearly shot Erik on sight yesterday, but here I am, completely turned on by him, and trying to fend him off at the same time.

"Ms. Harper, please. I didn't mean..."

"I told you no. Now go away, Sinclair."

"I'm sorry. I didn't mean to...I'd never hurt you, Ronnie."

Oh Lord. The sound of my name rolling off his tongue causes every nerve to explode in tingles, and it makes me want to throw open the door and drag him into my room. Into my bed.

What the hell is wrong with me?

"Good night!"

When his bedroom door closes, I force myself to breathe and move again. This guy has some sort of hold on me that I don't yet understand, but overcoming it is a priority. I move away from the door and set my gun on the dresser. When I pull open the drawer, I rifle through my clothes lethargically as I recall every look and every word spoken between us, trying to find the moment when everything changed. The one I can point to and say, 'Yes. I should have known my life was going to be different from that moment on'. But all I see is his face. I feel his hands on me and the sound of his voice rings in my head, causing the blood to surge through my veins at warp speed once again. *Fuck!* This is useless. I move to the bathroom and turn on the water.

I need to release this tension in a long, hot shower. Shit…I just need *release.*

♟

Trembling in the cold and darkness, I hear nothing except the sound of my breathing as I hang here whimpering, shackled by my hands and feet. Hot tears stream down my cheeks and drip into my ears. The ache in my joints increases with every hour that I remain suspended by leather and steel.

The gag is drying out my mouth, and I'm parched, fiending for water that's being ritually offered, then denied. Another method of torture he uses to keep me quiet.

The sudden blast of cold air streaming from the ceiling vent covers my naked skin with goose bumps, and my muscles shake uncontrollably. Everything in my soul wants to cry out, to scream through the gag so that someone will hear me. I don't care who, just anyone. But I don't, I know what will happen if I do. Just take it, I tell myself. Endure it until he tires of you. Maybe he will let you go, or Jeff and the police will find you. Wait until you have an opportunity to fight back.

Trying to calm myself does no good. He's here, and the harsh fluorescent lights switch on, blinding me after being in near darkness for I don't know how long. "Have you been good my pet?" His voice grates on my shattered nerves, like nails on a chalkboard. My head yanks back as he pulls me by the hair, and I whimper a yes. He's in no hurry. He likes to drag it out, going about his business in his dungeon as I hang here, unable to run.

"I must feed my pets." He steps close to me, and I shake, fearing whatever new torments he's about to unleash on me. He gently pulls a wriggling mouse out of a small, black bag, and holding it by the tail, he lets it drop onto my naked stomach. Watching in horror as the creature scampers around my torso, I can feel its sharp claws dig into my skin as it moves. It nears my face, and I try to turn away in revulsion, but it's no use. I have nowhere to run, no way to protect myself. His cackling laughter angers me, and I fight harder,

pulling against the chains. He grabs the mouse off me and walks to the back of the room, and I hear him talking to them.

"Here my pet, here is your meal." The cages open, and I hear the faint squeaking of the mouse and others like it as he feeds his reptiles. When the door closes, he appears at my side again quickly.

"Are you hungry my pet?" His question is diabolical. He does not intend to offer food. "ANSWER ME! Or I will punish you." I nod my head yes. "That's better. If you please me, you may earn a meal."

Everything goes black as he blindfolds me again. I'm struggling to free myself, knowing what is coming. My legs pull against the chains, and I'm screaming through my gag. He pulls my legs wider, and then the pain comes. Over and over, the pain comes and I fight him, pulling against the restraints the best I can. Then it stops, and I sob.

"You're a very bad girl," he cackles as I hear the ratcheting sound coming from the ceiling. My legs slowly fall to the ground, but my muscles are weak, and I stand upright, hanging painfully from my hands. I hear the cane swish through the air as he swings it. Wham, searing pain, and my skin splits open. Please Master, not again as I beg through the gag. I have to get out of here. Please, let me go Kincaid. I whimper.

Let me go.

LET ME GO!

KINCAID LET ME GO!

"Whoa, Ronnie, what the fuck is going on?" I feel hands grabbing my arms, shaking me. "Ronnie, stop! Stop!" Tearing the blankets off, I scramble to my feet and run toward the door. I make it into the hall, and I'm running but strong hands catch me. My fists fly at him as I twist around and swing at what's holding me.

"Ronnie, stop, it's me!"

"Jeff, please. Get me out of here!"

I'm shaking, trying to tear myself away from his grip. "We need to run before Kincaid comes back."

"Open your eyes, luv," his voice is gentle, and his hands are warm. "Breathe, Ronnie. Calm down or you'll pass out."

Why are we standing still? We need to go. My voice trembles, and when I try to speak, it's weak and hoarse. "Jeff? Oh god . . . "

He scoops me up, and I'm cradled in his arms. My head rests against his chest, and I listen to his heartbeat. Loud, strong, and steady.

"Jeff, please don't leave me alone," I whisper against his skin. He lowers himself onto the couch with me in his lap. I want to run, but I can't. I'm trapped in the protective vise of his arms.

"Easy. Just breathe. You're safe."

I pant loudly, causing my heart to race and my pulse to pound endlessly in my ears. My body shakes violently, and I couldn't walk right now if I tried.

Wait, what are you doing? We need to get out of here!

"Easy. I've got you."

Warm hands comfort me, running up my back each time I inhale and slowly back down each time I exhale. My head rests on his shoulder, and the fine stubble along his jaw is scratchy against my cheek. I like it. It feels better than the fear.

"Please don't leave me Jeff."

"I won't."

I pull my knees up, making myself smaller in his arms as I try to contain the tremors. His hand grips my thigh. My gasps come slower now, and the thunderous heartbeat is quieting.

"Breathe," he whispers.

His hand rises along my spine once more and tangles into my hair, cupping the back of my head. I bury my face in his neck. My lips press against his skin, feeling the slow pulse of his heart underneath. I wallow in his delicious spicy, citrusy scent, which calms me, like a drug.

I don't want to run.

Wait . . . That scent.

Please Lord, don't let it be him.

Please. I'll be good. I'll go to church again.

After a few seconds of silently praying to myself, I peel open my lids and the outline of the tattoo across his chest is faint in the dim room.

"Erik?"

I hold my breath. My heart stops.

"Yes."

100

My heart lurches up into my throat again and my body tenses. He must feel it because he reacts instantly. "It's okay," he pulls me in closer. A gentle kiss lands on my forehead and then my nose.

His hand slides up my thigh.

Just a little.

When he stops, his grip tightens.

Just a little.

His breathing increases.

Just a little.

That hand in my hair lifts my face. His nose brushes along mine, and his stubble skips across my lips.

Oh—Oh my.

Oh my god.

I think a finger traces the outline of my lips. Maybe it was his lips, I can't be sure. I'm shaking again. My heart is racing again. This can't be healthy.

I'm up in the air again, slowly moving down the dark hall to my bedroom. He deposits me gently on the bed.

I'm crushed. Embarrassed. I want him to go.

The light blinds me, and when I open my eyes, he's in the closet, pulling out another blanket. He drops it on the floor and then steps toward me, lifting the bed covers as I look up at him. I'm a mess, but he doesn't say a word.

"Get in."

I do as I'm told, and I roll on my side, facing the window so he won't see the traces of fear in my eyes.

"You kept calling me Jeff." He strokes my hair, and I refuse to answer. I have no idea what I was saying, and I shrug in response.

"What happened to you Ronnie?"

I hold my breath in an attempt to fight back the pain. But it's no use. The tears come in loud hiccupping sobs as he sits behind me stroking my hair and reassuring me. After a beat of silence, he continues.

"You told me when I met you that I'd have to learn to trust you. Now it's your turn."

Okay, I think, but I remain silent, unwilling to discuss the horrible dream or my horrible past with him. Not tonight, not ever.

"Sleep now baby girl."

I nod, hoping no more dreams will haunt my sleep.

♟ CHAPTER TEN

Startled, I sit bolt upright in bed. I rub the sleep out of my eyes and lie back down. Another dream maybe. Then I hear the slow, low rumble of his snore-like breathing. I roll over, and he's on the floor, wrapped in a makeshift sleeping bag he fashioned out of the blue comforter. He looks peaceful. My heart swells, but I resist the urge to let out a loud *'awwww'*.

He stayed.

I prop my head up on my elbow, and I watch him until the sound of the back door opening snaps me to attention. I grab my phone and glance at the time, eight a.m. Leaning over the side of the bed, I grab Erik's arm and shake him awake.

"Erik. Wake up!"

"What's wrong?" His voice is raspy, and his head drops heavily back down to the pillow.

"It's after eight. Dan is in the kitchen."

"Shit." He jumps up and dashes across the hall into his room, leaving a mess of blankets on the floor.

"Dan, is that you?" I yell as I awkwardly hop across the room with one leg in my gray sweatpants.

"Yeah. Just making coffee," he yells back.

I shut the door silently, pull off my nightshirt, and switch into a black t-shirt instead. I swallow hard, trying to calm my ragged breath. Thank God he didn't find us in here together. I take a few more minutes to collect myself before I walk into the kitchen.

"Morning," I smile. "Sleep well?" He finishes pouring the water in the machine.

"Yes. It's nice to sleep late once in a while." Opening the fridge, I try to make myself useful.

"Eggs for you Dan?" I pull out the carton and set it on the counter.

"Sure, if you're cooking."

I pull out a bowl and a whisk and start breaking eggs. When Erik finally appears, I smile at him nervously.

"Good morning, Mr. Sinclair." I say, as I whisk the eggs. Erik walks in looking calm and composed, but as soon as our eyes meet, a huge smile spreads across his face, in a *"I've-got-a-secret"* sort of way. It's contagious, and I smile. Thankfully, Dan is sitting at the counter, checking his e-mail and doesn't notice.

"So what is the plan for today?" As I pour the eggs into the pan, they begin to sizzle, and Dan waits for Erik's input.

"Well, we don't have to be at the set until three p.m. It's all night shots today."

I serve myself some eggs and let the guys get their own. I might be the defacto chef, but I'm no waitress. As Dan and Erik talk about the schedule further, the only thing on my mind is getting to the gym. Perhaps Dan can stay with him while I work off the stress that has built up since I set eyes on my client. It would be nice to get away from both of them.

"Mr. Sinclair, do you have a gym you regularly use?" They both stare at me as I interrupt their conversation.

"Yes, it's not far from here. Why? Do you want to go today?" he asks, and then takes another bite of egg.

"Yes. I need a good workout." The expression on his face changes, he's staring at me salaciously. I'm almost certain he has other ideas in mind, which don't involve wearing workout clothes. Or any clothes at all.

"Dan, are you coming with us?" I ask, knowing that if go out alone with Erik I might never make it to the gym. He realizes what I'm doing of course, and he stares at me, perhaps hoping to change my mind. Ignoring him, I shift my focus to Dan, who seems hesitant.

"Sure, I suppose. After all, you can't go into the men's locker room."

I laugh. "Says who?"

The three of us are out the door by nine and on our way to Fitness Compound Gym. We walk into the brightly lit warehouse style building with exposed ceiling girders and ductwork and red-and-black striped walls. The music, which is pumping from the speakers high on the walls, drowns out the sound of people running on the treadmills or grunting while they lift weights.

"What's back there?" I ask. At the back of the building, there are two rooms separated from the rest of the gym by large glass windows. Both rooms have kettlebells, ropes, and various workout gear lining the walls. As we walk, Dan wanders off to the weight machines, settling on the leg press. He begins to grunt as he flexes his massive thighs, and then jumps off to lower the weight. Erik and I watch and laugh. Fortunately, Dan is too far away to hear us.

As we debate the purpose of the room, a tall, darkly tanned instructor walks inside. A woman would have to be blind not to notice the muscles of his well-defined biceps and shoulders and how they stand out beneath the black tank top.

"He's former military."

Erik looks at me then back at the instructor. "How do you know?"

I smile. "Only Marines wear a high and tight that high and tight." As I step to the door, I read the flier taped to the glass, it's exactly what I'm looking for.

"This is a training room for Krav Maga, ma'am," he says as he pulls a mat free from a large pile in the corner.

"Yes, I saw the flier," I turn and point back toward the door.

"Have you tried mixed martial arts before?" he asks.

I nod, and he smiles and holds out his hand, "Patrick Wilson."

"Nice to meet you Patrick. And your rank?"

He smiles and turns to pick up another mat. "Is it obvious? Master Gunny, retired." Erik stands to the side watching our rapport, a little perturbed.

"Gunny, this is Erik Sinclair." He walks up to us, and I notice the swagger right away. He takes on the same cocky, imposing demeanor when he's in character. I sigh, hoping that this won't turn into another dick-measuring contest.

Patrick extends his hand again. "You up for this Erik?"

He nods confidently. "Sure."

"We have a few more minutes before the class starts, so if you'd like to warm up on the treadmill or elliptical, you can come back in about twenty minutes."

As I turn to go, Erik presses his hand to the small of my back. He does it unconsciously, but he needs to stow it.

"Mr. Sinclair, you need to keep your hands to yourself." I whisper, and he glances at me from the corner of his eye, smiling. Dan is grunting it out on the weight machines, and much to my relief he's unaware of Erik's inappropriate gesture.

"What did you get me into?" He laughs and steps on the treadmill, and I join him on the adjacent machine.

"I'm going to kick your ass Sinclair." Pressing the buttons on the large control panel, I start slow, but quickly work up to a good stride. He matches me for speed, and run in tandem for two-and-a-half miles.

When we return to the martial arts room, four more students waiting to get started. Patrick and his co-instructors, Max and Martina, divide us into three groups, making it easier to give us individualized attention. Patrick starts out with a quick introduction to the equipment and the fundamentals of Krav Maga, along with the basic stances.

"Let's start with some tagging and blocking counter moves." Patrick can tell I have a bit of experience, so he spends more time teaching Erik the basics: covering groundwork, sparring with him, and getting him used to countering and avoidance.

"You're catching on quick Sinclair." Patrick gives Erik a break and comes back to work with me, going over more advanced techniques.

"Okay, tag me here, and then spin around while hooking your arm into mine. You can crouch. Get your center of gravity low, now you can flip me." Showing me the series of moves one by one, I get it down slowly.

"Ready to go full speed?" I nod and get in my stance. Patrick is excellent at blocking and countering, making me work hard for the flip. But I get there—eventually. I crouch down, pull him by the arm over my back and down to the ground, and punch the air, "YES!" I shout, and then extend my hand to Patrick, helping him to his feet.

"Good job."

Grabbing my towel and water, I tag out leaving Erik to work with Patrick for a few minutes. Patrick works with Erik patiently, showing him the most useful positions for tagging.

"Show me the flip you taught Ronnie."

Patrick looks a bit hesitant. "Well, Ronnie has a bit more experience and . . ." Resting his hands on his hips, Erik stands straight up, looking annoyed that he's not being taken seriously.

"Bring it on, man." He swipes at the sweat on his upper lip with the pad of his thumb.

Wonderful, let the dick measuring begin. Patrick steps up the workout, and to Erik's credit, he keeps up tolerably well. Learning the series of moves before the flip is a bit harder for him. After about ten minutes of trying, he finally masters the moves.

"Good job, Sinclair." Patrick offers him a high-five and laughs.

"Now, let's have you do that with Harper." Pointing at me, I put my water aside and step on the mat. I get in the ready position, waiting for Gunny to give us the go-ahead. He lifts a well-muscled arm in the air, and as I wait, I taunt Erik a little.

"You ready for an ass—" Before I can finish, Erik runs at me. My feet leave the floor as he ragdolls me, sending me sprawling on the mat. He pins me with his heavy torso, my arms spread out above my head. He's knocked the air out of my lungs.

Gunny yells at him, in his best Marine drill Sergeant voice. "Get up, Sinclair!"

Erik jumps up to his feet, and Gunny steps up close. Close enough to put the fear of God in Erik.

"Are your parents siblings, Sinclair?"

Erik is defiant and folds his arms across his chest.

"I asked you a question. Are your parents fucking siblings?" Gunny's booming voice startles the other instructors and the students, and they all turn around to watch.

"No, Gunny."

"Then why are you so fucking stupid! PULL YOUR HEAD OUT OF YOUR ASS!" Patrick's face is red and the veins are popping out all along his forehead and neck. Only when Erik nods, does Patrick move aside. I get ready again, smirking and loving the ass chewing he just took.

"Now it's your turn, Sinclair. I'm going to take you down."

"I love going down." He smiles at me wickedly, and Gunny raises an eyebrow at both of us.

"You two need to get a room. Okay, Go!"

Erik lunges at me, and I shift, pivoting around to throw him off-balance mentally. As I slip behind him, I push my foot into the back of his knee, and send him sprawling on the mat. He springs to his feet, looking undeterred as he wipes the sweat off his brow. He maintains his stance, and I shift, side to side, awaiting his first move. Erik moves forward and tags me, just touching my shoulder.

"Gotcha." He yells, but I pivot again, twisting around behind his back to tag him in the back of his shoulder. Wrapping my arm around his neck, I pull him down at an angle toward the mat, hooking my leg around his. One good yank and he's on the floor.

"HA!" I force him down on his back and pin his hands on either side of his head as I straddle him.

"Okay, you win," he says, breathing heavily.

I stand up, and Gunny pats me on the back. "Nice job."

Erik sits up and takes a few breaths before climbing to his feet. "Not bad Sinclair. Nice work for a beginner. We're done for today's session."

In serious need of water and a towel, we both relax and try to cool off. Gunny traverses the room, talking with the other students, and finding out how they liked the class.

"You're tougher than you look. I guess we didn't need to hire Dan after all." His admission surprises me. It's the first time he's complimented me on my skills. Perhaps a good ass whipping is what he needed to have confidence in me.

"So maybe now you'll trust me to keep you safe?"

He smiles at my snarky jab and shakes his head. "Yes. And you can throw me down and climb on top of me anytime."

My mouth drops open and silently bounces along the floor, but I have no opportunity to answer him or even scold him for his lewd comment before Patrick makes his way back to us.

"Here's my card. You can find the class schedule and a bit of background information on the different martial arts disciplines on the gym website. Are we going to see you in class again?" He looks at me, hoping to gain a new student.

"I don't know about him Gunny, but I'm game." Erik shoots me a terse frowns as Patrick walks away.

"See you next week." Gathering my towel and water, I head toward the door with Erik following behind.

"Don't think I can handle it, eh?" he says, and I laugh at him, but I stop when he smacks me on the butt—hard. I yelp at the stinging smack, and I turn around quickly, my eyes wide and my lips pressed together. He laughs at me.

"Walk," he says pointing out to the main gym.

"Where's Dan?" Erik stops and looks around, but he's nowhere in sight.

I shrug. "Maybe he's in the men's locker room?" We walk over to the far side of the gym, and as we round the corner to the locker rooms, we see Dan. He's talking to a woman. She's entirely too made up to be here for a workout. It's clear she's the type that comes to the gym to hook up, not to get sweaty. Judging by Dan's body language, he knows it.

She's propped up against the wall, and Dan is standing in front of her. He's leaning against the tile wall with his meaty arm cleverly placed above her head, and he's flexing, trying to impress her. She's batting her false eyelashes at him, pandering heavily to his ego. Erik looks at me and we both laugh. Without a word, Erik sashays toward Dan and his new friend.

"Hey Dan, honey. We should go now." Erik flounces up next to Dan, putting on his best lispy drama queen impression.

"Ooh, look at your big muscles." He practically salivates as he squeezes Dan's arm and suggestively licks his lips. Dan's eyes grow wide with panic. His potential hook-up is shocked, and her mouth gapes.

"Um, see ya later, Dan." She darts beneath his arm and runs off.

I can't contain my laughter as I watch her hurry away, and neither can Erik. "Oh my God!" I'm doubled over with laughter, and Erik can't speak. Dan is bright red, and his arms folded across his chest as he glares at both of us while we laugh.

"You two are fucked up," he scowls, but his anger is fleeting. He can't keep a straight face any longer and smiles, shaking his head.

"Let's go Romeo." Erik gives Dan a shove in the direction of the men's locker.

"We'll shower at home." Erik insists as he disappears.

As soon as we get back to the house, Dan goes inside first, making sure everything is safe. When he waves a hand out the front door, Erik and I come inside. "Okay, ladies first," Erik says as he points down the hall. I gather my things and disappear into the bathroom. I step into the steaming hot shower and lean against the wall. The water streams down over my head and back. It feels like hot needles, melting away the strain from the workout.

Lingering in the shower is not a problem. Dan is keeping an eye on things, so I remain longer than necessary. It's the only place I have to get away from him, where it's quiet, and where I can think. Even after the workout, last night weighs on my mind. There was no sign of hesitation or pity from him at all. But inside, I felt it. It's that cold dread I feel whenever I reveal too much, too soon. He saw it all last night.

Ok, not all. There's more. So much more. But he didn't bring it up, and I don't think he will. Thank god.

When I step out of the shower, I towel off quickly. My confidence is back, now that I've convinced myself he's going to leave the issue of last night exactly where it is. In the past.

When I return to the kitchen, Erik is busy at the island, putting out salads and ingredients for cold sandwiches. He's removed his sweaty shirt, and watch, fascinated as every beautifully toned muscle flexes beneath his skin. While he's unaware of me, I finally get a look at the Lords Skeleton tattoo. The gruesome skeleton sits on a throne, partially clothed in a purple robe, wearing a tilted and tarnished gold crown. It's massive, and stunning. Just like the man it's attached to.

"Oh, hey boss." Dan says. He's outed me, and I move quickly to the seat beside him, hoping Erik doesn't realize I was admiring his body.

But I think he does, because when I look at him the glint in those blue eyes and the just-messy-enough-to-be-sexy hair is enough to make me forget how to breathe.

"See, I can cook." His smile spreads wider across his face. I melt, knowing the longer I look at him, the more I'll get lost in those eyes. *I want to drown in those eyes.*

"I'm going to get a shower." Dan smiles and walks off. I'm silently praying for him to return, because every second we're alone gives him the opportunity to flirt.

"So how long have you known that FBI guy?" Erik asks. He's looking at me, wearing nothing but those sweatpants and a smile.

"I've known John since I was four years old." His eyes grow wide. Apparently, he wasn't expecting such a long friendship.

"Really? Wow, I thought he was just someone you used to work with." He takes a large bite of his sandwich, and I talk as I push the lettuce around the plate with my fork.

"Our families were close growing up. I'm Godmother to his eldest daughter." I try to keep focused on his face, but my eyes linger on the golden skin encasing the perfectly chiseled pecs and his rock-hard belly. I want to feel the contours of the peaks and valleys with my fingers and run my tongue along the furrow in the center. I want to follow it all the way down to–*Lord help me*, he has that V. I tip my head down, and look at him on the sly, my eyes following that gorgeous ridge of muscle from his hips all the way down to . . . *there*.

"I'm going to get a shower," he says as he walks out of the room. Smutty thoughts invade my brain once again, and the image of him naked, wet, and soapy starts a tingle rocketing through my body.

Just as I finish my food, Dan returns. He fixes himself a sandwich and sits at the island to eat.

"So what's the plan, boss?"

I watch at him as he chews, and I shrug. As far as I know, we don't have to be to the set until three p.m. "I'm not sure. I don't think Mr. Sinclair has any plans. We don't need to leave until two." He nods at me and talks with a bite of sandwich in his mouth. God, he's gross.

"Okay. Mind if I take my food and go relax?"

"No. Go ahead. Be ready at two please."

As the door closes, I can hear the soft padding of Erik's bare feet against the floor.

"So are you going to tell me who Kincaid is now?" he asks quietly. I spin around, stunned that he would ask such as question with no warning. My insides tighten, and the food I just ate might make a return appearance.

"No," I squeak, feeling ambushed.

He steps toward me slowly, as if he's approaching a wounded bird. "You kept screaming that name last night. Begging him to let you go."

My jaw clenches hard, and I try to push past him. I need to escape this, but I can't. He's like a six-foot tall block of solid marble. Everywhere my body makes contact with his sings with electric tingles, even where his strong hands wrap around my biceps.

"Why won't you trust me?" he begs. His eyes are full of anguish, and the ache in his voice is enough to make even the hardest, coldest parts of my heart give in. Though he doesn't understand what he's asking, and I shake my head in refusal. I already know what will happen. He'll pity me.

"I could have taken advantage of the situation last night. I didn't. I couldn't," he declares, as if I should be thankful to him for his integrity. Does he expect a fucking medal for that?

"Am I supposed to be grateful? Fuck you, Erik."

Finally, I push past him, and make my way toward the hall, but he catches me by the wrist.

"My god! What did he do to you?" He spins me around, and I look upon a face twisted by pain. My heart feels as if it's going to burst and launch itself right out of my chest as his eyes search me for an answer. He is desperate to know why I'm rejecting him, keeping him at arm's length. What he doesn't understand is I've kept my emotions and my heart locked away for the last five years, and it's going to take more than one night to hand him the key.

"I can't Erik. Please don't ask me to." My heart starts to pound, and my chest constricts tightly. The pain spreads down my arms, it spreads down to my legs, and I feel it all over again. The pain Kincaid unleashed on me every time he . . .

"Wait!" He attempts to follow, but I slam the bedroom door closed, trying to keep him out, but there's no point. I gasp for air under the crushing weight of my panic, and every vessel in my body dilates to cope with the increased rush of blood. Within seconds, the room constricts into a tiny, circular pinpoint. My sobs become loud hiccups as my breathing races faster and faster. Then everything tilts at an appalling angle. I'm off my feet, and my head lolls back with the movement, but I don't know where I am. Something soft is under me, and I feel a warm rush of air on my face and muffled voices.

"Breathe baby. I'm here. Breathe."

The bright light in the room finally penetrates that small black pinpoint. The feeling slowly returns to my limbs as pinpricks of sensation erupt in my fingertips and my toes when I shift my weight. I'm cradled in Erik's arms. His hands gently stroke my head, running down the length of my back, stopping briefly to trace small circles against my skin.

"You're safe. I'm not going to let anyone hurt you."

I breathe, filling my lungs with much-needed air. His voice, his aroma, and the steady thumping of his heart calm me. He's like a light, guiding me home in the darkness. Just like last night.

"I won't ask you again. I promise," he whispers as he cradles me against his chest.

"I'm sorry, Erik."

I can't hold back any longer and the fat tears spill from my eyes and roll down my cheeks. They drip onto his skin, and I watch them roll down his pecs and into the groove between his abs. My fingers trace the line of my tears down the soft rippling skin of his abdomen. His large hand clasps mine, stopping me before I venture too low. Suddenly, I'm back in the present.

Lifting my head, warm, soft lips kiss away my tears and move slowly across my cheek to my chin, stopping only to linger at the corner of my mouth. My lips part and a small, shuddering breath escapes. Every inch of my body vibrates, and I'm aching for his mouth to make contact with mine, but he moves.

Away.

Resting his forehead against mine, he exhales while his thumb wipes away the wetness on my other cheek. He swings around, lowers me to the mattress, and lifts the blankets to cover us both. Lying on his side, he slips his arm underneath the pillow while his other hand traces the contours of my arm, moving from my shoulder to my fingers. When he stops, his hand comes to rest on mine, before gently weaving our fingers together.

♚ CHAPTER ELEVEN

When I wake up, I'm alone and chilled from the loss of his body heat. Shifting my weight, I slip my legs from under the blanket and straighten the sheets. I reach for my phone and check the time. We still have an hour before my alarm goes off.

"Erik?" I call out to him, hoping he retreated to his own room. I'm not sure how long he's been gone, and I'm not sure when I started calling him Erik. He appears in the doorway in a moment.

"Feeling a little better?" he smiles as he walks in and sits on the edge of the bed. The short nap has calmed my nerves, but I know it's time to tell him something. He deserves my trust, even just a little. I sit up, leaning against the iron bed frame, and knit my fingers, squeezing and twisting them together in anxiety.

"I truly hope you never find out what Kincaid is like. You have no idea how horrifying he can be." My willingness to reopen the subject has taken him by surprise. He shakes his head and places a hand on top of mine.

"I don't want to know," he says.

I nod at him, and I realize that if I tell him the truth, he might not feel the same way about me. "Good, because it's not an image you want in your head, believe me. I don't want anyone to look at me with pity in their eyes."

He inhales sharply, and his grip on my hand tightens a bit. "What? Pity? I could never feel pity for you! I admire you. Whatever he did to you, you survived, and that makes you strong, and smart, and brave. You didn't give up, and you're not sitting in a strait jacket in a corner somewhere drooling and twitching."

114

Right now, I think I could love this man. But I wonder if he'd still want me if he knew how close I came to a straitjacket, especially in the beginning. And lately, I feel like I'm going to end up right back there. My past is quite literally coming back to haunt me.

Lying down on the bed, he moves next to me, and lays his arm around my shoulders. "We all have demons honey. We all carry around baggage," he says.

"My demons have bigger teeth than most," I lament, and I smirk a little, trying not to bring down the mood. But I know inside the same psycho who almost wrecked me is after him, even if John hasn't proved it yet. I feel it in my bones, and I'm afraid Kincaid will manage to destroy everything and everyone I care about.

He squeezes me a little tighter, and I willingly shift so that my head is resting on his chest. That calming, slow and steady heartbeat is ringing in my ears again.

"Are you still in love with her?" I ask calmly, and I tilt my head up a little as a smile spreads across his face. I've clearly given away my feelings without saying so explicitly. He seems happy about that, but his expression changes quickly.

"No. I hadn't been in love with her for a long time." He rolls on his back and sighs as I kick myself for opening up the wrong subject.

"We had become more like friends for at least the last year. I just didn't know how to end it. I was a coward."

He looks my way, and I urge him on silently with a soft squeeze of his hand. "Things got really bad after a friend's wedding last year. She got the "marriage bug" and figured after she caught the bouquet, that I'd eventually ask, but I didn't."

Great. I'm falling for a commitment-phobe. We're perfect for each other. I can't consummate, and he can't commit.

"She brought it up about seven, maybe eight months ago, wanting to know if there was any hope of getting married. That's when I realized I didn't want to get married. Well, I didn't want to marry her."

Ouch. I cringe. Maybe I've been too hard on her.

"She moved into the Brentwood house for a month, then came back and we tried to work things out. But she wouldn't budge and I had to end."

So, that explains why his dossier mentioned Catriona. They were trying to work on things, trying to keep their relationship problems private and out of the tabloids.

"So what was your last job like?"

I smile. "Michael Cummings."

He shrugs, so I continue, "You know, the CEO of Cummings Financial. The one who was in the news last year for the Ponzi scheme."

His expression changes to surprise. "Oh, yeah. I remember. Didn't something happen recently?"

I nod. "Yes. Some people who invested money with the financial advisors in his Miami office had relatives in the mafia. They lost millions, so they went after Michael. They killed his ex-wife instead."

"That was you? You were there?" His eyes widen, and I realize I probably shouldn't have told him about this. After all, a woman died. But once I explain what took place that night, and how Nicole Cummings was responsible for her own security, he seems to let it go.

"So, tell me about the dresses you bought" For him, this subject is far better than mafia hits and Ponzi schemes, but not I'm the one who's uncomfortable. It's the one and only time I've caved in to the ridiculous demands of a client and I hate admitting I lost. Even though Cecelia was an immense help, I still feel as if I'm going to make an ass of myself and let him down.

I groan and roll my eyes. He holds out a hand and raises his eyebrows, prodding me for more information, but I'm at a loss. I couldn't describe them to Cecelia, and she knows what they look like, so how am I going to describe them to Erik? Sitting up, I grab my phone off the nightstand. Part of me doesn't want to show him, I sort of like the idea of keeping this a surprise. But he's a pest. He won't quit until he's satisfied. I pull up the photo gallery and find the pictures Cecelia took of me.

"Here," I say, handing him the phone. His eyes get wide, and his smile is beaming as he looks at a picture of me in the aqua gown with the complicated bodice. The shot is a bit blurry, and it's mostly of the back of me, but he seems happy.

"I like the color," he says as he swipes to the next photo of me in the black-and-white dress. "Wow. You have legs, Ms. Harper. Nice ones. Who knew?" he jokes. I grab the phone from him and bury my face in my folded

116

arms that I've been resting on my knees. "You're going to look stunning in that dress," he says as he sits up, resting his back against the bed frame.

His compliments make me shy and self-conscious, especially since I'm not the girlie girl type. The most I know how to do is put my hair in a ponytail and put on some lip gloss. Somehow, I manage to express my fears, and he reassures me, insisting that all of these things can be arranged with a few phone calls. I suppose anything is possible in Hollywood, even turning me into a proper woman.

Regardless of his assurances, I'm fairly certain I'll have a major malfunction on the red carpet, and a million paparazzi will be there to capture a nip-slip or an image of me sprawled out on my ass. It will go viral in seconds.

"So I get the sense that makeup and dresses are not normal things for you?" he smiles. He's just bordering on sarcasm.

"Yes. I was a bit of a tomboy growing up. I have two younger brothers, so I was always playing cops and robbers instead of playing with dolls," I admit.

He laughs a little. "Same thing I was doing."

Smart ass.

"So what about you? What is your family like?" This is the first time any conversation of ours has been mutual. Right now, we can talk openly and learn about each other naturally, instead of in the rearview of the Escalade.

"My mum was a dancer and my dad served in Vietnam. He was an American and when the war ended he came back here and found things weren't so good for Veterans. He hated living on the reservation so he came to England. He met my mum, they fell in love, and got married pretty fast. She quit dancing and had my brother soon after, and I came along few years later. We moved around a lot, since my dad couldn't keep a steady job." He presses his lips together in a wistful smile. And when I ask what his dad was like, his eyes go dark and sad. The shades come down, but he continues, even after I tell him not to bother.

"We moved a lot: Brighton, Essex, Newcastle, and then Birmingham. By that time, I was getting in trouble a lot, and Dad had left."

Well, there's something we have in common. "Were you close to him?" I ask, and then instantly regret my question when he sighs.

"No. I never saw him again after that. He disappeared," he says. This time, the bittersweet longing is gone. I detect a fair bit of anger, and I watch his face. The fine muscles in his jaw are tense as he recalls a difficult period in his life.

"I'm sorry. I shouldn't have asked." I feel awful, and I try to smile at him, but it's an uneasy smile. He sits quiet for a moment, staring at his hands. Then he rouses himself, and his normal demeanor and quick wit return.

"Nothing like a walk down memory lane, huh?" He smiles and reaches for my arm, dragging me to his side, and wrapping himself around me. It's Erik who needs comfort this time and as much as I want to offer him solace, I find it difficult. This is the first time he's opened up about anything, and I'm floundering, searching for the right thing to do or say.

His hands reach up for my ponytail, pulling it free of the elastic band with one hand while weaving his fingers into my hair with the other. He rakes his fingers from my scalp to the ends in long, unhurried strokes, watching as the strands fall to my back. His eyes are distant, and his face is blank. He seems lost in a memory, something painful from years ago. Not knowing what to do or say, I push myself up and out of his grasp, breaking the awkward silence. I hop off the bed and walk nervously to the closet.

"It's almost time to leave," I say, opening the bi-fold doors.

He swings his legs off the bed, resting his palms on the edge of the mattress. "Let's continue this later," he says, smiling.

"Mr. Sinclair, are you threatening me with another date?" I tease, as I turn around to face him. He's on his feet and stops a few steps in front of me.

"Ms. Harper, you are a beautiful, intelligent woman. But I'll admit, you have me at a loss. One minute, you're vague and unreachable and the next you're taunting me with my own words. Figuring you out is quite a challenge."

His intense gaze penetrates me, and I feel warm—as if I should be on my back with my legs spread to him. He might get his wish because that look could make me do almost anything.

"W-Was this a date?" I stammer, becoming more nervous by the second.

"Hmm, perhaps. But doesn't a good date end with a kiss?" He smiles broadly as he closes the distance between us, sending me backward a few steps. My butt makes contact with the chest of drawers, the handles poke uncomfortably into my back.

Fuck. He's better at this than I am. Way better. I stammer a few syllables and take fast, halting breaths. I'm literally caged by him as he rests his hands on either side of me and when he presses his rock hard body against me, a flush heats my skin. His fingers skim down to my waist, and with barely any force, he manages to take complete control of me.

"Erik . . ."

His hand glides up my arm, brushing my neck until his fingers weave into my hair. Tugging gently, he tilts my head until I'm looking up into his eyes.

"Say my name again."

"Kiss me." It's nothing but a lusty whisper, a plea.

He growls, and his words come out in a raspy purr. "Mmm, I like that better than my name."

He raises my chin, dipping his head toward me and at the same time, moving closer, inch by inch, drawing out the moments until our lips make contact. When he presses his soft, warm mouth against mine, the kiss is tender, restrained and oh-so-deliciously slow. Erik turns his head just enough to seal his mouth over mine, and I open to his demanding kiss, allowing his warm, silky tongue to see out mine. We're locked to each other, his hand weaving into my hair, cupping the back of my head gently, and I feel my way up his body, my fingers finding a home around his generous biceps. The kiss is so electric and so consuming that nothing distracts us.

Except the squeaking of the door and Dan's voice.

Shit.

"Uh, sorry Mr. Sinclair . . . boss. I . . . "

I drop my gaze, trying to hide my face in Erik's shoulder, but he gently pulls away and walks out of the room following Dan. Even though they're gone, my hands fly to my face, covering my warm red cheeks as I strain to hear their conversation. By the time Erik returns, my embarrassment has cooled, and my senses have returned. At least a little.

"We can't do this Erik," I mutter.

"Don't worry. He's not going to say anything."

He leans forward, trying to get another kiss. But I shy away.

"No. Go," I stand defiant and point toward the door. He laughs.

"Oh come on—" He moves again, but I hold my hand out, pointing to the door with even more emphasis.

He grumbles as he leaves. I take two or three deep, cleansing breaths as I try to calm my heart rate. I'm so embarrassed. Working with Dan is going to be nothing but awkward now.

♟

"Hello, Dan," I say cheerfully as I walk into the kitchen carrying my holster and gun. Dan doesn't say a word, but he raises his eyes from his sandwich and nods. The tension in the room is thick, and I wonder if he's waiting for me to scold him. But there's no need, because did nothing wrong. The worst I could do is reprimand him for his lack of manners. Trying to be normal and upbeat is the best way to go, I think.

"You ready for a long night?" I ask as I sip my coffee. He glances at me quickly then averts his eyes. He hesitates before answering.

"Yes. I suppose so," his voice is low and terse, and given the opportunity, he might be very judgmental of what he walked in on. He finishes the last bite of his sandwich.

"So, are you going to ride on the process trailer tonight?" he asks, talking with a mouthful of ham sandwich. My stomach turns watching the contents of his mouth as he talks.

"I guess so. You can teach me about this since you've done it before. I have no idea what to expect," I say, hoping that pandering to his ego will erase this awkwardness. Maybe he'll forget about it by the end of the night.

"Make sure you bring your coat and gloves. You'll need them." I nod at him, and even though I don't know what a process trailer is, I walk down the hall to retrieve the new coat I bought. It was one of the things I added to the clothes shopping list. When I return, Erik is in the kitchen talking to Dan. They seem perfectly at ease with each other. It must be a guy thing.

Erik looks relaxed and comfortable in his well-worn jeans and a blue thermal Henley. It's unbuttoned just enough to reveal the sexy furrow between his pecs, and as my eyes graze over his body, I bite my lip involuntarily, recalling the feeling of his mouth on me. He notices my stare and smiles—he's happy he caught me admiring his body. But I quickly realize I'm playing with fire–we just got caught, and I need to at least try to act like a professional.

"So are we ready to hit the road?" I ask, hoping to get my mind back on business. Dan nods as he takes the sip of his drink. As they wait for me by the door, I slip on my holster and coat.

"Here are the keys, boss." Dan hands them to me and he steps outside first. "Not too chilly out so far." I remotely unlock the Escalade and Dan takes the SecPro from the trunk to inspect the car. As I pass by Erik, his unpredictable hand lands on the small of my back.

"Stop it," I whisper as I pull the driver's door open. My heart is thumping out of my chest as I slip into the car. When I look in the rearview, I can see him, wearing a huge smirk, and I just want to reach back and smack that grin right off his face. As I pull away from the house, the car is quiet. Dan is checking e-mail and Erik sits in the back, sipping his coffee and reading his script. We're halfway to the set when Erik resumes his interrogation of my past.

"So tell me about your parents, Ms. Harper."

Dan turns his gaze my way with a raised eyebrow. As if the kiss he walked in on wasn't enough, now he has to listen to Erik and I getting to know each other. I'm sure he must be feeling like a voyeur.

"Ah, what?" I look back at Erik over my shoulder, and that smirk is still plastered on his face. My stomach churns in an uncomfortable way, and when I hesitate, he chides me.

"Come, Ms. Harper. Did we miss the lesson on sharing in kindergarten?" He smiles.

Incorrigible bastard. "Fine," I huff.

Dan snickers beside me then turns around to Erik. "You know what "fine" means, Mr. Sinclair?"

"Yes. It means I'm in the doghouse," he laughs, and unfortunately, Dan's distraction doesn't last long.

"So please, your parents, Ms. Harper."

Why he insists on calling me Ms. Harper is beyond me, after what Dan witnessed earlier, it shouldn't matter. "I'd rather not talk about it," I snap, closing the subject. My life is slowly opening to Erik, but not to Dan. He doesn't need to know about all my demons.

"The lady doth protest too much, methinks."

I laugh and look at him in the rearview again. Gone is the smirk, and in its place is a dazzling smile.

"I thought you promised, no Shakespeare?" I whine.

He laughs at me. "Touché, Ms. Harper. But continue, please." His tone is commanding and sexy, and my insides flutter. I want to jump over the seat and do things to him that I haven't done in the back of a car since I was a teenager.

♚ CHAPTER TWELVE

"Holy Shit! Hold on." As I merge onto the highway, some crazy asshole in a tricked out burgundy Monte Carlo SS flies across the acceleration lane on my right and cuts in front of me at high-speed. No one is beside me or behind me in my mirrors, and I swerve to avoid a collision.

"Goddamn stupid asshole." My heart is pounding as my grip on the wheel remains tight.

Erik exhales loudly. "Jesus Christ. And this is why I ride a motorcycle." The Monte Carlo is ahead of me as the acceleration lanes merge into the flow of traffic, and I increase the speed to catch up to the car. I'm itching to pull alongside it and give the owner a piece of my mind with some not so polite hand gestures.

"Are you worried about something?" Erik asks as I change lanes, bringing us alongside the Monte.

"No, just checking him out. The tint on those windows is very dark, which can't be legal." The Monte suddenly slows down, disappearing in traffic behind me. The move is odd, and it tells me whoever is driving doesn't want to get out ahead of me.

"Dan, keep an eye on our six. Make sure that guy doesn't ride up on our tail." He nods and keeps his focus on the side view mirror.

"Sure thing boss." The traffic on I–5 highway is heavy, but it's moving at a steady pace. If there is any trouble, maneuvering between cars will be tricky. I barely make it a mile before Dan is yelling.

"Coming on us fast, boss!"

Shit! I step down hard on the pedal and the engine screams. We surge ahead of the other cars, and I weave in and out of traffic, hoping to lose the asshole in the tricked out '80s behemoth. Dan looks behind us again. "I don't see him boss."

I exhale a bit and keep an eye on the rear view. Erik looks ashy and nervous.

"I think we lost him," he says, looking out the back window. About two minutes pass before I see the damn Monte Carlo alongside me. Fuck! I stomp on the brake, and the Monte zooms far out ahead of us. I weave through cars, my front bumper nearly kissing a BMW's rear end, but I make it to the right lane. "Hold on!"

"Nice driving boss!" Dan smiles.

"Dan. Get the office on the phone." Dan pulls up Cole Security in the contacts list and dials. When Marci picks up, I waste no time with pleasantries.

"Marci, get Jeff on the phone now."

"He's not here honey. He hasn't been in the office since yesterday." Terrific. Now is not the time for Jeff to go missing.

"Is Hunter there?"

"Yes, I'll transfer you." The line goes silent for a moment, and then I hear Hunter's voice.

"What's wrong Ronnie?"

"I've got a possible unsub. The guy cut me off on the highway, now he's following me down I–5. Can you pull me up on GPS?"

"Yeah, doing it now." Within seconds, Hunter has me on speakerphone, and he's traced our location. "Okay, found you. How far back is he?"

Dan and Erik both look behind us. "He's about six cars back, boss." The Monte is hanging back for now, but it's weaving in and out of its lane. He's stuck behind a slow moving car, boxed in by the surrounding traffic.

"Hunter, can you conference in John, please?"

"Yeah sure. Hang tight." The phone goes quiet for a moment, but within a few seconds, John's voice comes through the speakers. "Hey sis, are you okay?"

"Yeah John. We're okay for now."

"Are you okay, boss?" Dan asks quietly, trying not to alert anyone. I nod and try to reassure him. I don't want John or Erik worried that I can't handle the situation.

"Yes, I'm fine," The car goes quiet again, but not for long.

I just happened to catch the Monte weaving in and out of traffic behind us at high speed seconds before Dan starts yelling at me again. "He's back boss."

"John, I'm coming your way. How far am I from the 405, Hunter?" I'm yelling and driving at the same time. Trying to keep everyone safe.

"You're about a mile from the 405," Hunter says.

"Keep going Ronnie. What kind of car is it? Can you get a plate?" John asks for the typical information, but we've been ahead of the Monte most of the time. I rattle off the make and model but have to admit I didn't get the plates while I had the chance.

As I approach the 405 exit, I have no choice but to slow down. I cut through traffic, but I'm far enough ahead of the Monte to make it onto the freeway safely. But I don't lose him. We put maybe a quarter mile between us when I see him merge onto the 405.

"He's still behind us, John."

"John, she just got on the 405. Can you get the highway patrol and a police chopper?" Hunter asks.

"Yes, but this could be over before they get in the air. She's only got a few miles to the FBI office," John says.

"Damn, I need to get out of this traffic." I mutter and continue to cut between cars, ignoring how dangerously close I come to other vehicles. I slip in behind a Mercedes, then shoot out again once an opening appears. The move puts more distance between the Monte and me.

"Mr. Sinclair, check our six, let me know what he's doing."

"Check our what?"

"Our six o'clock. Check our back!"

Erik looks out the back window. "Shit! He's getting closer again."

When I get stuck behind two slow-moving cars, I flash my lights at them, but they are oblivious. I have to move onto the shoulder to cut in front of them.

"He's stuck about two cars behind, but he's weaving. Looks like he's trying to get out from behind them." I stomp on the gas, and the car lurches forward.

"WHOA, this thing can move!" Erik yells as he tries to steady himself.

"I can't find anything about a Monte Carlo SS. Are you sure about the model Ronnie?" John asks.

"Yes. Don't you remember the Mafia boys driving around the neighborhood in them back in the day."

"Oh my God yeah, back in the 80s. Now that's strange."

I hear Erik gasp in the back seat, and I look into the rearview fearing the Monte has gotten closer.

"Back in the 80s? Ah, how old are you?" Erik asks curiously. With all his questions about my past, we never got around to discussing my age.

"Thirty-nine." I grumble. He laughs and raises his eyebrows.

"Hot damn, I got me a cougar!" Dan turns back to look at Erik, laughing at his comment.

Oh my god. Now is not the time!

Trying to concentrate on the Monte, I cut off a Ford Focus and move into the left lane. He checks behind again.

"Mr. Ford Focus didn't like that. He just flipped us the bird."

Stepping down on the pedal, the engine screams and the car lurches forward slamming us back into our seats. There's less traffic, which is good for speed, but the Monte has plenty of room to catch up with me.

"Shit, John he's keeping up."

"Just keep him off your tail. You're not too far from me. I've got the highway patrol on alert, but you may get to Wiltshire before they finish their donuts and get their asses moving."

John is right. This thing could be over in the next thirty seconds.

"Don't worry. You know how to do this. Hang in there and try to keep this guy off your six."

I'm holding my speed at ninety and weaving in and out of traffic. Every time I pull away and leave the Monte behind, he eventually catches up.

"How much farther to Wiltshire?" I speed up again, and the Escalade leaps forward, the tachometer needle barely ticking higher. I glide into the left lane, and some idiot in a Honda decides to pull in front of me.

"CRAP!" I yank the wheel to the right and zoom past the Honda, but it's no better. I cut across three lanes to the right and then back, tearing past five cars.

"Nice driving!" Erik yells through his clenched teeth.

"You've got four miles Ronnie." Hunter is still on the line, still watching me on GPS.

"John, anything from DMV?"

He's quiet for a few seconds. "No, it could be registered in any state. Until you can get a look at the plates, there's no telling."

"Okay, but the Monte Carlo is an old car. There can't be that many still on the road."

"Yeah, but that kind of search is going to take some time."

I look in the rearview. He's closing in, and I push down harder on the pedal.

"Over one hundred John. This guy is coming on fast." My heart races into my throat as I see the intersection looming up ahead. Laying on the horn, I hope to clear the few cars ahead and barrel through the merge lanes without killing us.

"Dan, turn on the hazard lights." The tactic works, the few cars in the left lane move toward the right, and I make it off the interstate and onto the loop leading to Wiltshire Boulevard. Erik is white knuckling the grip handle in the roof, and a sheen of sweat has bloomed on his forehead.

I hear Hunter talking directly to John in the background, letting him know we're off the highway. "You've got a traffic light ahead of you. You're going to have to weave a lot," Hunter advises. I lay on the horn the whole way, and the cars move as I barrel through a red light.

"Hunter, how much further?" I scream.

"Thirteen hundred feet. Turn right on Veteran Boulevard. Make a sharp right into the parking lot."

The Monte Carlo manages to catch up as I weave through more traffic. Fortunately, some old woman in a Dodge Dart pulls behind me as I approach the traffic light. I laugh a little, knowing he's stuck behind a slow driver. *Son of a bitch!*

"Hold on!" The tires screech as I take the hard right at high speed. I manage to correct the fishtail as we near the parking lot entrance.

"Cut your speed Ronnie, or you won't make the turn into the lot," Hunter yells.

"This is going to be tight!" I cut the wheel to the right again, but the speed is too much, and the back end skids, smashing hard into a large tree.

"Fuck!" I shout as I right the wheel and step on the gas again. The tree topples as we pull away. I drive into the lot and back behind the building. We're safe in the loading zone, and I put the car in park.

"You there Ronnie? TALK TO ME," John yells in panic.

"Yes, were fine," I say as I check on Dan and Erik. They're shaken but not hurt. "But the tree is not so good."

"Everyone breathing?" Hunter asks.

"Yes." My body sags with relief, and none of us can find anything to say.

"Hunter, I'm going to need another vehicle. Can you come down here?"

He laughs. "How bad is it?"

"It's drivable, but fairly crumpled," I admit.

"Yeah. I'll be there in a few minutes," he says.

John is still shouting instructions in the background to the agents who took off in pursuit of the Monte Carlo. It isn't long before he appears on the loading dock with a couple of other agents following him.

"Hey boss, here comes the cavalry," Dan says.

I step out of the car as John approaches. "Good job!" He holds up his hand, and I smack it, high-five style, but he grabs me in a tight hug and lifts me off the ground. Over his shoulder, I can see the unmarked cars take off after the Monte. Even from a distance and the blueish white smoke from the burning rubber lingers in the air and the squeal of the tires is loud.

"Keep following him. Get a plate number," he barks orders into his phone. John disconnects the call. "Follow me. We can wait in one of the conference rooms until Hunter arrives." We step inside the loading bay door and pass through the bowels of the FBI field office. John leads us to the main lobby, stopping at the giant FBI logo laid into the floor as he presses the button for the elevator. In a few seconds, we step into the empty car and the doors close sweeping up to the fifth floor in a few seconds.

"First car chase?" John asks. Erik runs a hand through his tousled hair before folding his arms across his chest.

"Yes. And television is nothing like the real thing. In case you were wondering," Erik huffs. Preparing a person for a situation like this is impossible, but Erik held himself together well. The doors open, and we follow John down a long hallway and then through a maze of cubicles and offices.

"Ronnie did a fantastic job. She was one of the top students in the driving courses." He says and I smile, remembering the few fun times I had with the FBI. He's also trying to make Erik feel better, which he needs now.

"Yes, she did. She's amazing," Erik says as he looks my way. John looks at him with a hint of suspicion before opening the double doors to a large conference room.

"Let's have a seat in here." Inside, a dozen leather chairs flank the enormous wood table. We all have a seat as John reaches into a small refrigerator in the corner and hands us each a bottle of cold water. Sitting in the large leather executive chair, I suddenly feel tiny. "I'll be right back," John says leaving the room. He's only gone for a moment, and when he returns, he has a brown FBI folder in his hand.

John sits across from me and opens the folder. I stop drinking my water. "John can we wait until Hunter gets here? I'd like to keep him informed. We couldn't find Jeff today." John nods, he's clearly surprised.

"What did Hunter say about it?"

The adrenaline hasn't completely worn off yet and my hands are slightly unsteady as I rub my eyes.

"He didn't know where Jeff was either. Ordinarily, he tells the receptionist where he is going, but she knew nothing." He rubs at his chin and taps his fingers on the folder. I'm sure that new information has something to do with Jeff.

"So when are you planning to go to Vegas?" I ask, but he raises his eyebrows and sighs.

"Don't know yet. You know how the Bureau works. It takes days to get approval for these things. I'm half-tempted to foot the bill for this one."

Dan appears confused, as does Erik. They weren't privy to the conversation I had with John in the office the other night.

"What's going on?" Dan looks at me, but I shake my head.

"Let's wait until Hunter gets here, Dan."

He nods and stands. "Where is the men's room?" John stands with him and as he walks out in to the hall, and Erik follows. John returns and has a seat.

"So is there any way we can get Dan out of here once Hunter arrives? Whatever this new information is, I'd rather not have Dan involved." John stares at me and rubs his temple. My request is odd considering he was just at the house the other night, and Dan heard everything.

"What's up Ronnie?"

"I don't know John. There's something I just don't trust. I don't want him involved in this, especially where it concerns Jeff and the business. It's none of his business."

"Sure. I'll have one of the agents bring him down to the parking lot to take his statement." I nod at him, and he pulls his phone from his pocket.

"Agent Wilcher. Yes, meet me in Conference room 212." He ends the call. "It's done."

Within a few seconds, Dan is back and takes his place at the table. "Where's Erik," I ask. I'm not overly concerned, he can't get into too much trouble around here.

"Erik is out in the hall. He's trying to explain everything to Mark."

When there's a knock on the door, I turn, expecting to see Erik, but instead, a man I vaguely recognize from my time with the FBI steps into the room.

"Agent Grilli, what can I do for you?" Agent Wilcher says as he stands in the doorway. When he speaks, I remember the voice and the face. He was a new recruit when I left the bureau. He's young, good looking, and one cocky bastard–and one of those people I disliked as soon as I met him.

"Could you escort Mr. Royce downstairs and take his statement?" Dan's gaze shoots from John to me. I give him a nod, and he stands without a word and follows Wilcher out the door. Once John and I are alone, his mood changes.

"So how are things going with lover boy?" he smiles.

I shoot daggers at him with my stare, but I laugh when he starts singing "Bow Chicka Wow Wow."

"You're ridiculous!" I slap him hard on the shoulder, but it's nice knowing he'll always be a big brother—forever my protector. "Nothing is going on John." I'm relieved that John accepts my answer. The door opens again, and Erik appears. He sits down and sighs.

"Is everything okay?" I ask as he puts his phone on the table. He nods at me but says nothing when John's phone rings. He picks it up and answers gruffly.

"Agent Grilli. Yes, show him up. Conference room 212. Yes, keep Dan Royce busy. Yes. I'll let you know." Within two minutes, Hunter appears in the room.

"Scott Hunter, this is Erik Sinclair. And you know John," I say as he reaches over to shake hands with them both.

"So what is going on?" Hunter asks as he takes a seat in one of the leather chairs.

John speaks up first. "I'll assume you are up to speed on the details of Mr. Sinclair's case?" John asks.

Hunter nods quietly.

"Were you aware of the hacking attempt at Cole?"

Hunter nods again. "Yes, but the last I heard about it was earlier in the week when Ronnie flew into town."

John briefs Hunter on everything he has discovered so far—including Jeff's connection to the house in Henderson, Nevada and Miranda's former neighbors. The look on Hunter's face registers skepticism at first, but when I fill in more details of Miranda Cole and Jeff's history, he listens carefully. He may not have known this much about Jeff until now and when I tell him Jeff lied to me about the death of his mother, Hunter is visibly angry. He recognizes right away what it means—Jeff has been lying. Not just to me, but to everyone. A deep sense of betrayal shows in his eyes. For me, it's even worse. Twenty years of friendship and loyalty have been erased in a few short days. I feel more foolish and naïve than I could have ever imagined. The betrayal lances my heart.

"So we did some more digging. We cross-referenced legal records, probate, and vital statistics for Miranda, Jeff, and Kincaid," he says pointing to the folder. "Take a look at what we found." John slides the brown folder across the table to me first. When I open it, I'm shocked by what I see.

Utah Bureau of Vital Statistics, Record of Live Birth

Name: Byron Turner Kincaid

Date: 21 November 1962

Place of Birth: Modena, Utah

Mother: Miranda Turner

Father: Byron Kincaid

Attached to the page is another paper, it's an amended birth certificate. Kincaid changed his name to Vincent Turner in 2009. He was trying to hide his identity! My heart is racing, and I can feel the sweat starting to bead on my forehead. As my hands begin to shake violently, Erik reaches over and clutches my free hand.

"How could this be? I don't understand," my voice shaky and pained. John shakes his head, and his eyes are filled with concern.

"It seems like he changed his name right after you—" He halts his words and looks from me to Erik. I shake my head, and he realizes what I'm asking. Say no more about my connection to Kincaid. Not now.

"This guy is taunting us now. He wanted us to find the truth. He led us right to him by using his mother's old home."

"Are you okay?" Erik whispers to me, he seems lost and confused. He knows we're dealing with a psycho, but hearing that name, the same name I was screaming the other night is probably a shock. Hearing that Jeff is connected to the tormentor of my dreams, the same demon I mentioned earlier today raises the fury in him.

"Wait a minute. Do you mean this guy is Jeff's brother?" he says looking to John. But before John can answer, Erik whispers to me. "Is this the same guy you were dreaming about?"

I look down at our still clasped hands, and I shake my head, "Not now Erik, please." He nods, and his mouth is pressed into a frown.

"Why didn't this come up in the last five years?" Hunter asks, he's as stunned as I am. John cocks his head and hesitates. Admitting the bureau failed me is not easy for him.

"Look, all I can tell you is that back in 2008, the bureau was knee deep in the Amerithrax investigation, we got a huge black eye over Bruce Ivins. Then we got tied up in the Khalid Sheikh Mohammed and The Holy Land Foundation cases. Unfortunately, this case was . . . pushed to the back burner. The leads went cold after the original agents were reassigned."

He takes it personally, even though he wasn't assigned to Los Angeles back then. Their dismal failure and all the missteps in my case leave me searching for a thread of hope. I desperately want to believe there has been some mistake, and that Jeff is not as bad as he looks on paper.

"We still don't know if this is Jeff's mother though, right? What are you doing to verify this is the right Miranda Cole?" My question seems incredibly naïve, even to me.

"I've got agents pulling more records. Obviously, we need marriage and divorce records to confirm the relationship. But honestly, at this point, I'd say it's a foregone conclusion. The neighbors confirmed the name of Miranda's first husband, which matches the name on the birth certificate, and they recall there were two sons, though they didn't offer names."

It all fits. There's no denying it. Hunter's eyes are grave, and a shaky hand covers his mouth as he scans the same paper. Perhaps he's trying to find some flaw in the logic, some mistake, just as I had.

"Excuse me. I need to use the bathroom." I push back from the table and head down the hall, hoping to make it inside the ladies' room before I start crying. Running the cold water, I wet a few paper towels and place them on my neck. As I stare at myself in the mirror, I can't believe I'm standing here. I can't believe Jeff could actually be involved with this. Every instinct I have is screaming the same thing: this is wrong. He wouldn't do this to me, to Hunter, or to an innocent person like Erik. My head is spinning, threatening to lay me out flat on the floor if I don't get control of the rising panic. I manage to pull myself together and when I emerge from the bathroom, Erik is waiting for me in the alcove.

"Hi. I just wanted to make sure you're all right. You've been gone a while." His eyes dart from my face to the wet paper towel that I pull from my neck.

"I'm okay."

"I know this has to be difficult for you." He steps closer and wraps his hands around my upper arms.

"Yes," I whisper as I fidget nervously with the cloth. He pulls me closer and slips his arms around me, but my hands remain at my sides as I stiffen. I don't know how to react.

"Relax. Just let it happen. It's only a hug," he says calmly. He pulls back a little, and I'm surprised when his soft lips meet my forehead. It's impossible for me to look up. Looking in his eyes would either end with me in tears or his lips pressed to mine. His hands slip down my arms, and he takes my hand, pulling me behind him down the hall.

Halfway to the conference room, he weaves our fingers together. And I let him. It's comforting and sweet. But all too soon I have to let go.

♚ CHAPTER THIRTEEN

"Hunter, do you have keys to Jeff's place?" I ask as I sit in my chair. He nods. "Yeah, why?" Jeff regularly gives a set of key to his right hand, in case of emergency.

"Get over to his place and see what you can find. When you're done there, go through his office."

"If you find anything, we can't use it. We'd have to get a warrant first," John says. My instructions are making him nervous.

"Don't worry about that right now John. I'm looking for anything that will lead us to Jeff. If Hunter finds something related to Miranda, we'll let you know." I direct my attention to Hunter again.

"Do you have a list of GPS units?"

He nods. "Yes. Jason Brenner is keeping track of the GPS system now. Why?"

"Account for all the units. Track every single one. Jeff's work car is traceable if the GPS unit is working. If we find the car, we find Jeff." John slips a notepad and a pen across the table, and Hunter starts scribbling furiously.

"See if you can trace Jeff's work and personal phones too." Hunter keeps writing as I speak.

"He could be using a burner phone, Ronnie," John adds, throwing a whole new level of complexity into the situation. He raises an eyebrow and shrugs at me. "He's not stupid Ronnie. I briefed him on some of this information a few days ago."

He's right. Jeff is probably long gone.

"Anything else, boss?" Hunter's words are not cynical or sarcastic. He knows we have to do everything we can to find Jeff while we keep Cole Security running.

"Yeah. The keys to the car," I say as I hold out my hand. My joke must have taken the edge off, because he smiles.

Hunter slides them across the table. "It's a black Mercedes CLS63."

"Are we done?" I ask John as I stand.

John nods and gives me a quick hug before leading us back down the hall. On the way to the elevators, I can feel the fatigue in every muscle in my body as the stress of the last two hours takes over. It's turning every movement into a monumental task, and I know the drive to the set will be long. Before we get into the elevator, John shakes hands with Erik and then exchanges phone numbers and e-mail addresses with Hunter.

When we reach the lobby, Dan is waiting with Agent Wilcher. "Let's go, Dan." We walk to the parking lot. Dan gets in the passenger seat and Erik climbs in the back. I put the car in gear and take off, merging back onto the highway headed toward North Hollywood. My nerves are on high alert, and I suspect Dan feels the same. I frequently catch him checking the mirrors, both of us more aware of the cars around us. It has an effect on Erik, the few times our eyes meet in the rear view, instead of the usual intense gaze, he immediately looks out the back window.

When we reach the set, it seems empty. Most of the parking lot is vacant, and the cameras are nowhere in sight. "Where is everyone?"

"They are headed out to a remote set, Ms. Harper," Michael says as he walks back to unlock the gate.

Erik urges me to pull in anyway, and I park behind his trailer.

"I have to go to wardrobe and makeup," he says before jumping out of the backseat with his scripts. Dan is out of the car, following behind as I cut the engine and make my way to the front of the trailer. As soon as I step inside, Dan and Erik are ready to leave.

"Why don't you stay here. You look wrecked," Erik says, laying a hand gently on my shoulder. He's right, of course, and the brief glimpse of my face in the bathroom mirror at the FBI building scared me. But I have to do my job, whether I feel like it or not. I shake my head to protest, but he stops me.

"Dan, come with me to wardrobe. Ronnie, you stay here and rest for a bit."

He drops his hand to his side, and as usual, I refuse to listen. When I take a step toward the door, he grabs me by the wrist.

"Don't argue with me. We'll be fine." Dan steps out the door, and Erik smiles at me, giving me a quick wink as he disappears. I sit on the couch and everything that has transpired in the last three days hits me. The magnitude is almost crushing, it's more than most people could handle, and my whole life seems to be on the edge of disaster. All it will take is one small push and everything will go to shit.

I sit on the couch, and as the silence overtakes me, the anger rises, like the slow, rolling burn of a lava flow. All the plans I've made for the future disappeared today. My best friend is gone and the realization I never really knew him is the bitterest pill to swallow. The perfect little sphere of safety I had created for myself up in San Francisco, thinking Kincaid was no longer a threat was an illusion. He's been lurking all along, just waiting for the opportunity to unleash more terror on me.

♟

My parched throat burns, and the ache in my limbs is unbearable. I don't know how long I've been here, but I'm sobbing, and my arms are bound behind my back with leather shackles. The bullwhip dangles in front of me, dancing along the gray concrete floor as his hand twitches. It's a threat, and I dare not look up. I know what will happen if I do. He grabs me by my hair and pulls me up off my knees, but I still won't make eye contact.

Not a sound comes from my mouth, not a gasp, not a whimper. I won't give him the satisfaction. The pain in my scalp increases as he drags me over to the padded wood bench he likes to sit on, but I can't keep up with him. My shackled ankles won't let me move that fast.

"MOVE FASTER, PET!"

I shuffle faster, and he stops in front of the bench. He pushes me down to my knees again, and the bench creaks loudly as he sits. The bile rises in my throat as I hear the metallic sound of his zipper—it signals what he wants, what he will force me to do.

"Open your mouth, pet." I clench my jaw in defiance, and he smacks me hard across the face. I whimper as he grabs a handful of hair at the root, pulling me closer to him.

"Open, now." He yanks my hair hard, and I can feel strands tearing from my tender skin. My mouth opens in a pain reflex, and it happens. I gag at the force of it, and he pulls back, only to shove my head back down. The rage builds inside me, and I don't know how much longer I can do this before I break and do something drastic.

"Faster bitch." He thrusts himself into my mouth faster, and the tears stream down my cheeks. My entire body trembles with hatred. I slow my movement, even though I know what will happen. I pull away, and his hand flies out, striking me hard. He slaps me repeatedly. As I take my punishment, I rest on my thighs, feeling for the metal clip between the leather ankle cuffs. I gently unfasten it, freeing my feet as he continues to hit me. He is in a fury and doesn't notice my movements.

"Enough punishment, my pet?" His hand clamps onto my throat, I'm weeping, and blood is dripping into my mouth. I can taste the salty metallic flavor of it. He sits again, grabbing me by the hair to force me once again. I bite down on him, trapping his flesh between my molars and incisors, and instantly, he lets out a blood-curdling scream.

He thrashes me, ripping at my hair, and punching me, trying to free himself. It's no use. I am like a rabid dog, and I bear down with every ounce of strength I have. He screams as my teeth cut deeper into his flesh. The sound is deafening. *"AAAAAAGGGHH!!! You bitch! I'm going to kill you!"*

I hear the sound of it a second before it hits. The cane contacts my skin, and it feels like a rope of fire stretching across my back from left to right. This time I let go, and I scamper to my feet, spitting out a mouthful of blood. I watch with a sick delight as he tries to staunch the bleeding with his hands. He pays no attention to me, and it gives me the advantage. I tackle him, hitting him squarely in the center of his chest. He flies off the bench, smashing his head hard on the concrete floor below.

I can hear his skull bounce as he screams and curses me, but I don't let up. I stomp and kick relentlessly, doing as much damage as I possibly can. I deliver my last kick to his face, hitting him square in the nose. It breaks, and he blacks out as the blood pours from his face. I sit on the floor, having given myself just enough time to bring my legs through my cuffed hands. Within seconds, my wrists are unclipped, and I run toward the door. I stand my ground for a moment, but he's still lying on the floor—bleeding and unconscious.

I grab the whip and cane, taking it up so he has nothing to strike me with. All too soon, he regains consciousness, groaning and trying to stand. I run, *making my way out into a long hallway. As I run, the corridor seems to lengthen, like one of those special effects in a horror movie. But I hear a voice calling me, and it's familiar. "RONNIE! RONNIE! It's Jeff!"*

I sit up, shaking as I remember the last day I was in Kincaid's dungeon. An unsettling feeling washes over me as my grogginess clears. I recall Jeff's face that night. He was walking down the hall so calmly with his arm at his side. He had no vest, no weapons of any kind, and he wasn't in a defensive posture with gun drawn as he should have been. Why?

Could this be the dream distorting the chaos of that night, turning it into something completely unreal? Most of my memories of Kincaid's dungeon are vague—nothing more than fuzzy glimpses and flashes of Kincaid walking into the room or taunting me with food or water that he never intended to give me. The rest of the time he kept me drugged so that he could do with me as he pleased.

As I try to compare my dream against my recollection of that last night, nothing seems out of place or exaggerated. No, it wasn't a dream. It's my subconscious trying to tell me something. Why didn't I see this before? Why didn't I realize something about Jeff was out of place?

I look around, recalling where I am. We left the set after Erik was finished with makeup and wardrobe and drove out to La Tuna Canyon. Dan didn't raise any objection to splitting up the night's duties. I took the first half of the night and he took second shift.

Even in the back seat of the cab, the ride was windy and cold. But the crew needed the windows open and the icy wind racing through the canyons kept the interior of the truck like an igloo. Ironically, the scene they were filming involved a car chase and firing at police. The second half of it had squad cars chasing Erik in a Mustang. I had to sit on the sidelines for that. The only person that could be in the car with Erik was the cinematographer.

When the grogginess clears, I look around for my coat, but I find Beth, sitting at the dinette with a book in hand.

"Hi Beth. I didn't realize you were here." I say as I stand.

She slips a pretty rhinestone bookmark between the pages and sets it on the table.

"I came in about a half-hour ago. Are you all right? You were thrashing around on the couch. I was going to wake you." Her eyes are full of concern, and I'm sure Mr. Cohen must have told her about the car chase today. She sits on the couch, looking cozy in her turquoise cowl neck sweater, and then folds her hands primly in her lap. I can tell Beth wants to talk, so I take a seat next to her.

"I'm okay. It was just a rough day." I smile a little, hoping to take the edge off her worry.

"I've been wanting to apologize for what happened." Her eyebrows turn upward, "When Erik told us what happened with Melissa and the phone call with your boss, I was horrified. I had no idea she would stoop so low. And when he explained how he feels about you, everything about that day made more sense and..."

I listen to her talk and for a moment, still expecting her to question me about the car chase, so her words don't quite register...until the part about Erik's feelings.

I shake my head and blink wildly, "Wait...what? How does Erik feel about me?" The confusion in my voice must surprise her, and she presses her lips together. She just revealed a huge secret, and it doesn't take her long to backpedal.

"Oh, what I meant was—" she stops speaking and lowers her head. There's no point in trying to cover it up, just as there was no point in trying to hide my awkward moment with Erik. I stare at her, cocking my head to one side and smile.

"Beth, just tell me. Please." I ask, lowering my voice to a steady calm tone. I'm not mad at her, after all.

She sighs, smiling. "Erik told Mark that he wanted to kiss you. He's very . . . smitten with you," she laughs. I try not to join her laughter, but inside I'm all giddy like a teenager.

"You're the first person he's been interested in since, well, you know," she says, her eyes rolling at the mention of Miss You-Know-Who. This time I laugh. But inwardly, I'm embarrassed. She knows more about how Erik feels than I do.

"I promise, Mrs. Cohen, whatever his feelings, I'll keep him safe," I say, holding my breath a little. Her eyebrows slant, and her mouth forms an "O". She reaches for my hands and pats them.

"Aw, honey. We know that. We trust you." She smiles at me in the same way a doting grandmother would, and I'm satisfied that she and Mr. Cohen aren't thinking ill of me or worried that I'm too wrapped up in falling for Erik to be of any use protecting him.

All too soon, my thoughts return to Jeff and his appearance in my dream. It gnaws at me, and I need to call John. "Beth, could you excuse me? I need to make a phone call to the FBI." I know it's freezing outside, and I'm asking a lot. But she shakes her head.

"There's a changing room back there you can use honey."

I get up, walk to the back, and close the door behind me. I have a seat on the armchair and call John.

"Hey Ronnie. I called you earlier, but you didn't answer," he sounds groggy.

"Sorry John. We're out in La Tuna Canyon filming. Anything on the unsub?" I can hear him shifting in the blankets. He's talking softly as he explains, trying not to wake Theresa.

"We found the Monte Carlo in an industrial park next to a small executive airport. There are a lot of storage units over there, so he pulled in there and stashed the car. But we got something on the plate. It's fake. The number, get this—it's Canadian," the sound of amazement in his voice is not lost on me.

"Are you joking? How the hell does anyone get a blank California plate and stamp a Canadian number on it?" I laugh.

"I don't know Ronnie. It's creative, I'll give him that. Now at about eight p.m., a single engine private plane was stolen from that airport." John's information is surprising.

"Were you able to track it?"

"No. It was a small private aircraft, and the transponder was turned off. Does Jeff know how to fly?" he asks.

"I have no clue John. I don't remember him ever taking flying lessons, but it doesn't mean he hasn't. I've been gone for a few years remember? Speaking of Jeff, I need to ask you something."

"Shoot, sis." I hesitate a bit, dreading what I'm about to say. "Do you recall me talking about the night Jeff rescued me from Kincaid?"

"Yes. Why?"

"I had a dream about that night. Jeff was walking down the hall when I escaped from Kincaid. He didn't have his gun drawn. He was just walking casually down the hall. Not in a defensive posture or anything. He was wearing jeans and a shirt, no vest, and no gear of any kind. It just seems odd to me now."

"Oh, sis. Don't put too much stock in a dream."

"John, everything about this dream was exactly the way it took place that night. Every word out of Kincaid's mouth, everything he did to me—every kick and every punch was the same. Except for the one thing I never thought about much, and that's Jeff. How did he get there, why he was so calm and relaxed? Maybe I blocked it out, I don't know."

"Ronnie, there's no way for us to know what Jeff was doing there that night. He's gone. There's a real possibility that the unsub could have been Jeff, not Kincaid." My stomach churns. Fortunately, there's nothing in there for me to bring up. For a brief second in his office, the thought occurred to me that it could have been Jeff chasing us, but the shocking revelations about Kincaid pushed Jeff and the unsub to the back burner.

"John, what if Erik is not the real target." The line goes quiet, and I hear rustling, but I'm not sure what he's doing.

"Sorry. I'm getting out of bed. I woke up Theresa. What are you thinking?"

"I don't know for sure John. If Jeff is Kincaid's brother, there's no telling how long this has been going on. Jeff could be behind the letters and the hacking, hoping the case would lure me back to Los Angeles." I lean back in the chair and stare at the ceiling, hoping he will find some major flaw in my theory.

"Ronnie, stop. There's no answering these questions. You're what-if-ing this to death. Yes, Jeff might be holding a torch for you. But that doesn't mean he's going to dangle you like a carrot in front of a deranged rapist. So let's flesh this out. According to your theory, he knew where you were the first time Kincaid held you, right?" He stops, letting me answer.

"Yes."

"It may have been staged, with him swooping in at the last minute to look like a good guy. But in the end, did it make you fall in love with him?" He asks.

"No," I grumble. He's right. And I feel like a fool for letting my thoughts spin out of control.

"Okay then. Let's not put the cart before the horse here. Something is up with him, I'll agree to that much. He's been lying about his relationship with Kincaid. But I'm not willing to speculate any further right now. Not until we find him and question him," he says with a note of calm authority. I'm silent. There's no point is beating a dead horse, at least not tonight. He's heard me out, and that's all I can do for now.

"I have one more request," I ask.

John sighs. I'm sure he'd rather be in bed than talking to me at this hour. "Shoot."

"Can you run a background check on Dan?" I ask meekly, trying to lower my voice in case anyone is listening

"Sure. I'll see what I can find. What are you thinking?"

"I don't know, John, it's just a gut feeling. Dan has said and done some odd things. Jeff hired him, so who knows what the truth is. I doubt Dan will be upfront if I ask."

"Good point. I'll get Wilcher started on it in the morning. Do me a favor though, call Hunter. I haven't heard from him. I'm hoping he's just busy going through Jeff's place. Let me know tomorrow if he finds anything."

As nice as Theresa is, I'm sure she's not too happy with me. I've kept him on the phone for a while. "I will. Good night, John. I'll talk to you soon."

When I walk out of the back room, Beth and Erik are sitting on the couch talking. His cheeks are pink from the icy wind, and when he smiles at me, Beth notices. She pats him on the shoulder before she stands. "I'll see you later," she says, as she gives me a reassuring wink on her way out the door. Now that we're alone, I can talk to him about my theory. I need to tell him about Kincaid, and my dream is the best way to ease into it. Even if my theory about Jeff is wrong, my presence could be putting Erik at risk, and he has the right to know. Gearing myself up for a tough conversation, I move toward the couch, but Erik starts questioning me before I say a word.

"Beth told me you had a nightmare. Are you all right?" He looks concerned and taking my hand, he pulls me down beside him.

"I'm fine. There're things we need to talk about," I say as he frowns. He's worried and anxious to hear about my dream and my phone call to John.

"What is it?" he prods.

"My dream was about Kincaid. About the last night he had me, before I escaped." His face goes blank and hard except for the fire in his eyes. I've only seen it once before, when I felt like a blast wave hit me. He swallows hard and his hands turn to fists.

"What? You escaped from Kincaid?" His voice is shaky, and he reaches out for my hands.

"Yes. I remembered something about that night. Something about Jeff. I don't know if I'm dreaming or remembering," I say, my voice shaking.

He stares at me, his eyes full of anxiety, knowing only what I've told him so far, that Kincaid is a monster.

"I realize you told me you didn't want to know. But my dream raises some new questions, and some new angles to this whole case."

The door opens abruptly and Dan walks inside. "Car is all warmed up. Ready to go?"

Erik sighs and rubs at the stubble on his cheeks, he's only heard a tiny portion of the story, and he's worried now. But it will have to wait until Dan is not around.

♚ Chapter Fourteen

Once we're in the house, Dan makes his way to the back door. "Good night," he grumbles as the door slams behind him. He's clearly still annoyed about his exclusion at the FBI offices today but he'll just have to get over it.

Now that we are alone, Erik will want to continue our conversation. He drops his backpack near the door and pulls out his street clothes. He didn't bother to change before we left the La Tuna Canyon, and he hangs up the fleece hoodie and leather jacket near the door.

"I'm going to get a quick shower. But we're not finished." He stares, waiting for a reply. For the first time, I can see the spark in his eyes that goes along with the commanding tone he unleashes on me at times. I nod and lower my eyes, dreading the difficult conversation that is looming.

I follow him down the hallway and close the bedroom door behind me. Resting against it for a moment, I try to collect my thoughts, since this won't be an easy story to tell. Within a few moments, I'm stripped down and in the shower with the hot water streaming over my head and down my back, washing away the stress of the day. For now.

When I finish, he's already in the kitchen, setting up a small kettle for tea. "Would you like a cup?" I nod and sit on the couch.

"I talked to John. They found the car hidden in a storage unit near an executive airport. It's the same airport a single engine plane was stolen from this afternoon. And the license plate on the vehicle that followed us was a fake." His eyes grow wide. Apparently, even he knows that's hard to manage. He carefully walks into the living room with two cups of steaming hot tea in his hands. I take a cup and sip from it.

"I'm sure John and the FBI people are on top of it. So please, tell me what's going on."

My heart slams against my rib cage. *Just start talking, just get the words out*, I tell myself. "Five years ago, I was on a job, protecting Miranda Cassidy. Remember her?" He nods but says nothing. "I was on the job about a month. Miranda had an appearance at a club, and it was at the club that her stalker showed up. I had dressed up to look like her, and at the event, he grabbed me instead of her."

I set my cup on the table, and I hear him mutter the word 'Jesus'. He has no idea how much worse it's about to get.

"And it was Kincaid?" he asks, holding his breath. I can see the muscles in his jaw begin to clench.

"Yes."

He looks away as I talk about how Kincaid kept me shackled and beat me. His shoulders begin to slump, and his gaze is focused on something in the distance. When I get to the worst part, how Kincaid drugged me and raped me, his eyes have narrowed into thin slits, and his hands are clenched into tight fists. He doesn't say a word, he just lifts a hand to his eyes and wipes across them before looking back at me. Somehow, I managed to get it all out without breaking down, but I'm not so sure about him. What I've told him sounds like something from a horrifying news report. And I'm sure that by the end of this conversation, I'll see the pity in his eyes. But when he drapes his arm around my shoulder, I'm beyond surprised.

"You're an incredibly strong person to survive that. I'm in awe of you." He pulls me into his arms and kisses my hair, inhaling deeply before I pull away a bit.

"Now what does Jeff have to do with all this?" His quiet strength surprises me. He's heard the worst of it, and he's ready to take more.

"That night, while Kincaid was unconscious, I ran down a hall trying to find my way out. Jeff was there. He didn't have a gun or a vest, and there were no police. I suppose I never really thought about why he was there. Maybe I blocked it out, or I didn't think there was any reason to suspect Jeff. It was all a blur. I want so much to believe this is all a jumbled nightmare, but the more we learn, the more I think Jeff knew where I was the whole time."

He gasps as I finish my story. I can't sit still, so I get up and pace the room. I wrap my arms around myself, trying to hold in the hurt, trying to keep it from exploding. The possibility that Jeff knew where I was, and what his brother was doing to me, is too horrifying to think about. He sighs, coming toward me slowly.

"You've got to let him go," he pleads quietly. It's a hard thing to hear because I want to believe there's something good in the man I've looked up to all these years. How could I have been so wrong, and what does that say about me? Something like defiance rises in me, I still feel the need to defend him, the years of friendship and loyalty are hanging on tight.

"He's my best friend, Erik. He saved my life in Afghanistan. He took care of me after . . . after." My voice croaks, on the edge of tears, and I realize my loyalty has me sounding naïve and foolish.

"I'm sorry Ronnie. I know this hurts. But you'll have to face it eventually. Even if Jeff does turn up, there's no denying the evidence. He lied to you and put both of us in danger."

My chest constricts with a pain so acute I can barely breathe. I'm not just outraged over my own safety. The idea that Erik could be hurt, or taken away from me is like a knife through my heart. It's a feeling I've never experienced, and I don't know how to handle it. Every inch of my body is shaking with rage.

"Easy Ronnie," he says tenderly as he pulls me into his embrace. He makes me feel protected and safe. It's very much the opposite of how I feel every time Jeff hugs me, and I realize something deep in my subconscious always knew and was repelled by him.

"It will be all right," he says confidently as I lean my forehead against his chest. "You've got me now."

He pulls my hair back from my cheek, and his fingers drag softly against my neck. "Goosebumps," he whispers, as his fingers skitter down the ultra-sensitive flesh along the curve of my neck.

Breathe. Just breathe. My insides flutter, and I clutch his biceps. I need to hold onto something real and keep myself grounded or I might expire on the spot.

"Ronnie," he whispers into my ear.

The way my name rolls off his tongue sounds like sex—like he's making love to each letter. It's my new favorite thing. Ever.

His hand slides up my waist, and his breathing changes. It's fluttery and ragged, like my own. That hand makes it to my neck, wrapping around it while his thumb slides along my jaw. He lifts my chin and stares down at me, and my eyes come to rest on his beautiful mouth.

That mouth moves.

"Baby,"

I melt. I think I like the sound of that more than my name. And then he kisses me. His mouth is warm, wet, and gentle. He crushes me into his chest, and he moans as he nibbles at my lips. That soft little moan rockets through me, and I open to him. His tongue dips tentatively inside my mouth, gently caressing, tasting, and exploring. I can't remember when a man tasted or felt this good. This is better than Christmas morning, a hot caramel sundae, or a diamond ring. I moan softly, inhaling his scent and breathing back into him. He responds by gripping me tighter as his hands move to cup my backside. Our hips lock together like puzzle pieces. Our fit is incredible, and I can feel his arousal.

My heart is pounding faster than it ever has and I break away because I can barely breathe. He groans a little and then breathes his words across my lips.

"Your lips are so sweet."

My mouth opens and a little fluttery laugh comes out, and he takes advantage. His lips are on me again, and I'm moving backward so quickly I have no time to think. My back meets the wall, and he's kissing me, possessively eating at my mouth, and I open wider to give him more.

I'm his. He just doesn't know it yet.

He sucks my earlobe into his mouth, sending shivers down my spine, and then releases as he whispers in my ear.

"I want you in my bed, baby. Stay with me tonight."

His voice is low and dominant, and my body responds. My sex clenches and the small muscles deep inside me ripple with excitement. I can't deny how much I want him—how he makes me feel, but my mind is in the way. I'm afraid of how intensely I feel about this incredible man, so quickly.

"No." I whisper softly, not offering an explanation.

"I want you. So much, I can't breathe around you."

"I can't." It takes every ounce of my will to say no to him. I must be insane for turning him down. But I'm not ready, and I'm not ready for him to know why.

146

"Please, be patient with me, Erik."

He stares at me, and he must know I'm holding back. His eyebrows knit, and I drop my gaze and pull away.

"Hmm, it's very late." I slowly walk backward toward the hallway. "Good night." I turn and duck into the bedroom, closing the door behind me. I jump into bed and turn off the light, but within seconds, my phone vibrates loudly against the nightstand. I look at my texts, it's not Sarah or John. It's from Erik.

Erik: I love the way you taste.

My heart races. I reply.

Me: **bites lip**

There's no reply, and my head barely hits the pillow when my phone vibrates again.

Erik: Good night, good night. Parting is such sweet sorrow, that I shall say good night till it be morrow.

Me: One kiss and you spout sonnets? Good night, Romeo.

I squint at the bright early morning light coming through the blinds. My alarm is going off and I fumble blindly for it. I stab at the screen to dismiss the shrill noise and set it on the nightstand. It's eight, and we don't have to be at the set until noon.

Slipping into some sweats, I pad softly down the hall and into the kitchen. I setup the coffee pot and wait, enjoying the quiet and solace while it brews. It isn't long before the smell makes my stomach growl. I haven't eaten since sometime yesterday morning, I think. After a chase through Los Angeles, my stomach was in no mood for food.

It's a beautiful day, and the sun is shining through the back window. It's the first time I've seen the property in daylight, and I have a few hours to survey the buildings and perhaps go over some things with Hunter. He can take over in Jeff's absence, and I have faith that with his background, he can run the office and keep on top of all the ongoing contracts. My main priority is to get the security system installation back on track. I pick up my phone and dial the office.

"Good morning Marci. Is Hunter in the office yet?" She's quiet and haltingly starts to speak.

"Um, yes Ronnie. What is going on? Where is Jeff?" She sounds agitated, and I hadn't counted on talking to the troops, but one of us needs to keep the employees informed. Otherwise, we might end up a two-man shop.

"I don't know Marci. We're looking for him. Everything will be fine. Hunter and I will run things in Jeff's absence." I can hear her sigh and then the phone clicks several times before he answers.

"Scott Hunter."

"Hi Hunter. How's it going?"

"Morning, Ronnie. I checked the GPS system. Jeff's last recorded location was at a dentist's office a few days ago. I stopped by his house last night. My keys don't work." He stops talking and my mood sinks. Finding Jeff's car would have been a huge help, but now it's a dead end and so is the house.

"There's only one way we're going to get in there, Hunter."

"Yes, I know. I'll call the police and report him missing," he says.

"I'll call John. He'll have to get a warrant to enter the house and trace his phone," I say, as I take a sip of my coffee. Despite this latest bit of bad news, my stomach is growling. "We also need to go through the company's financial statements. Jeff mentioned something strange the other day. He said we couldn't afford to lose the contract with Olympus. I would bet the company has money problems." He's silent again, but I hear the computer come to life as he switches me to speakerphone.

"Now that might be a problem. I don't know the passwords for that stuff."

"Get a hold of Alex Harris. He can get into those programs. I wonder how he's doing after the surgery."

"What surgery?" he asks, sounding confused. My heart lurches up into my throat, how is it possible that Hunter didn't know about this?

"Jeff told me Alex was in the hospital with Appendicitis and that he was trying to contract the security system install."

"Wow, he never told me. Let me go, I'll call Alex and get back to you." I disconnect the call and set my phone on the island, staring at it for a moment. The lies are piling up faster than we can handle. It's gone way beyond a simple miscommunication at this point. Back in the military, even Jeff's superiors used to call him anal, so for him to disappear without putting Hunter or me in charge is bizarre. And now the lies about Alex. Why the cover-up? Did he intend to delay the security system for some reason?

As I sip my coffee, I realize staring at my phone won't make it ring, nor will it stop the growling in my stomach. I peer into the fridge looking for something to eat.

"Good morning." I turn to find Erik standing at the edge of the hall, hair disheveled and smiling with that sexy charm I find hard to resist. He comes up behind me as I cook my egg and looks over my shoulder as his fingers come to rest on my waist.

"Mmm, looks good."

Something tells me he doesn't mean the food. His lips meet the curve of my neck, and his stubble tickles the sensitive spots along my shoulder.

"Are you hungry?" I ask playfully. He turns me, and I'm pinned between him and the island. Reaching for my chin, he lifts my face to meet his gaze.

"Yes. And you look positively delicious, Ms. Harper." Our lips meet, and the kiss is hotter and more passionate than last night. Erik is wrapped around me like a snake, our tongues twisting and grinding as we taste each other. He cups the back of my head in his large hand, holding me as he pulls back and nibbles at my lips, stopping only when my phone starts to vibrate noisily against the granite. I grab it anxiously, hoping for some small shred of good news.

"Hi Hunter."

"Hey, I spoke to Alex. Are you sitting down?"

I choke back a lump as I turn off the stove. "Yes." The muscles in my chest constrict tightly, in anticipation of bad news.

"Jeff gave him a week off. He knew nothing about the security system installation."

My plate falls from my hand and clatters on the granite counter top as my stomach sinks to my shoes. "What the fuck is going on here!" I yell into the phone. My stomach roils as I realize my best friend has intentionally put me and my client in danger, lied to everyone, and involved innocent people in this crazy situation.

"I don't know Ronnie. I'm as confused as you are. Alex is on his way into the office, can you get down here?"

"Yes. I'll stop by the office a bit later," I promise as I hang up with Hunter. I quickly gather what remains of my sandwich and have as seat at the island. When I look down at the plate, it's a managed mess, much like my life, and suddenly, I'm not so hungry anymore. I pick up my phone to call John and when he answers, I can hear the kids in the background. Teresa must be getting them ready for school.

"Morning, sis. What's up?" Part of me wishes John weren't on this case. I don't want to see those two kids, who I love like my own, made fatherless by Kincaid.

"Well, no luck on the GPS, and Hunter couldn't get in to Jeff's house. The locks were changed. He's calling the local police to report him missing. I think it's time." My words trail off, and Erik looks at me, confused.

"Yeah. I was thinking the same thing last night. I'll call the office and get a warrant started," he says.

"Who are you going to assign to us?" I ask. John goes quiet for a moment, and I'm afraid of what he's going to say.

"The only guy I have free right now is Wilcher."

"Really? He's such a dickhead," I groan. Erik laughs as he takes a sip coffee. He won't be laughing once he spends some time with Agent Wilcher.

"Look, he's all I've got for a few days until I can request more agents. My other two guys are working on the physical evidence and the vital records stuff," he says, irritated.

"Okay, John. I know it's the best you can do," I say, hoping to smooth his ruffled feathers.

"I'll send him out there ASAP. Anything else, sis?" he asks.

"Yep, for now. Bye, John." I disconnect the call, and Dan walks in the back door.

"So what's the story, boss?" Dan looks at both Erik and me. I'm sure he's wondering why we both appear so tense.

"No sign of Jeff. FBI is getting warrants." I stand and put my plate in the sink as Dan makes himself something to eat.

"That's not good. Now I'm wishing I was still with Millennium."

Huh . . . I thought he was subcontracting? Maybe I should have asked for a background check sooner.

I look at Erik before I walk to the door, and he shrugs a shoulder. We're clearly thinking the same thing. When I step out onto the deck and breathe in the crisp morning air, I round the side of the house, moving toward the outbuildings. Looking to the left, I take in the length of the property, the long valley and the high ridge that surrounds it. The trees are mostly pines, but a few have turned autumn gold, the grass is dead and brown, and it crunches under my feet as I walk toward the barn. When I push back the door, I notice the upper loft. There are leftover bales of hay somewhere, and the damp, green smell fills my nostrils. The back of the barn has several small windows that look out onto the rest of the property. Directly behind it, the land starts to swell upwards at a steep angle. The top of the ridge is barely visible through the window.

I hear Erik walk in, and I turn and lean against the window. "So, what did Hunter say?" He reaches a hand up, brushing my bangs from my eyes.

"Nothing good. Jeff is a ghost, the security installations were intentionally delayed, there may be financial problems. Honestly, I don't think it could get any worse."

Being openly fatalistic and over-dramatic is not my style, but with him I find it hard to hide my worries.

"What is it? Something else is on your mind," he says as he taps a finger between my eyebrows, and I laugh. But I still worry about telling him my theory and I prepare myself for his reaction. Like John, he may not see the validity, or even worse, he may decide I'm right, and want nothing to do with me. Bringing it up before I have real evidence may do more harm than good, but there's no getting around it now.

"I'm starting to think you're not the target at all. I think Jeff either put me on this case to draw Kincaid out, or he put me in this situation so he can play the rescuer. Whatever his motivation, I think I'm the target." The words burn as they leave my mouth and he stares at me blankly, then rubs at his face with one hand.

"So what does all this mean?" His mood shifts suddenly, the slight smile he had earlier evaporates.

"It means that I think I'm a danger to you. We may have to find you another security arrangement. If my hunch pans out, you can go back to your life, and the FBI will take care of me." He's shaking his head the entire time I'm talking. My words aren't penetrating his thick skull at all. "Erik, we just don't know the extent of Jeff's involvement. He could be trying to catch Kincaid himself, or he could be masterminding this. He could be the one sending the threats. There are so many variables here I can't even count them. Unfortunately, we can't interrogate Jeff to find out. And I'm not sure I trust Dan either."

His eyes snap from the floor to my face. I've never mentioned my suspicions before now. Erik turns away from me and paces a bit, eyes down, raking the hair back from his forehead. He covers the large open space several times as I wait in agonizing silence. The fear overtakes me silently as I wait for him to speak. I can't blame him if he decides that he was wrong about me, or that this is all too much to handle. An aching loneliness descends on me. Once again, Kincaid is destroying my life.

He stops, moves toward the door, and pulls it closed. The only light streams in through the grimy window, lancing the empty expanse of the barn in half. Erik strides toward me resolutely in the damp gloom, takes me by the waist, and walks me back into the wall.

"Okay, just stop. Thinking this way gives them the power. I'm not going to let them win, and I'm sure as hell not going to give you up." The fire in his eyes ignites the desire within me, and his hands cup my face. Our mouths seal together, and our bodies are pressed as close as possible while still clothed. When his tongue dips into my mouth, stroking and flicking against mine, my body arches with the intensity of our connection, and our lips part. His mouth drags across my chin moving slowly down my throat, tasting my skin inch by tender inch. He thrusts a hand into my hair, tipping my head back further, as he nuzzles me with more urgency.

"You. Taste. So. Good," he mutters between sweet kisses. I smile against his mouth, and my ragged breath escapes as his lips hover above mine for what seems like an eternity. He's holding me hostage, and I can't think, I can't move. All I can do is feel . . . him. One more gentle kiss touches my lips and he pulls away, dragging my bottom lip with him.

We are still wrapped around each other when the door rumbles loudly along the track and bright sunshine illuminates the barn. We both turn at the same time and are met with Dan's embarrassed face, again. "Sorry, boss. Agent Wilcher is here."

Erik puts distance between us, turning his back to the door as he wipes at his mouth. When he turns back toward me, our eyes lock for a brief second, and a look of silent apprehension passes between us. Dan turns to go, and as I step past Erik, his hand makes contact at the small of my back. It's the epicenter of a thousand tiny tingles that spread down my legs.

How in the world does he do this to me?

♚ CHAPTER FIFTEEN

Agent Wilcher is waiting in the living room, and he rises from the couch when we enter the house. Almost nothing about him has changed. He still oozes the same smug attitude, and his dark soulless eyes are the same. The only slight difference is his overly chiseled face shows a few more lines. He's good looking, and he knows it. What's worse, he's the type that doesn't let you forget it.

"Harper," he nods with a cold stare.

"This is Mr. Sinclair," Erik reaches out a hand, and I notice immediately that he doesn't offer up his first name as he did with me. Erik looks him over suspiciously before taking a seat on the couch.

"I've been working on your case for a while Mr. Sinclair. I guess you're involved now too?" He shoots me a questioning look. I'm sure John didn't tell him the truth of my connection to Kincaid. He wouldn't without my permission.

"Yes. I think I always was," I smirk. Wilcher stares at me for a moment, looking slightly confused, but I ignore it.

"We're headed to the set in an hour. Dan, you can help out with general security today while Wilcher sticks with Eri—Mr. Sinclair."

Dan and Wilcher catch my overly familiar slip, and Wilcher's eyes dart between the two of us as I shift in my chair. I'd gladly deal with Wilcher and his attitude if I could get rid of Dan. At least Wilcher is trustworthy.

"And where will you be?" he asks abrasively. I narrow my eyes to thin slits, letting him know his remark is inappropriate.

"I have some things to take care of today at the Cole Offices." Leaving him no room to question me, I get up, and Erik does the same.

"Would you like a quick tour of the property?" Wilcher nods and follows Erik out the front door. I'm amazed by how well Erik has come to know me in such a short time, and that he can decipher my moods so easily. It's frightening, awakening all sorts of insecurities, but he's sweet and thoughtful at the same time.

I walk down the hall and close the bedroom door. Changing into my clothes, I watch through the blinds as Wilcher, Dan, and Erik move from the stable to the barn and then disappear behind the house.

Within a few minutes, I'm dressed and the voices of Wilcher and Dan are reverberating through the garage opposite my room. He's asking about Erik's motorcycle and from the sound of it, Dan is claiming it was his idea to ground Erik. *What a little bastard!*

When I walk into the living room, Dan's eyes flick toward me nervously as he shrugs on his jacket. As far as I'm concerned, the lie is a minor transgression. Certainly no reason to fire him, but with all the other odd things about him piling up, it only adds to my worries. We all leave the house, Erik and I get in the Mercedes and Wilcher and Dan follow us to the set in his car.

When we pull up to the set, Michael opens the gate. "Dan and Agent Wilcher from the FBI are in the car behind us. He'll be coming to the set every day."

Michael nods and scribbles the name on his clipboard. "Yes, ma'am," he says as he pulls open the gate. Once we park and meet at Erik's trailer, I give Dan and Wilcher instructions for the next few hours. Dan is to supplement the security on set while Agent Wilcher will stick with Erik and get to know the schedule and the layout of the set. When Erik and Wilcher take off, I let Dan know explicitly that under no circumstances are they to let Erik sign autographs outside the gate. He stalks off in the opposite direction, grumbling and angry as he takes up his new post.

I have enough time to call John, leaving him a message about Hunter before I grab the keys to the Mercedes. I'd rather get this trip to the office over with, and my nerves are on edge as I pull off the lot and pass the haunting piece of property where the warehouse once stood.

In the lobby, it's cold and stark as usual. But it's quiet, and that unnerves me. Even Marci is shy and tense. "Hi, Ronnie," she says, without her usual smile. I feel bad for her. It would be natural for her to be worried about her job right now. No one could blame her if she started looking elsewhere.

"Morning, Marci." I smile, hoping to calm her.

"What's going on? Jeff still isn't answering his phone. Have you found him?" she says, rambling.

"No Marci, but we've reported him missing and are doing everything we can to find him. Have you noticed any strange behavior from him recently?"

"Not that I can think of." She stares at me blankly. There's no telling how long he's been hiding things, and she may have to think back over months, possibly even years.

"Do you remember any strange packages, keeping odd hours, maybe strange phone calls?"

Her eyes light up. "Yes. There were a lot of phone calls from some doctor. It stopped two or three months ago. He was arguing with whoever was on the phone one day. I could hear him yelling through the glass. He kept saying something like, sedate him, or keep him sedated."

That information alone is worth checking into since Alex can scan through our phone equipment to pull logs of all calls in and out of the office. Marci offers up another idea - she can search Jeff's appointment logs and calendar while I'm busy with Hunter. If anything, it will keep Marci's mind off Jeff's disappearance. Whether we get any useful information out if it is a huge leap, but Jeff's old habit of keeping handwritten appointment books may turn up something we can use. Before I walk into the office, I thank her, offering as much encouragement as possible. Going out of my way to lift her mood is worth it since she has such a good rapport with the employees. By the time I leave her desk, she's smiling again.

At least one of us is.

"Morning, Hunter. Alex, you're looking very . . . healthy," I take a seat on the couch and smile. Alex nods and raises an eyebrow.

"Hey Ronnie. It's good to have you back. Are you back?" Alex has a dry, sarcastic sense of humor, and it's hard not to like him. He's extremely smart, graduating from Berkeley at twenty, he's a prodigy, and one of the best Network Engineers I've ever met. And it doesn't hurt that he's tall, young, and fit.

I nod and smile. "Yes. I suppose I am. So what have you two found?" I ask. They both frown, and I know the news is going to be devastating. Saving this sinking ship might be tougher than I thought.

"You were right about the financial angle Ronnie," Hunter says as he turns his chair toward me. "There's been money flying out of the company accounts for years, to the tune of several thousand dollars a month. We barely have enough to keep the company going for a month—maybe two, if we're careful," he says. I can see the worry in his eyes. He's thinking about the employees, just as I am. They have families to support, and I don't want to let them down.

"Where is the money going Hunter?" I ask. I have my suspicions, but I'd rather have evidence. Alex jumps in and describes what he's found in the last few hours. Jeff has been funneling money from the main bank accounts to a separate account. What he was doing with the money is unclear.

"I think we need to get an accountant, Hunter." My suggestion is met with agreement, but we don't discuss it further. Marci knocks on the door and I wave her in, but she pushes the door open timidly.

"What is it Marci?"

"Um, I was going through my appointment and visitor logs. I found something." She hands me a receipt and written across the top is the name Desert Lawn Funeral Home.

"It was stuck to the back of one of Jeff's appointment books, and it got sandwiched between his book and my visitor log."

"Thank you, Marci." I smile and wait for her to leave the office before I hand the paper to Hunter.

"This is dated June 26, 2013. His mother's name is on here." His eyes are wide with shock.

"Yep, it's for his mother's funeral. He lied to me five years ago." We all sit quiet for a moment, absorbing the bad news.

"Alex, as soon as Hunter has all the access he needs, start putting together a security system for the Lords of the Street set." I reach into my bag and pull out a schematic of the lot. "It's an easy job: two entrances and plenty of locations to install cameras." He takes it from me and briefly looks it over.

"Now, Mr. Sinclair's house is a big job." I pull out the photos and blueprints of Erik's property. Alex flips open the brown folder and sees the photo first.

"Holy crap, that's a large property," he grumbles as he scratches at his short brown hair. I nod, and I figure there's no time like the present to make it worse. I describe the property and the lack of lights along the driveway or near the outbuildings. When I'm done, Alex lets out a exasperated grumble.

"I'm going to need additional electric for this. You want infrared and standard cameras outside?" he asks as he makes notes on the blueprint.

I nod again. "No cameras inside though," I say. That's Erik's specific request, which is one thing I plan to accommodate.

"I can get an alarm system installed and some outdoor cameras quickly— perhaps tomorrow. Is that good?"

"Yes. That's fine."

Alex turns to Hunter. "The exterior lighting and infrared are going to take some time. I have to order them. Do we have money for this?"

Hunter frowns. "Yes, but just barely."

"Let me talk to Erik—Mr. Sinclair. He can help foot the bill for this." Hunter stares at me for long seconds, confused by my stutter.

"Olympus Television needs to cover the cost of upgrading the security at the set," he says. Regardless of the threat against Erik, the show is becoming more popular every season, bringing more chance for problems.

"How much do you plan on telling Erik?" Hunter asks, and I stare at my shoes. Erik knows so much already, but I don't want to be indebted to him to save the company. Mixing business with personal relationships never works out well for anyone.

"I'm not sure. His life is on the line here. I don't anticipate he'll refuse. I'd better get back to the set. Call me if you find anything new." I walk out the door and thank Marci on my way out.

As I pull out of the parking lot, I immediately call Sarah, who answers on the first ring.

"Hi Sarah. You busy?"

I hear the telltale beep of her car alarm, and realize she's probably on her way back from lunch. "Nope. I'm just headed back to the university. How is the job going?" she asks.

"Ah, things could be better," I admit quietly. She'd never say I told you so. Not to me.

"What's wrong, I can hear it. It's bad isn't it?" The tension returns to my shoulders, and I'm dreading the words I'm about to say.

"Yes. Sarah, you were right about Jeff." She is silent, and my mind races as the quiet descends on the car. With Sarah, silence means bad things.

"Good Lord, what's happened?" she sounds anxious. I can feel my nerves wind up like a coiled spring as I start to explain the new information about Jeff and his hidden relationship to Kincaid. She's horrified by the news.

"I don't understand why he kept this from me, Sarah. We've been friends for so long. He had so many opportunities to tell me about his family. Everything we went through, Iraq, Afghanistan—nothing about him was true. It was all lies." Admitting it aloud hurts.

"Ronnie, he was probably embarrassed. Many times, people who have mental illness in their family keep it hidden. There's a stigma attached to it in this country. And obviously, his brother is far worse than the average person who's dealing with depression or Bipolar disorder. His brother is a psychopath. I might hide that from people too."

While I understand her point of view, it does nothing to lessen the sting of betrayal or the reality that the person I was briefly married to and friends with for so long is someone I never knew at all.

"Sarah, I have to ask you something. Can a dream be a replaying of events, like a memory, more than a jumbled nightmare?"

"I suppose so. Why?"

"I had a dream about the night I escaped Kincaid's dungeon. Everything in my dream was exactly as it happened that night. But what struck me most was Jeff. His behavior in my dream was unusual."

"What was strange about it?" I hear the sound of voices in the background, but within moments, they disappear. The jingle of keys and the closing of a door let me know she's in her office.

I take a deep breath and explain the dream, and Jeff's odd appearance that night to her. Once I'm finished, I hold my breath, waiting for her assessment. She's probably going to tell me I'm crazy.

"Oh Ronnie, this could be your subconscious mixing things up, definitely. The only way to be sure would be to put you under."

Wonderful. It's not what I was hoping to hear. Sarah and I tried hypnotherapy in the early days. There was a lot I couldn't remember, since Kincaid kept me heavily drugged. It was a helpful tool in figuring out just how much I endured. But we never touched on Jeff because we never thought we had to.

"You might need to fly down here," I suggest. It's not a scenario I'm hoping for. If I need her down here that badly, it means my situation has taken a terrible turn.

"If you need me to, I will. So how are things with Erik," she asks, wasting no time getting to "the good stuff".

"Um . . . Good," I giggle.

She quickly becomes irritated with my hysterical laughter. "Tell me," she yells. I calm myself enough to tell her how things have changed with Erik, going from a harmless but awkward moment in his trailer, to full-scale flirting, and even talking me into dressing up for him. She's amazed by the last part, but instead of asking how I feel about it, she has one and only one question.

"So has he kissed you yet?"

I laugh so hard, I'm nearly crying. "Yes," I admit.

"Hot damn! Succ-sess!" she shouts. I'm happy she's so happy. At least I don't have to admit I had a panic attack only a few minutes before the big event. But she still manages to caution me.

"Just don't jump in the deep end here. Take things slow," she says, sounding too much like my mother.

"Slow is my only option, Sarah. He knows about Kincaid," I admit. In a way, I'm proud of it.

"Wow. You told him! I'm amazed. He must really be hot!" I'm glad she can't see me because I just rolled my eyes.

"Oh calm your hormones Sarah," I laugh. "He knows, but he doesn't know about my other little problem."

She's silent for a moment, and I fear she'll tell me to be honest with him. The thought of telling him that I'm deathly afraid of sex is almost as bad as being face-to-face with Kincaid.

"Well, you can tell him that because of the danger, it's best that you wait. Or you could be honest with him," she says, just as I expected.

"I'm going to have to face this fairly soon. He's not going to wait forever. Besides, what if he runs? What do I do then?"

"Then he isn't the right man for you."

I wish it were that simple. In Sarah's world of cold, analytical psychology, it is that simple though. I hope she's right, and I tell her so, trying to bolster my shaky optimism. But all too quickly, her break is over and she is heading back to her class.

"Please call me if you need me. I don't care what's going on, I'll get down there," she says.

"Thanks, Sarah. Talk to you soon."

As I drive through the streets of Los Angeles, one of Sarah's affirmations repeats in my brain: Everyone is responsible for their own behavior. People may treat you like shit, but it's how you react to it that gives them the power. I need to remember that. As I stop at a red light, the phone rings. "Hi, John. How is it going down there?"

"Hi, Ronnie. We're still working on the connection between Jeff and Kincaid. Then I'm on the road tomorrow."

"Did you get the warrants?" I ask.

"Yes. I'm going to Bullhead City first. Are you going to meet me out there?"

"I don't know. I haven't talked to Erik about it yet. Besides, we found some new information."

John groans loudly. "Okay, what is it?"

"We found a receipt from the funeral home that buried Jeff's mother. He buried her in Bullhead City, Arizona. And there has been money flying out of the Cole bank accounts for years. Our IT guy is trying to find out more. Hunter and Alex Harris should be calling you soon with whatever they dig up."

"All right. I'll have Agent Jacobs request a warrant for Cole's records. It's just a formality, but we need to get that information. Oh, and I have the background report on Dan."

My stomach does several somersaults and my fingernails dig into the steering wheel. "Give me the quick and dirty, John."

"Well, there's nothing in the background report that is a cause for alarm. His employment history is a little spotty though. Seems like he was fired from the L.A. Police department then bounced from job to job before working for Millennium."

"What? I thought . . . " I hear a lot of voices in the background, and John drops off for a moment.

"Hey Ronnie. I'll e-mail the report to you and Wilcher. I have to go. I'll call you from the road."

John hangs up as I pull into the set, and I see a large crowd of people standing in front of the gates. It's a normal occurrence at the Lords set, and since I don't see Erik, I pull through the gates when Michael opens them. I park behind the trailer and quickly call the office.

"Hey Marci, can you put Hunter on, please." There is a beat of silence before I hear the click of Hunter picking up the line.

"Hi Ronnie. What's up?"

"I just got off the phone with John. He's going to file for a warrant to get the financial information from Cole. Can you text me the contact number for Millennium in Jeff's files?"

"Sure. What's going on?" he asks. Talking about my gut instinct with Hunter is not something I've done very often, and I'm a little hesitant.

"Ah, I've just got a bad feeling Hunter," I say, vaguely.

"Come on Ronnie. Talk to me. I know we haven't worked together directly over the years, but there's no time like the present, right?" Hunter's gentle persistence wins out, and I blurt out my suspicions about Dan and the little bit of information I already know.

"I want to talk to Dan's boss at Millennium. Jeff hired him. Even if there's nothing there, I'd rather rule out any problems."

"I think it's for the best Ronnie. We can't afford to keep him either way." It's a fatalistic viewpoint, but it's reality nonetheless. I sigh.

"Oh, I've got Alex working on the bank account we found. Jeff transferred money to it from the primary Cole accounts and then made payments to a doctor, a nursing home, and money was transferred directly to an account at a different bank."

"Whatever you find, call John about it, because we're not going to be able to find out who that other account belongs to without a warrant. By the way, I'll probably go out to Vegas for the weekend. John wants me around to ID Jeff's mother."

"So are you going to take Erik with you?" he asks. I'm little amused by his familiarity. Maybe he's trying to tell me something.

"Yes. Of course. I can't leave him with Dan." I grumble.

"Are you sure this is a good idea, going out there alone?" He sounds worried, and in truth, so am I.

"I'm the only one who can ID Jeff's mother. The more info we have, the faster this case will be over with."

"Well, Alex wants to get his team started on the set tomorrow and the house as soon as possible. He's going to work on the house himself," he mentions. In a day that has been otherwise difficult, this news is a relief.

"We can give him the keys and let him work the entire weekend if that's okay with him," I suggest. When I step out of the car, I hear the commotion. A throng of female voices are calling out for Erik, but when I look around I don't see him. As I round the corner, I notice the tight crowd of people yelling and pushing to get closer to my client, who is at the epicenter of the throng. Fans surround him as they thrust books and papers at him to sign.

Son of a bitch!

"Shit, I have to go, Hunter. Text me that info." I disconnect and run toward the gate. When Erik sees me, he knows I'm not happy. Dan is standing off to the side, leaning against the gate with his arms folded, casually watching the crowd. Wilcher is a bit more proactive, standing in front of Erik, trying to control the pace of the signature requests. I push my way into the center of the group.

"Sorry folks, autograph session is over. Mr. Sinclair has to go back to work." Some of the women close by groan in disapproval. Now, I'm the enemy, and I'm about to rob them of their chance to meet their hero. Erik stares at me as he scrawls his signature across the cover of Breathless for a cute blond.

I grab him by the arm and drag him past the iron gate. "What the fuck is the problem?" His tone is castigating, and he probably feels like I embarrassed him in front of the fans, but it's for his own good.

Jesus, I sound like my mother.

"I told Dan no autographs outside the gate. After the last two days, you're crazy for taking a chance like that."

He shakes his head. "I asked Dan if it would be okay, and he said yes."

I don't say a word as I walk around to the trailer. He runs up the stairs ahead of me, and I slam the door shut, turning the deadbolt lock.

♚ CHAPTER SIXTEEN

"We may have a problem with Dan." I throw my bag down on the dinette in a huff, and he stares for a moment.

"Why, because of a few autographs?" He shakes his head at me and snorts. He's mocking me now.

"No, smart ass. He lied about his employment. I had John run a background check on him. All I know so far is that he was fired from the L.A. Police department," I say angrily. "Now, he's totally disregarding my instructions. I just don't trust him." I watch Erik closely, waiting for the moment the realization hits. When it comes, he finds it hard to believe.

"He wouldn't . . . no." He shakes his head and stares out the window, looking back toward the gate. "This is just a misunderstanding, right?"

"Look, until I know more, I don't want you going anywhere with him. Don't say a word about this either." He nods at me as I watch Dan walking up to the trailer through the window in the kitchen.

Hold your tongue, Harper. Remember your military bearing. I barely get out of my coat when my phone vibrates. Hunter has texted me the name and phone number of Dan's boss at Millennium, Richard Alfaro. Erik sits on the couch and stares at me, still a bit confused and angry

"So what are you going to say to him?"

"I don't know yet. But I don't want him around anymore. He certainly can't go with us to Vegas."

"We're going to Vegas? When?"

"This weekend. Agent Grilli is going out there to do some interviews. He wants me there to ID Jeff's mother."

Erik sighs and then shrugs. "Well, I suppose it isn't a problem. It's better than sitting around waiting for some psycho to show up."

His words have me at a loss. Nothing seems to get to him or even give him pause—not even when he's in danger. I rub my eyes, trying to wipe away the stress, but Dan has seen fit to show up at the worst time. I reach over and unlock the deadbolt when I see Agent Wilcher and Dan climbing the stairs.

As soon as Dan enters, the atmosphere becomes awkward and frosty. Erik doesn't acknowledge him and gets up from his chair. "I have to go to wardrobe."

Dan moves to follow Erik, but I stop him. "No need Dan. I've got this." He stares at me a moment, bewildered.

"Ah, okay, boss." He and Wilcher stay behind as I follow Erik out the door. He walks briskly ahead of me, his hands jammed in his pockets. He turns, and his eyes are on fire.

"Why did you leave him behind?"

I stop in my tracks, surprised by the turn in his mood. "It's better for now. I need to make a few phone calls, and I'd rather not have him lurking around. Please do me a favor—don't tell anyone about Vegas. We don't need that information getting back to Dan."

He nods, and when he disappears inside wardrobe, I decide to call to Richard Alfaro. After being transferred twice and sitting on hold for five minutes, I finally manage to get through to his receptionist.

"Hello, Mr. Alfaro's office," the overly cheerful voice says.

"Yes, hello, Mr. Alfaro, please." The receptionist asks who's calling, and I give her my name and company.

"Hold Please." As I wait, my eyes scan the area. The throng of autograph seekers has dissipated, and the traffic on the set is starting to quiet down. Most of the actors are leaving for the day. When Miss Sunshine herself comes back on the line, she informs me that Mr. Alfaro is not available now.

"Please have him call me back. It's about his employee, Dan Royce." She takes down my number, and then the line goes dead. As I disconnect the call, I turn to see Dan and Wilcher walking toward me. He sits on the bench across from me, looking calm and smug.

"So what's up boss? Where's Erik? I figured you'd be stuck to him like white on rice."

Little fucker thinks he's funny, but I don't. If you want to go there asshole, bring it on. "So why did you disregard my instructions today, Dan? I explicitly told you nothing outside the gate." I try to appear calm, but the words boil on my tongue before they leave my mouth. He looks nervous and stammers an answer.

"Um, I . . . ah. I didn't think it was such a big deal boss." He's dumbfounded by my anger. Wilcher, however, looks ready to throttle Dan as he stands behind him. Wilcher's jaw is tense, his eyes narrow as he listens to Dan speak. Apparently, we share the same opinion of Dan—dumb as a box of rocks.

"When I tell you to do something, you do it. No questions asked, and no deciding for yourself. Understand?" He nods silently and stands up. As he turns, I catch the irritated look on his face. His transgression was a stupid mistake, and if I had no other suspicions about him, I'd let the incident go. Wilcher sits down and apologizes immediately.

"I should know better. I'm sorry, it won't happen again. By the way, I just received the report on him." I pull my phone from my pocket, just as Erik runs down the stairs of the wardrobe trailer.

"Yes, Alessandro hold on!" Erik's voice is panicked and his eyes are wide as he runs toward me.

"What is it?" I demand as he thrusts the phone at me.

"It's my agent." He says.

"Mr. De Luca, how can I help you?"

"Yeah, we got a box this morning. It's addressed to Erik. You need to get down here." He sounds panicked.

"Has anyone opened it?"

"Yes. There are dead rats inside!" My stomach turns as I recall Kincaid's love of the dirty little creatures. The sweat breaks out all over my body as the adrenaline surges through me.

"Mr. De Luca, call the police. Get your employees out of the building now." I disconnect the call and give the phone back to Erik.

"Wilcher, get John on the phone and get down to Performance Artist International. They have a suspicious package. It's at 3000 Olympic Boulevard."

"I'm on it," he says as he jogs back toward the car. Erik is visibly shaken and sits at the bench with his elbows resting on the table.

"What happens now?" he asks.

"CSI will take the box into evidence," I say as I pull out my phone to text Hunter about the new threat.

"That's it?"

"Yes. Then John and Wilcher will start running down leads. We just have to wait."

With all the commotion, I barely noticed Mr. Cohen standing behind Erik. There's no need to explain what's going on, he heard the whole conversation, and the look on his face tells me he's worried.

"This is getting out of hand. Who is behind this?" he asks.

I look up at Erik, and there's a moment of recognition between us, a quick tightening of the eyes, a slight nod of the head. I don't know, but he realizes I'm not going to be specific.

"The FBI has some theories, but nothing solid yet, Mr. Cohen," I lie flawlessly, leaving out the worst of the details. There's no way I'm going to talk about Kincaid with him.

"Is that the reason for the FBI agent?"

I nod. "Yes, sir. We have a team of Cole Security technicians coming tomorrow to install a security camera system. One gate guard isn't enough anymore."

Mr. Cohen looks perturbed, and he lays into me. "Why didn't anyone inform me? This is my set after all!" His face is stiff with anger, and it's the last thing I want to deal with right now.

"You'll have to call Olympus, Mr. Cohen. They agreed to it and are footing the bill for the system." I stare him down, unwilling to let him walk all over me. Mr. Cohen nods and crumples his lips, turns toward Erik, then pats him on the back.

"All right, Ms. Harper. I'll take your word for it. Erik, can you get over to the ADR Studio and take care of that voice over? It's maybe an hour of recording." Cohen and Erik look at me for approval.

"That's fine. Dan will be here, Agent Wilcher will be tied up at PAI for the next few hours."

Cohen seems pleased and walks away. The pressure is off, at least for a few minutes.

"So what are you going to do about Dan?" Erik asks as we walk to his trailer.

"I'm waiting for John to e-mail me a copy of the report. Wilcher has a copy, but he never got a chance to show it to me. I'm not going to make a move until I read the report or talk to his old boss. He could be sitting on valuable information that will help us put a stop to Kincaid. So I need you to put on your poker face."

Erik runs up the stairs and into the trailer to gather his belongings while I wait. When he returns, we walk around back and I open the trunk to inspect the car. I make my way around the undercarriage with the SecPro, and everything is clear. Propping up the hood, I carefully check the engine compartment and make sure the GPS unit is secure.

"Mmm, now that's a beautiful view." The sound of his voice startles me, and I rise, smacking my head on the underside of the hood.

"Fuck! Could you not do that, please?" I rub the aching spot on the top of my head as he laughs. Dropping the backpack next to the tire, he steps in front of me.

"Let me see." He gently weaves his fingers into my hair and a sexy smile spreads across his lips. He tips my head up as he slips his muscular thigh between my legs. My body reacts instantly, tensing in all the right places as his hips press into mine. Kiss me, dammit. But he won't. Not here.

"Yeah, you have a nice lump here, but nothing serious," I smirk a little as he continues to look down at me.

"I could say the same about you." I bite my lip. I shouldn't say things like that. But I can't help it, the man makes my heart race. He licks his lips seductively and dips his head a bit closer to mine. I can feel his hot breath wash over me.

"Naughty girl," he whispers.

Fuck. He's better at this than I am.

Much.

His hands slip from my hair, and he walks away. I'm left aching for his touch, watching him intently as he reaches up and lowers the hood of the car and it closes with a *thunk*.

"So you ready to put that beautiful ass in the car so we can get out of here." I'm speechless, and a sexy grin appears on his face as soon as he notices.

"Erik, you can't say—" He opens the driver's side door for me.

"Oh, hello kettle. I'm pot," he says, shutting me up. He's such a smart ass.

"Just get inside. I'd like to get this over with," he says playfully. I open my mouth, but I realize it's pointless. He's in the mood to tease and torture me, reminding me of how much I like him. The truth is there has never been a moment when I didn't find him attractive, even before we met.

As I buckle in, he appears in the passenger seat beside me.

"Please sit in the back."

He looks at me and cocks his head to one side. "Really?"

He's a sarcastic bastard, and I just don't have the energy to fight. I sigh and turn the key then back out of my space.

"If you need to shoot someone, just give me the gun. I'll do it." He laughs, but I don't find it funny at all.

"Oh please, you couldn't hit the side of a barn."

He scoffs at me but doesn't reply. Once we get on the road, Erik decides to continue his probe into my background.

"So, what made you want to join the military?"

It's not that I mind these chats, but they feel so one-sided. As much as he's learned about me, in comparison, I know very little about him. I'll be damned if I'm going to fall into something with a man I barely know. Even if it is the devastatingly handsome Mr. Sinclair.

"Well, I finished high school, did some college, but I wasn't sure what I wanted to do. When the Gulf War broke out, I joined."

"And that's it?" he asks. I nod, smiling.

"Yep. What about you? What about your high school years?" Erik snorts and stares at me, then takes a deep breath before he starts to speak. Oddly, being in the spotlight is uncomfortable for him. He may be on television and movie screens all over the world, but he doesn't like talking about himself. He plays it very close to the vest.

"Well, after my dad left, I was in secondary school. I started getting in trouble, fighting a lot, that sort of thing. But I managed to get into drama college a few years later."

"Do you have siblings?" Of course, I know the answer, but I'd rather hear it from him.

"Yes. I have a younger sister and brother from my mom's second marriage."

"So what was your dad like?"

"My dad, he was a bad boy, a bit of a gangster. He was tough on us." He goes quiet, rubbing his index finger along his chin.

"Ah, so that's where you get it from."

His head snaps in my direction. "What do you mean?"

"You have some of that bad boy thing going on, that's all." I'm sure he's heard that before. After all, he's the perfect person to play the character of Axel. Erik doesn't get to expand on his story as I pull into the parking lot of the ADR Studio.

He leans over the console, gently grasps me by the neck, and pulls me to him for a quick, chaste kiss. Leaving me with a devastating smile, he jumps out of the car. I follow inside, and it's dimly lit and quiet. A solitary receptionist sits at a curved black and gold console in front of a small seating area. The three lights above her cast an eerie glow on her blond hair. She looks up from her work and smiles at Erik. "Hello, Mr. Sinclair. They're waiting for you in studio four."

We bypass the waiting area and head down the corridor. As we turn down the hall, every door is closed, and an illuminated sign indicates whether the room is in use. Each sign is lit until we reach the last room. He opens the door for me and ushers me inside with a hand at the small of my back. I'm past the point of getting used to the gesture, I'm starting to like it.

The inside of the room is large with padded walls and a large table covered with colored buttons, dials, and sliders. Two sound engineers sit at the board loading the video onto the screen, which is behind a large glass panel.

"Tom, Mitch, how are you this evening?" Erik shakes their hands, and they don't notice my presence until Erik introduces me. When I take off my coat, my gun is clearly visible. This, the engineers notice, and their eyes dart between Erik and me. "It's okay. She's security."

"You can have a seat, miss," Tom says to me. The couch is large and comfortable looking and as I sit, Erik smiles at me as laying his jacket on the couch.

"This shouldn't take too long." He turns toward the engineers, and they hand him a few sheets of the script before he disappears behind a glass door. Putting on the headphones, he stands in front of a large microphone. The scene starts to play on the screen, and the engineers give Erik his cue. He starts speaking his lines and within seconds, he gets out of sync with the video footage.

"All right Erik, let's take it from the top." Mitch restarts the video, and they start again. This time Erik gets it right. As I listen, I can't help being drawn to him, even though he's speaking as Axel. His tone and command of the words are enthralling and I walk closer to the mixing board to get a better look at him through the glass. I can't take my eyes off him as he acts out the scene, handing out kill orders to his underlings, Vasquez and Rolando, as if it were a grocery list.

He has the bark of a drill sergeant, the swagger of a gangster, and the grace of a CEO. Erik has never been any of those things, and that kind of presence has to come from somewhere. I find myself captivated, intoxicated, and completely aroused. More so than I've ever been in my life. I've seen that dominance in him before, the night John arrived unexpectedly. What seemed like petulant, childish behavior was simply Erik controlling the situation.

As I watch, my mind goes into overdrive. Something inside me wants to him to dominate me, to touch and control me, to make me feel what he wants me to feel. I bite my lip as my eyes roam over his body, watching the way his frame changes as he talks, mimicking the posture he has on-screen as he reprimands an underling. His shoulders pull back and his biceps flex, his voice becomes gravely, deeper, and even more intimidating. My body responds to it, I'm aroused by the sight of his tall, lean body moving and responding to every word, every muscle flexing as he speaks.

I catch his gaze landing on me from time to time and my heart quickens, my sex clenches viciously. I'm a puddle and my God, how I want him.

"Good work, Erik. We're going to load up the next segment so you can come in."

Erik walks back into the booth and leans over the board, talking to the two engineers for a moment. They both get up silently and walk out of the room at his behest. My heart thumps in my chest once the door closes. The way he's looking at me could set me on fire. Erik walks toward me with the languid grace of a panther and his eyes rake my body as he moves, invisibly backing me up against the wall. There's no fight here. I've already surrendered.

Placing both hands against the wall, he cages me and stares me down. "What's going through that beautifully wicked mind of yours?" His eyes roam my face and settle on my lip, which is caught between my teeth.

"Nothing," I squeak.

A hand slips off the wall and runs down the length of my arm, gently moving aside my suit jacket until I feel the warmth of his skin through my shirt. With one step, he closes the distance between us and presses himself against me. My nipples harden, and the need unfurls low in my belly. His lips hover above mine for what seems like minutes, and his eyes devour me as he waits.

I'm panting. I'm aching for him. He tilts his head and seals his lips over mine in a possessive, frantic kiss. The kind of kiss that truly lives up to all the anticipation.

A movie kiss.

The kind they probably teach in drama school—How to bring a woman to her knees 101.

The force of his need tilts my head back, and I can't contain the groan as his hand rises up my body. It moves like a snake, slithering up my waist, then over my breast, gently squeezing me before cupping my cheek. He pulls back, and I stare up at his hooded eyes.

"The next scene is a sex scene baby. You going to be okay with that?"

I nod, blinking. My brain is still scrambled from that kiss.

"Good. By the time I'm done we're going to need a hotel room." His words are purring in my ear, and I exhale in a fluttery groan. He runs his hand down my chest again, stopping for a moment to pinch the tight bud at the front of my breast, and I flinch.

"God, I want to strip you down and make love to you right here, right now," he groans. He pushes his hips into my belly, and I can feel the hardness there, and for the first time in years, I'm ravenous enough to let him do it. Kissing me quickly, his lips linger on mine for a moment, and I breathe him in, not wanting it to stop. But it does. And he's gone.

The engineers walk back into the room talking loudly over their cups of hot coffee. Erik flashes me a crooked smile.

"Let's get this wrapped up boys."

We're barely on the highway when the phone starts ringing. "Hello?" I don't recognize the number immediately.

"Ms. Harper? Richard Alfaro from Millennium, returning your call," he says in a gruff tone. Erik sighs, I can see the apprehension in his face.

"Yes, Mr. Alfaro. I have some questions about an employee of yours, Dan Royce." The line goes silent, and then I hear him clear his throat.

"Ms. Harper, I'm at a loss. Dan Royce is no longer my employee. There's not much I can tell you about him."

My hands grip the wheel tightly, and my anger boils inside. "I'm sorry, I was under the impression that he worked for you," I ask.

"Yes, he did work for me. But right around the time Olympus Television contracted security for Mr. Sinclair, we had some problems with Mr. Royce."

"Would you care to elaborate, Mr. Alfaro?" I ask, hoping he will clear up this mystery.

He hesitates and grumbles into the phone, and based on his response, I'm assuming the story isn't good.

"Right about the time Olympus began bidding for security contracts, our HR person found out that Dan was let go from the L.A. Police Department. Then a coworker brought up some serious issues about Dan's work habits, so we started investigating him. We monitored his e-mails and found he was already in contact with some of the companies that were bidding. We're not sure how he got the information, but it violated the Non-Compete clause in our terms of employment, so we let him go. It sounds like he managed to get himself hired by Cole Security."

"So you've never spoken with Jeff Cole about Mr. Royce?"

"No, Ms. Harper. We were aware Olympus was hiring security, and once we got the word from Mark Cohen, we had no further involvement."

I'm shocked. Perhaps Jeff simply guessed at the security setup for London, or Dan told him what to say.

"Mr. Alfaro, I'm assuming that Millennium has security setup for the London and Los Angeles premieres?"

"Of course, Ms. Harper. We'll be taking care of both. We have drivers and guards licensed to carry weapons in London arranged for Mr. Sinclair." I loosen my grip on the wheel, relieved that I won't be in a foreign country unprotected.

"That's good news. Thank you for the information, Mr. Alfaro."

He disconnects and I breathe again. I can't carry a weapon in the U.K., which puts me at a disadvantage. Although, I doubt Jeff or Kincaid will make it to London. Kincaid has been on every BOLO list for five years, and now that includes the no fly list. Regardless of the security arrangements, it doesn't explain why Jeff lied about needing to arrange Dan's employment with Millennium.

Erik reaches across the console and grabs my hand. His warm fingers weave between mine and we sit in companionable silence for the rest of the trip.

♟ CHAPTER SEVENTEEN

When we arrive at the house, Wilcher's car is already in the driveway. After the scare at the PAI offices, I'm sure he has quite a lot to tell me. I park the car and turn off the engine, the sound of our mutual breathing is the only noise in the car. Erik turns suddenly and releases my hand.

"We should go inside," he says quietly and slides out of the car, while waiting for me to follow. We walk up the porch together, hand in hand, and he pulls me along behind him into the house, not caring what Wilcher thinks. The move doesn't provoke Wilcher however, who is sitting on the couch, devouring an In-N-Out Burger. He nods at me and then wipes his mouth with a napkin. "Mr. Sinclair," he says tersely.

Erik nods at him and walks past without a word, heading down the hallway to the bedroom.

"What's the matter with him?"

I sit in the chair across from Wilcher, and he continues with his meal. "Richard Alfaro from Millennium called on the way here. He confirmed that Dan hasn't worked there in a while." Taking a quick sip from his cup, he hands me a folder containing the report I hoped to see before we left the set.

"Take a take a look at his work history, it seems like the L.A. Police Department let him go last year," he says, taking another sip. I skim through the first two pages and I close the folder. After the phone call with Richard Alfaro, the report really isn't necessary. I toss it onto the table and Wilcher looks at me with raised eyebrows.

"Not going to read it?"

"What would you do Wilcher?"

"Fire his ass," he smiles. He's got no love for Dan after today's screw up.

"Exactly," I smile.

Erik walks to the end of the hallway, looking more relaxed in a comfortable pair of jeans and a gray Henley sweater. His hair is just disheveled enough to be heart-stoppingly sexy. "So what's the story on Dan?"

"We'll let him go tomorrow morning before it gets too busy on set. He has a gun and some gear I need to take back."

Erik walks toward the kitchen, casually dragging a finger gently along my shoulder as he passes. "You got the keys from him right?" he says, looking toward Wilcher as he reaches into the fridge. When he returns, he hands me a bottle of water.

"Yes, but he could have made an extra copy for himself days ago," Wilcher says.

I look at Erik and I know what I'm about to say is going to cause problems with his ex. "We have to change the locks," I say quietly. Erik rolls his eyes, stares at the ceiling, and huffs in response.

"It's not too late to go to the store. We could get them done in a couple of hours," Wilcher says as he checks the time on his phone, then looks to me for approval. When I nod at him, he cleans up the remnants of his dinner and returns to the living room.

"Do you mind if I take the Mercedes?" Wilcher asks, being more polite than usual.

"No. Here's the keys." He takes them and walks out the door and Erik frowns.

"You're not coming?"

"No. I'm going to let you two get better acquainted," I giggle.

He smiles and bends over to kiss me. "I'd like to get better acquainted with removing your clothes later," he smiles, and then runs a finger gently across my jaw. "Be back soon."

The house is quiet as I walk back into the living room, and I'm relaxed and happy after a long hot shower. I fix myself a plate of left over salad and a sandwich as my thoughts return to Dan. He's in a position to cause so much trouble, and if he's in contact with Jeff or Kincaid, they're probably watching our every move. The thought chills me to the bone, and all I want is to get rid of him as soon as possible. As I finish my food, I wonder again where Jeff may be hiding. No matter how many times I call, it's always the same thing—straight to voicemail. But it doesn't stop me. Like a fool, I dial and hang up one more time. *Forget it, Harper.*

When I've tortured myself long enough, I move into the living room and sit on the couch. As I reach for the remote, Wilcher's bag catches my eye. It's beneath the coffee table, and a brown folder is sticking out of the top. As I pull it out, a picture slips from the folder and falls to the floor. It's an evidence photo from PAI of the box Mr. De Luca reported. A close-up photo shows the logo 'RNP 2012' stamped into the bottom. Setting it aside, I open the folder and flip through the pile of pictures. Most are views of the outside the box, but the next picture shows the interior, painted black with a red skull on the inside lid. Two dead rats lie in the bottom.

It's Kincaid. The rats. That was his thing.

My chest constricts and I take a deep breath. The last three photos are different from the rest, and it takes a minute for me to decipher what I'm seeing. It's the same box, but with other smaller photos laid on top. As I look closer, it's a woman, trussed up on leather shackles and chains, blindfolded, gagged, and a man is standing in between her spread legs. Jesus Christ.

The next photo is clearer and closer, and I stare at the unbound woman, lying broken and helpless on a bed.

It's me. I'm that broken and helpless woman.

He fucking took pictures!

I flip through all the photos haphazardly, some of them falling to the floor as I realize he couldn't have taken these. My heart pounds–someone else was there. Someone watched as he raped and tortured me!

My vision starts to constrict, and the ringing starts in my ears. The pain comes back to me, and I feel things, excruciating things I thought my mind and body had forgotten. The sensations flood my brain; the cold, the smell of the room, the sound of the wriggling rats crawling on me, the foul odor of his breath, and his rough hands on my skin. And the pain.

The haze of the drugs.

And more pain.

I stand, and the room tilts at an odd angle. The weight on my chest is crushing, and I stumble to the hall, but I don't make it. I sink to my knees. Everything goes black.

"Get her up!"

"No, don't move her, she could be hurt."

I hear muffled voices, but my foggy brain is unable to distinguish who is speaking. I can barely feel my limbs, but the tingling in my lips and face mean my body is slowly coming back to life.

"Ronnie. Ronnie! Say something."

My eyes flutter open, and I see him, out of focus, but I feel his warm breath. He's stroking my hair gently, telling me to breathe, and that I'm safe.

"Sarah," I whisper, maybe. I can't tell if I've truly made a sound. They talk back and forth, deciding if they should call an ambulance. I feel as if I'm a prisoner in my body, and I'm screaming but no one can hear me.

"Phone . . . Sarah," I mutter, hoping they understand.

"Okay, baby."

Again, they talk among themselves, and then the room moves. I'm up in Erik's arms. He brings me into his room, which is cool and dark, and my lungs fill with his soothing scent. After setting me down on the bed, he turns on the lamp.

"Can you tell me what happened?" he asks, worried.

"Pictures . . . in Wilcher's bag."

"I'll be right back." He stands and disappears.

Sensation slowly returns to my limbs, replacing the painful, tingling sensation brought on by my panic attack. Though, I find it far more tolerable than the embarrassment which is growing in my gut, knowing Erik is about to see those horrible pictures. The thought brings on the tears, a tidal wave of them, fat and hot, they sting my eyes and burn my cheeks as they fall to the pillow beneath my head. Up until now, my past has been words, things he hears but could never truly imagine. Unfortunately, that's all about to change, the minute he looks at those photos. It will be real, a real woman, lying on a bed, damaged and used as a sexual toy, the object of a mad man's sick fantasies.

"I understand what you're saying. I won't pressure her. She's safe with me, I promise," he says.

His words should be reassuring, but they are hard to listen to. He knows now, all of it. Between the pictures and Sarah, there's nothing left to hide. And that means the inevitable is coming. Trying to shield myself from it, I roll over and wrap myself in his blue comforter as the minutes pass by slowly.

When the door opens, he walks into the room and says nothing as he sits on the bed. The quiet in the room could suffocate us both, as he waits, maybe trying to find the right words to put an end to this misguided infatuation between us.

I swallow my pride, if only to get it over with. "What did Sarah say?"

"She told me a little bit of everything. About your friendship, your therapy, and how far you've come in the last few years."

I try to ignore the humiliation as it washes over me. The tears sting my eyes as I try to choke them back. Desperate to unravel myself from the blanket cocoon I've wrapped myself in, I barely hear him talking about his conversation with Sarah.

"Did you see the pictures?" I cry.

He hesitates. "Yes." The single word is an anguished whisper. My heart shrivels in my chest, knowing he will see me as that broken and abused woman in those pictures. But that's my fault. I opened myself up to him, but only a little. I can close up that wall. Whimpering and struggling, I pull myself free of the blanket and walk toward the door.

"Don't run away," he croaks. He's hurting, I can hear it. I'm one step from the hallway when he stops me.

"Ronnie. Come. Back. Here. Please." That low, commanding tone of his rumbles through me, turning my legs to jelly. My heart races when he talks to me that way. It's something I never thought I'd respond to, but I'm reined in and calmed by the sound of his voice. Leaning against the door frame, I take a deep breath.

"You're running because you think that bothers me?" he says quietly. Those images would disturb almost anyone. Somehow, he's able to ignore it, and I'm amazed by the strength of his will. I look back, and he's behind me. His breath falls silently on my shoulder and his fingers pull back the hair I'm hiding behind.

"It doesn't bother me, because I see an amazingly strong women in those pictures. Someone who kept fighting and never gave up. Why would I want to give up someone who I have more respect and admiration for than I ever thought was possible. You're the same woman who took my breath away the moment I saw you."

My shoulders slump under his firm grip, and I melt against him. He sees me differently than I ever would have guessed, and I close my eyes, still struggling to believe that I deserve such a sweet and sexy man who would want me, in spite of my terrifying past.

"I don't see the woman in those pictures. I never will." I turn in his arms and lower my head, pressing my face into his t-shirt. His strength and warmth comfort me as I listen to the steady rise and fall of his breathing, his thoughtfulness moving me in a way no one ever has. He can be such a pain, yet say such wonderful things, perfect things that make me feel safe and best of all, wanted. The sudden thought of anyone ripping this man away from me is so painful it causes my fingers to claw into his biceps. The urge to cry and release it all becomes overwhelming.

"It's okay baby. Everything she told me, it's all okay."

Sobbing, I collapse against his hard body, and he lifts me and carries me to the bed. He climbs up onto the mattress and then lowers me gently. All the pain of the last five years comes out in a torrent of whimpering sobs as I cling to him, burying my face in his neck, but all I hear is his gentle reassurance. "Let it all go baby."

I press myself against him and my legs interlace with his. My hands fumble for the hem of his t-shirt, frantically seeking the warmth of his body. The delicious feeling of his skin against mine and his hard body pressing up against me are the only things that could rid me of the deep ache inside me. His skin is like velvet on steel, stretched tight over the curves and furrows of his well-defined chest. I flatten my palms and push his shirt up, almost to his chin as I press my lips against his perfectly formed pecs, kissing slowly from one side to the other. He reacts, his breaths come quicker and I can feel his frantic heartbeat against my lips. When I look up at him a subtle change darkens his eyes, a sudden fog passes over them, and his hands grip my wrists.

"No, baby. It's not the right time for this. I don't want to use sex to make you feel cared for and safe."

I suddenly feel foolish as he looks down at me, his eyes gently searching my face. I squirm in his arms, but a quick jerk of his bicep against my back pins me. His face is a mask of silent strength and fierce protectiveness I've come to adore.

"Don't think for a second that I don't want you." He says with enough quiet determination to make me believe him instantly. But his lips twitch in response to the touch of my hands as my fingers climb over his shoulders.

My lips press against his, eager to feel his desire as my tongue tries to coax his out, but it doesn't take him long to catch on, and he breaks our kiss.

"Don't argue," he says quietly with that commanding tone. I laugh softly as he lays a gentle kiss on my forehead and then reaches back to turn off the light.

"Sleep now, baby girl."

His voice in the darkness is the last thing I hear. All the stress of the day leaves me, and I'm asleep in what seems like moments.

I wake in the night, burning hot and my sweat-drenched clothes cling to me uncomfortably. I'm imprisoned by Erik's heavy limbs, my leg is pinned between his, and his arm is slung across my waist. Desperate to free myself from his grip, I force myself to move slowly as I try not to wake him. Once I'm free, I slide off the bed and into the bathroom, quietly closing the door behind me.

The enormous tub dominates the room. It's an impressive marble creation, elegantly sculpted from one giant piece of rock, beautifully veined in hues of ivory, gold and bronze, and it's bathed in soft light from above. I turn the corner to find the large glass-encased shower. The toilet is next to it, enclosed in a small cubicle, and I'm thankful for the privacy.

When I return to the bedroom, the soft glow of the bedside lamp illuminates his features, casting dark shadows along the sharp lines of his jaw and nose. He lies on his side, waiting for me. Struck by the incredible symmetry of his features and the insanely ripped muscles in his torso, I completely forget that I removed my heavy sweatpants in an attempt to escape his body heat. He sits up, tossing back the blanket, revealing more of his body. He looks so enticing, I could be completely naked right now, and I wouldn't notice.

"I didn't mean to wake you." I say, watching as his eyes rake me, from my head, down my bare legs, then to my feet. He's removed his clothing as well, and the carelessly thrown back sheets reveal his blue boxer briefs.

"What happened to your sweats?" he asks, his lids heavy and his voice raspy from sleep.

I move closer to the bed. "I took them off. You're like a human electric blanket wrapped around me. I was hot."

He smiles and nods toward the door behind me. "Get one of my shirts from the closet." I turn and step into the closet, and as I take a quick look at Catriona's clothes, I realize it's useless. Clearly, she's either incredibly slim, or has very small breasts, because not a single shirt of hers fits me. My choice is obvious, it's one of his shirts or nothing. And nothing could get me in trouble.

Just past the elegant black and gray suits are his dress shirts, all neatly pressed and still wrapped in plastic from the cleaners. Beyond those are his more casual shirts, and I find a purple and black plaid, which isn't too heavy. I pull off my sweatshirt and shrug into his shirt, buttoning it to the top. Fortunately, it's long enough to skim the top of my thighs and cover my backside. I turn off the light and step out, hoping he doesn't mind. He smiles, but it disappears quickly and he licks at the seam of his lips. He beckons me closer with a couple of fingers.

I go.

I stand in front of him and he reaches out for me, his large hands gripping the back of my thighs. Pulling me in between his legs, he looks up at me with those inky blue eyes. My insides unfurl with something like desire mixed with a healthy dose of fear.

"Erik . . . " I want to tell him to go slow, but I can't spit out the words. There's no way I can tell him how far he can go if I don't even know myself. He must sense my nervousness, and he takes my hands as he moves back on the bed, making room for me.

"Get in," he smiles. I crawl beside him, and we lie facing each other with his arm draped around my waist. He kisses me gently while his hand finds its way into my hair, pulling me closer with each nibble. I open my mouth and run my tongue along the seam of his lips, and he opens for me as our tongues meet, twisting around each other in a slow, sweet dance.

Both arms find their way around me, one hand in my hair, the other gripping the small of my back. I'm anchored to him, as he pulls me even closer, each kiss slowly chipping away at years of pain and fear. Skin against skin, our heat melts together and our breaths mingle. The riot of sensations builds quickly and soon overwhelms me. I break the kiss and nuzzle my head into his neck, sighing and maybe shaking a little. His hands caress my back, up and down, slow and reassuring.

"Don't be afraid, sweetheart. I'll only go as far as you can handle. Sarah told me what to do and not do." His words are low, soft, and calm, but even with that reassuring tone, I can't hide my surprise.

"What exactly did she suggest?" I prop myself up on my elbow.

"She said the best way to get you comfortable with me is to go slow. Touching and displaying affection is fine, but no sex. Kissing is fine, but no sex. Intimacy, but no sex."

I stare at him for a moment, trying to absorb what he just told me. I'm shocked they talked about all this, and I don't know whether I should be angry at her, or grateful. He'd never force me or hurt me, that I'm sure of and suddenly I feel comfortable enough to weave my fingers into his hair as I pull him to my mouth for a soft kiss, and he responds, wrapping himself around me. His hand finds my thigh, and he pulls my leg over his hip, hooking it around his.

Wet lips travel along my jaw, and dip into the collar as he nuzzles my neck. My skin is on fire as thousands of tingles rocket just underneath the surface, concentrated right where his lips make contact at any given moment. Soft squeaks and moans vibrate in my throat as he nibbles and kisses his way across my collarbone. He reaches up and opens a button and then another. He pushes the shirt open, giving him greater access to my cleavage, but he can only go so far. He kisses down my chest until he's stopped by my white sports bra. I was still wearing it under my sweatshirt when I fell asleep.

"Are you okay?" he breathes and then kisses my forehead.

"Yes," I whisper as he lays another soft kiss on my lips. He gazes at me, his eyes covering every inch of my face, his fingers trace along the contours of my cheek, my jaw, and my throat, memorizing every curve and every line. I feel almost embarrassed as he inspects me, waiting for him to find the flaws. When I try to bury my face against his chest, he laughs.

"What is it?" he asks, as his fingers find my chin, gently lifting my face to his. I close my eyes and shake my head. There's no way I can tell him that I've recently been comparing myself to his ex, a tall slender woman with very little up top. We're on opposite ends of the spectrum, and I wonder what he sees in me and my "baby got back" type of body.

"Oh, I see. You don't think you're beautiful," he says teasingly, causing me to blush more. "Well, you're just going to have to get used to it baby," he says and kisses me quickly. Those fingers make quick work of the buttons and when he pushes the shirt off my shoulder, I feel even more exposed than I did a moment ago. Coaxing me onto my back, he looks me over, his eyes following the path of his roaming hands. He smiles from ear to ear as he lazily traces circles around my belly with his fingertips. When I try to cover my lightly padded midsection, he stops me.

"Why are you covering up?" He pulls at my wrist and when I try to look away, he quickly captures my chin between his thumb and index finger. His determined stare melts my fear.

"I don't like my belly," I admit.

"That's ridiculous. You're beautiful."

"It's too . . . round," I say, complaining about the one area of my body I hate, especially as the years creep up on me.

Resting his palm on my belly, he squeezes a little and then slides his hand along the waistband of my underwear to my hips. "You women all think you're fluffier than you really are," he says, capturing a handful of my backside as he squeezes again. "I like this. Skeletal women do nothing for me baby. I'd rather have a little somethin' to hold on to." He kisses me gently and stops. The tip of his nose rubs against mine and our eyes meet. "You're perfect," he whispers against my lips. Now I know he's delusional. I shake my head and laugh.

"Oh, is that how it is?" He props himself up on his elbow, then bends down to nuzzle my neck. "This right here is the most perfect earlobe I've ever nibbled on."

His fingers trace over the curve of my shoulder. "This arm? So soft, skin as smooth as a baby," He kisses gently down my arm.

"These hands. Soft and deadly at the same time." He kisses my palm and my fingers caress the stubble along his jaw. Scalding tears begin to well up in my eyes as I watch him. I'm in awe, as he moves along every part of me, describing what he loves and why I'm perfect. To him. Even my toes. He must have spent a full five minutes describing how each one of my toes is perfect.

"This back. It's beautiful, strong and holds up so much responsibility. And . . ."

His fingers trace over the large patch of skin just below my shoulder blade. It's bumpy and raised, quite different from the rest. He goes quiet as he inspects it, moving lower to touch the long, roping scars that cover my lower back, all remnants of Kincaid's horrific beatings.

"Erik, please. Just forget it," I say as I shrug the shirt back over my shoulders.

"No, I'm not . . ."

I swing my legs over the side of the bed, trying to escape the embarrassment, but he wraps his arms around me, capturing me before I can sprint back to my room.

"No, don't run. You don't have to explain," he whispers in my ear. His hands clasp mine, and he wrestles the shirt free of my grip, pulling it off me completely as my eyes fill with tears.

"These are your badge of honor, baby. Wear them proudly because you survived it. And you're beautiful."

The alarm wakes us both from a deep sleep. Erik rolls over, freeing his limbs from mine as he reaches for his phone. I peel my lids open and watch him through hazy eyes. He's beautiful, even from the back. He rolls over and reaches for me as a smile lights up his groggy face.

"Good morning beautiful," he says as he smooths my messy bedhead.

I snuggle against him for a moment, not wanting to leave. Last night was wonderful, Erik was sweet and romantic and playful. But the same old problems came back to haunt me. As I look out the window, I long for the day when this won't be part of my life. When I can successfully say I've put it behind me.

He didn't give in when I tried to sidestep the issue of the scars. The horrible truth that a lunatic carved his name on my back and beat me bloody quickly put a chill on Erik's sexy, playful mood. He wrapped himself around me like a vine, trying to get close enough to blot out the disturbing images. For most people, the idea of someone doing something that vile only happens on television shows.

"I suppose we should get up," I mumble against his skin. He groans a little, but he sits up and waits as I swing my legs off the bed. I slip my sweats on again and look back.

"Not getting up?" I joke.

"Uh . . . " he glances down, and even covered by the sheet, I can see the effects of his morning . . . arousal, and he wears an embarrassed grin.

♟ CHAPTER EIGHTEEN

I decide not to tease him and return to my bedroom to dress. I'm content and relaxed, and for the first time, unconcerned if anyone finds out about my relationship with Erik. Why should I care about Dan, a worthless excuse for a security agent and Jeff, a dangerous liar. They mean nothing to me now, and it's time I started living for me, doing what makes me happy. While keeping our relationship low-profile and out of the tabloids is smart for now, I'm not going to hide forever. I've spent too many years hiding, and I'm finally waking up and moving out into the sunshine. And it feels good.

As I step out into the hallway, I can hear Wilcher in the kitchen. "Morning Wilcher." He nods as he pours water into the coffee maker. I retrieve the canister of coffee from the closet and hand it to him. As I pull out a cup of yogurt from the fridge, Erik walks into the living room and drops his backpack near the door.

"So what's on the agenda?" Wilcher asks.

"Firing Dan."

Both of them gape at me, stunned by the bluntness of my response so early in the morning. I'm all business today. And I've had about enough of people betraying me.

"Wilcher, can you stay here and finish installing the locks, please?" I ask. He glares at me for a moment and I can anticipate his argument; he's FBI, not the local handyman.

"That's not my—"

"Just do it. I need to take care of Dan myself. I have a company to run," I snap. I walk out of the kitchen leaving Erik and Wilcher to their coffee, not caring what objections he may raise in my absence.

In my bedroom, I pull out the large bag containing my gear, and dig through it looking for the small Taser. When I find it I slip it into my messenger bag. As I collect the rest of my gear, I hear Erik talking. Wilcher is pleading his case, but Erik is not budging an inch. I make it out the door with the vests in my hand and neither of them notice me as they discuss whatever Wilcher is griping about. Once I return to the living room, Erik is outright yelling at Wilcher.

"Fuck off man. You have no business judging her or me for that matter." He slams the mug that he never filled on the counter, and the handle breaks off in his hand. "Just do what you're told," he yells. Wow. What happened?

He turns toward the door, not realizing I'm in the room and stops in his tracks. His face is contorted with frustration, and his lips are pressed into two hard lines. I raise an eyebrow at him, and he brushes past me, walking out the front door. I turn and stare at Wilcher, wondering what he said to get Erik so upset. Walking up to the kitchen counter, I pull on my holster.

"Damn, I thought seven years in the FBI would have taught you to rein in your attitude. I guess nothing changes," I say with a smirk. He snorts a reply, which I ignore as I walk out. This was going to happen eventually, I just didn't think it would happen so fast.

As I walk out the door, I'm surprised to see Erik sitting in the driver's seat. He looks up at me and it's obvious he's still a bit steamed from his exchange with Wilcher. "Gimme the keys," he says, holding his hand out the window. I don't argue.

I buckle in and he takes off down the driveway, turning sharply onto the main road. Unfamiliar with such a powerful engine, he stomps on the gas, and I'm thrown back into my seat. "Take it easy."

He laughs at me and cocks an eyebrow. Once we're on the highway, I bring up the awkward topic of money, and the state of Cole Security's bank accounts.

"I'm going to need you to write a few checks," I blurt out. I figure there's no better time for this. No matter when I do it, asking for money from a man you've been intimate with is awkward.

"For what?" he asks, confused.

"To pay for the clothes, the dresses, and the security system for your house. The company is almost bankrupt. We can't afford to pay the employees unless you help cover those costs." I say my guts twist with humiliation. He thinks for a minute, rubbing at the hair on his chin, making me wait for long minutes before speaking again.

"I think I can manage that. After all, I want you to look like a princess at the premiere." He pauses, and a wicked smile spreads across his face. "A princess with a Glock . . . between her legs."

Holy fuck, the look in his eyes could melt the polar ice caps. A stuttering laugh comes from my mouth, he knows how apprehensive I am, but he's not going to give up on the idea.

"Keep it up, caveman. I'll show up in overalls and a Duck Dynasty t-shirt."

He laughs, grabs my hand, and kisses it gently. But his mood changes, he becomes pensive.

"Can I ask you something?" he says as his eyes flick to me. He seems hesitant but I nod.

"The other night at the ADR studio—I touched you, I got a little . . . um, suggestive with you. But you didn't panic. Why?"

I exhale with a grumble. *How do I answer this?*

"I'm sorry. Forget it," he says, taking my hand and kissing it again.

"No. I'm not mad. I'm trying to find the right words. At the studio, I wasn't bothered by it because I knew nothing was going to happen. You wouldn't take the chance of someone walking in on us, not with the way you feel about gossip and the tabloids. When we're alone, there's no safety net. I'm vulnerable and naked. And it just feels like we are moving . . . a bit fast. Does that make sense?" I ask.

My reasons are simple, yet they make getting to know a man very complicated. It's more than wanting to go out on a date or spending time together. Although, having the time and space to date like a normal couple would be a luxury. I'd love to get to know him normally, at my own pace. But dating someone like Erik is not easy. He's the kind of man every woman dreams of—a drop-dead gorgeous bad boy with a sensitive side, and he's interested in me. I suppose I should take what I can get.

"Yes. It does. I'm sorry if I . . . "

He doesn't get a chance to finish. "You haven't," I smile.

"So in an ideal situation, how would you want things to progress with a guy?" he asks.

"I don't know Erik."

He sighs loudly, frustrated by my need to protect myself. I feel lost, and my natural reaction is no reaction, so I shut down.

"Please Ronnie. I'm not sure how to move forward without frightening you," he pleads. I look at him as he drives, and my heart leaps around in my chest. His thoughtfulness amazes me sometimes, and here I am, giving him nothing to work with. Thinking back to my life prior to Kincaid seems like ancient history, I barely remember my last real date.

"Well, slowly. I mean, I was never the type to jump into bed with a guy right away. Maybe some romantic dates, just spending time together. No pressure."

He nods, thinking. "Hmm, so romantic and creative. Nothing too fancy?"

"Exactly."

Unfortunately, pulling off a quiet, under the radar date with a high-profile celebrity is a difficult task. Fans recognize him and having a bodyguard in tow everywhere we go would put a damper on the romance. He's silent a bit longer, and I worry that he's come to the same conclusion I have. Openly dating is difficult, if not dangerous.

He stops in the middle of the street and waves out the window at Michael and Dan. They're both staffing the gate today, and there's a small group of technicians in blue uniforms on ladders directly on the other side of the iron fence that surrounds the property. Though I should be relieved, the sight of Dan has my nerves on edge. It's only a small comfort to know that if anything goes awry there will be working cameras to capture it.

Erik parks behind his trailer, and as we walk inside, he notices the vests in my hand. "Wow. You need those?" he asks.

"Yes. I'd rather not get shot."

"When are you going to do this?" Erik drops his backpack on the dinette and walks toward me. The concern is etched on his face, and tiny lines form around his eyes. His hand sifts through my hair before he cups the back of my neck and pulls me in close. I inhale the scent of him, a delicious mix of spicy citrus, his skin, and leather, and I want to drown in it.

"As soon as I talk to Hunter. Before the set gets too busy, in case things get ugly."

He nods and leans down for a slow, deep kiss, and his soft lips glide gently over my mouth. It feels so good to be in his protective embrace and to be kissed by him that nothing else matters. The world and all its problems could fall away, and I wouldn't care as long as he keeps kissing me.

"Better make the call," he whispers against my ear. He moves away quickly and I'm left trying to recover my wits. I pull off my coat and strap on the vest, then cover it with my trench coat. Dan would notice it if I didn't cover up, and the sight of it would raise an alarm for him.

"I'd like for you to go," I ask as I button my coat.

Erik looks at me and his eyebrows tick up in surprise. "Are you kidding me? There's no way I'm going to leave you alone with him." I can hear the bitterness and disgust in his voice. He feels betrayed by Dan and protective of me. It's a bad combination.

"Then you'll need to wear this."

He groans before he reaches out for the vest. "Do I really—?"

Erik doesn't finish because he knows what my answer will be. He nods, pulls off his jacket and flannel shirt, and in a minute, he's strapped the Kevlar around his chest.

I slip my phone from my pocket and dial. After the second ring, Hunter grunts a hello, making me smile a little. He must have had a long night.

"Morning Hunter."

I watch Erik from behind as he shrugs into his flannel and jacket again.

"Anything on Dan?" I ask.

"No. Jeff could have paid him in cash. There's no way to know if Dan owns the account until John gets a warrant. But Alex said he'd check the security footage to see if Dan is on there," he says. It's a great idea. It would prove a prior relationship easily.

"By the way, Wilcher sent me the background report on Dan." Hunter exhales sharply into the phone. Even he seems perplexed by the depth of Jeff's lies. "You going to get rid of him?" he asks.

"Yes. As soon as I hang up," I say as I slip my gun into my coat pocket.

"Then get to it. And be careful. Call me when you're done."

"Will do Hunter."

I put the phone down on the table and reach into my pocket. I hold the small device in my hand as Erik looks at me, confused.

"What's this," he asks.

"Be careful, it's a Taser."

He frowns and sighs. He's not the weapon type, I can see it. He'd rather throw punches.

"It's the next best thing to a gun. If anything happens, at least you can protect yourself," I look up at him and try to force a smile. But it fades quickly. He hesitates a moment before he reaches out and takes the Taser from me.

"Okay, how do you use this thing?" he breathes. It takes about five minutes of instruction before Erik feels comfortable using the Taser, showing him the safety release, the trigger and explain the best points of contact on the body.

"Okay. I think I've got the idea." He turns the safety on again and slips it into his pocket. Even though he says he's okay, I can hear the stress in his voice. The muscles in his neck flex and clench as I dial Dan's number.

"Dan Royce . . . oh, morning boss."

"Morning, Dan. Come on down to the trailer. I need to talk to you about some stuff."

I shove my phone into my pocket. "Let's go."

Erik follows me outside, and we descend the stairs just as Dan walks in behind the last group of cars rolling through the gate. As he jogs up to us, my shoulders tense.

"Morning boss, Mr. Sinclair." After his monumental fuck up yesterday, he seemed on his best behavior this morning. "Any news from the FBI?"

Erik looks at me and shifts nervously from foot to foot. "No Dan. I have some other things to discuss with you. Why did Jeff hire you?"

Dan's eyes dart back and forth from me to Erik. "You know why," he says, with a hint of defiance.

I huff. "It doesn't explain why he'd hire you or how he knew you. It doesn't explain why he'd even bother with you if you'd been fired from the L.A. Police Department."

Dan's hands drop to his sides, and he smirks as I flip off the safety of the gun hidden in my pocket.

"Checking into my background I see. You should be more worried about Erik, and yourself. Besides, what does it matter?" He suddenly seems cocky—almost defiant.

"Take off your jacket, slowly. Remove the holster and set it on the ground."

Dan pulls off his brown suede jacket and drops it on the stairs. "This is a fucking joke, right?" he smirks. The holster and gun land with a thud on the concrete between us.

"No Dan. What is your relationship with Jeff, and how much do you know about this case?" I demand.

"He hired me to work with Erik and keep Kincaid away from him." Dan just inadvertently confirmed my suspicions. Jeff knew all along that it was Kincaid behind the threats.

"Did you have anything to do with delivering the threats and the boxes of lingerie?" Erik decides to jump in against my wishes. His question is one I would have asked, but coming from him, it's totally unexpected.

"I'm not going to answer that," Dan smirks and shakes his head. He might not be too bright, but he knows not to incriminate himself any further, and that only angers Erik.

"You motherfucker!" he yells. I pull Erik back by the arm, and his free hand rises up instinctively. He stares at me for a second, realizing that he nearly hit me, and he instantly backs down. I shake my head at him, trying to let him know there's no point in getting angry.

"Give me the keys, Dan," I demand. His sarcastic smile is infuriating, and as his hand disappears into his pocket, my heart starts to pound. Dan realizes this is over and nothing he says will change my mind. He tosses two key rings to the ground, one for the house and one for the set.

"You know something, you're a fucking cunt," Dan hisses at me and it's the only excuse Erik needs to rush him. He crouches down low as he runs at Dan, forcing a shoulder into his sternum, using the Krav Maga techniques he learned the other day.

"Erik! NO! Get off him!" He has Dan on his back, and he is throwing rapid punches, making contact with Dan's mouth and nose. Dan tries to fight back, but he only makes contact once or twice. I wrap my arm around Erik's neck, bracing it with the other hand, and I put him into a chokehold. He stills immediately, and I drag him off Dan and let him fall backward to the concrete as I pull my gun from my pocket. Dan scrambles to his feet and starts to run toward us, but the Glock aimed at the center of his chest stops him.

"Okay . . . Okay." Dan is out of breath and bleeding, but he puts his hands up and takes a few steps backward before turning and running behind the trailers to get into his car.

"Stay here!" I yell at Erik, as I cut between two trailers. I watch as Dan jumps into his car and backs out of his space. The tires squeal as he stomps on the gas, taking off for the gate and almost hitting Michael as he races out onto the open street. Running back to the trailer, I find Erik—bruised and bleeding slightly from his lip—still waiting where I left him. His breathing is uneven and fast, and his eyes flare with anger. As soon as Erik sees me, he stomps up the steps and flings the door open, which bangs loudly against the wood railing behind it. He is either agitated from his fight with Dan, or he's mad at me for pulling him away. It's clear he can fend for himself, and I can only imagine how much damage he would have done if I hadn't interrupted.

He flops down on the couch and lets out an angry grunt. His biceps flex as he balls his hands into fists and punches at the cushions on the couch. From across the room, I can see the redness bloom on his cheek, even though the stubble. He's going to need ice or it will become a dark bruise very fast.

"I'll be right back."

I run to craft services and the young Asian man goes to work filling a bag with ice. While I wait, I send a quick text to Hunter, just to let him know it's done. I take the bag of ice and run back to the trailer, and when I reach the steps, Michael is waiting for me.

"What happened with Dan, Ms. Harper?" he asks, out of breath.

"He's a fake, Michael. He lied about his background. He won't be back and don't let him on set. You'll need to get those locks re-keyed." Michael nods at me and turns to go as I walk up the stairs. When I step inside the trailer, the mood is gloomy, and Erik is still simmering with anger.

"I got you some ice," I say, trying to calm my breathing. I sit next to him and place the bag against his cheek.

"That's not necessary, I'm all right," he tips his head to the side and looks at me with frustration. He tries to pull my hand away, but I scold him.

"Don't argue," I say, as he gives a little laugh. "You can't do that again Erik. You're going to get yourself killed. No more protecting me, understood?" He lolls his head toward me, and I remove the ice from his face.

"Look, no one talks to my . . . I don't let anyone talk to women that way." His nostrils flare, and there's a flash of fury in his eyes, but in a second it's gone. I wish I knew what was behind this protectiveness, this raging desire to keep a woman safe.

"Erik, they're just words," I plead. He shakes his head adamantly and cuts me off.

"Baby, you'd better get used to it because I'm not going to change. I've been this way since I was a kid. My dad . . . " He turns away and doesn't finish his sentence. But I have a feeling I know.

"Was your father abusive?"

He slips his arm around me and his hand comes to rest on the small of my back, a spot that seems perfectly made for him. My skin starts to tingle from the warmth of his hand, and every ounce of my focus is drawn to the sensation.

"Yes," he whispers as his hand moves up so his fingers can sift through my hair. His eyes look distant and lost, almost as if he's remembering something painful.

"What is it, Erik?" I ask, hoping to bring him out of his melancholy.

"My mother had hair just like yours when I was a kid," he says, pausing a moment. "My father got drunk one night. They were arguing, and he accused her of cheating. Even though she insisted there was no one else, he didn't believe her and as punishment, he tied her to a chair and cut off her hair." He takes a deep breath and exhales when he hears my gasp. The mental image is terrifying, and now I understand his protectiveness. He pulls me close, and his arm bands around me tightly. I rest my head against his chest, and I feel like it's the first time I've been able to breathe in hours, maybe days. It's the first time since I set foot in this town that we're alone, truly alone where there's no need for either of us to hide our feelings. He kisses my forehead gently and then pulls away.

He walks into the small bathroom and flips on the light. Dropping the bag of ice into the sink, he yells back to me.

"Mark is not going to be happy."

♟ CHAPTER NINETEEN

M r. Cohen and Adriana carefully inspect the darkening bruise on Erik's jaw and the cut on his lip. "Yeah, this is difficult to hide. I can cover up the bruising, but the swelling is a problem." They continue to talk as I take a seat in the corner and dial Hunter.

"Hi Ronnie, are you okay?"

"Hi Hunter. Yeah, we're fine," I say, explaining the full ordeal with Dan.

"Jeez, what a prick. But I'm glad you're both safe. Hey, I put in a call to the people at Olympus. I put the ball in their court about hiring extra security."

I'm relieved. Even with the cameras, Michael can't manage this set by himself until the show wraps.

"Thanks, that's great news. Oh, I spoke to Mr. Sinclair this morning. He's going to cover the cost of the security system," I say. "Perfect. That should keep us going for a little while." The relief in Hunter's voice is clear, and when the idea hits me, I figure he might be agreeable to a business proposal.

"So how would you feel about an outside investor? Because I was thinking of calling Michael Cummings," I admit.

"That name sounds familiar. Wasn't he your last client," he asks.

"Yes. He might be willing to invest."

"Hmm. You going to tell him what's going on?" He sounds apprehensive, and I immediately realize why. Even though I was able to build a comfortable working relationship with Mr. Cummings, explaining to him that my ex-husband and boss has bankrupt the same company I'm asking him to invest in would be awkward. And a long shot, at best. My stomach sinks to my knees as I cave in to the idea that maybe it's best to let the business go. Finding an entrepreneur willing to invest in a company in this much trouble would be unlikely.

"Ronnie, I didn't mention this before, but I have some money." Hunter says. I'm confused and I remain silent for a beat.

"What are you suggesting, Hunter?" If he's offering what I think he is, we might be able to save the company, and our reputations. With my early retirement from the military, my reduced pension pays my rent, allowing me to save a good portion of my salary. But I don't have enough to fund Cole Security by myself.

"Well, I've had some family money sitting in the bank for years earning interest. It may take a few days, but I could pull it out."

"Well, hello partner," I laugh.

I can almost hear his smile through the phone, and Hunter never smiles. "Are you sure you want to do this?" he asks.

"Yes. I've been saving my military pension all these years. Are we really doing this?" I ask, excited. My nerves are tingling. I never dreamed I'd be plotting the hostile takeover of Cole Security when I rolled out of bed this morning. Running the company with Hunter gives me everything I want, everything I've been working toward. Except for one thing. I'd have to move back to Los Angeles. Sarah might not like it, but Erik will be thrilled.

"I suppose so! But look, I'll do this is on one condition. You run things," he says surprising me. He's clearly been thinking about this over the last few days.

"Hunter, you probably have more available cash than me, and—"

"Ronnie, money isn't the issue. The other day at the FBI office, you took control of the situation. You knew exactly what needed to be done, and you didn't wait for someone else to do it. It was impressive. You think well under pressure, and you'd make a great CEO."

The responsibility that just landed on my shoulders is immense and I don't want to let him or the employees down. And if he were to lose every penny of his savings, I'd never forgive myself, because if it's me at the helm, it would be entirely my fault. Yet, I can't turn away from the challenge or the renewed hope I'm feeling. A whole new world of possibilities is opening up to me, and I think I should grab it. My life seems to be feast or famine lately.

"I'm flattered Hunter," I say as my mind swirls fear and excitement. "But, I don't think I could do this without you. I haven't been around much the last five years. You know the employees far better than I do, and they respect you. So regardless of money, I'd feel more comfortable if we shared the big decisions, equally."

"You got it," he laughs. It's good to hear my new partner happy. "Let me go, I need to call Paul and get him started on this," he says, anxious to get the business out of Jeff's name and under our control.

"I need one more thing, Hunter. Do the initials RNP sound familiar?"

"No. Why?"

"The box that arrived at Mr. Sinclair's agent yesterday had the initials RNP 2012 stamped on the bottom. Maybe there's something in Jeff's files or a check paid out to some business named RNP."

"Okay, let me write this down," I can hear him shuffling around and opening doors before he speaks again. "RNP 2012 you said? I'll have a look and let you know."

Hunter is happy, but unfortunately, I've given him another mystery to solve.

I follow Erik back to his trailer, and we wait for a production assistant to drop off some script changes. Taking Adriana's advice, Mr. Cohen decided against any close up shots of Erik due to the swelling and his split lip. A young woman knocks on the door and peeks inside.

"Mr. Sinclair, here are your script changes." She smiles sweetly and disappears. He looks at the small number of pages she handed him.

"I think I'll be done just after lunch," he chuckles. He sits next to me, dropping the script on the couch. I have no complaints about a short day. Our weekend trip to Nevada is sure to be long and tiring, so I'd love to hit the gym again before we go. Releasing the day's stress would be a huge help, for both of us.

"Maybe we can go to the gym?" I ask.

He presses his lips together and nods. "Hmm, maybe," he says.

I raise an eyebrow and cock my head to the side; he's hiding something. His hesitation changes to a heart stopping smile as I stare at him.

"What are you up to?" I ask, holding my breath.

He turns serious, and his eyebrows rise. "Nothing," he says, pretending to be affronted.

I laugh and shake my head and he cocks his head so he's mirroring me. "You're laughing at me?"

"No."

"You, Ms. Harper, are a terrible liar."

I giggle more. "No, it's just . . . You're planning something. I can see it." I point a finger at him, and he grabs my hand, pulling me into his lap for a kiss. His open mouth seals over mine, and his tongue darts between my lips, touching and stroking inside me desperately. The kiss becomes frantic, and my hands roam his chest, feeling the taut muscles beneath his shirt flex under my fingers. The kiss only lasts a few more seconds before he winces and pulls away, rubbing his thumb over the cut on his lip. I rest my head against his, breathless and dizzy from his intensity, every inch of my body drowning in desire so strong I feel consumed by it.

"We should . . . the door isn't locked," my voice is a raspy whisper, and while some part of me wants to remain cautious, his playful teasing makes me desperate to have him.

"Okay beautiful."

He calls me beautiful like it's my name. I sigh against his skin, and he nuzzles me, running his nose along my cheek toward my ear. "We'll continue this later."

I slip off his lap and he stands, offering me a hand up off the couch. He's made my legs wobbly, and I need it.

"Time to go," he smiles. He holds my hand as we walk to the door, but drops it as soon as we step outside. The cast is gathered off in the distance, the security crew is working on the cameras near the gate, and Michael is at his usual post. Everything seems right in the world for a change. As we walk toward the far end of the set, Mr. Cohen and several of the principal cast have gathered and are waiting for filming to begin. Then I see Melissa lurking on the fringe of the crowd. She's wearing an outfit that's more revealing than usual, her black lace bra is clearly visible under the thin white tank top, and her jeans look like the tightest skinny variety on Earth. Erik walks off, giving me a quick wink as he joins the crowd.

While he's filming, I have plenty of time to make a few calls. I find my usual spot at a picnic bench near craft services and have a seat. My first priority is Sarah.

Me: Hey, hun. I hear you told Erik quite a few details about my past. While I would have liked some say in the matter, I understand why you did it. I need some advice. Txt me when you're free.

As I watch Mr. Cohen talk to the actors, everyone takes their places. He and the camera operator work out the blocking and camera angles while Melissa and Erik move into their positions. Erik turns my way, and the displeasure shows on his face as he raises an eyebrow and frowns. Ever since Melissa's underhanded stunt, Erik's working relationship with her has been tense at best.

Mr. Cohen calls for action, and the group starts to talk and move around. I begin to dial John, but I stop halfway when Erik walks toward Melissa and takes her in his arms. My heart pounds with anxiety and the jealousy spikes hot and bitter in my belly. He moves in for a long, passionate kiss, as I grit my teeth, unable to look away. The other day, watching Erik kiss her was like watching a train wreck. Today, I want to cut the bitch. Even though he's just acting, that he has no interest in her, it doesn't change my irrational reaction. Sarah would tell me it's pointless to get upset about this, but watching him kiss a woman I loathe makes me sick, and it's probably even worse for him. He has to kiss a woman pretending to be his wife for the show but who he hates in real life. A woman who is also best friends with his ex-girlfriend who just happened to try to get his current love interest fired. The whole situation makes my head spin.

When Mr. Cohen calls cut, I release my fists, and the blood returns to my clenched fingers. Melissa walks away, and Erik waves me over. I walk up to him and we turn away from the crowd of actors. Trying to hide my uncomfortable reaction is impossible, and if I'm honest with myself, if that kiss had gone on any longer, I might have flown into a jealous rage.

"You okay Ronnie?" He sounds concerned, I see the worry in his eyes, and his hand reaches out for me involuntarily, but he stops before touching me. He knows he can't.

"Ah . . . yeah." I keep my head down, but my eyes scan around me for anyone who can overhear. "I just didn't expect to feel so . . . I don't know."

He keeps his head and his voice low. "You know I don't feel anything at all for her." I look up briefly and nod. "The only woman I want to kiss is you, babe," he whispers. My heart leaps out of my chest, and I find it hard to keep my mouth from hitting the floor. He always manages to say the perfect thing, driving his point home with a reassuring smile.

"Stop it," I growl through my teeth, trying to look mad even thought I'd rather jump into his arms and kiss him.

"I'd better go back," he turns, jogging toward the pub. When I turn around, Melissa has her arms folded across her chest waiting for me wearing a smirk on her lips. Her smirk turns into a smile, albeit the fake, forced kind and she waves. All at once, her relationship with Catriona makes sense. They're both scheming harpies. Politely ignoring her is futile and she makes her way toward me as fast as her legs will carry her.

"Good morning. Are you okay?" she asks, looking concerned. But that concern is artfully contrived. I can see it in the phony smile that doesn't touch her eyes.

"I'm fine. Why?" I ask, hoping she'll unwittingly reveal her intentions.

"Are you sure? You looked like a ghost after that kiss," she smiles venomously at me, but I can feel the thinly veiled animosity in her words. "He's a fantastic kisser," she says breathlessly with a flick of her hair.

The bitch is goading me!

"Really?" I raise my eyebrows with a smile. "Did you tell his ex that?" I ask. At this point, I have no interest in putting on pretenses for this woman and no interest in backing down. A rueful smile spreads across my lips. It's a silent 'bring it on bitch'.

"Oh, of course. We share everything. She never liked being here for the sex scenes though. It's hard enough watching someone you love kiss another person, let alone watching while they perform a love scene in front of you. But let me tell you, from what I've seen he must be fantastic in bed," she drags out the last few words then stares at him salaciously, and it takes all I have not to punch her in the throat.

"He still loves her you know," she says staring at him in the distance.

"Well, I'm sure they will work it out. It's none of my business," the words barely make it past my lips before she continues needling me.

"I thought Erik would offer her a place to stay after the house was destroyed. But he didn't. Probably because you're there," she sighs.

"Well, I'm only concerned with his safety. What goes on between them has nothing to do with me," I state, emotionless. Trying to keep my feelings out of this little ambush is getting more difficult by the second. I stuff my hands in my pockets and ball them into tight fists. If I don't, I might hit her. Hard.

When she turns to look at me, her face goes from smiling to scowling, and her lips curl back like a snake ready to strike as she spits her words at me.

"Oh, who are you kidding, missy." Her stare turns bitter, her eyes narrowing into thin slits as she glares at me. She takes one step closer to me and it's one step too far.

"I'm going to do everything I can to make sure you get nowhere near him," she warns.

Too late. I scoff and smile as I take a quick look into the distance. Erik is waiting for Mr. Cohen to start the next shot, but he's watching us, looking worried. I turn back and look down at Melissa, and even with as short as I am, I tower over her.

"Are you threatening me, Miss Tyler?" I stare coldly at her.

"No. Of course not," she says, doing her best to sound innocent. But she looks me up and down, her eyes full of disdain, and her cloyingly sweet reply can't hide her true intentions.

"Good. I'm glad we understand each other. I'm sure Mr. Cohen would be upset if I had to add you to the list of suspects."

Her face blanches and she swallows hard as I stare at her, unwilling to give up the space to her. "Excuse me Ms. Tyler. I need to call the FBI."

She huffs, her eyes darting from me to the crowd and back before she walks off, leaving me alone at the table.

Checkmate.

My racing heart starts to calm a little as I sit at the picnic table. When I turn back to the group, Erik is standing off to the side while Mr. Cohen films a scene with two of the actors. Erik has his phone to his ear, and he doesn't seem upset, but I keep an eye on him as I dial John.

"Agent Grilli."

"Hi John. Where are you?" I ask.

"I'm in Bullhead City. So how is Wilcher working out?"

Now this is going to be an awkward conversation. I knew Wilcher was a pain in the ass, but openly fighting with a client is unprofessional.

"He's an asshole, John. But you knew that. He picked a fight with Erik this morning. He was furious, yelling at Wilcher telling him to fuck off," I mention.

John groans. I hate to burden him with this, but sitting in a car for six hours with the two of them just isn't going to end well.

"All right. I'll do what I can to get him replaced when I get back," he groans. I'm relieved. John knows I wouldn't ask if I found him only mildly irritating. At this rate, Erik is liable to sucker punch Wilcher, and that could make our situation even more difficult.

"Do I have to take him with me to Vegas?" I ask meekly. It's not my style, but I'll have to sweet talk John to get my way. He's silent for a moment, and then I hear him muttering to himself.

"You know you two alone is not a good idea, right?"

"John, we have to drive through the desert. What could Wilcher possibly add to the situation to make it safer? He can't do anything more than I could."

He grumbles some more unintelligible expletives as I listen and laugh a bit. "You know I'm going to catch hell if anything happens?" he barks at me.

"Nothing is going to happen."

"Hmm. Famous last words," he groans.

It's not like John to be fatalistic. But he cares for me, so I try my best to reassure him. "I'll take every available precaution. Hunter can track me on GPS, and I'll bring the satellite phone if you want."

He grumbles again. "Okay. Fine. Just let me know where you are every step of the way."

"I will, John. Hey, I have to go. Erik is taking a break from shooting."

"Okay. Tell Romeo I said hello."

"I love you John, but fuck off." I say.

He laughs and disconnects. As I slip my phone into my pocket, Erik walks up, looking every inch the bad boy he portrays, and my heart leaps into my throat. It seems like I grow more addicted to him and his sexy charm with every passing minute.

"So what did John have to say?" he asks. As we walk toward his trailer, I'm unaware of how close he is until I feel a finger reach out and gently brush against my hand.

"Stop that. People are watching." I whisper, hoping little miss devious didn't see it. He laughs and smiles, looking at me from the corner of his eye and I figure it's best to keep my conversation with Melissa to myself for now.

"Oh, John said that we don't have to drag Agent Asshole along with us to Vegas. He's agreed to replace Wilcher when he gets back."

We step into the trailer and as I shrug off my coat, Erik is behind me. He takes it and folds it neatly over a chair.

"So are you going to tell me what happened between you and him this morning?" He slips his arms around my waist as I snuggle against his chest. He inhales deeply as he nestles his nose in my hair.

"Just defending my lady's honor."

I turn abruptly, shocked by what I'm hearing. "Are you joking? What did he say?"

He dismisses my question with a shake of his head. "It's not important now."

I fold my arms, hoping he'll give in to my pout. It's not something I normally do, but if I remember right, pouting is a standard female bargaining tactic in relationships.

"Are you pouting?" He asks as his lip twitches, almost imperceptibly.

"I don't pout." I turn around and face the dinette, hoping he'll take the bait. Sidling up to me, his hands caress my shoulders, gliding down my back before he wraps himself around my waist.

"I like it, it's . . . sexy." He nudges me, and I giggle. Gently kissing along my neck, his lips leave a wet trail up to my ear.

"Sexy, huh? I must remember to pout more often."

His mouth hovers over my ear and the goose bumps rise as he softly growls against my skin. I close my eyes, but he turns me roughly. I open my lips to him, awaiting the twisting and thrashing of his tongue against mine. My muffled moan becomes audible as his lips leave my mouth. His hand tugs at my hair, gently tilting my head back as he leaves a trail of kisses over my chin, to my throat, and back up again.

"I want you," he whispers raggedly against my ear. "But I'm still not telling you. No matter how much you pout."

I push him back playfully, pursing my lips and crossing my arms in front of me. He laughs loudly, and that boyish, playful grin infuriates me. He's toying with me and enjoying it far too much.

"Caveman!" It's my only defense. My calculated move failed miserably, but I should know better than to try my hand at acting in front of an actor. His eyebrows twitch, and a wicked smile lights up his face as he stalks toward me. He grabs me and I let go of my irritation. It probably wasn't entirely genuine anyway. My phone rings just as he leans in for a kiss.

"I need to take this Erik." He nods and lets me go.

"Yeah, Wilcher. What's up?"

"Hi. I'm done with the locks. Catriona's here." I groan. I should have known that another shoe was about to drop when Melissa confronted me. Hopefully, she isn't in a rage, because the last thing I have time for is more shredded clothes.

"What? Stay with her, please. Last time she showed up unannounced, she wreaked havoc."

"Unannounced? Mr. Sinclair called me and told me she was coming."

My jaw locks and I turn around, glaring at Erik as I speak. "Okay, just keep her away from my clothes. And no sense in coming down here. It's going to be an early day."

"All right. I'll see you later," he says as he hangs up.

I set my phone down and Erik puts both hands in the air as I walk toward him, wearing a scowl on my face. "Are you freaking kidding me?"

"Okay, before you chew me out, let me explain!" he pleads, laughing.

Now I know who he was talking to while the others were shooting. I raise my eyebrows and pucker my lips, he'd better start talking. Quickly.

"I didn't want her showing up over the weekend while we were gone."

"You need to tell me these things Erik!"

He nods, looking apologetic again. "I'm sorry. I was just trying to avoid a major problem for the security crew." I try to swallow my pride and let it go. He didn't want to subject Alex and Hunter to another crazy rant courtesy of Catriona and Melissa. Fortunately, he doesn't know about the conversation I just had with her, and perhaps Catriona's calm appearance at the house means she hasn't heard about it either. He grabs my by the arms, looking down at me with that smoldering bad boy grin, and I melt into a puddle, as usual.

"I'm sorry, it won't happen again," he whispers against my lips.

I nod, looking up at him through my lashes. He makes it impossible for me to be mad at him.

"Now let's go. I have a few more scenes."

When we arrive at the house, the gate is open. My fingers tighten on the wheel as I scan the front of the house through the trees. Wilcher's sedan is parked farthest from the porch, and a dark green Jaguar is behind it.

"Is that Catriona's car?" I ask.

"Ah. No. That's a friend of mine. I asked him to stop by," he says, smiling.

I park the car and cut off the engine. "Seems like you made lots of calls today."

He unbuckles in a hurry, walks around to my side of the car, and then pulls the door open for me. I take his hand and step out of the car.

"Don't forget the satellite phone." I walk around the car and wait for him as he retrieves it from the backseat. It needs a charge before we hit the road tomorrow.

♚ CHAPTER TWENTY

As Erik opens the front door for me, I step inside and inhale the most delicious aroma, and for a second, I'm back in Queens, in my family's favorite restaurant that we frequented when I was a child. But I'm drawn from my culinary memories to the person standing in the kitchen, who is clearly not Wilcher.

Erik tries to help me off with my coat, but I reach for my holster instead. "Who is that?" I ask nervously. When he steps out from behind the counter, I recognize him. He's one of those rock star television chefs. Fabio something-or-other. I let my guard down as I let Erik take my coat.

"Where is Wilcher?" I ask.

"I told him to stay in the guesthouse for the evening, if he wants to keep his job," he smiles. I huff in surprise as he pulls me by the hand toward the kitchen.

"Veronica Harper, this is Fabio Mazzanti, a good friend of mine."

Fabio smiles as he finishes chopping peppers and then wipes his hands on a towel hanging off his shoulder. He reaches out to take my hand and kisses it gallantly.

"*Piacere. Belissima,*" Fabio says, introducing himself.

Erik's lips crumple a bit. "Hey, don't be getting so friendly with my girl, Fabio." He points two fingers at his eyeballs then turns them in Fabio's direction, who laughs at the gesture. Erik's words turn my insides to jelly. Wow, I'm 'his girl'.

Fabio's generous smile and dark skin remind me of the people I grew up with, and the thick accent tells me he's definitely an Italian native.

"Cosa stai facendo qui?" I say. Fabio is here to cook, but I suspect there's more to it than a lesson for Erik.

Erik's eyebrows rise up, surprised that I can speak Italian fluently. Fabio smiles and nods at Erik before he replies to me.

"Erik può rispondere a questa." Fabio says, taking himself out of the conversation, suggesting I should ask Erik instead.

"Okay, you two. Speak English, please," Erik says as he holds out a hand, ushering me into the dining room.

As I turn around, I see the warm glow coming from the once empty room, and it's filled with multilevel stands that are holding vases, stuffed with creamy white peonies at the top and bottom and groups of ivory candles in the middle. The empty built-in shelves are sprinkled with the same ivory candles in every imaginable size. Erik pulls out a chair for me, and I sit at the beautiful table, which is set with white linen and bone china edged in silver. The flickering candle light reflects off the stunning crystal wine glasses, causing the previously homey, simple dining area to be transformed into an haute cuisine restaurant.

Erik looks at me, waiting for me to say something. "You were busy today!" I say a little breathlessly. He just smiles as he takes a seat next to me.

"Well, you said you wanted romantic and simple. This is the best I could do," he says humbly as I watch the candlelight dance across his features. He looks every inch the handsome leading man he truly is.

"The best you can do?" I say, as I drink in everything around me, and appreciate how much thought he put into this. "This is incredible. No one has ever done anything like this for me."

I rest my elbows on the table and lean my chin on my clasped hands. He's overwhelmed me, and I'm suddenly feeling shy.

"Then all those men were fools." He reaches out and tucks my hair behind my ear and I'm reminded that it's the simple gesture that started all of this. "They didn't know what they had."

I feel my skin grow warm, and it's impossible not to bite my lip. His fingers drag along my jaw, and he pulls me in for a quick kiss.

"Bacio, Bacio." Fabio says in his melodic Italian accent. I pull away and cover my mouth with my hand, embarrassed. Fabio is back with dinner, and his uniformed waiter follows behind with two white bowls. He places them in front of us.

"What is this?" Erik looks up at him.

"Gnocchi with Prosciutto, chanterelle mushrooms, and peas," he answers in heavily accented English.

"*Grazie*, Fabio," I say as he smiles and walks away, leaving us to our meal. Erik picks up a fork and digs into his food, and I watch as he enjoys the first bite.

"What is it? You don't like it?" He asks nervously. But I shake my head and eat. He has no idea how impressed I am. No one could deny he put a lot of effort into this, and it's not just the beautiful flowers and candle light that shows his thoughtfulness. Here I thought I'd be staring at some indecipherable haute cuisine, something I could barely pronounce. Instead, he's made sure I'm getting exactly what I asked for. Simple. Romantic. He was listening.

What more could a girl ask for?

After dinner, he leads me to the double French doors that open onto the back yard. When we step onto the patio, I'm speechless as I watch the flicker of candles dance along the walls of the small alcove where the iron fire pit and an oversized chaise lounge now sit. "What did you do?"

Erik smiles as he walks to the square iron and slate fire pit and sets the wood alight. The dry logs catch quickly, and a warm glow begins to smolder in the center.

"Sit."

When I turn and sit on the chaise, I notice the television from the living room is now sitting on the large outdoor coffee table. He picks up a large fleece blanket from a table behind us and we snuggle underneath it.

"Ma'am, sir." The waiter Fabio brought with him hands us two mugs filled with hot chocolate spiked with Amaretto and then disappears back into the house. Erik turns on the television and the small DVD player sitting next to it, and within a few seconds, the movie starts.

I begin to laugh as I recognize the music instantly. "The Godfather! Really?"

He stares at me, his eyes wide with apprehension. "Oh no. You don't like it?" He looks worried and reaches for the remote.

"Are you kidding. I love it," I smile.

He exhales, sounding relieved. "Good. Because it was either this or Pride and Prejudice."

His choice of movies has me laughing. Nothing could be more perfect. We sit and watch the movie while the fire grows, keeping us warm. I'm wrapped in his arms and the blanket, and the stars fill the sky by the millions. By the time Sonny dies on the causeway, we're busy kissing like teenagers. The loud gunfire startles us both, and I feel him smile against my forehead as he reaches over and turns off the DVD. The fire is dying and our spiked hot chocolates are gone.

"Let's go inside." He takes me by the hand and leads me into the kitchen, then locks the back door. The house is warm, and quiet, and the kitchen has been meticulously cleaned. Fabio and his team must have left before we turned off the movie. As he walks toward me, the dim light of the kitchen makes him look sinful and deadly. I lean up against the refrigerator and my heart begins to pound as he takes my hands and wraps them around his neck.

"Stay with me tonight," he whispers as he kisses me softly, turning me into a puddle. I open my mouth and sigh as I look down at his chest. I don't know how to tell him no. Why ruin a perfect night?

"Erik I think I should sleep alone tonight."

A small sound of displeasure comes from him, but the thought of attempting to confront my fear, with him, tonight is a recipe for disaster. He may be disappointed right now, but he will surely be even more so, later. But how can I say no to him after all the thought and care he put into tonight?

He groans a little and then tries once more. "Please, I'd love to wake up with you in my arms."

"Okay."

Changing into his plaid shirt from last night, I walk into his bedroom. He's patiently waiting, sitting on the edge of his bed wearing only his boxer briefs. His blue eyes light up, and a dazzling smile spreads across his lips when he sees his shirt has become my new favorite. I walk to him slowly, and when I stop in front of him, he spreads his thighs and pulls me in between.

"You look better in that shirt than I do," he says with a slight wickedness in his voice, his gaze greedy and hot.

"Open." He brushes the top button with the tip of his finger.

"I thought you didn't want to . . . "

"Don't argue," he whispers. I slip the top button open.

"Another."

The one-word commands leave me breathless, but I do it and Erik watches as I open the second, and then a third, exposing my generous cleavage. One finger skims down the center of my body, from the dip at the base of my neck to my belly. Before I know it, he leans back, yanking me down roughly on top of him. *I love playful Erik.*

My hair falls softly around his face and he cups my cheeks, gently pulling me into a soft, lush kiss. He plunges his tongue into my mouth, at first slowly stroking and swirling around mine, then faster, turning the kiss wildly passionate. His soft moans spark my arousal, and my blood surges through my veins, superheated and raw with need. Powerful thighs wrap around mine, and he rolls me on my back, pinning me to the mattress with his long, lean body.

I yelp, and I can't catch my breath. The feel of his weight on me, his hands interlaced with mine holding them tightly at either side of my head, and the feeling of being defenseless beneath him is too much to bear. The surging arousal swiftly turns into panic.

"Wait, no. Erik. Please get off me." I beg, wrestling my hands from his grip and then pushing at his shoulders as he slides off me.

"I'm sorry. I didn't realize," he says, watching for my reaction.

Neither did I. Pulling the shirt closed with my hand, I turn away from him.

"Baby, don't be embarrassed. Sarah mentioned there might be things that trigger panic attacks." His hand runs down my arm, caressing and soothing me. Snuggling up behind me, he wraps his arm around my waist. Erik's lips make contact with the soft skin behind my ear, and a shiver runs down my spine.

"We just have to go slow," I say as I turn in his arms, and when he opens his mouth to speak, I stop him. "Don't argue."

A breathtaking smile spreads across his lips and his eyes return to the dazzling blue that I find impossible to ignore. My mouth locks onto his, and my tongue dips into his open mouth, stroking and sliding against his. I weave my hands into his thick, silky hair, gripping, and pulling him tighter to me. He more than moans into my open mouth, he growls into me, and every cell in my body responds to it. The tender muscles of my sex tighten savagely, fueling the arousal. He gently rolls me on my back, slinging a thigh over mine, his hand resting flat on my bare belly as he lies beside me.

"How slow?" He props his head on his hand and kisses each of my fingers and I shrug, unsure of what he's asking. "Maybe a safe word would be a good idea?" he suggests.

My insides tighten uncomfortably at the thought. What little I know of BDSM includes the practice of safe words, an escape mechanism when sexual play goes too far. The idea of delving into that territory frightens me and I shake my head wildly, hoping to dissuade him.

"It's just a word, baby," he says, lifting his brow as he tries to convince me. "It would give you a way to take control, and turn something negative from the past into something positive."

His self-assurance amazes me, and for the moment, I feel comfortable enough to set my apprehension aside. The man has an innate ability to calm me, and I find myself caving in to his gentle coaxing. I want to open up to him, to give in to him, to let myself trust, and fall in love with him. He waits patiently as I think over his suggestion, and the more I look at him the harder I find it to resist. I'm suddenly in awe of him, and how much it seems he cares for me. My heart feels like it's about to burst, and something like joy overtakes me as he stares at my face. I want him to look at me with those eyes forever.

"Breathless."

He's amused by my suggestion. "Are you sure?"

I nod and his smile disappears. His mouth crashes into mine and he kisses me greedily, possessing me, making sure I'll feel the warmth of his kiss, and the depth of his emotion beyond just tonight. It's the kind of kiss a woman never forgets, the kind that reaches the deepest parts of her soul.

His lust ignites my heart, sending flames shooting through every inch of my body. I'm on fire, and I want him, as he wants me and I feel the strength of my fears waning, bending and giving in to his powerful will, like a tree bends in a strong wind. His hands push aside the soft cotton of the shirt, and it rasps across my tight nipples, driving me insane. Our tongues circle in unison as my breast swell and my nipples harden even further under his skilled hand. I gasp at the feel of his scorching hot mouth against my skin as he works his way down, nuzzling and nibbling as he moves until he captures my tight nub between his lips. Each soft suck and flick of his tongue sends a sharp jolt through me, and it's made even stronger as his other hand joins in, rolling and tugging my other nipple in sync with his mouth.

"Is this okay?" he asks, never taking his eyes off mine as his tongue darts out and flicks and rolls my nipple gently. Watching him pleasure me, physically and emotionally is the most erotic thing I've ever felt. At that moment, I'm completely and utterly lost to his desires, to his sinfully sexy body, and to his sweet, overprotective nature. And no matter how many times my fears raise their ugly heads, I'll come back, over and over again, for more of him. Until I conquer this.

"Yes," I whisper. My breath comes out in a ragged flutter as I gaze at him and my hands slip into his silky black hair as he goes back to work, kissing and nibbling at my body. He's so gentle, so patient that it feels like an eternity before he moves his mouth from my breast and licks a straight line down to my navel. My back arches from the tickling, wet sensation and I feel his smile against my skin.

"You're so beautiful. I've never wanted a woman, the way I want you," he whispers. His words unleash a flood of emotion inside me, joy, anticipation, pain, and loneliness are all released at once, and mingle with the physical, the feel of his touch, the heat of his skin and the intoxicating smell of his body. It's powerful, and the tears sting my eyes as I watch him explore, resting his weight on his hands as he hovers over me. The soft stubble on his chin and the flicking tongue in my navel make me flinch and gasp. He takes advantage of my squirming and makes a place for himself between my open legs.

He reaches up, and cups both breasts in his hands, squeezing me gently as he resumes his attack on my skin, his lips trailing from one hip to the other along the waistband of my panties. The gentle tug and twist on each nipple makes me cry out, and he rises again, clamping his teeth around one sensitive tip. He bites down, but not hard enough to be painful, and my neck arches, pressing deeper into the pillow as I gasp.

"You're breasts are so beautiful and firm," he says as he settles between my legs again, never breaking eye contact and never letting go of my body. My hips rock, almost in time with each twist and tug of my nipples, and I realize I'm wet and aching for release. When he dips his head between my legs, he presses his nose into the saturated cotton of my panties and inhales the scent of my arousal. A ferocious growl rumbles deep in his chest, and I can feel it racing down to my toes. My breath heaves and my heart thumps wildly against my ribcage.

Oh no . . . not now . . . please not now. Dammit!

"Breathless."

Looking out the blinds at the inky darkness, I notice the stars. They are still visible and twinkling, the same stars we cuddled under earlier in the evening. He's sleeping soundly beside me, half-naked and beautiful.

And he's mine. Wow. Erik Sinclair is . . . *mine*.

What was I thinking last night, safe wording him? I must be crazy. I move closer to him, and he rolls over, pulling me into his arms. My bare breasts press against his rock hard chest, and his smooth, hot skin feels like velvet against me. His hand skims up my spine and a million tiny tingles erupt as his fingers move.

"Good morning beautiful." Pressing his lips to my forehead, I inhale the unique, intoxicating scent of Erik, which is even better first thing in the morning. I look up and offer my mouth to him for a kiss, and he takes it. My fingers dig into his biceps, and he moans into me. I take advantage of it, and my tongue lashes at his open mouth, exploring him eagerly, stoking his early morning lust that is pressing hard against my thigh. Trailing kisses over my jaw, he nuzzles my neck and gently nibbles on my earlobe.

"Did you bring a baseball bat to bed?" I joke.

His cheeks turn pink, and I'm flattered knowing it's a reaction to me. My hands skim over the contours of his muscular arms, but he sighs loudly when his alarm rings.

"Fuck," he grumbles. He lets go of me reluctantly and climbs out of bed. Stopping in front of me, he picks up the plaid shirt from the floor. I look up at him, and from my vantage point, his stiff cock straining against the material of his boxer briefs looks positively enormous. I bite my lip and raise an eyebrow as I take the clothes from him. He smiles wickedly and disappears into the bathroom.

I shrug on the shirt, button it halfway, and then return to my bedroom. Opting for a pair of jeans, I slip into them and a suitable casual shirt. I'd rather be comfortable if I have to drive and wear full gear for six hours.

Opening a duffel bag, I pack my toiletries and a few extra days change of clothes. I fill my second bag with the gear I need: a Taser, vests, both guns, enough loaded clips for a small army and the satellite phone, which is fully charged and ready to go.

The house is dark, so I turn on the lights in the living room and leave my bags near the door. Setting up the coffee pot, I watch as it sputters to life and the aroma of brewing coffee makes my stomach growl. But I can't get my mind off this weekend. The interviews and evidence gathered will hopefully answer many more questions than they will raise. I'm so consumed with theories about Jeff and Kincaid that I flinch when I realize Erik is standing in the kitchen doorway, silently watching me.

"I'm sorry, I didn't mean to startle you. You seem preoccupied."

I unfold my arms and move toward the counter, ready to pour myself some coffee.

"Are you okay?" He steps closer and every muscle in my body reacts, my insides bubble with an intense sexual energy every time he looks at me. He grips my bicep and lays a gentle, wet kiss on my cheek.

"Yes, I'm fine," I smile halfheartedly as he reaches out a hand, pushing away stray wisps of hair from my forehead. I close my eyes and sigh, and he leans in for a kiss.

"Don't worry. Everything will be okay." I nod and reach for my cup, but before I can pour my coffee, my phone starts to vibrate.

"Morning Hunter."

"Hi. We're outside."

I move toward the door and open it to find Hunter, Alex, and Jason standing on the porch with Starbucks in hand. Erik walks to the door, and he greets Hunter.

"Come in." They all file in and congregate in the living room.

"I'm Erik Sinclair," he says to Alex and Jason as they introduce themselves, take a seat on the couch.

"So Mr. Sinclair, I assume Ronnie told you we'd be staying the weekend to get this system installed. Is there anything we need to know?" Alex asks as he takes a seat in the blue chair across from Erik.

"No, not really. My ex-girlfriend is half owner, but I doubt she will show up here," he says. As I listen to Alex talk about the security system with Erik, Wilcher comes in through back door.

"So the crew is here. How long is this going to take?" he says, grumbling a little as he pours a cup of coffee. I can't imagine what he has to be annoyed about so early in the morning.

"I'm not sure. Most of the weekend, I suppose. They are going to crash here," I say as Wilcher follows me into the living room.

"Alex Harris, this is Agent Robert Wilcher. Hunter is in charge, so if you need anything, please contact him."

I sit next to Alex on the couch. "If you hadn't heard, I fired Dan Royce yesterday. If he shows up here, please call Hunter or have Agent Wilcher escort him off the property."

"Mr. Sinclair, would you mind showing us around the property?" Alex and Jason stand, and I nod at Erik, letting him know it's okay to go. He's perfectly safe with them, but Wilcher follows them anyway. It leaves me alone with Hunter, and it's a good time to discuss business before we leave.

"I have some documents for you." Hunter takes three blue folded papers from his bag and hands them to me. "Agent Jacobs stopped by the office yesterday to deliver them. He also served us."

I look at Hunter and frown. We knew it was going to happen, but it's still a shock. The company itself is evidence. A jumbled mess of electronic records and files, that when put back together will tell us how devious Jeff has become. It's a picture I don't really want to see.

"This one is for a psychiatric hospital," he says as I take the paper from his hand.

When I look at the document a little closer I notice the name; Rawson-Neal Psychiatric printed on the front. Holy shit!

"RNP?"

"Yes. The doctor that Jeff was paying practices there. His name is Dr. Polidori. John spoke to the doctor already, and he's confirmed that Kincaid was there for years and then released in July."

I'm silent for long minutes, trying to process that Jeff was hiding his brother in a mental institution all this time. Bastard.

Hunter throws an arm around my shoulder, breaking me out of my swirling, angry thoughts. It's an unusual gesture for him.

"I'm sorry Ronnie. I realize what this means," he says. I shake my head. Every bit of new evidence is a shock to me. Something in me still wants to believe we've got it all wrong. Jeff can't possibly be this bad.

"How are you so calm about this, Hunter?" I ask, knowing he's generally quiet, but maybe he's hiding behind his military bearing. He pulls his arm away and rubs his thighs nervously and frowns.

"I don't know. Maybe I'm not handling it yet. Same as you really. Even if there's a plausible explanation why he disappeared, I don't think I can ever trust him again."

I can see the disappointment on his face for the first time. "We'll figure this out Hunter," I say as he nods and smiles.

"I hope so. If anyone can pull us out of the hole we're in, it's you. I have faith. So did Sinclair write a check?" he asks, returning to his business-like demeanor.

"Yes. I spoke to him about yesterday."

"Okay. I'll pull him aside before you leave." Hunter seems satisfied and a little relieved. With Erik's money and Olympus footing the bill for the set, the company can keep running for a little longer.

"Here are the keys to the property." I hand them to Hunter, and he slips them into his pocket. Our conversation ends as soon as everyone else walks through the kitchen door, chatting noisily about the additional electric needed for lighting the driveway.

"Mr. Sinclair? May we speak in private," Hunter says as he approaches Erik. He nods, and Hunter follows him down the hall to the office. I shake off the depressing news and stand from the couch. Taking the two bags out to the car, I open the trunk and put my clothes in the back, then set the gear bag in the back seat. When I turn back to the porch, Alex is waiting with Erik's luggage.

"I've got it," he says as he drops the bag into the trunk and closes it. A sudden apprehensive look appears on his face as he rests his hand on the car.

"What is it Alex?" I ask.

"Is that FBI agent always such a jerk?" He says, looking annoyed. Alex can be self-assured and sarcastic, but he's the type of guy everyone gets along with. Yet, it didn't take long for Wilcher to piss off even him.

"Yes, unfortunately, he is. Just do your best to deal with him."

Within a few minutes, Erik appears on the porch, followed by Hunter. They speak a few words to each other and then shake hands. Erik slips into the passenger seat as Hunter meets me on the driver's side.

"Call me on the sat phone if you have any questions," I say.

"Will do Ronnie. Have a safe trip and call me when you get there."

I slide into the car and pull out onto the driveway, slowly making my way toward the open gate. The car is quiet, and for a few minutes, we both watch the sky change. The sun is just starting to color the horizon, and the early morning haze morphs into a pink-orange glow.

♟ CHAPTER TWENTY-ONE

Before we're on the highway, Erik's mood changes. He shifts uncomfortably in his seat and rakes his hair back from his eyes. I recognize those signs, he's preoccupied with something.

"So you used the safe word on me last night. Why?"

His abrupt question leaves me speechless. I hadn't counted on him asking me why I used the safe word. When I recoiled, he didn't flinch, when I stammered trying to offer an explanation, he quieted me. He didn't pressure me, and I was grateful, but confused. I wanted to surrender to him, to give myself to him, but that same cold, tight panic welled up in the center of my chest once again, stopping me cold.

"You're mad?" I ask, and as the nervous energy surges through my veins, my grip tightens on the wheel.

"No Ronnie. Not at all!" He reaches for me, and I take one hand off the wheel, and I warm to his gentle, soothing touch. "I just want to know what you were feeling."

Did the man just ask me about my feelings? Did I hear him right? "Well, fear mostly. The last man to touch me . . . " I stop, thinking I don't have to explain any further. He does pressure me this time, but in the gentlest of ways.

"I know, baby. But I'd never hurt you. Please, let me be your safety net."

His words tear at my heart, this back and forth must be incredibly confusing for him. I want to make it better, to be better, for me and for him. But the self-loathing and fear beaten into me five years ago won't let go.

"Erik, I'm such a mess. I can't understand why you'd . . ."

"Why I want you? Because when I broke up with Cat, I realized I'd been dating the same type of woman repeatedly. The same clingy, dependent, shallow type of woman that's everywhere in Hollywood. Then you showed up, and you're all defiant, and witty, and intelligent. You're the complete opposite of clingy and dependent. So yes, I want you. Yes, I want to get you naked and do ridiculously naughty things to you. I realize I'm probably moving a little too fast at times, but I'm aware of your boundaries. I'll take you right to the edge baby, but I won't push you. You have to take that step."

Holy fuck. He went from sweet to scorchingly dirty in a nanosecond, and I don't know how to answer him. Everything he said sparked an incredible range of emotions, so strong, that I can't think straight. When I realize my mouth is hanging open, I close it, and he laughs a little. Fortunately, he's not waiting for an answer. I'm still trying to figure out what he means by the edge. *The edge of what?*

I keep my eyes on the road, but my thoughts are consumed with his panic inducing words, and the one thing I keep thinking is that he's mine, he wants me. What am I waiting for? He's sweet, protective, and make-my-panties-catch-fire gorgeous. Certified-ovary-killer gorgeous.

And he's asleep.

I laugh quietly to myself, but in truth, I'm grateful for the quiet as the road stretches out before us. The gold and reddish-brown leaves and neatly manicured lawns of Santa Clarita eventually give way to the parched brown landscape of the desert communities as the highway grows more desolate. Scrub brush covers the barren ground as we pass by the occasional roadside rest stop.

I bring the speed up to ninety. The faster we get to Bullhead City, the better. Erik is dozing beside me, and the first rays of sun are beginning to streak over the mountains as we pass through Victorville. I put on my sunglasses and pull down the visor as the sun rises over the eastern horizon. We're an hour into the drive when Erik wakes and straightens up in his seat before pulling down the visor to block the strong sunlight.

"Where are we?" he asks as he pulls his sunglass from his breast pocket.

"We passed through Victorville a few minutes ago. We'll be in Barstow in a half hour." The sound of his voice is a welcome distraction. The last hour of analyzing the future of Cole Security Services, my past with Jeff, and a possible relationship with Erik has me longing for conversation.

"Do you need a bathroom break?" I ask.

He rubs a hand over his face, trying to wipe the sleep from his eyes. "Yes. I need to stretch my legs a bit. I'm not used to sitting in a car this long." The warmth of his hand settles on mine, and he lifts it to his lips, kissing each knuckle gently. Something low in my belly tingles at the contact, and his words repeat in my head, how he's going to push me to the edge. I figure that can only mean one thing, but I'm hesitant to ask.

I let off the gas pedal as I pull into a large gas station. It caters to truckers and tourists, and the enormous parking lot is filled with big rigs. I turn off the engine in front of a pump, and he releases my hand so I can reach into the backseat for my vest. I can feel his hot breath against my cheek just as I turn around and it causes tingles to race down my spine.

Keep your mind on business, Harper.

"Here, put this on," I say as I lay the heavy vest in his lap. He looks at me, somewhat stunned. I've deflected his little flirtation, and the effect he's used to having on me is suddenly gone.

"Why do I need this?" he asks.

"Safety. Put it on under your flannel." He strips off the red and black long sleeved shirt, revealing his familiar white tee. My eyes immediately fix on his biceps and the thick roping of veins in his forearm. I bite my lip and repress my desires. *Don't let his beautiful body distract you.*

I secure my vest and step out of the car, leaving him in his seat. "Stay here," I say as I close the door. When the tank is full, I get back inside and park the car in a spot closest to the double glass doors of the store.

"So how are we going to do this? The loo, I mean," he smiles.

"Oh. I'm going to find the manager and have him clear out the men's room. Stay by me and don't wander off please."

We walk into the store, and as I make my way through the myriad tourists, I decide most of them are harmless. It's mostly retirees on their way to spend a few days gambling in Vegas or perhaps buying souvenirs for friends on their way to Lake Havasu. No one seems to recognize us and nothing incites any particular alarm as I walk through the store in search of the manager. When I approach the counter, I find him. He's a man in his fifties, with a comb-over, and a crooked blue tie covering the buttons of his shirt that are straining to contain his large belly.

"Are you the manager?"

He nods and looks at me nervously as his eyes come to rest on my gun. "How can I help you?"

218

When he steps up to the counter, I explain our situation, and he happily agrees to check the men's room for me. We follow him to the back of the store toward the cold beer case.

"The restrooms are back here," he says. The two wood doors are separated by a water fountain, and the yellow ocher walls are smudged with dirt. He steps inside the men's room, and I can hear the metal doors of the cubicles banging open. Within a moment, he returns. "It's empty," he says as he holds the door open.

Erik and I enter, and the stench of urine and pine-scented disinfectant makes my stomach churn. It smells like the subways in New York.

"Use a stall, please," I ask before he's fully unzipped.

He shrugs as we both disappear into the small cubicles. He finishes before I do, and I hear the water running as he washes his hands. As I step out, he's standing by the sink. I wash mine, and as I look in the mirror, I notice he's staring at me. Well, he's staring at my backside.

"Stop it," I mutter. His eyes fly up, and he smiles at me in the mirror. He fidgets with the brown paper towel a bit then tosses it in the garbage can.

"What?" he says innocently as he grins down at me, looking unbelievably edible. As soon as we walk out the door, the manager hurries back to the front of the store. I make it three steps away from the door before Erik manages to grab me. Pulling backward by the hand, I mumble some expletives as he spins me around into his arms. His mouth meets mine, his lips parting just enough for our tongues to join in a twisting, writhing dance. I moan into him as he kisses me. He pulls away and rests his forehead against mine for a second, giving me a chance to catch my breath.

"Erik, pl . . . please. Not here." I look up at him, but his hot gaze is unrelenting.

He kisses me once more, "Mine," he whispers against my lips. With one simple word, he manages to scramble my brain and make my heart do the samba. When he releases me, I exhale a loud shuddering breath. I straighten my vest and walk out of the claustrophobic alcove on wobbly legs.

"There's not much between here and Barstow," I say, peering into the deli case of ready-made sandwiches as I pick something that looks marginally edible. While I'm waiting for him to fill a giant size soda cup, my phone rings. When I finally wrestle it from my pocket, I frown at the unknown number blinking at me.

"Hello? Who is this?"

The voice on the other end sounds like a man, but the conversation is so broken I can't understand a word he is saying. "I can't hear you. Call back in about fifteen minutes." We should be within Barstow city limits soon, and maybe we'll have better cell service. Disconnecting the call, I slip my phone into the back pocket of my jeans. As I follow Erik to the register, I set my items on the counter. The manager rings us up, and just as I hand him the cash, Erik's phone rings. He has the same problem as I did.

"Yea, can't hear you. Call back and leave a message. Cheers." He hangs up abruptly and puts his phone in his pocket.

"Same thing?" I look at him, a bit worried.

"Yeah, couldn't understand a word." He looks at me for a moment and shrugs. He may be unaffected by it, but the hairs on my neck are standing at attention. The cashier hands me a large bag and we turn to leave. We're barely at the car before Erik is complaining.

"Can I take this thing off now?" He climbs into the passenger seat and closes the door, then sighs in frustration. The vest is uncomfortable and hot, and he's not used to it.

"Yes. Go ahead, but keep it within reach." He doesn't think to ask why, but my instincts are pinging. Someone is desperate to get in touch with us. It's someone who knows both our numbers and knows we're together. Something is going on, and I don't like driving blind. As we get back on the road, I press hard on the pedal, bringing the speed back up to ninety. I'm sure whoever was in such a hurry to get us on the phone will leave a message. It can't be Hunter or John. They both have the number for the satellite phone. But I decide to concentrate on matters that I have some control over. Erik is taking a sip of his soda when I verbally accost him.

"You can't do that kind of thing in public places Erik."

He turns toward me, and the smallest smile touches his lips. "Fine. Do ut des."

"What?" I giggle nervously.

"I give something, and you give something in return. I'll be a good boy in public, now it's your turn," he smiles.

My thoughts return to his comments earlier, and I wonder if I can turn this game to my advantage. "Go," I have no idea what he's going to ask so I brace myself.

"Favorite place in the world."

I exhale sharply. I'm relieved it's not some embarrassing truth-or-dare style question. "Oh wow. I've been so many places. Um. I'd have to say Capri."

"Why?" He shifts a little in his seat, trying to face me more.

"It's so beautiful there. The island has this wonderful fragrance. It's the lemon and olive trees and the scent of basil in the air. And the colors of the buildings, they climb the hills all painted pale pink, blue, and yellow. I love it there," I say, suddenly calm and relaxed as I go along with his game.

"So what's your favorite place?"

"My mum's kitchen." He doesn't elaborate, and I prod him to tell me more.

"Why?"

"Hmm, it was the best place to be when I was a boy. My grandparents and cousins would come over on Sundays, and she would make a roast and Yorkshire pudding. My mum is an excellent cook. It was just fun, good memories."

"Are you excited to go home next week?" He rubs his cheek and sighs.

"Yes and no. I'm not a fan of London. Besides, this trip is all about work. Mum is coming to visit, but it won't be a vacation," he says.

"So what is your mom like?" I ask, he doesn't talk about her much.

"She's strong. After my dad left, she had to raise us on her own. She went back to dancing to support us, and she also worked at the grocery store and a bookstore, wherever she could to make a little money."

Our shared history sparks a feeling of closeness. We both watched our moms struggle to raise their children.

"She was a dancer? I bet going back to ballet was tough after having two kids."

He sighs and lowers his gaze. He almost looks embarrassed, and it's the first time I've seen that. "She wasn't that kind of dancer," he admits.

Dammit. I just stuck my foot in my mouth. He stares out the window, and I quickly try to cover my mistake. "It sounds like she did whatever was necessary to care for her boys. No one could fault her for that." He looks at me again, with something like gratitude touching his smile.

"I think she will like you," he says sweetly.

She will like me? Oh sweet Jesus. I hadn't considered the possibility that I'd be meeting his mother. Well, I had, but as his security. We definitely need to talk about this. I'm not sure I'm ready for him to introduce me as . . . as what?

"So what are you going to tell her, about me I mean?" I grip the wheel a little tighter, waiting for a full-blown panic attack to hit me.

"I don't know. I hadn't thought about it much," he says, rubbing his chin.

"And what if she hates me?" I ask, sounding worried.

"Well, I'm a big boy. She didn't like Catriona much, and I managed to stay with her for five years. Maybe I should listen to my mum a bit more," he laughs.

Well, I think I like his mom already. "So what were you talking about earlier, when you said you'd push me to my breaking point, but not beyond?" I just willingly broached the second panic-inducing topic in as many minutes, and I look at him hesitantly.

"Are you sure you want to know?" he asks. Now I'm even more apprehensive, but as with many other things related to Erik and this case, I figure there's no turning back.

"Yes."

"After Sarah told me about what you've been through, and that she worked on some aversion therapy with you, I thought trying some BDSM techniques would be helpful for you," he says, looking out the window. My mouth drops open and falls into my lap as I stare at him in disbelief. This has to be a joke.

"Hey! Eyes on the road," he yells and grabs the wheel to keep the car from drifting onto the dirt shoulder. I'm lucky there's no one on the road.

"Maybe I didn't explain to you well enough what Kincaid is into," I say, angrily. He looks at me and I can see the distress in his eyes.

"Before you rip me to shreds, please think about it. Maybe if you're the one in control, if you make the rules, it might help you conquer this," he says, pleading.

He can beg all he wants. This is not something I'd ever consider. Definitely not without Sarah's guidance. "Did you mention your idea to Sarah?" I ask. He nods, covering his mouth with his fingers. When he doesn't say anything, I know she vetoed the idea. But I ask anyway.

"Well, what did she say?" I'm afraid he'll want to try this anyway even if Sarah advised against it.

"She said in theory, it could work. But she didn't want me to attempt anything like that without her supervision. Which I thought was totally inappropriate," he says, shaking his head in frustration.

"Erik, she's a licensed therapist. She's got a sex therapy certification too." He turns and seems more hopeful, though I haven't agreed to anything.

"Oh, I see," he says, shifting in his seat.

"So you never tried any BDSM?" I ask.

"Well, things weren't going so well with me and Catriona when I got the part in the movie. Plus, after reading the books she wasn't shy about telling me what she thought about them. It wouldn't have been something she would have tried considering the way the story ends."

Now I wonder what exactly is in those books. "They don't have a happy ending?" I ask innocently.

"No. Cameron goes too far with Bianca and she suffocates. He brings her back, but that's it for her. She walks away at the end."

He waits for a reaction, but I remain impassive. It's easy to brush it off when we're talking about characters in a book. Real life is far more complicated.

"You've never tried anything like that? I mean, before . . . "

"Me? No," I huff. He should know better than to ask me that.

"And you want me to play dominant? Even though you're going to be playing one in a movie," I ask, totally confused.

"Yes. If you wanted to try it. But I'm fairly certain I can get you to submit without all the contraptions and props," he says with a self-assured smile. "Don't get me wrong, I like toys, but I have no need to cause you in pain. I have no need to strike a woman."

For him, this admission is bittersweet. With his history, his memories, he could easily fall into an abusive relationship. Somehow, he's managed to steer clear of that, and perhaps playing the role of Cameron is an opportunity for self-exploration. A way of letting go of the past, just as I have to let go of mine.

"But you're willing to do it on screen?"

"Yes. It's a way to deal with the overbearing, aggressive type of male I saw growing up. I went the opposite way. But it still bothers me, I react violently when I see a man treating a woman that way."

I try to keep myself from panicking, but I can't help thinking of all the ways trying something like this could go horribly wrong. Delving into this lifestyle, with our combined history could tear us apart, and set me back even further than I am right now. It requires a level of trust and familiarity with your partner that Erik and I don't have.

"Look, this is just an idea. I don't need a flogger and handcuffs to push you a little further each time. That's the goal of aversion therapy anyway, isn't it?" he says.

Jeez, one conversation with a therapist and he's an expert.

Before I can spiral down too far, my phone starts making noise. We're approaching the city limits of Barstow, and now we're both getting messages of all sorts. He picks up his phone as it begins buzzing in the cup holder.

"I've got a few messages too." I pull into the first empty lot I find and put the car in park. As I go through the texts, one of them is from Sarah.

> Sarah: I just wanted to talk to you about the other night. Call me when you can XOXO

I'd love to talk to her, but I'd rather not do it right now. Erik knows far more about me than I would have envisioned before we met, but there are still things I'd like to keep private. While Erik listens to his voice mail messages, I dial Hunter.

"Hi, Hunter. What's going on?" My stomach is in knots, hoping that there hasn't been any trouble since we left.

"Hi, Ronnie. Everything is going according to plan. I left the crew at the house with Wilcher and went back to the office. I found something. There is a charge to the Black Card."

I blanch when I remember the thousands of dollars I spent on dresses, but with Erik footing the bill, it should ease the financial pain.

"Jeff rented a storage unit. It's in Cedar City, Utah, paid in full for six months."

I'm silent for a moment, trying to come up with a reason why he'd pay for a storage unit so far away. What could be in there? "Where the hell is Cedar City?" I ask.

"It's a small town off I–15, three hours north of Las Vegas."

"Okay. Thanks for letting me know. I'll call John. He'll have to get a warrant to get in there. One more thing, Hunter. Can you confirm if a background check was ever completed for Melissa Tyler?"

Erik turns abruptly and stares at me. I never told him about my confrontation with Melissa.

"Sure, I'll check and let you know," he says.

"Thanks, Hunter. I'd better get back on the road. We're still far from Bullhead City." Assuming that was the worst of the news is wrong, and he stops me.

"That's not all Ronnie. Dan called the office. He seemed very agitated."

My jaw locks and a knot forms in my gut. "What did he want?" I ask as Erik looks at me, wondering what is going on.

"He wanted to know where you and Erik were. He said to be careful in Bullhead City."

My stomach turns into a brick and my heart pounds. "How could he possibly know where we are?"

"I don't know. I called Alex, and he's checking the network remotely," he says.

"Hunter, do me a favor, keep track of us on GPS. If we go anywhere other than Bullhead City or Vegas, something is wrong."

"Gotcha. I'll let you know if anything else happens. Be safe." I disconnect, and Erik looks at me with huge eyes.

"What happened?" he asks anxiously.

"Dan called the office. He knows where we're headed. He said we need to be careful." I admit, and the anger is evident in my voice. I'm sure he can see it in my face. He frowns, and his complexion seems a few shades paler than normal.

"I had a bunch of voice mails, and it sounded like Dan, but I couldn't make out a word."

Now the phone calls we got outside of Barstow make sense. It was Dan calling to threaten us or warn us of some type of danger. Although, I highly doubt it was the latter.

"Let's get out of here. We've got about two hours to Bullhead City."

He nods at me, and I can see the worry in his eyes. He's as alarmed as I am, but he tries to hide it as he sits silent next to me, eating a chicken salad sandwich from the gas station. My stomach is starting to growl a little, but I need to concentrate on the road and any potential danger.

♟ CHAPTER TWENTY-TWO

I take off and about ten minutes pass before my phone rings. It's Dan. Son of a bitch. I decide to answer it. Really, the worst he could do over the phone is anger me.

"What do you want?' I do nothing to hide the irritation in my voice.

"Where are you?" he demands.

I laugh, I have no intention of telling him anything. "That's none of your business. Don't call me—" He cuts me off.

"Look, Kincaid can find you. I don't know how. Just don't go to Bullhead City. Jeff has tried to keep a lid on Kincaid, but he's lost track of him. The last place he went was the cemetery in Bullhead City."

I laugh at him, but he's silent. "Do you really expect me to believe a word you say? Fuck off, son of a bitch." I hang up and Erik stares at me, highly alarmed and tense.

"What did he say?" he asks.

"He warned me not to go to Bullhead City. He said Kincaid might be there."

He shakes his head and rubs his face with both hands. "Do you think he would go to so much trouble to warn us if he just wanted to hurt us?" he asks as he rubs his temple with his fingers. There is truth in his question, and as much as I want to believe Dan has good intentions, my gut is telling me otherwise. He has something to hide, and if he didn't, he would have answered my questions yesterday.

"I don't know what he's up to Erik, and I'm not about to believe a word he says." My phone starts to ring again. Erik picks up the phone and looks at it, it's Dan calling back.

"No, don't answer it."

He sighs, and the call goes to voice mail.

Even though I push our speed to one hundred, the next ninety minutes drag on slowly. There's a long stretch of desolate road ahead of us, devoid of police cars, gas stations or traffic of any kind, and the thought makes me nervous. Erik is snoozing in the seat beside me again, and I wonder how he falls asleep almost anywhere.

With one hand on the wheel, I pull off the plastic seal covering the chicken salad sandwich. I take a bite while trying to hold the wheel and watch the road at the same time. I'd rather not stop in Bullhead City. We'd stand out—strangers with bulletproof vests and guns always do. The sooner we make it to Vegas, the safer we'll be. As we cross over Route 66, the satellite phone rings. This time the call is welcome.

"Hi, John. I have some news. We've had some trouble—" As I open my mouth to tell him about Dan, he interrupts.

"Don't stop in Bullhead City. Just get to Vegas."

My heart begins to pound. John doesn't act this way and I can hear the anxiety in his voice. "Why? What happened?" My voice wakes Erik, and he sits up in his seat as I put the call on speakerphone.

"What is it Ronnie?" Erik asks. He stares at me as I wait for John to start talking, growing more irritable as the long seconds of silence tick on. I can vaguely hear other voices in the background along with the faint sound of police radios.

"John, what the fuck is happening out there? John!" My words are less than tactful, but my situation has put me at a disadvantage. Being in the middle of nowhere, and far from any sort of help makes me twitchy.

"I'm here at the house in Henderson. Miranda's old place. It's the neighbors. I wanted to talk to them to see if they remembered anything more about Jeff. They're dead . . . they've been dead for a few days."

The news sucks the air from my lungs, and the car suddenly becomes claustrophobic. Kincaid was never a random killer. He has very particular tastes and thrives on the cat and mouse power play with his victims. Two elderly people would never be a challenge for him. Perhaps he knew we were getting close to finding out the truth. Right now, the only one who can answer that is Kincaid, but I have no interest in having a casual chitchat with him.

John keeps talking, describing the murder, but it isn't long before the gruesome details sicken us both.

"That's enough John. I don't want to hear anymore," I plead as the chicken salad sandwich threatens to come up.

"Sorry Ronnie."

"I was trying to tell you earlier that Dan called. He warned me to be careful in Bullhead City. He said Jeff was following Kincaid through Vegas but had lost track of him."

"Do you have Dan's number?" John asks.

"Hold on, John." Erik pulls out his phone and brings up the contact for Dan.

"Yes. Are you ready?"

"Yeah, give it to me."

"952-555-0143"

"I'll see what I can do about tracking him. Now what were you going to tell me?" John asks.

"It's about Dan. When I fired him yesterday, he said Jeff hired him to keep Kincaid away from Erik."

"So your theory about being the true target is probably disproved." He's got that I-told-you-so sarcasm in his voice. And like any big brother, he enjoys being right.

"John, I'm surprised at you. You're going to take Dan's word?"

"Oh, shut it, Ronnie. By the way, we dug up some information on the Monte Carlo. Ready for this?" He pauses, giving me a minute to think. I'm not ready, but I doubt I have a choice. "It was registered to Vincent Turner in Bullhead City, Arizona up until four years ago. After that, it's registered to Jeff Cole."

Fuck. I suddenly feel stupid as I realize that my absence allowed Jeff to keep his brother's identity hidden. He was doing everything he could to hide him for the past four years, and I never saw it coming.

"Hey kid, I've gotta go. Just get here as quickly as possible. Don't make too many stops, you know the drill."

"Yes, I know. I have Hunter keeping an eye on our location. We will be there as soon as we can." I say, trying to reassure him.

Erik is already busy reprogramming the GPS to take us to Las Vegas when I hang up. As I set the phone in the console, he notices my shaking hand as I grip wheel. Erik sits silent, perhaps grasping the full horror of the situation for the first time. His voice breaks, filled with a quiet sense of rage, of powerlessness.

"This is awful. Their poor family." Erik stares out at the mountains as they fly past us.

"I know. John warned us about this . . . " I realize nothing I can say will dampen the blow of cold-blooded murder. But leaving him to brood over this is not the answer. "None of this is our fault, Erik." He stares out the window and mumbles, barely acknowledging me, but I don't want leave him wallowing in guilt. "This is typical . . ."

"Typical?" he glares at me, his face filled with horror, as if my words are ice-cold and unfeeling. "You law enforcement people are all alike. You're all hard-nosed, cold, and suspicious. He killed them for no reason, and you're worried about it being typical."

I recoil from him and the withering heat of his stare. He thinks I'm devoid of feeling—cold and unmoved. That hurts. I want to comfort him somehow, to return the compassion and caring he's showered on me the last few days. He's devastated and feels responsible but letting him sink into an all-consuming grief is not helpful.

"Erik, there's nothing about this that doesn't bother me. The hardest victims to get over are the defenseless ones—the children and the elderly. You can't see it, but it stays with me."

He looks at me again, and his face has softened somewhat. He sighs and covers his mouth with his hand. "There's nothing we did to cause this. But what happened to those poor people, it isn't unusual. You need to be ready for it. It's inevitable."

"There has to be a way to stop him!" He's angry with me again. But I don't let him take it out on me this time.

"Yes. There is. We put a bullet in his head! But there more going on here. Hunter and I found several accounts that Jeff was funneling money into. He was paying to keep his brother in a psychiatric hospital in Las Vegas. Hunter gave me the warrant, and we're probably going to meet with Kincaid's doctor while we're there. You're going to hear the same sort of thing from the doctor, and probably a lot worse. Their crimes escalate to feed their addiction. It's like a heroin addict, who eventually needs more and more to get the same high."

His eyes graze over my face, trying to understand my point of view. What I haven't told him is that I'm scared, almost petrified. Kincaid won't stop at rape this time. He could kill me, or even worse, he could kill Erik while I watch. He's just that deranged. But I can't admit that. Not now. He'd just become more protective of me.

My long silence has unnerved him. "Ronnie, are you okay?" He's shaking my hand, trying to get my attention. I've barely noticed how much time has gone by and how many miles we've driven since I talked to John.

As the signs for Ludlow appear, the GPS starts chirping instructions. It's taking us through the Mojave Preserve. The drive is desolate, but there is a visitor center in the preserve if we run into trouble. Once we make it through Kelso and Cima, it isn't much longer to Vegas.

"Erik, in the glove box is the extra Glock," I say, as he stares at me. "If anything happens, if I'm incapacitated in any way, you need to defend yourself."

I'd rather not put Erik in a situation where he'd be left alone to defend himself, but I have no choice now. He looks at me for a moment, sighs, and then opens the glove compartment. "The safety is on the—"

"I know where it is." He sounds a bit tense, as if I'm treating him like a child. "Dan showed me a few things the other day. Ironic, huh?" He lifts his left leg a bit and slips the Glock underneath his thigh.

Somehow, I'm not surprised. Dan apparently went against my orders more than once. He knew that clients don't carry weapons under company rules, and I explained to Erik that there was no time to instruct him. Now I wish I had.

"Yes, it is ironic. Now put on your vest," I say as he moans and grumbles, reaching into the back seat for the vest.

"Oh, stop whining. I'm still wearing mine. You won't have time to get it on if there's trouble."

As he struggles to slip into the vest in his seat, he looks at me from the corner of his eye. "Don't worry, baby. Nothing's going to happen."

The signs for the main road through Mojave Preserve signal the start of the long desolate trek through the desert dunes. As the GPS continues to squawk directions, the first car in hours passes us. As it disappears in the rearview, so does the chance of any assistance. There's no one out here, not for miles.

A sudden movement out of the ordinary and large cloud of dust catches my eye as I look in the mirror. I see nothing but the milky brown sand of the Mojave. The passing car kicked up a huge cloud of dust, but something about it doesn't sit right. As I look out the passenger side mirror, the absence of dust behind the Mercedes bothers me. That car should not have stirred up so much debris unless it ran off the road.

As the distance increases, it's impossible to tell if the car is off the pavement. Taking the exit, I cut the speed a little as the road curves slightly, but as the curve ends, I see it. A car is coming up fast in the rearview, and it looks like the same one that passed us a few minutes ago. I can't imagine why they would turn around. Erik notices it too and looks at me, hoping for guidance.

"Just be ready for anything." I take a left turn hard, and the car fishtails a bit on the dirt and gravel lying in the road. The tires kick up a wall of dust, temporarily obscuring the view of the car behind us.

"Shit! He's right beside us!" Erik yells as I turn to my left, clearly seeing the car for the first time. The flat gray paint blends in with the dusty bland colors of the desert, only the dark tinted windows standout.

"Get that gun ready, Erik."

He obeys immediately and pulls the gun from beneath his leg, flicking off the safety, and holding on to the grab handle with the other hand.

"There's no telling who this is or what they want." My best guess is garden-variety thieves. A nice new Mercedes would make an excellent score, and there's nothing to get in their way out here. We probably look like an easy target.

As we approach the overpass, the road is too narrow for both cars to pass, and I stomp on the pedal, trying to get out ahead of him. The engine screams as the car surges forward, and then I hear the loud crunch of metal. The back-end fishtails to the right. He's run his front end into the rear driver's side forcing me up the concrete slope supporting the highway overpass.

"Fuck! Hold on!" I jerk the wheel to the left, bringing us back down on the road again. The gray car is still there, and I hear a shot. They are firing at us! This guy is after more than the car. He keeps up his speed and hits me again, and this time I spin completely under the second overpass. The car slowly inches past us, blocking us off from the open road. I sit, with my foot on the brake, my fingers digging into the wheel. I'm just waiting, like a bull waits for the matador to move.

The seconds tick by with agonizing slowness, and my gut is demanding I ram him. After all, this is an armored car. Even up against a 1990s Chevy Impala, I'd wager that this beast would do some significant damage. But I think better of it since I can't afford to strand us in the desert.

Then the door opens, and a tall figure steps out of the passenger side door. I see a man's head first, but the hair. It's almost familiar. When the man turns, the shock registers, and then quickly fades into rage.

It's Dan!

I throw the car into park and growl at Erik to stay put. There's no way I'm letting him get in the middle of this. This is all about revenge–pure and simple. Dan has no business being out here, and the only way he could have traced us to this very spot is by gaining access to the GPS System. It confirms my suspicion that the hacking attempt wasn't an attempt at all. It was an inside job.

I stand behind the open door of my car and point the gun in his direction. "What the fuck do you want, Dan?"

He raises his hands as if he were under arrest and starts to walk around the back of the car. "Don't move. Stay where you are!" I shout to no avail.

He stops and wears the cocky smirk he had the other day. The one that makes me want to cap him in the knees. But I'm distracted by Erik, who's opened the door, and is now standing behind it, gun drawn.

"Get back in the car, Erik!" I don't even look toward him, I can't. Getting sucked into an argument will get us both killed.

"Yeah, get back in the car Erik. This is between me and her," Dan taunts.

Erik looks at me briefly, but stands his ground. He's not going anywhere, regardless of what I say. He certainly isn't going to take orders from Dan.

"You just had to go looking into my background. You have no idea what you're dealing with here, you fucking bitch," Dan yells. His words mean nothing to me, but I know Erik. Those words will enrage him.

"Who's in the car Dan?" I ask, ignoring his animosity. Getting information is more important.

Dan smirks. "It doesn't fucking matter. Get the hell out of here and go back to Los Angeles, or this time, it won't be just Kincaid that works you over," he spits.

Rage blinds me and for a moment, nothing exists but me, my gun, and Dan. He moves again, this time faster, jogging toward us. I step past the armor-plated door of the Mercedes, just as Dan stretches his right arm behind him as he moves, clearly reaching for a weapon.

"Get down Erik!" I shout. Firing two quick shots, I hit Dan in the abdomen, sending him back a pace. But he keeps moving. More shots ring out, one, two, or maybe more. I hear Erik yelling and the racing of the engine.

Shit! I have to get up. But the pain shoots through me like liquid fire and it races across my eyelids as the blackness consumes me.

When I open my eyes all that I see is the gray steel and concrete underside of the highway overpass. I take a deep breath and the pain shoots through my torso. Perhaps only a few seconds have elapsed, because when I force myself up, Erik is still standing behind the car door, protecting himself behind the armor plating.

My client is still alive.

I can't say the same for Dan.

Thank you for reading my first novel. I sincerely hope you enjoyed reading about Ronnie and Erik, as much as I enjoyed writing about them. They are a fantastic couple that I've fallen in a little bit in love with, and I hope you have too.

Stay tuned for the next two novels in the Ultimate Betrayal Series. Erik and Ronnie must face their demons, together. And they have bigger teeth than most . . .

About the author

Born and raised in New York, Catrina is a U.S. Veteran, wife, mommy, controller of chaos, domestic engineer and cook. She loves wine, good books, good food and especially anything slathered in Nutella.

Always a storyteller, she enthralled her friend with tales of her wild daydreams involving the latest hot boy band (okay, they weren't called boy bands back in the 80s. They were called Duran Duran), but she never wrote them down.

She eventually grew up and embarked on a not so exciting career in the military, followed by an exciting career working in IT for a few major U.S. corporations and traveled the world. And instead of meeting in their hometown, she met her husband in Cyberspace while he was in Korea. Marriage and having a child afforded Catrina more time to read, one of her former passions, and eventually, to begin writing. With the support of her family, she's released her first novel, Ultimate Betrayal: Revelations and is working on the follow up - Nightmares.

Connect with me

Twitter: @CatCourtenay
Facebook: www.facebook/AuthorCatrinaCourtenay
Website: www.catrinacourtenay.com

45347793R00138

Made in the USA
Charleston, SC
19 August 2015